Praise for A FISHY

A Fishy Tale is another triumph by John J Jessop. It is a laugh out loud story of the exploits of the private investigation firm run by Dr. Jason Longfellow and his wife Chelsea as they try to solve a series of murders of prize-winning fishermen in rural Virginia. The story speeds along as you follow the hands-on approach to crime solving employed by the intrepid Dr. Longfellow. In addition to the swashbuckling action A Fishy Tale sparkles with the interactions between Dr. Longfellow and his nurse wife. The humorous comments and actions between these two are fun of love and very relatable to anyone that has been married. **Rick Spees, Author, Capitol Gains**

John J Jessop has weaved a tall (fish) tale with unbelievable characters that are as relatable as if they were real. And events are told in a way that makes the reader become part of the story. You'll take the bait and more in Jessop's newest and best work yet. **Ben Berkley, Author, The Selfish Giant**

When a couple of brothers pull a ninety-pound fish out of a Virginia lake, they know that something strange is 'goin' on.' Jason and Chelsea Longfellow, amateur PIs, dive into the mystery of what might connect the soggy body of a businessman, several missing fishermen, and a medical biotech company. John J. Jessop propels 'A Fishy Tale' with the speed of a Nitro Z21 Bass Boat toward its shocking conclusion. **Henry G. Brinton, Author, Windows of the Heavens**

A FISHY TALE

A Fishy Tale

©Copyright 2023 John J Jessop

ISBN 978-1-7358178-7-3

This is a work of fiction. The characters are both actual and fictitious. With the exception of verified historical events and persons, all incidents, descriptions, dialogue and opinions expressed are the products of the author's imagination and are not to be construed as real.

Published by:

JJJESSOP LLC

A Fishy Tale

John J Jessop

JJJESSOP LLC

Other Books by John J Jessop

Pleasuria: Take as Directed

Murder by Road Trip

The Realtor's Curse

Guardian Angel: Unforgiven

Guardian Angel: Indoctrination

DEDICATION

To my wife and daughters, who lived with me on a mountain lake for many years and put up with my sometimes-wacky sense of humor. We had a lot of fun, and I hope you have the same fond memories of that time as I do. And to my wife and youngest daughter for all your help and support in the writing of my Medical Biotech Murder Mysteries. If Dr. Jason Longfellow, PI, were a real person, he'd be very lucky to have you all as his family.

Chapter 1. The Fishing Tournament

Tod Carlson and his brother Bill, professional fishermen known as the *Carlson Brothers*, had heard from kinfolk that record-sized fish were being pulled from Smythe Mountain Lake. Tod figured that was why the Blue Ridge Bass and Beer fishing tournament had over two hundred registered participants this April. The Carlson Brothers never missed this tournament, the event's slogan being *If you don't catch a bass, there's still plenty of beer*. They had placed second last year and were odds-on favorites to win. Tod's cousin had whispered rumors of fishermen disappearing and unknown danger in the lake; the locals were trying to keep this quiet. Tod's gut screamed at him to skip this year, but a fifty-thousand-dollar grand prize would go a long way towards paying off serious gambling debts.

Tod and Bill launched their Nitro Z21 Bass Boat with 300 HP Mercury motor from the SML State Park boat launch at six o'clock on Friday morning. They fished until two in the afternoon, rested, ate dinner, and Tod made sure they were back on the water by nine that night. They raced towards the big water up near the dam at a brisk sixty miles per hour with Tod at the helm. Tod grinned when he saw his brother hanging onto the steel seat frame for dear life.

Bill said, "You crazy bastard. Slow it down. It's too dark to go this fast. Remember last year, you didn't see that shallow marker and tore hell out of our propeller first night out. That cost us precious time, or we might have finished first."

Tod, yelling over the roar of the engine, "Chill out, Big Brother. What the fuck's your deal? We gotta get to our spot before some other asshole gets there. That's what the three-hundred horses are for. Besides, I know this lake like the back of my hand."

"More like the back of your head. Slow the fuck down!"

At that moment, the bottom of the boat skidded over a small shallow spot near one of the islands. Tod and Bill were thrown forward as the boat decelerated rapidly and the large outboard engine bounced once over the sandy bottom. Tod readjusted himself in his seat at the helm as the engine dropped back into position, the propeller caught water, and they continued on their way.

Tod saw Bill get up off his knees, where he had landed when the boat temporarily bottomed out. Bill said, "You really are an asshole. You're gonna kill us. This is a bass boat, not a freakin' dune buggy. It ain't built to go on sand. I'm guessin' the prop's okay since we're still movin'. But I swear, if we have to replace it again, it's comin' out of your half of the winnings."

Tod grinned sheepishly and gunned the large outboard.

Tod's Uncle Jed had filled him in on the history of Smythe Mountain Lake. Construction had begun in the late nineteen-sixties to form a huge mountain lake by damming up an isolated area of southern Virginia where two major rivers flowed together. When the lake filled, it had formed a forty-mile-long expanse of deep, crystal-clear water with shimmering reflections of sun and blue sky. Upstream the lake was bordered by thick deciduous forest, grassy meadows, and farmland. Downstream towards the dam where the two rivers met, the deep blue water, up to two hundred feet in some areas, was outlined by the beautiful Blue Ridge Mountains. This included heavily-pine-forested shoreline that rose dramatically into steep, sheer, rugged terrain, ending where the pointed mountain tops reached towards the sky. The result had been a pristine mountain lake filled with spectacular views in all directions, a vacationer's dreamland. As Tod had discovered, the mountainous topography also resulted in shallow areas that devoured propellers and wrecked engines of boat-owners who liked to go fast.

Uncle Jed, having lived there from the beginning, clearly thought the lake was a spectacular thing to behold. But he told Tod that boat and jet ski traffic had increased significantly, and runoff from excessive shoreline housing development had caused algal blooms in a few smaller coves during peak summer heat. The lake was currently healthy, but this could be a sign of bad things to come. Something needed to be done. Tod knew the lake was famous for its fishing, with an abundance large and smallmouth bass, catfish, perch, muskies, sunfish, and carp. Its greatest prize, the striped bass, or striper, averaged 11-15 pounds, could reach 20 pounds, with the current lake record a little over 50. The Virginia Department of Wildlife Resources re-stocked the lake with stripers periodically to keep the tournaments busy, fueling the local economy. Tod had visions of a first-place trophy on his mantle and prize money in the bank.

The brothers reached their first spot of the night, a deep hole off a large island in the big water near the mountains. Tod jerked the throttle into neutral, and the boat decelerated abruptly.

Bill yelled. "For God's sake! You're gonna break my neck. What the hell's gotten into you? You don't want to sink us here in two hundred feet of water, Asshole."

Tod, a big grin on his face, "Quit yer' bitchin', Big Brother. You should learn to swim. We caught a couple of big ones here last year. All we need's a school of shad, and the tail slaps of those stripers comin' up to feed. I'm startin' with a bucktail. That worked for me last year."

"I'm gonna try a redfin. There's enough moonlight to see, but it's kinda cloudy. Them stripers like it really dark. But it is what it is."

Tod could barely see Bill's silhouette as Bill lowered the trolling motor from the starboard bow and guided them quietly along the shoreline. Tod pointed over the starboard side of the boat.

"Listen, Bill. I hear the tell-tale churning of water, a school of shad. Get us over there."

Tod felt the boat stop, and heard Bill say, "Hot damn! Did ya' hear that? Tail slap. The stripers have arrived."

Tod baited his line and watched as Bill pointed the boat in the direction of the action. As the boat moved forward slowly, they both began casting and reeling.

Bill whispered, "I got one! Feels like a big one. Finally! We've had lousy luck so far today, but I think we've stumbled onto the motherload."

Tod could see his brother's tall, lanky silhouette in the sparse moonlight, his long blonde hair blowing in the cool night breeze. Tod chuckled to himself as he pondered how people had a hard time believing they were brothers. His older brother Bill took after Mom, long, lean, blue-eyed, blonde-haired form with a pretty face. Tod, on the other hand, favored Dad, brown hair, green eyes, short, stocky, block-shaped form, face more like a boxer who'd lost a lot of fights than a professional fisherman. Bill appeared to be working hard, his pole bent in half. Tod laid his pole down, picked up a flashlight, and shined it on the water.

"Keep the tip up. Get him close to the boat. I'll snag him with the net. You've got a freakin' monster, Big Brother. I'm thinkin' 'bout what I'm gonna do with my half of the prize money."

Bill fought with the fish for several minutes before reeling it in next to the boat. Tod shined a flashlight on the object in the water.

Bill said, "Look at the size of that thing. Get the net on it. We don't wanna lose this one."

Tod bent over to net the fish and almost fell in. He felt Bill grab him by the jacket. They struggled together to haul the large fish into the boat.

"I think you've done it, Big Brother. You've caught the Moby Dick of stripers. I'll bet this one breaks the record. It's gotta be over fifty pounds."

Bill said, "I'd say he's at least sixty, maybe more. Let's get him into the tank and get back to castin'. Maybe he's got a big brother out there."

Tod held the net while Bill untangled the fish. It took them both to load it in the storage tank. Then, they continued fishing.

Bill said, "Damn. Every time I cast, I catch another one. I got four keepers and a couple of little guys I threw back. I'm ready to move on to the next spot."

Tod said, "Give me a minute to land this big boy, and then I'll start her up and we can move on. I've caught three more in the thirty to forty-pound range, bigger than anything we've pulled out of this lake before. We're gonna clean up; first place for sure. Cha-ching!"

Tod netted his fish, put it in the tank and started the motor. "We've saved the best for last, just around the bend from the dam. Where we caught our biggest striper last year,"

Tod flew between the two islands in front of the dam doing seventy. He smiled when he saw Bill hanging on tight to his seat frame, looking terrified.

"Dammit Tod! You're gonna get us killed. You came awful close to that little island on the left. I wanna win this tournament and live to tell the tale."

Tod rounded the bend, decelerated rapidly, and killed the big Merc. He said, "Chill Big Brother. We're here. Set up the trolling motor. I think I hear shad in the water just ahead."

Tod watched as Bill put the trolling motor in the water and inched the bass boat forward towards the shoreline. Bill pointed and said, "Just over there. I can hear the little bastards."

Tod heard several tail slaps. He said, "More stripers. This must be our lucky day after all."

Tod felt Bill move the boat closer to the slapping sounds. He could barely see the school of shad, what little moonlight there was bouncing off their shiny scales as they skimmed the surface. He saw Bill cast his lure, begin reeling, and his pole jerked so hard he almost lost it.

Bill said, "Jesus! I think I've got a whale by the tail. Feels like it's gonna break my pole."

Todd, excited, yelled from the stern, "Keep the tip up! This one's bigger than the other one. Do NOT lose it."

"What d'ya think? I'm gonna let it go on purpose? Get the net ready in case I do manage to get this beast up to the boat."

Tod watched impatiently as Bill fought with the fish, finally reeled it within sight.

Bill said, "Tod. Shine the spotlight on that thing. It's a monster."

"I'm not swimmin' in this lake anymore. That thing looks like somethin' from the ocean."

Bill, exhausted, "Brother, come help me. I can't hold it any longer."

Tod moved up beside Bill, took hold of the pole, and helped him pull the fish to the boat.

"Reel like a sonofabitch. I think he's wearin' down!"

Together they managed to haul the striper up next to the boat. The fish didn't have much fight left. Tod shined the light on it, noticeably larger than the fish they had caught so far.

"My God! That thing must be seventy or eighty pounds, maybe even ninety, and the size of a small man. I don't think it'll fit in the tank."

Bill said, "Just help me haul it into the boat. I'll get it in the tank, no worries."

It took half an hour of struggling, pulling, and wrestling to get the gigantic striper into the boat. Tod was impressed when Bill finally managed to stuff the fish into the tank.

Tod moved to the stern and sat down to catch his breath. "This is crazy. The fish aren't supposed to be bigger than we are."

Bill smirked. "Quit yer bitchin'. We're a shoo-in for first prize with this monster. And he might be bigger than you, but you're the runt of the litter."

Tod said, "We've fished here lots of times, and we've never caught anything like this. We've got a fifty and an eighty or ninety pounder in our tank. There's something strange goin' on here."

"The only thing strange is that we're gonna win this tournament, and you're complainin' about it. You're not just a 'glass half empty' kind of guy. You're a 'glass is broke' kind of guy."

"Bite me! And I might be the runt, but I'll kick your ass any day of the week."

Bill said, "Get your rear in gear, and let's get to fishing. We're gonna set the world's striper record tonight."

As Tod stood up to cast his lure into the school of shad, the boat suddenly lurched. Tod almost fell overboard.

Tod said, "What the hell? Quit screwing around. You almost put me in the water."

Tod heard Bill from the bow, "I didn't do nothin'. Something banged into the boat. Maybe we hit a log or a rock. I'm sittin' here in the dark trying to untangle my line so I can get this lure back in the water. I'm goin' for a hundred pounder."

Just as Bill finished speaking, a large object banged hard against the starboard bow. The boat rocked violently. Tod fell and landed on his knees next to one of the stern seats.

Tod growled, "What the fuck? That came from up front. Did ya' see anything? I dropped my pole in the lake. Grab the light and see if we ran into a log, shallows, somethin' up there. I'm gonna try to get my pole before it sinks to the bottom."

Bill grabbed the hand-held spotlight and stood up, looking over the bow into the water for rocks and logs. Tod struggled to get to his feet, found his flashlight, and started looking over the side near the stern for his fishing pole. As Tod scanned the water, something large hit the bow again. The boat listed violently, and Tod saw his brother fall overboard, spotlight still in his hand. Tod bent down, grabbed the side of the boat, and held on for dear life. He heard Bill scream once as he hit the water, another muffled scream near the shoreline, and then nothing.

Tod started crawling towards the bow, afraid to stand for fear of ending up in the water himself. "Bill! Where the hell are you? Are you okay?"

No answer. Just the rustling of the shad, the chirping of crickets, the sound of a light breeze and of small waves washing against the shoreline. Then, Tod saw the battery-powered spotlight, still lit and floating half submerged ten feet from the bow. He stood up, leaned over the side, and shined his high-powered flashlight on the spot. Terror slowly crawled up his spine, along the back of his neck, up the back of his head, and blurred his vision. He saw his brother's body, upper half on the shoreline where he had tried to crawl out of the water. His hips and legs were still in the water, surrounded by a large pool of a dark substance.

Oh my God! Is that blood? His eyes started to fill with tears. He yelled, "Bill! Bill! Are you okay? Talk to me, you Bastard! Get up and answer me!"

Something very large crashed into the bow of the boat, and Tod went over the side, his flashlight flying out of his hand. He struggled to swim back to the boat, but a hard object collided with his head. As he lost consciousness, something strong grabbed his pants leg and pulled him underwater. Helplessly sinking deeper and deeper into the cool water, his last thought was, *Are you fucking kidding me? We're supposed to win this year.*

Chapter 2. Money, Money, and More Money

Dr. Jason Longfellow, pharmacologist and amateur PI, and his wife Chelsea sat at the kitchen table in their home in Northern Virginia. It was late March, on a Saturday night at eleven thirty, and Chelsea felt cold despite the hum of the heat pump working overtime. They were drinking coffee and talking quietly to avoid waking their daughters.

Jason, a forty-eight-year-old man of Dutch descent, had worked for the US Food and Drug Administration as a drug reviewer for twenty years. Chelsea had found herself a tall man with deep blue eyes, now less slender than when they first met. She still found his sculpted chin and rapidly graying sandy-brown hair attractive; she was happy he had any hair at all. His prominent and slightly crooked nose, broken in childhood, gave him a rugged look. They had fallen madly in lust, and then in love, in their first month together and she still found him physically attractive. He had proven to be loyal, protective, a good provider and father to their children. She liked the way he made her laugh with his often-goofy demeanor, most of the time.

"How are you doing, Chelsea? It must be difficult. I know how much you loved your mother. But she went quickly. Probably didn't feel a thing. You might say it was kind of a blessing."

Chelsea, Jason's wife of twenty-three years, was of Swedish descent, a natural blonde with clear blue eyes, a perfectly formed nose, and smooth, unblemished skin. Jason had told her he had at first fallen in love with her full, beckoning lips and dimpled chin. But she knew if he was honest, it was her perfect ass that had sealed the deal. At the moment her ass was not the issue; her chin quivered as she fought back tears.

"Jason, I know you're trying to console me. But I'm guessing Mom did feel something when that bus hit her."

Chelsea still loved Jason dearly. But the lack of a filter between his brain and his mouth could turn from entertaining to infuriating in a heartbeat. Since he'd insisted on a ridiculous second career as an amateur PI, she had become less patient with him. Neurotic and OCD, he sometimes carried on long conversations with himself, sometimes in his head, other times mumbling aloud. He was often better off, and safer, talking to himself...like now. She desperately wanted to whack him one to shut him up.

Chelsea sipped her strong, black, dark-roast coffee. She would never understand why Jason bothered to drink that weak decaf swill he was currently choking down. No flavor, no caffeine, what was the purpose? The stupid coffee wasn't the issue either. She felt overwhelming grief and needed consoling. But was Jason up to the task?

Jason said, "Yeah, but the bus knocked her and her walker half a block. The EMT said she was probably dead before she hit the sidewalk."

Chelsea sobbed loudly, struggling to keep back the tears. "You're not helping. The only consolation I can take from this terrible accident is that Mom was miserable and had been drinking heavily again. It's been years since my father passed away, but she still missed him terribly. She never got over it when he died suddenly from pancreatic cancer. The blood sample showed that her alcohol content was way over the legal limit when that bus hit her."

Jason said, "You should sue the medical equipment company that sold her that walker. They never provided any warning about the potential hazards of drinking and walking with a walker. You can also take some consolation from the fact that alcohol is an anesthetic; she was probably so drunk she didn't feel a thing when the bus hit her."

"Jason, please stop talking. I tried to get her to stop drinking. I work, so I couldn't constantly protect her and pour her booze down the drain. I should have put her in a nursing home."

Chelsea had met Jason's faults—difficulty dealing with stress, indecisiveness, a lack of understanding of the female gender, and no social skills. She could now add inability to console a loved one to the list.

Jason took a large gulp of his decaf coffee. Chelsea had a fleeting wish that he'd choke on it. That might shut him up for a hot minute. Jason kept talking.

"Well, she's buried beside your dad now. It was a nice funeral service, with lots of attendees. That *Six Feet Under* funeral home does a good job. I heard their motto is '*We plant family more than six feet under, so they can't come back to haunt you*'. I'm amazed they were able to manage an open casket. Every bone in her body must have been broken. But she looked great. I'd swear she frowned at me when I walked by the casket. She never did like me very much."

Chelsea knew Jason had grown up with an abusive alcoholic father, and his self-esteem wasn't all that great. He often needed her emotional support and assurance. He lived a stressful life—a tedious government job, and a long, daily commute on the Washington Beltway. Chelsea also understood that being married to a strong-willed woman, namely her, could be difficult. It didn't help that their daughters Lizzy sixteen, Lilly fourteen, and Lucy eight, always sided with her. But she *was* always right.

Chelsea said, "Mom liked you okay. She and Dad just didn't think you were good enough for me. To their minds, with a Ph.D. you're not a real doctor. Dad believed he was the real deal, an M.D., a specialty in neurosurgery. Mom wasn't too happy with your part-time PI thing either. It's a good thing Dad was gone before you started on that kick. A fake doctor *and* an amateur private eye? He might have put a hit out on you if the pancreatic cancer hadn't gotten him first."

Jason sighed, "Good to know your family held me in such high esteem. Again, I'm sorry for your loss. But, on the bright side, you were their only child. Which brings me to the ten-million-dollar inheritance. Jesus, Chelsea! Ten million dollars! Neither one of us need ever work again!"

He mumbled to himself, "That old lady used to call me the 'idiot son-in-law'. I didn't realize it until now, but I have always been rooting for the bus."

Chelsea squinted her eyes, gave him a fierce look. "What did you say?"

"Nothing Dear. I was just clearing my throat."

Chelsea had met Jason at Georgetown University Medical School, he a graduate student in the Pharmacology Department and she a nursing student. She started out as an intensive care nurse, reached ICU burnout after a couple of years, and moved into hospital administration. This inheritance was a life-changer. Neither of them would have to work anymore. She doubted Jason could pull that off for long though. A workaholic, he often needed work as a distraction to help him avoid uncomfortable feelings from his childhood. Without a job, he'd eventually wander off in search of a murder to solve. She had no idea where he got this obsession with amateur sleuthing. He used to watch that old show *Murder, She Wrote*, but surely that couldn't be it.

"Jason, I know Mom was a pain, especially when she started drinking again. But she was my mother, and I loved her."

"Me too. I especially loved the way she kept trying to hook you up with single or divorced doctors. She introduced you as a widow, even if I was standing there next to you." He mumbled to himself, "Yay bus."

"Jason, in all fairness, she thought you were completely daft when you got your private eye license. She was determined to find me someone sane to replace you. The fact that she was drunk all the time didn't help. That neurologist, Dr. Fanning, was quite the catch. Good-looking, a world class practice, and very wealthy."

Chelsea had a faraway look in her eyes. She took a sip of her thick, highly caffeinated brew.

"Chelsea! Stop it! He married that Victoria Secret model. You dragged me to the wedding."

Chelsea smiled when she saw Jason's face redden with a flash of anger. He took another gulp of coffee and spilled some on his T-shirt; another coffee-stained shirt for the rag bin.

"I do. I remember you walking around in your suit and tie with your tongue hanging out at the reception. I'm surprised you didn't fall over it and break your neck. I couldn't believe it when I saw her flirting with you right before the wedding ceremony."

It looked to Chelsea like Jason was about to lose it. Sometimes she liked to poke the bear. Chelsea had a jealous streak. She had noticed that some women found Jason's combination of height, intelligence, clumsy charm, and child-like innocence to be very attractive. She was often quick to stave off any flirtatious attention directed at Jason by other females.

"Why would I fall over my tie? I'm not that clumsy, and it only hung down to my belt."

"Not your tie, your tongue."

"Come on, Chelsea. You saw all those models. I'm only human." He grinned, "And besides, you like my tongue."

Chelsea took her last sip of coffee. It always amazed her the way Jason could be angry one minute, then quickly turn it around with humor. She ignored the tongue comment.

"Yeah, too bad you're only human. I'm thinking I would have liked you better as a monkey."

Jason raised his coffee cup, mock toasting her last comment. He said, "You gave me the cure. That's on you."

Chelsea had a brief and unpleasant flashback of their family road trip the previous year. They were traveling cross country so Jason could interview for a lucrative job in the medical biotech industry. Chelsea approved of the lucrative job thing. But by then, Jason had already convinced himself that he wanted to pursue the PI thing full-time. Unfortunately, she had discovered that while he excelled at drug development, he lacked the observational skills and attention to detail required to succeed as an amateur detective. Yet in his mind, he might very well be the next Sherlock Holmes, with Chelsea as his "Watson". Truth be told, in this version, Watson ended up solving most of his cases while struggling to keep Sherlock alive.

"Jason, you certainly were a lot more fun back then. Maybe we should take another road trip. But right now, Mom's gone, and I need to figure out what to do with my inheritance."

"Don't you mean *we* need to figure out what to do with your inheritance?"

Chelsea stood, walked over to the coffee machine, and made another cup of dark roast. She realized she might have trouble getting to sleep tonight. But her grief would probably keep her awake anyhow, that and Jason's snoring. She sat back down and carefully took a sip.

Chelsea said, "*My* mother, *my* inheritance, *my* decision. I want to get out of Northern Virginia. It's too crowded here, all the traffic, hustle, and bustle. It's just too much. I'm exhausted from working and trying to raise our three daughters under these conditions. One of the nurses at work and her husband just bought a second home on a lake in Southern Virginia. Smythe Mountain Lake...something like that."

Chelsea watched as Jason got up, went to the coffee maker, added water, a K-cup of decaf, and pushed the button. He turned to speak to Chelsea without putting a cup under the dispenser.

Jason said, "Sounds kind of snooty to me. Probably lots of *real* doctors there."

Chelsea shook her head as she watched him turn around, dive for his cup, and shove it under the dispenser just as it began to spew out scalding hot coffee.

She said, "I looked online. It's a beautiful lake in the mountains, very isolated and peaceful. After living in this crowded city, it sounds perfect. With the inheritance money, we could buy a place there and retire, at least for a while. We would probably want to get jobs eventually. I'm a nurse and could always get work. There are a couple of colleges in the area. Maybe you could get a job as a college professor, or something. What do you think?"

Jason sat down. He looked flabbergasted, his hand shaking as he put his cup on the table.

"Gee Chelsea, I don't know. Maybe I could get a job as a Walmart greeter. Or maybe I could do some consulting work. I have an ex-FDA friend who gets hired by drug companies to help them get their drugs licensed through the Agency. You can work out of a home office, and all you need is an airport nearby. I could make good money. But do we really need the money?"

Chelsea said, "I think Walmart greeter is sexier. If I invested carefully, we would likely never have to work again. I just think we'd get bored doing nothing. I'm also not sure I could stand our being together twenty-four seven. We'd need to stay busy…to keep me from strangling you."

Jason looked sad. Then Chelsea saw him smile, and his eyes lit up.

"Chelsea. I have a great idea. I've got my PI license and have already been working cases part-time. I'll set up my own private detective agency, do it full-time. You could work as my assistant, *Dr. Jason Longfellow, PI, and Associate.*"

Chelsea smiled back. "That's a thought. Only, since it's my inheritance, how about '*Chelsea Longfellow, PI, and Associate*'? I think that has a nicer ring to it, don't you?"

Jason, sad again, "Chelsea, the PI thing was my idea. I have a PI license and CCW permit, and I've already solved several cases working part-time."

"Yeah, a PI license off the internet. I could do that too. If I remember correctly, I solved the great cheese caper during our weird cross-country road trip. And you thought an armed mosquito killed that realtor in Florida. I must admit, the idea of investigating murder intrigues me too. Maybe we could work together. But you should be *my* assistant. What d'ya think, Husband?"

Jason said, "Let's find a Walmart near the lake, and I'll fill out an application for greeter while we're down there."

Chapter 3. House Hunting at the Lake

As Jason had expected, once Chelsea made up her mind she didn't mess around. She put a deposit on a rental on Smythe Mountain Lake for early June, after school let out for the summer. The day arrived, and the Longfellow family headed for the lake in Chelsea's SUV. Four hours into their trip Jason found himself driving on a narrow, curvy country road in the boondocks. Chelsea was arguing with Matilda, Jason's GPS, as usual.

Matilda said, "Go two miles and turn right on Road."

Jason said, "Turn right on Road? Road as opposed to what? Donkey trail?"

Jason had expected to see some sign of the lake by now. He knew Chelsea didn't trust Matilda. He wasn't surprised when his wife dug a map out of the glove compartment.

Chelsea said, "We've been on this road for over an hour, and I haven't seen any sign of water, or civilization. Matilda's going to drive us into this mystery lake, and my SUV won't float. We need to get settled into our rental before dark. No telling what's in those thick woods."

Jason started humming the theme song to the movie *Deliverance*.

"Jason, stop it. You'll scare the children. And you suck at making banjo sounds."

"Not likely to scare our little angels. Two of them are watching a movie. Lizzy's asleep."

Chelsea pointed at the road ahead.

"Jason, look. There's a sign that says *White House Corner, 5 miles*. That's where the realtor's office is located."

A few minutes later Jason saw a sign that read *White House Corner City Limits*.

He looked around. "Chelsea, sure you want to move here? All I see is a tackle shop, a beauty parlor, and a country store with a gas pump from the sixties. Where's this realtor's office?"

Matilda interrupted. "Turn right in half-a-mile and your destination is on the right."

Jason said, "Thanks, Matilda. It's good to see someone's on the job."

Jason cringed as Chelsea wadded the map into a ball and threw it at him.

"*Someone's* on the job? How about you and Matilda sleep in the car tonight?"

Jason turned right and started looking for the realtor's building.

"Just kidding. You'd have found the realtor. I'm sure you were about to tell me where to go."

"You got that right."

Jason saw a small brick building with a sign stating *White House Realty*. He pulled into the parking lot and parked next to the only other car there, a Jeep Wrangler with the top down. He watched as Chelsea got out and went into the building to get the keys.

When Chelsea returned, Jason said, "Do you have an address for Matilda?"

"We don't need Matilda. The realtor said it's only ten miles from here, on the water."

"And it was a real live realtor? Not a character out of *Deliverance?*"

"She was alive, in her late twenties, tall, blonde, and quite shapely. You'd have liked her."

"I knew I should have gone in to get the keys. I need to stretch my legs. What's her name?"

"Her name is Julie Thompson. She told me our rental has a spectacular view of the lake. If you'd gone in for the keys, I'd have had to come in to get you. It wouldn't have ended well."

Jason started the SUV and turned onto the main road. Chelsea turned off Matilda, gave directions herself. Twenty minutes later Jason pulled into the driveway of a two-story log home. He exited the car, woke Lizzy, and unplugged the other two from the TV/DVD player.

"Come on, girls. We're here. We need to unload the SUV and get settled in before dark."

Jason, loaded down with luggage, followed Chelsea. She opened the front door and turned on the lights. He entered and looked around the fully illuminated room.

He said, "I love these log cabin style houses with an open design. This room is massive, a combination dining and living room, and look at that large stone fireplace."

Chelsea stepped in and said, "I love the cedar plank walls, the vaulted ceiling with those gigantic wooden beams, and all the ceiling fans. Look, the loft runs the full length of the house."

Jason struggled with three large pieces of luggage. "I'm guessing the bedrooms are upstairs. I'm gonna get a hernia. You ladies do not travel light."

Jason continued to grumble as he struggled up the stairs. "Chelsea, please turn on the ceiling fans. Your bellboy is sweating like crazy."

"Oh, Jason. Look at that beautiful view. Quit complaining. I could have packed more stuff."

Jason turned his head to see the view, missed a step, stumbled, and dropped a suitcase.

Lizzy said from across the room, "Dad, be careful. That's my bag. It's got my makeup in it, and you might break something."

Jason grumbled. "Yeah, like my neck. "

Then he saw the spectacular view. The lake side was all glass, with an expansive view of the lake and mountains in the background. A wooden deck ran the entire length of the house.

At the top of the stairs Jason saw four separate bedroom doors.

He heard Chelsea yell from downstairs, "This place is fully updated, a kitchen with stainless appliances and beautiful granite counter tops located next to the dining room area."

Jason mumbled to himself, "That would be useful if my wife ever cooked. Only time she fixes a decent meal is when she has bad news."

Jason heard Chelsea and the girls walk up the stairs. Lucy said, "Where's Daddy?"

Jason saw Chelsea look in the bedroom. "Jason, it's not nap time. Finish unloading the car."

"With all your stuff, I won't finish before tomorrow's breakfast. How about some help?"

"Those bags are too heavy for the girls. I'm tired from arguing with Matilda. Suck it up and finish. I'll get the girls settled. It's cute you think I'm fixing breakfast in the morning."

The sun was setting as Jason finished hauling in the last of the luggage. He found Chelsea downstairs sitting on a sofa, looking out the window.

Chelsea said, "I could stare at this forever. We need to find a house with a view like this."

Lizzy, also sitting on the sofa, chimed in. "Boring. We're in the middle of nowhere. Isn't there anything to do around here, besides go bear hunting or fall in the lake?"

Lucy, sitting next to Lizzy, said, "Yeah, boring. We need to play."

Jason said, "No worries, girls. We're here to find our own lake house." *We should buy this one. We're already moved in since I just hauled everything you own in from the car.* "But we'll take some time to play. This rental comes with a boat. Maybe you can learn to water ski."

Chelsea said, "Good idea, Jason. We can also swim off the dock. Won't that be fun?"

Lilly said, "My friend Lisa told me there's an arcade store in town with ski ball and bowling. You get tickets when you play, and you can turn in your tickets for prizes."

Lucy squealed. "Yay, prizes! Let's go there now."

Jason cringed. "Calm down, Lucy. Daddy's tired. Tonight, we're going to have some dinner, and rest. Tomorrow's our first big day of house hunting."

Chelsea said, "It's very quiet here; almost too quiet. Most of the houses appear to be empty."

Jason said, "We're ahead of peak season. This is a one season lake, and people don't start coming here until late June. Besides, we're doing this to get away from crowds, right?"

Jason headed upstairs to wash up. With the choice of two bathrooms, he took a hot, relaxing soak in the one with the hot tub with water jets.

In a while, Chelsea informed him through the bathroom door that the hot dogs and beans were ready. He dried off, dressed, and headed downstairs. Everyone sat at the kitchen table.

Jason said, "Hot dogs and beans. Yum. Don't worry, girls. I'm sure there's a local pizza parlor around here. Every small town has one."

After dinner, they watched *The Lion King*, as per Lucy's request. By ten o'clock, all three girls were in bed. Jason and Chelsea sat at the living room table drinking coffee and talking.

Chelsea said, "My friend, Victoria, recommended a realtor that works this part of the lake near the dam. The lake's deepest here, with the best views, wide water, and the mountains."

Jason got up to pour himself another cup of coffee. Chelsea had only made one pot, her thick heavily caffeinated brew. He looked for some milk to make it palatable.

He said, "Just so this realtor is sane. I'm kinda wary after condo-shopping in Florida."

"Jason, I'm sure everything's fine. There's a more laid-back feeling here than in Florida. And by the way, Florida's another example of why it should be *Chelsea Longfellow, PI, and Associate.* I basically solved the case while you ran around hurting yourself trying to prove how manly you are. I'll give you one thing though; you were right that Florida is a dangerous place. It ought to be a lot different here on this beautiful, isolated mountain lake."

Jason reached into the refrigerator, turned to look at Chelsea. "We solved that case together. You just figured it out a little sooner than I did, but I almost caught the killer. More importantly, have you ever heard of caramel-flavored almond milk coffee creamer? I'm gonna give it a try."

He poured some creamer into his coffee and stirred it with a spoon.

He sat back down. "I'm with you, Chelsea. This lake sounds great. No alligators, crazy manatee, sharks, hurricanes, salt water, or massive rust. I'm not sure about poisonous snakes."

"Relax, Jason. Vicky gave me a book on Smythe Mountain Lake. There are rattlesnakes that mostly stay on the mountain, copperheads that hide in the leaves, and black snakes that are harmless. Vicky assured me it's safe to take the kids water skiing, let them swim in the lake."

Jason said, "Not just the children. Florida tried to kill me too. This place sounds like heaven in comparison. No giant things in the water to eat you."

"Yeah, you can relax. Your OCD should settle down. No need to do so much counting."

"That would be nice. But, what about pythons? Are there any pythons in southern Virginia?"

"No, Dear. That's the Florida Everglades. No pythons in Smythe Mountain Lake."

"That's good. If there were pythons, I'd need a bigger gun. I read about this thing called The Judge. It's a revolver, shoots four-ten shotgun shells and forty-five caliber rounds."

"Jason, no shotgun-shell-shooting handguns. We'd be safer with pythons."

Jason took a sip of his coffee, made a face, and poured the rest down the sink.

"That's awful. I should have known. Almond milk? What's that about? This is the country. Milk's supposed to come from cows, not nuts." He put the cup in the sink and sat down.

Chelsea said, "The thought of you with a handgun that shoots shotgun shells? That's nuts."

"No worries. Since there's no pythons, I won't need the Judge. I can get shot shells for my little revolver to dispatch rattlesnakes, copperheads, and water snakes. Problem solved."

Chelsea said, "On a less violent note, I've been thinking. We're planning on quitting our jobs, living off my inheritance, and retiring here full-time. But you're a workaholic, I like to keep busy, and I'm guessing we'll get bored after a while. There're also the winter months. Being stuck alone with you twenty-four-seven? You can be irritating, and you might not survive that."

"How is that less violent? But you're right, we might get bored, and I do like surviving. I could take up hunting during the winter. I'm a wilderness kind of guy."

"Yeah. I saw how well you did in the Florida swamp. You're not much of an outdoorsman."

Jason said, "Am too. We have my jacked-up four-wheel-drive pickup truck. I'm sure we could find some off-road trails out here in the boonies. Snow and mud might be fun."

Chelsea shrugged, "That's true. But we're not going to spend the entire winter off-roading. We need to put some serious thought into this if we're going to move down here."

Jason's eyes lit up. "I could start my own PI business, like we discussed when you first brought up moving down here. There's the small town of Bedford, only a little over a half-hour from here. I could rent an office there to hang out my PI shingle. People would love to hire me to solve murders, adultery cases, burglaries, meth labs, find lost pets, and who knows what else."

Chelsea grinned, "Actually, I was kind of hoping you'd say that. I enjoyed solving...I mean helping you solve your previous cases. So, we agree, we'll rent an office in Bedford and put up a shingle, "*Chelsea Longfellow, PI and Associate*". We can work together. It'll be lots of fun."

Jason was sad. He'd walked right into that one.

***

Bright and early next morning, Chelsea stood in the door to Lizzy's room and yelled, "Rise and shine! Today we find our dream house. Start our new life of peace and quiet."

Lizzy grumbled, "Mom! Are you insane? It's eight in the morning. I need at least ten hours."

Chelsea heard movement as Lilly and Lucy climbed out of their bunk beds and shuffled to the door of their bedroom.

Lucy said, "Yay Mommy. Let's go swimming."

Lilly mumbled, "Stupid lake! Stupid house hunting! I wanna go back to bed."

Chelsea heard Jason walk up behind her. He said, "Let's go. Mommy got a big inheritance, and we're gonna live the good life."

Lizzy spoke up. "You mean we don't have to go to school no more?"

Lucy repeated, "No school? Yay!"

Chelsea smiled. "They have school out here in the boonies too."

The girls all said in unison. "No fair!"

After breakfast, Chelsea herded everyone into the SUV, made sure they buckled up. She gave Jason directions to the realtor's office. He started the vehicle and pulled out of the driveway.

Chelsea said, "The realtor that Vicky recommended is Carmen Schlump. She works for *LoveTheLake Realty*. They're a local business. Not one of those giant realty chains."

"Just so it's not *ReallyRealty*. I'm done with them."

Chelsea grinned. "There is a *ReallyRealty* office here at the lake. Want me to call them?"

Jason shook his head and frowned. "No thanks. Their realtors in Florida were terrible, but that's a different book...I mean story."

Chelsea said, "I know, Jason. I was there, saving your butt. And speaking of that, you're driving too fast for this curvy road. Are you trying to kill us? Please slow down."

"Don't worry, Darlin'. I've got this...Oh crap!"

Chelsea screamed as Jason hit the brakes and swerved to miss a family of deer. The SUV bounced into the ditch. Jason sat there shaking.

Chelsea turned around and looked at the girls. "Are you all right? Daddy just tried to kill us."

Lilly said, "Bad Daddy. You almost ran over Bambi."

Lucy said, "Yeah, bad Daddy. Poor Bambi."

Chelsea said, "Idiot. I told you to slow down."

Jason said, "Sorry, but I think those deer tried to kill *us*. Did you see the way the big one with the antlers looked at me? I think he was threatening me."

Chelsea said, "Well, you did try to run over his family."

Twenty minutes later, Jason pulled into the parking lot of a small, whitewashed brick building. A large sign read '*LoveTheLake Realty. We'll try to get you the best price, but you can't put a price on happiness*'.

Jason said, "I don't know about this Schlump person, but I'm not thrilled with their motto. And Bambi's parents should teach her not to run in front of cars."

"Jason, it's just a business sign. Vicky told me Carmen Schlump found them the perfect house at a great price."

Chelsea exited the SUV. Jason walked around to meet her and opened the door for the girls.

He said, "Watch out for killer deer. This is a place where the deer and the cantaloupe play."

Lucy said, "Mommy, what's a cantaloupe?"

Chelsea said, "Jason, stop scaring the children. There are no killer deer. Just a crazy man at the wheel. And it's deer and antelope…oh…never mind."

Lizzy said, "Oh Dad. Isn't a cantaloupe a kind of fruit?"

The girls exited the car. Everyone entered the building. Chelsea walked up to the counter.

"Hello. I'm Chelsea Longfellow. This is my husband, Jason, and our children Lizzy, Lilly, and Lucy. We have an appointment with Carmen Schlump to look at waterfront properties."

The young woman sitting behind the counter stood and shook Chelsea's hand. She was in her late twenties, a tall, slender brunette, dressed for summer in a pink cotton blouse and short dark blue cotton skirt. Chelsea glanced at Jason. He was checking out the young realtor's ample cleavage and long slender legs. She was clearly displayed in the front of the office to take control of weak-minded men. Chelsea gave her husband her threatening *behave yourself* look.

I'm gonna kill him.

Chelsea's face turned red as Jason stepped forward, bumped her out of the way, and shook the young realtor's hand.

"Hello. I'm Dr. Jason Longfellow, PI. As this lady…er…my wife…said, we're here to look at waterfront property. Perhaps this Schlump person is busy, and you could take us on the tour."

Lizzy turned to her sisters, "Daddy's in a lot more danger than Bambi was. He's gonna die."

The young realtor said, "Pleased to meet you, Dr. Longfellow, PI. I'm Carla Schlump. Carmen is my mother. She will take you on the tour. She's elderly. You'll relate to her better."

Chelsea moved to her left, hip-bumping Jason out of the way, and said, "If Carmen is anything like her daughter, I like you both already. Now that my husband, Grandpa Longfellow, has introduced, and made a fool of himself, please let Carmen know we're here."

Carla turned and walked towards the back of the building to a bay of offices.

Jason whispered to Chelsea, "That wasn't nice. What's this *grandpa* stuff? I'm only forty-eight. Country folks are known for their friendliness. I just wanted to get off on the right foot."

"It wasn't her foot you were staring at. And, if you don't get your male hormones under control, you're going to need to have my foot surgically removed from your butt."

Lucy said, "Ha, Ha. Mommy said *butt.*"

Carla returned with Carmen, a tall brunette, hair graying around the edges. She looked like an attractive but plumped up version of her daughter.

"Welcome to Smythe Mountain Lake. I'm Carmen Schlump. You've already met my daughter, Carla." She extended her hand to Chelsea and nodded at Jason.

Chelsea smiled. *Interesting. The daughter works on the weak-minded man, and Mom here puts me first. These women know what they're doing. I'm going to have to keep Jason under control if we're going to get a decent price on a house.* "Pleased to meet you, Carmen. Vicky told me good things about you. I'm hoping you can help us find our dream house."

"We'll do our best, Mrs. Longfellow. This is a good time to buy. There are lots of properties on the market. We've already discussed what you're looking for, and I've put together a list of things to show you. Let me get my purse. Carla, please get some waters for our guests."

Carmen led them outside to her giant SUV, built like a tank. The Longfellow family piled in, Chelsea took the shotgun seat and left Jason in back with the girls.

Chelsea heard Jason grumbling. "Already chatted with Mrs. Longfellow about what *she* wants in a house. Put together a list of properties…without asking me. I'm drowning in women…wife, daughters, realtors."

Chelsea ignored his rant. She said, "So, Carmen. What are we looking at this morning?"

"You wanted waterfront, in the one to one-point-five-million-dollar range. This one sits on a lot with a gentle slope to the water. It's a six bedroom, six bath, two level cedar log house, three thousand five hundred square feet. It has vaulted ceilings, large, open living space, upgraded kitchen, a cute sleeping loft, and spectacular view for one point two million."

Jason yelled from the back. "Money is no object. My wife just inherited a ton of money."

Chelsea frowned. *Idiot.* "Jason, children and husbands should not be seen or heard."

"That's not how it goes."

"Just ignore him, Carmen. He tends to exaggerate. My mother passed away recently, and I inherited some money. Since it's my inheritance, I'll be calling the shots."

Carmen winked at Chelsea, "Sorry for your loss. And I already figured out who's in charge."

Jason started to speak. Chelsea turned her head and saw Lizzy elbow him in the side.

Lizzy said, "Dad. Don't make Mom any madder. Out here in the boonies I'll feel safer with you sleeping in the house than the car. A bear might get in. It'd eat you first cause you're big, old, and slow. Then it'd be full, and we'd be safe. Don't you want to keep your children safe?"

Jason frowned, "Your concern for me is…underwhelming. I'll try not to make Mommy mad, so I can sleep in the house and provide foraging bears with a large meal, so they won't eat you."

Chelsea was terrified by the way Carmen drove the curvy country roads in her huge SUV. She accelerated wildly through the curves, tossing everyone around like rag dolls.

Jason said, "These curvy roads would be fun to drive in a sports car."

Carmen said, "Maybe. But I love my giant SUV. At sunset there're herds of deer out, and I play *dodge the deer*. I've already hit four this year, and they just bounce off."

Just then, Chelsea pointed ahead and yelled, "Deer! Deer! Lots of deer in the road."

Carmen slammed on the brakes, throwing everyone forward, seatbelts straining. She said, "I told you. And it's still daylight. There're whole herds out at sunset, and they're all suicidal."

Lizzy mumbled out loud, "No wonder they're suicidal. The poor things are bored out of their minds stuck out here in the middle of nowhere."

Jason mumbled, "Note to self. Try to avoid death by suicidal deer."

Carmen said, "Oh, pish-posh. It's fine. You just need a large enough vehicle. Even better, my husband is a hunter. He carries a thirty-thirty rifle in his truck. If he sees deer on the road, he stops, shoots a couple, and hauls them home to fill up the freezer. Problem solved."

Chelsea looked at the realtor out of the corner of her eye. "There're men around here with rifles in their trucks that stop and shoot at deer? Isn't that dangerous for other drivers?"

Carmen shoved the SUVs accelerator to the floor. Chelsea was thrown back into her seat.

"Y'all must be city folk. Out here, we do things a little different. If it is a pest, shoot it." She winked at Chelsea. "That goes for two legged pests too. Jason, do you hunt or shoot?"

Chelsea shook her head. *Oh no!*

Jason smiled. "I am a licensed private eye. I have a CCW permit and a little revolver thingy."

Carmen laughed, "What caliber is this little revolver thingy?"

"It's a thirty-eight. I want to get a twenty-two. I understand they're easier to shoot."

Carmen said, "You need a real handgun, like a forty-four magnum. If you're gonna live here, you'll also need a deer rifle…minimum a thirty-thirty, also good for a coyote, bear, or mountain lion. You'll need snake shot for that thirty-eight revolver, for the rattlers and copperheads. A twenty-two works on them destructive squirrels. They're tasty if you fry'em up just right."

Jason, panic in his voice, said, "Chelsea, did she say bears, coyotes, and mountain lions? Rattlesnakes? Copperheads? And destructive squirrels?"

Before Chelsea could answer, Carmen yanked the wheel to the right. The huge SUV bounced over a shallow culvert and into a gravel driveway. She pulled up in front of a garage and parked.

"Our first stop of the day. Fifty-three Rattlesnake Lane. This is a very nice property. Just came on the market. Give me a minute to find the key, and I'll meet you at the front door."

Chelsea watched as Carmen took several small devices out of the back of the SUV.

"What's she doing?", Chelsea asked.

Jason said, "I'm not sure. Looks like she's placing speakers on the ground around the SUV."

Chelsea saw Carmen walk to the front door of the house, turn, and wave to them to join her. As they exited the SUV, they all heard an electronic high-pitched screeching sound and placed their hands over their ears.

Chelsea winced and said, loudly. "What on earth is that terrible noise?"

When they reached the front door, Carmen said, "Sorry. I'm used to the noise. It keeps the squirrels away. They'll chew through your gas or brake lines or make a nest in your engine. We've had incidents where the pests caused engine fires and a fatal brake failure."

Jason said, "Mountain lions, bears, snakes...and killer squirrels?"

Carmen opened the front door, and they followed her into the house, into a large foyer.

Carmen said, "My husband, Roy, has a pellet gun. He's killed at least forty of the little bastards…sorry kids…in the past couple of weeks. Last spring, he took our boat out, got half-a-mile from our dock and the outboard motor died. A squirrel had chewed through the gas line. Took two hours to paddle home. We hate squirrels."

Jason said, "We tried to buy a condo in Florida last year. There were alligators, sharks, poisonous snakes, hurricanes, and rust. Here there's dangerous squirrels, and suicidal deer?"

Chelsea smirked. "Don't forget the lions, tigers and bears, oh my!"

Jason said, "But squirrels? Really?"

Carmen said, "Sorry. I run my mouth too much. You just need a good pellet gun and a great aim. Problem solved. I'll focus on the positive side of lake living. The fishing has improved dramatically in the past couple of years. Smythe Mountain Lake is famous for striped bass. The stripers used to average eleven to fifteen pounds. This year record fish up to fifty pounds have been recorded. Are you a fisherman, Dr. Longfellow? There're lots of fishing tournaments."

Chelsea answered. "My husband isn't the outdoors type. He's not much of a fisherman."

Jason said, "Fish? At fifty pounds, that's a freakin' whale. It could eat a small child."

Lucy's ears perked up, and she started to cry. "I'm a small child! I don't wanna get eated! Daddy, you're mean! I wanna go home!"

Lizzy said. "Oh, Dad. Now you've traumatized poor Lucy. She's gonna need counseling."

Chelsea said, "Jason, stop scaring the children!" *Should have gone with Carmen's daughter, Carla. She'd have distracted Jason, so he wouldn't scare the children away from the lake. Idiot.*

Chelsea shook her head hopelessly as she watched Jason bend down and give Lucy a hug.

Jason said, "Lucy, Honey. I was only kidding. Bass are a kind of fish found in lakes. They don't eat people. Actually, people eat them. You catch them, chop off their heads, cut out their guts, strip off their scales, rip out their bones, and slice them into filets. Then you cover them with butter, breadcrumbs and fry them up in a pan."

Chelsea watched as Lucy's eyes got bigger. She yelped, "Chop off their heads? Cut out their insides, slice them into pieces, and eat them? Poor fishies! Daddy, you're a big meanie!"

Jason gently pushed Lucy towards Chelsea. "Here, take your daughter. She's hurting my ears. We should rent her out to keep the squirrels away from peoples' cars."

Lucy cried harder. Chelsea said, "Jason, I hope you enjoy sleeping in the SUV tonight."

Chelsea smiled as she heard Lizzy say, "Oh Dad. Now you can't protect me from bears."

Chelsea saw Carmen reach into her purse and pull out a chocolate bar.

Carmen said, "Lucy, if it's okay with your mom, would you like this bar of chocolate? Might take your mind off your father trying to scare you to death."

Chelsea smiled. "How about that Lucy? A candy bar for breakfast. See, the country's not so bad. Like Daddy finally said, after scaring you half to death, fish don't eat people, just worms. Right Carmen?"

"That's right. Just worms. And worms are icky. It's good to get rid of all the worms."

Lucy took the candy bar, "Bad Daddy. Can I sleep with you and Mommy tonight?"

Jason said, "Only if you want to sleep in the car."

The realtor cleared her throat, started her tour. "Come along, Longfellow family. We're in the foyer. Next is the living room. Notice the large open space, cathedral ceiling, cedar paneling, large skylights, and all glass on the lakeside to optimize the view."

Chelsea and family followed the realtor. Chelsea switched into house-hunting mode.

"Jason, this place is beautiful. Look at all the space. We'll need to buy more furniture."

Jason said, "Oh boy! Nothing I like more than furniture shopping."

Carmen continued moving through the house. "Notice the living room with fireplace and big screen TV. There's the L-shaped kitchen, granite counter tops, and state-of-the-art stainless-steel appliances, and a separate dining area. The master bedroom and two of the other bedrooms are behind the kitchen. The master bedroom's on the lake side. Great view. There's a small bedroom loft above bedroom number three, accessed by stairs from the hallway. The county wouldn't allow a sleeping loft, too dangerous in case of a fire. So, the builder called it a *mezzanine*."

Lilly said, excited, "I want the loft. I won't have to share a bedroom with Lucy."

Chelsea's face was all smiles as she looked around. "Jason. This is perfect. I love the open feel, there's plenty of room for all of us, and it's so clean and bright."

Carmen said, "Glad you like it. It's one of the nicest properties available at the moment. It won't stay on the market long."

Carmen led them downstairs via a staircase near the front door. She said, "This is another living room with what serves as a rec room attached. The lakeside wall is all sliding glass doors. There's a pool table in the rec room that conveys."

They followed her into a large room in the back. "This could be used as another bedroom. The current owner uses it as an office."

Chelsea saw the realtor open a door and gesture for Jason to walk through. Carmen said, "You'll love this, Dr. Longfellow. It's a large, tiled bathroom, with a free-standing seven-foot tub with circulating water jets. The separate luxury shower includes a rainfall shower head and body spray. Note the high-end vessel sink. And I think the Blue Moroccan tile is spectacular."

Chelsea watched Jason walk through the door. She was startled when he came running back through the door waving his hands in the air. He screamed, "Chelsea, help! Snake! Snake in the hot tub! He forgot to turn on the circulating jets!"

Carmen said, "What on earth? I was just here yesterday. There weren't any snakes then."

Chelsea followed Carmen into the bathroom. They both looked in the hot tub. Carmen bent over and picked up a baby black snake.

Carmen laughed, "Dr. Longfellow, that's the smallest snake I've ever seen, not much larger than a night crawler. The little fella must have gotten in through a gap in one of the sliding glass doors. It's a black snake. They keep rats and mice away. You should turn it loose on your lot."

Chelsea turned around and saw Jason stick his head in through the bathroom door. He said, "Well, it is a snake. It could have been bigger...a rattler, or even a python. Now I'll have to carry my snake gun when I go to the bathroom."

Chelsea giggled. "Jason, you're being ridiculous. That thing's so small it isn't even scaring the children. This bathroom is spectacular. Look at that gorgeous blue tile. And the tub…it would fit your six-foot-seven frame perfectly. My God, this place was built for us."

Jason elbowed Chelsea gently on the arm, shook his head, and frowned at her. She could read his mind from his expression. He wanted her to tone down her enthusiasm, or they weren't going to be able to negotiate a good price. Or maybe he was just worried about the snake.

Jason said, "The basement is an odd place for such a fancy bathroom. It's kind of dark. And how'd a snake get in? Maybe his mama's nearby waiting for her turn at the hot tub."

Carmen reached up, flipped a switch on the wall, adjusted a dimmer. Chelsea had to squint.

Carmen said, "Is that bright enough? And it's a lake, so there's snakes. Get used to it."

Jason shrugged and said, "I give up. These people thought of everything."

Carmen said, "There's also two heating and cooling zones, a separate heat pump for each floor, common for these high-end properties. The system's only two years old. The owners also installed a gas stove in the rec room for supplemental heat. You'll actually feel warm in winter."

On the way upstairs, Chelsea held Jason back to whisper in his ear. "Jason, I'm trying to find something to not like about this place, but I can't. It's perfect."

Jason whispered, "I admit, it's great. But we can't buy the first house we see. We still need to look at the dock. Also, maybe the snake's a bad omen."

Back upstairs, Carmen said, "We still need to check out the dock. What do you think so far?"

Jason took the lead. "Well, it is nice. But, that tile in the downstairs bathroom looked kind of cheap. And the mezzanine thing might be a problem."

Lizzy spoke up. "Dad, when Mom gets mad at you, maybe she'll let you sleep in the mezzanine thingy instead of in the car. Wouldn't that be a step up?"

Carmen said, "The porcelain tile was very expensive, a special order from Spain."

Chelsea looked at Jason, and he just shrugged.

They walked down to the dock, where they found over a thousand feet of waterfront. The view across the cove was extra special, an undeveloped mountain set aside as national park. The dock included a large boat house, a small refrigerator, and bays for two large boats.

On the way to the house, Chelsea whispered, "We can't let this place get away. It's perfect."

Jason answered, "It's bad luck to buy the first house you see. We need to keep looking."

"Jason, I know you. You want everything to be perfect. To my mind this property is perfect."

"But Chelsea. We went through the place so fast; I didn't get a chance to make sure the closet doors were closed. And I should count the kitchen tiles; has to be an even number. And make sure the faucets work and the toilets flush. On the plus side, there were no dead realtors."

Carmen obviously heard, did a double take. "Excuse me. What's this about *dead realtors*?"

Chelsea said, "No worries. We tried to buy a condo in Florida last year and suffice it to say that it did not go well. It has nothing to do with today. My husband is just being a pain."

Chelsea put on her stern face. "Jason, we're buying this house. Deal with it. Maybe I will consider letting you sleep in the mezzanine instead of the car when you misbehave, like now."

Chapter 4. Buy It, Quick

Carmen drove the Longfellows back to her office. The realtor gave Jason and Chelsea coffee in ceramic cups with the realty company logo stamped on the side. They sat in comfortable chairs in front of Carmen's large walnut desk. Jason struggled with his hot cup, spilled some on his shirt. Chelsea happily sipped the dark brew. Carmen offered to take the girls to the lunchroom for snacks, so Jason and Chelsea could discuss the house in private. Jason nodded yes.

Refusing to be outdone by his wife, Jason took a large gulp of coffee and burned his mouth. He winced in pain, saw Chelsea give him that grin that implied he'd done something stupid.

"Chelsea, I think we should keep looking. This place is nice, but we have a full two weeks to shop. Besides, if we make an offer today, we'll be buried in paperwork. Won't have any time to take the boat out and play. It's not fair to the girls."

Chelsea took another drink of coffee. Jason thought the pain receptors in her mouth must be broken. That office swill was very hot and tasted like the pot hadn't been washed in years.

"Jason, stop using our children as an excuse. You're the one who wants to take the boat out. My mother died and left us all that money. We already agreed to move here and set up a private detective agency. If we don't make an offer on this house, it won't be *Chelsea Longfellow, PI, and Associate*. It'll just be *Chelsea Longfellow, PI*. Now, what's our initial offer?"

Jason knew when he'd lost a battle to Chelsea, which was way too often.

"Okay. You win. They're asking a million two. I say we offer nine-hundred-thousand and see what happens."

Jason, irritated by Chelsea's smug smile, took another large gulp of coffee to show her who was the tough one, really in control here. He burned his mouth again and began to choke.

Jason was still choking, coffee spewing out of his mouth and nose, when Carmen joined them in her office. She sat down behind her desk. "Are you okay? That coffee is strong stuff."

Carmen handed Jason a paper napkin, and he wiped the coffee off his face. He didn't say anything, just looked embarrassed.

Carmen said, "Carla is watching your girls. They're such sweet children. You're doing a great job raising them, Chelsea. They're enjoying soda and candy bars from the snack machine."

Jason said, "Are you sure Carla's watching *our* girls? Doesn't sound like them."

Chelsea said, "Jason, hush. The girls are fine, and we have serious business to attend to."

"But I want a candy bar too. And some more of this delicious coffee." *Chelsea doing a good job raising our girls indeed. I'll show her.*

Jason caught the irritated look on Carmen's face. She took their coffee cups and returned a couple of minutes later with refills and a Snickers bar. Jason smiled. He thought he'd finally won one, until he saw the look on Chelsea's face.

Jason said sardonically, "Thank you. I really appreciate it."

He was further irritated when Carmen sat down at her desk, looked directly at Chelsea, and said enthusiastically, "How did *you* like the house? Nice property, and a great price."

Jason sat up straight, shoulders back, stern look, adopting his version of an aggressive male posture. He said, "You said there's lots of inventory. We've discussed it and..."

Chelsea finished his sentence, "We'd like to make a full-price offer."

Jason did a double take, spilling hot coffee in his lap. "Say what? Chelsea, have you lost your mind? And ouch! That coffee's hot."

Carmen didn't offer him napkins this time. He took out his handkerchief and wiped the hot coffee off his pants leg.

"Jason, did you see that place? We're lucky we got to it first. Next person who looks at it is going to snatch it up. It's my inheritance. I'm pulling rank. The place just felt right...like home."

The realtor gave Jason a smug grin, as if to say it was clear who wore the pants in this family. Jason wished he wasn't wearing any pants. His were soaked with hot coffee.

"But Chelsea."

"Jason, if you want to open a private detective business, you'll need seed money. And..."

"I know. It's your inheritance. Can we at least go back to *Jason Longfellow, PI, and Associate?*"

"Well, we might be able to add back the *'and Associate'* part. I'm sure Mother would want the business to be in my name. And, you'll have the *mezzanine*, so there's that."

Jason sat impatiently as Carmen started the paperwork. They signed on lots of dotted lines. Jason started to get indigestion. He knew they could afford it, but it was a lot of money. He always felt uncomfortable spending money; a large bank account made him feel safe and secure.

Carmen said, "I'll meet the seller's realtor at the house tomorrow morning at ten to present your offer. Should be a formality since it's full price. You all can meet me there too. Give you one more chance to look the place over. I assume you'll want a home inspection."

Chelsea said, "Sounds fine. Yes, we want a home inspection, to rule out any serious issues."

Carmen shook hands with Chelsea, and then Jason. They found the girls in the lunchroom frenetically chasing each other around, empty candy wrappers strewn everywhere.

Jason said, "Oh goodie. A sugar high. Tonight will be fun."

Chelsea said, "Jason, don't pout, be happy. We've found a wonderful lake house, and you get to be a full-time private detective's associate." She leaned over and whispered into his ear, "Next time, check out the realtor's daughter's feet instead of her chest, Grandpa."

***

Jason heard Chelsea's alarm at eight AM. He had trouble getting out of bed. The children had kept him up until after midnight jabbering and running around, still wild from the sugar high.

Jason and the girls entered the kitchen after brushing their teeth. He was fully dressed, the girls still in their pajamas. Jason saw a box of Krispy Kreme Glazed Donuts, three glasses of milk, and three small plates his wife had set out on the table. He smelled coffee brewing.

Jason yawned and stretched. "Oh goody. More sugar."

Chelsea said, "Stop complaining, stuff your face with donuts, and let's go check out our new house. We're supposed to meet Carmen there at ten."

The girls sat and munched on donuts. Jason grabbed a donut and took a large bite.

He said, "Are we going to meet the sellers there too?"

"Jason, it's not polite to talk with your mouth full. According to Carmen the sellers live somewhere in Maryland. They'll sign the paperwork electronically. Their realtor, a Mr. Hiram Oldenman, is handling everything."

Jason watched the girls finish their sugar-coated breakfast. Then they headed to their rooms to get dressed. He grabbed a couple of donuts to eat on the way. Everyone piled into the SUV. Jason munched and dribbled crumbs on his pants as he drove to their new house.

Chelsea frowned, "Jason, it's not safe to eat while you're driving. You're going to need a bath with all that donut debris you're dribbling on yourself. You are way messier than the girls."

Lucy said from the back seat, "Yeah Daddy. Way messier than us. We're ladies."

Jason made it clear he enjoyed licking the sticky glaze off each and every finger.

When they arrived at the house, Jason parked next to Carmen's SUV. Carmen met them in the driveway. She shook hands with Chelsea, nodded at Jason, and patted Lucy on the head. Jason heard the girls immediately start complaining that they were bored.

Carmen said, "Hello Chelsea, young ladies, and Jason. It's a gorgeous day to buy a house."

Jason grumbled, "She's a realtor. She'd say that in a tornado."

Chelsea's huge smile irritated Jason. She had won this round and was clearly celebrating.

Chelsea said, "Good morning, Carmen. It is a spectacular day. Is Mr. Oldenman here yet?"

Carmen said, "He should be here soon. He's no youngster. Been selling property for forty years, and some say he needs to retire. If he's not here shortly, I'll go looking for him."

Jason said, "Isn't he the seller's agent who listed the house? Shouldn't he know where it is?"

Carmen said, "One would think so."

While waiting, everyone walked around to the back of the house to look at the lake. Jason had to admit it was spectacular. He heard Carmen call Mr. Oldenman on her cell, and saw her shake her head in frustration, indicating no answer.

Carmen said, "I'll hop in my car, see if I can find him. He probably went to one of the other two places he has listed. They're not far away. I'll go ahead and let you in the house."

Jason was pleased the girls found ways to entertain themselves while waiting. The two older ones went on social media on their cell phones, while Lucy played a road racing game on her tablet. Jason was surprised they could get a decent cell signal this far out in the boonies.

Jason said, "This doesn't bode well. The seller's realtor can't find the house he's selling."

Chelsea said, "Stop grumbling. You're not going to ruin this for me. He'll be along soon."

Forty-five minutes later, Jason sat dozing in a living room chair. A loud noise like tires on gravel woke him. The Longfellows all went to the window and saw Carmen's huge SUV in the driveway. A very old man with long white hair and wrinkled leathery skin, wearing a wrinkled brown suit, and matching scuffed brown leather shoes, slowly exited the SUV.

Carmen led the man through the front door and introduced him. "This is Hiram Oldenman. Hiram, these are the buyers, Dr., and Mrs. Longfellow."

Jason shook the man's arthritic looking hand. Hiram said, voice and hands both shaky, "Pleased to meet you. Sorry for the wait. I musta' went to the wrong house this mornin'."

Carmen shook her head and sighed. "My bad. He has three other properties on the market, and I only knew about two of them. He was at the third. That's why it took so long."

Jason shook his head. *Their realtor has been here for forty years and can't find the property he's selling. I better read the contract carefully. God knows what we'll end up buying.*

Chelsea said, "No worries. He's here now. Jason wants to take one more look at the dock, and then you can present Mr. Oldenman with our offer."

Jason walked over to the couch and told the girls, "We're going down to the dock. Please stay here and behave yourselves. We'll be back in a few minutes. Lizzy's in charge."

Jason followed as Carmen led the parade down the path to the dock. Hiram's knees looked like they were about to give out as they all negotiated the mildly sloping lot. When they reached the dock, Jason heard a loud bump, bump sound, and went on ahead to investigate.

Jason turned to the group and said, "Look at this, a bass boat. This wasn't here yesterday. Does it come with the house?"

Jason felt Chelsea walk up beside him. "Jason, I don't think this boat belongs here. It's not tied to the dock, there's no bumper to protect it, and there was no boat in the listing."

Jason watched as Chelsea examined the boat more closely. Jason said, "Is that blood? There appears to be blood all over the gunwale and floor on the port side."

Jason moved in closer and bent down for a better look. He said, "I don't think it's people blood. It's probably fish blood. I choose to believe it's fish blood. We don't need no people blood. If I gotta investigate, how about a simple burglary or lost pet. Not another murder."

Chelsea got down on one knee for a closer look. "Jason, calm down. That looks like human blood, but I don't see a body. Maybe a fisherman cut himself and went to get help."

Jason, babbling, "Fact: the boat is here at the dock. Fact: it must come with the property. Fact: we just missed it yesterday. Fact: It's fish blood. If that's *human* blood, the guy must have cut off his arm. And don't forget the old law enforcement adage, '*no body, no murder*'."

Carmen said, "Fact, as Chelsea said, there was nothing in the listing about a boat conveying with the property. I agree with her. That's human blood, and lots of it."

Jason realized that Hiram had finally reached the dock and walked up beside them. The old realtor frowned. Jason heard Hiram mumble, "Oh crap. That's the third one this month. Stupid son-in-law just got out couple a months ago."

The old man looked at Jason, and Jason saw his frown morph into a cheerful smile. Hiram said, "Look, a bass boat. Do you need a boat? I'm sure we could include it in the negotiation."

Jason smiled. *Maybe I can turn this to my advantage.* He said, "I am a private detective. And I detect a bass boat with blood in it. If the blood is human, the amount suggests murder. Chelsea, I don't think it's a good idea to buy a house where a murder's just been committed. And it sounds like Hiram here might know something about it."

Jason felt the anger in Chelsea's voice, "Jason, this has nothing to do with buying the house. We should call the police, report the lost boat, and let them analyze the red stuff on the gunwale. There's no signs of a struggle, no blood up at the house, and no body. You just said yourself, '*no body, no murder*'. And why would poor old Hiram know anything about it?

He couldn't even find the place. Let's go up to the house and discuss our offer."

Hiram said, "Know about what? There's nothin' unusual about a boat conveyin' with a lake house. And I woulda found the place eventually, Missy. I just got a tad confused. Ain't you never been confused? Yer husband there sure looks confused. And my son-in-law did his time for killin' that rat bastard in a bar fight. He wouldn't kill no fisherman."

Jason said, "But Chelsea. Boat, blood, murder. Investigate. Should not buy murder house."

"Jason, you can investigate later, after we've bought the place. It's the perfect lake house."

Jason's OCD and neurotic tendencies had been set off by the bloody boat, and possibilities. But he could tell from Chelsea's tone he had lost yet another fight.

Jason said, "Okay, we can buy the house. But I want to go on record as saying we should look at some others first...preferably one without a murder boat. Also, after finding this blood, my gut tells me I should look for a body in that boat house. How's that for a detective's *associate?* And there's one-hundred-twenty-three deck boards on this dock, just so you know."

Jason noticed Chelsea's grin. She had clearly won this battle. He walked to the boat house door, saw Chelsea follow.

Chelsea said, "Okay, Associate PI Longfellow. Look inside the boat house, but you're not going to find anything. The boat isn't even tied to the dock. It just randomly floated up here."

Jason opened the door and walked in. He found a large, inflated tube, three sets of water skis, and a couple of wakeboards. Plastic folding chairs and cushions lined the back wall. A small refrigerator sat on a wooden counter behind a metal door that opened to the outside.

Jason found a rack of fishing poles along the side wall. "Chelsea, there's a bunch of fishing poles along with three tackle boxes, a cooler, and several life jackets." He took one of the poles out of the rack and inspected it. "This is the largest fishing pole I've ever seen. And these plastic lures, they're huge. This is the kind of equipment I would expect to be used for ocean fishing; for hauling in marlin, or sharks, or maybe a small whale. Not for lake fishing."

Jason noticed that Hiram looked hot, tired, and worried as he wandered into the boat house.

Hiram said, "What's going on Dr. Longfellow? Find any dead bodies? I haven't heard nothin' bout no murders on the lake, honest. I'm just worried if they's somethin' to it, the police'll be after my son-in-law since he just did time for murder. I'm hopin' it's nothin'.'"

"No dead bodies. But, what's with these gigantic fishing poles? Hiram, have you ever seen anything like this? What would you catch in a lake with a pole that big?"

Hiram grinned. "I ain't much of a fisherman. But if I remember correctly the husband does some deep-sea fishing. That's probably the equipment he takes with him when he heads to Virginia Beach. It's only a couple hours from here."

Chelsea said, "See Jason, no dead bodies. That boat just floated up here. Nothing to investigate. Besides, even if we had my PI business up and running, I'm not working any cases without a paying client. That's going to be my number one rule. We'll let the police handle it."

Jason followed Chelsea up to the house. He knew she was serious when she shooed the girls out of the living room, sat everyone down, and told Carmen to present their offer to Hiram.

Carmen said, "Hiram, I have good news. Mrs. Longfellow, the one with the money, likes the house. She made a full-price offer. You present the offer to your clients, and I'll help the Longfellows schedule an inspection. Place looks good. Shouldn't be any major problems."

Jason mumbled, "No major problems, except the murder boat."

"What was that Dear? You love the house? You can't wait to move in and start my new business, Chelsea Longfellow, PI?"

Jason sighed, "And Associate. Don't forget the Associate, with his office in the mezzanine."

"If you don't behave, you'll have to fit a desk and a bed into that tiny mezzanine."

***

Jason, Chelsea, and family went back to their rental house. Carmen had told them she would arrange a home inspection for the next morning. She would also phone the local sheriff's office about the abandoned boat, try to get it removed it as soon as possible. Carmen assured Jason the lake was safe. This was most likely a fishing accident.

Next morning, Jason and family met Carmen at her office. They left the girls with Carla, who had donuts and milk waiting for them. Carmen drove them to the house to meet the inspector. Jason was pleased she also provided breakfast for the adults.

Jason got impatient sitting in the dining room, waiting for the inspector to arrive. Carmen sipped some coffee, washing down a bite of onion bagel with cream cheese.

She said, "I couldn't get my go-to home inspector. I called a guy that my guy recommended. His name's Tom O'Connor. The bad news, the guy's twenty minutes late."

Jason saw Chelsea staring at the view out the lakeside window and smiling serenely. Chelsea said, "No worries, Carmen. I'm sure he'll be fine. By the way, did you call the police?"

"Yes, sorry, I forgot to mention it. I called after you left, and they sent someone out late yesterday afternoon. A Deputy Jim Harbinger phoned me last night. Their crime scene folks concluded the dock was not a crime scene. They said the empty boat must have floated up and wedged itself against the dock. They trailered it to the sheriff's office for further examination."

Jason said, "What about the blood? Human or fish?"

Carmen said, "Deputy Harbinger had no new information on that. He did make a vague reference to two similar incidents in the past month where fishing boats have turned up empty. I tried to get more out of him, but he said he couldn't comment on an ongoing investigation. I asked around and it sounds like a couple of fishermen have disappeared off the lake in the middle of the night. Please, keep this to yourselves. Not great for real estate sales. The deputy did assure me that the lake is safe."

Jason couldn't help himself. "More abandoned fishing boats, blood…and didn't someone say something about really big fish? What were they called? Stripers?"

Hiram snorted. "Nonsense. You must be a city feller if you're thinkin' what I think you're thinkin'. A striper's nothin' but a big bass. They eat worms, bugs, and little fish. There's nothing in this lake that would attack a man. And it wouldn't do the real estate business any good if people got the idea that something was eatin' fishermen. Calm down, take a breath, and let's focus on me gettin' my commission."

Jason started to panic. He stuttered, "S…Something eating fishermen? These stripers are that big? Chelsea, round up the girls and let's head back to Northern Virginia. I don't want to investigate our murders by something in the lake big enough to eat a person."

Carmen said, "Hiram. Would you hush. I think you've broken Dr. Longfellow. He's talking about investigating his own murder."

Chelsea smiled. "He'll be all right. He's prone to anxiety attacks over nothing. Jason, go into the bathroom and count a few tiles. You'll feel better."

Just then Jason heard someone knock loudly on the front door, and everyone jumped.

Carmen chuckled. "I guess all this talk about disappearing fishermen and murder has us on edge." Jason watched her get up to let the home inspector in.

Jason, ever the professional PI, said more calmly, "Without a body there is no murder. I still think that was fish blood. Granted, a lot of fish blood, but if they caught a fifty-pounder…"

Jason saw a short, heavy-set man with a round bald head and prominent beer belly hanging over his belt enter the room. He carried a small briefcase. Jason and Chelsea stood to meet him.

This guy must weigh over three hundred pounds. He'll provide a good test of the strength of the floor joists and deck boards.

The man nodded to Carmen, offered his hand to Jason, "I'm Tom O'Connor, home inspector. Y'all are lucky I had a slot open on such short notice. I got another appointment this afternoon."

Jason watched as the man opened the briefcase and took out a pen and a government form.

"This is the official county form I'll fill out as we walk through the house. I'll need to list any problems I find with the property. I'll let you know which things are minor, dangerous, and what needs to be fixed according to county building codes. Let's get to it."

Jason, Chelsea, and the realtors followed O'Connor out onto the deck. O'Connor looked around in an officious manner, and said, "Just as I expected. This deck is substandard."

Jason looked around, *The deck looks brand new to me.*

The inspector jumped up and down hard on the deck boards, and the deck shuddered. "We need to get off this thing, afore it collapses. I need to check underneath."

Jason caught Chelsea's eye and shrugged. *With the size of that beer gut, I'm thinking reinforced concrete would struggle to support him…poor deck.*

Jason and the others followed O'Connor outside and around the house under the deck. The inspector pointed up towards the underside of the deck.

O'Connor said, "Just as I thought. Those cross supports are only sixteen inches on center. And the deck is just attached to the house with a band board and some bolts. None of this is up to code. I know a guy who can fix this. Here's his card."

He handed Jason a business card.

Jason saw the confused look on Hiram's face. Hiram said, "Accordin' to the owners they just spent over forty thousand dollars re-doin' this here deck. And I'm pretty sure it meets county code since they needed a county permit for the redo."

O'Connor growled. "Listen, old man. I'm the expert. You're just a glorified salesclerk. Do you want me to continue, or are you gonna keep yappin'?"

Carmen said, "Hiram, let the man do his job. We'll get this sorted out later."

Jason and the others followed O'Connor into the downstairs family room through one of the sliding glass doors. Everyone crowded into a utility room where the furnace, water heater, and washer-dryer were located. The inspector pulled out a flashlight and examined a circuit box.

"This circuit box is all screwed up. It's got a 220 where a 110 should be, and there's no ground wire. I'm surprised this place hasn't burnt to the ground. This whole thing'll have to be rewired. My cousin's an electrician. He'll give you a good price to do the job. Here's his card."

Hiram said, "But they just had the place rewired for a generator by a bonified electrician…"

Jason saw the rotund inspector give Hiram an angry look. Jason began to panic. Collapsing deck, faulty wiring. They should run away, before the house collapsed or caught fire.

Next, O'Connor led them into the downstairs bathroom. Jason worried as the inspector ran water into the sinks, tub, and shower, tried the drain plugs and flushed the toilet.

"Looks like this drain plug on the tub isn't workin' right. It's leakin'."

Jason cringed as O'Connor reached down, yanked hard on the lever to engage the drain plug, and the lever snapped off in his hand.

"Well, this is crap. These fixtures are all cheap. I know a guy who's a plumber, and…"

Jason finished for him. "…he'll give us a good price to re-do the bathroom."

The inspector ignored him. "That's it for the house. Now, we need to check out the dock."

They all followed O'Connor down the gentle sloped hill to the dock. As they walked, Chelsea whispered to Jason, "Instead of home inspector, this guy's a 'home destroyer'."

Jason saw that the bass boat no longer sat alongside the floating dock. O'Connor stepped onto the dock, and Jason heard the inspector mumble, "What the hell? The bass boat's gone."

Jason whispered to Chelsea, "How does this guy know about the bass boat? This is supposed to be his first time here."

She whispered back, "He did make time in his busy schedule to take this job last minute. Now I wonder why."

Jason said, "Mr. O'Connor, I'm a private eye and never miss anything. How is it you know there was a bloody bass boat at this dock yesterday? What do you know about murder on the lake? Makes me wonder...well Chelsea wonder...why you dropped everything to take this job this morning. Were you hoping to retrieve the boat? Perhaps it's you who left it there. Who did you kill? Where are the bodies?" *He looks like he ate them. Oh no. A cannibal on the lake.*

Jason saw O'Connor turn bright red. The man started waving his arms and yelling. "Are you outta your freakin' mind? Ya' can't go around accusin' a fella' of murderin' folks with no proof. I took this here job cause I'm a helluva a nice guy and wanted to help you out. One of my fisherman buddies told me this place was up fer sale, and he thought they had a bass boat. I been lookin' fer one and thought I might get a good price. I don't know nothin' 'bout no blood."

Jason whispered to Chelsea, "This guy's surprisingly quick on his feet. I still think he knows something. I'm adding him to my list of suspects."

After that, Jason got the impression the home inspector was in a big hurry. He didn't find anything wrong with the dock or boathouse. Jason thought that either he knew something about the murders and wanted to leave, or he didn't have any friends or family that worked on docks.

O'Connor said, "That's it for my inspection. I'll finish my list, sign the form, and be on my way. You can write me a check. Add an extra twenty bucks and I'll forget you accused me of being a murderer."

O'Connor led everyone up the hill. On the way, Jason and Hiram fell behind the group. Hiram whispered to Jason, "This feller's a jackass."

Jason smiled. He was beginning to like Hiram the elderly. "I'm with you, Hiram. This guy is a real horse's ass." *Maybe I can use this to my advantage. Talk Chelsea out of buying the place because there's so much wrong…according to O'Connor the destroyer. I also need to check this guy out. See if he's got anything against fishermen.*

Hiram said, "I can assure that there's no electrical hazard, the deck is not about to collapse, and this here idiot broke the tub fixture. I'm surprised he didn't find anythin' wrong with the dock. We can sort this out, I promise you."

Jason had to push Hiram the rest of the way up the gentle slope to the house, where they all gathered in the living room. The inspector checked his signed form and handed it to Jason, along with more business cards of friends and relatives, plumbers, electricians.

"You've got yourself some serious problems here, but with the help of these fine local businessmen you can get this place in tip top shape in no time. I gotta run. My next appointment's in twenty minutes, and the place is an hour away."

As O'Connor started to leave through the front door, he turned to Jason and said, "By the way Mr. Big Shot PI, since you're accusin' me a killin' folks, I might as well tell ya' somethin'. My cousin Jackson fishes this lake. He told me t'other day he heard they's all kinds of rumors floating around. Robbers attacking fishermen at night, fishermen stumbling on boats sellin' drugs, some crazy SOB shootin' at fishermen in the dark, and even giant man-eating fish. Jackson says fishermen are getting spooked. There're concerns fishing tournaments might get cancelled this year. Far as I'm concerned, a few less fishermen's a good thing. During tournament season, them bastards take over my favorite drinking holes. Me and my drinkin' buddies can't find a quiet spot to throw back a beer or ten. But we prolly wouldn't kill a fella over a little thing like that."

O'Connor continued through the door. Jason watched out the window as the home inspector waddled to his truck, got in and threw gravel in all directions as he drove off.

Jason said, "I guess he's in a hurry to get to his next appointment. I'll bet he has a cousin who repairs gravel driveways."

Hiram said, "More likely he's in a hurry to get to lunch, and a six pack. Don't worry about his report, folks. Most of the stuff he listed ain't real. He didn't know his ass from his elbow."

Carmen said, "Sorry about this. My usual guy does a good job. I don't know how they expect anyone to know what they're doin' when all it takes is one short online course to get certified."

Jason spoke without thinking, "Yeah. Hiram and I had that guy pegged from the beginning. That deck's brand new, the electrical box is fine, and he broke the tub fixture. I can't believe that all the state requires is an online course to do his job." *Oh crap! I was gonna use his report to talk Chelsea out of buying this place. Stupid! I also think the guy knows more about these fishermen murders than he told me.* Jason mentally whacked himself on the forehead.

Chelsea grinned, and said, "You mean like your online course in private investigation, PI Longfellow? Are we sure *you are* a real PI?"

Jason was sad, again.

Chapter 5. Chelsea Longfellow, PI

Despite Jason's objections and the odd number of tiles in the master bathroom floor, the Longfellows finalized the purchase of their new lakefront home. Two months later, they had moved to the lake, settled into the house, and registered the girls for school. Chelsea loved their new lake house, with beautiful cedar log exterior, reclaimed oak cathedral ceilings, the open floor plan, the six bedrooms and even the mezzanine. Her favorites were the large deck with screened porch and the spectacular view of the wide water outlined by beautiful mountains. The seclusion up near the dam felt so peaceful. There were five houses on their cul-de-sac on large lots. Two of them were owned by people who lived there year-round.

Sunday morning, the first day of August, Jason and Chelsea sat at the table on their screened porch at eight AM having coffee and donuts. The girls still in bed, Chelsea was enjoying the peace and quiet. She chuckled as Jason took a large bite of chocolate covered cake donut, painting his face with chocolate frosting.

Chelsea said, "Jason, it's obvious you're enjoying that donut. On another note, I've completed the online course and have my PI license. I also filled out the application for my CCW permit. I need to take the three-hour gun safety course, qualify at the range, and submit everything at the courthouse. I called the sheriff's office, and they recommended an indoor pistol range. I signed up for their class. It starts tomorrow morning at nine. The owner said I can bring you along. Lizzy agreed to watch the girls for a few hours. Want to come to the range with me?"

"Sure. Why not? I could use a little practice. What will you be shooting to qualify for your permit? Would you like to borrow my thirty-eight special revolver?"

Chelsea had gone to a local gun store to buy a handgun without Jason. She wanted expert advice. Jason's firearms experience consisted of shooting a hole in the poop tank of their rental RV while fighting off two killers during an ill-fated cross-country road trip the year before.

"No thanks, Dear. I appreciate it, but I already have a handgun. I bought one at a local gun store called *Guns, Guns, and More Guns*."

"Why'd you do that? I could've helped you pick out something appropriate for a lady. Like one of those cute little three-eighty semi-automatics. Fits in your purse, and they come in pink."

"That's why I didn't take you along. I wanted a handgun that would bring down a hardened criminal, or a hard-headed husband. The man at the gun store helped me find something effective for self-protection against humans. I didn't get a PI license to hunt squirrels."

"So, what did you get?"

Chelsea led Jason into the bedroom. She reached up on the top shelf of her walk-in closet and took down a wooden box. She sat the box on the bed, opened the lock, and lifted the lid.

Jason said, "Chelsea. No, you didn't. Is that a Desert Eagle?"

She said, "I didn't think you'd recognize it, since you went with that little revolver thingy."

Chelsea watched as Jason took the pistol out of the box and felt its heft in his hand. He removed the clip to make sure it was unloaded.

"But Chelsea. We're private detectives, not elephant hunters. Have you ever fired one of these things? It shoots fifty-caliber rounds. I'm thinkin' the recoil would break your arm."

Jason replaced the clip, tried to pull back the slide. Chelsea smiled as he struggled against the strong spring.

"Au contraire, Husband mine. The gun store had a range in the basement. The nice man let me fire a Desert Eagle in fifty-caliber before I bought this one to make sure I was comfortable with it. I handled the recoil just fine. The weight of the gun absorbs most of it, and the barrel is vented. I hit the target consistently from fifteen yards. And there's no round in the chamber."

She took the large pistol, pulled back the slide using her entire hand to grip it, like the salesman showed her. She enjoyed Jason's look of surprise. "See, the chamber's empty."

"How are you going to carry that thing, in a backpack, or a suitcase? It won't fit in a sexy thigh holster like in one of those spy movies."

Chelsea released the slide, placed the handgun in the box, locked it, and put it in her closet.

"I bought a large purse, just for Bertha. It'll hold her, a couple of loaded clips, and my wallet. If I get tired of carrying it, sometimes a nice husband will hold his wife's purse for a while."

"Oh no. You know how I feel about that. I'll do anything for you *but* hold your purse."

"Yes, Dear. We'll see. But you're right. It's probably not safe to put such a large handgun in your hands...Jason, did you just growl at me?"

Next morning at nine, they arrived at *A Gun for All Occasions*, a gun store and pistol range in downtown Bedford that ran gun safety classes with the range time required to qualify for a CCW permit. Chelsea sat through a three-hour lecture on gun safety, while Jason spent the time looking at the gun displays. She was concerned at what mischief he might get into.

Chelsea saw Jason at the door just as the lecture ended. She walked up to him and said, "Ready for lunch?"

Jason said, "Hell yeah. I'm starving. Let's eat."

They spent some time walking around downtown, looking for a place to eat. They passed a furniture store, hardware store, bank, Midtown Café, the sheriff's office and a very large, limestone courthouse. Chelsea was impressed with the cleanliness of the streets and the well-maintained brick and limestone buildings. They ate at the Midtown Café.

Chelsea sat across from Jason in a wooden booth in the front of the restaurant. She handed him a menu. "Look at the menu. This is your kind of place, burgers, burgers, and more burgers."

Jason said, "I'm having the number one burger, fries, and a milk shake. What about you?"

Chelsea scanned the menu a second time. "I'm gonna try the fish sandwich. Maybe it's a bass from the lake. You should take up fishing. Then you could catch us a fish dinner."

Jason said, "I could borrow your hand cannon and shoot one. That thing could kill a whale."

"Jason, there's probably not a lot of whales in the lake. Let's order. We need to get back for this afternoon's session."

After lunch, they returned for the qualifying portion of the class. They took the elevator to the basement. Chelsea thought the range looked well-maintained, with thick cement walls, five shooter's lanes, and a strong ventilation system. She shared a lane with Jason. She knew he had carried his revolver in an inside-the-pants holster, unloaded according to range rules. He took out the revolver and placed it on the shooter's shelf with the cylinder open.

The instructor entered the room and Chelsea introduced Jason. "Jason, this is Mr. James Johnson. Mr. Johnson, this is my husband, Dr. Jason Longfellow. Jason has his CCW permit, and the owner said he could take a little range time with me today. Is that okay with you?"

"That's fine. You need to qualify first. Once you've done that, your husband can fire off a few rounds. What are you shooting today?"

Jason's thirty-eight-special lay on the shooter's bench. Chelsea's Desert Eagle lay next to it, chamber open, empty clip next to the gun.

Chelsea pointed. "These are our handguns."

Johnson said, "Okay Chelsea, show me what you've got. Let's put on our ear protection."

Chelsea picked up the clip for the Desert Eagle and started loading it with rounds.

Johnson said, "Whoa there, Little Lady. Do you think you can handle that hand cannon?"

Chelsea saw Jason wince. She knew what he was thinking. He was concerned this guy was talking down to her while she was heavily armed.

Chelsea just smiled. "I'm fine. I've already fired one of these, and I liked it, a lot."

She filled the clip, shoved it into the Desert Eagle, jacked a round into the chamber and aimed at the paper target with the silhouette of an armed bad guy fifteen yards down range. She held the pistol as she had been taught, her left hand supporting the grip and her right shaking hands with the grip while pushing forward firmly to stabilize the weapon. She sighted the target, both eyes open, and gently pulled the trigger straight back. The massive pistol went off with an explosion that shook their entire shooter's station. The bullet hit the silhouette center mass. She fired four more times, forming a nice group around the first shot.

Chelsea saw Johnson shake his head and smile. "Ma'am, that's some of the finest shootin' I've ever seen. I'm thinkin' you've done qualified for your CCW permit. I'm gonna mention you to the Bedford ladies' shooting team. They could use someone for the large handgun category."

"Thank you, Mr. Johnson. I'm new to shooting, but I'm very competitive by nature. If my husband can do it, I'm determined to do it better. Speaking of my husband, Jason, you're up."

She knew Jason was a perfectionist, and not good under pressure. He would want to show this instructor he was the better marksman of the two. She smiled demurely.

Chelsea heard Jason grumble to himself, "No way Chelsea can shoot better than me. How the hell did she do that, and with that hand cannon?"

Her smile brightened with self-satisfaction. She watched as Jason walked up to the shooter's table, his hands shaking noticeably as he loaded his revolver. He dropped the first two rounds on the floor. Finally, he closed the cylinder, took the shooter's stance, aimed, and squeezed the trigger. The shot went wide to the right. He fired four more rounds, only hitting the silhouette once. He opened and emptied the chamber, placed his gun on the table, flipped the switch to move the target back to the shooter's station, and sighed with frustration.

Johnson looked at Chelsea and chuckled. "I get that you're competitive with your hubby, but the bar ain't that high. I'm guessing you'd have done even better with his revolver. Why'd you choose that hand cannon?"

Chelsea grinned. "First of all, if I'm going to be an armed PI, I wanted something that will be effective against criminals. Second, when I compete with Jason, I don't just want to win, I need to crush it. If I show any signs of weakness, he gets all protective, and that drives me crazy. And if he makes me mad, I need something to convince him to sleep in the car."

Johnson said, "That hand cannon oughtta do it." Then the shooting instructor turned to Jason and said, "My wife gets pissed at me when I drink too much, but her weapon of choice is usually a broom. A Desert Eagle? Jesus, Mother and Mary."

Chelsea was surprised when Johnson took Jason's target down and put up a new one. Johnson said, "How's about you give it another try? Buck up, Dude. You don't wanna let your lady do you like that. Grow a pair and show her what you've got."

Chelsea watched as Jason looked down at his small revolver. He said, "I'll be back in a minute. Gotta get something from the SUV."

Chelsea yelled at him as he walked briskly out of the room, "Jason, what did you do?"

A couple of minutes later, Chelsea saw Jason come running back into the range with a large box in hand. He placed it on the shooter's shelf next to his empty revolver. He opened the box, reached in, and pulled out a revolver so large that it barely fit in his hand.

Johnson chuckled. "Dude, you've got some stones after all. I haven't seen one of those for a while. The *Judge* ain't it? That thing'll shoot five Colt 45 rounds, five 410 shotgun shells, or you can mix and match'em. It's a handful and a half."

Jason smiled, "That's right. I'll be shooting 410, and I'll throw in a single Colt 45 round for good measure. Now we'll see who can obliterate those targets."

Chelsea watched as Jason loaded his mammoth handgun, sat it down on the shelf pointed down range, and flipped the switch to move the new target out to ten yards.

Jason said, "You might want to put on your ear protection. It's gonna get loud."

Jason picked up the revolver and fired off four of the 410 rounds, destroying the paper target. He said, "What do you think now, Wife? Your grouping might have been better than my thirty-eight-special. But with my new friend, Blaster, I don't need to worry about grouping."

Chelsea noticed that Jason had cocked his huge revolver for the last shot, the remaining Colt 45 round. He had placed the revolver on the shooter's table with the barrel aimed down range. She cringed and stepped back when he started throwing his arms in the air and doing a happy dance while singing, "I won. I won. Oh yeah, I won."

As Jason danced, Chelsea saw his rear end bump the revolver and knock it off the table. It hit the floor and went off, the fifth round flying down range. Chelsea stood there with her mouth open. She saw Johnson dive to the floor. Jason bent over, pick up the huge revolver and stood there staring at it.

Jason finally spoke, "Probably shouldn't have cocked it before setting it down. At least I had it pointed down range. No harm, no foul?"

Chelsea finally recovered from shock, reached up and whacked him on the back of the head. "Idiot! You could have killed us."

Chelsea turned to Johnson, on his feet again. He said, "Dr. Longfellow. You should let yer wife carry the firearm for your PI business. Her Desert Eagle's big enough to protect the both of you. I got a nice taser I'll sell you. When you tase yerself or your wife, at least it won't be fatal."

Chelsea nodded her head and said, "Not a bad idea. What do you think, Associate?"

Chelsea almost felt bad when she saw the pitiful look on Jason's face. He looked crushed.

Johnson said, "Dr. Longfellow. Maybe shooting sports just ain't yer thing. There are other ways fer a man to relax and have fun round these parts. For example, what about fishin'? You should buy yourself a bass boat. They's tournaments at the lake most months, 'ceptin' dead of winter. The striper fishin' has really picked up in the last few years."

Chelsea was glad to see Jason perk up, despite the fact he'd almost killed her. Jason said, "Hear that, Chelsea? I should buy a bass boat. Maybe I'll get one with a 250 HP Mercury engine so I can go really fast. I'll bet with a little practice I could win one of those fishing tournaments."

Johnson said, "Yes, Sir. Lately fishermen have pulled stripers out of the lake up to fifty or sixty pounds. One of them marine biologists recently said in the paper that if the stripers keep growing, they'll be the size of sharks. Good thing bass don't eat humans. Right?"

Chelsea heard Jason's voice change to high anxiety, "Chelsea, if we're gonna get a bass boat, sounds like we're gonna need that hand cannon of yours."

Johnson said, "It'd be better if y'all didn't carry any firearms on yer fishin' boat, especially on overnight trips. Ya' never know who you might run into out there in the dark, and it'd be better if y'all didn't panic and shoot anyone."

***

Chelsea had her PI license and CCW permit, and the family was settled into their new lake house. School hadn't started yet, and the girls spent most of their time at the dock. Chelsea had noticed that after the shooting range debacle Jason's enthusiasm for PI work had diminished. He spent his time lifeguarding for the girls. He did try his hand at fishing.

On Saturday, the family had a cookout at the dock using the new charcoal grill and picnic table Chelsea had bought. Jason grilled hot dogs and hamburgers, Chelsea bought some potato salad, and they sat at the picnic table to eat. Everyone else drank soda, Jason went for beer.

Jason had already consumed three beers. Chelsea knew he didn't handle alcohol well.

After lunch he said, "Chelsea, the girls have been swimming off the dock. I've been watchin' them, and I haven't seen any giant fish. I'm gonna get a fishing pole out of the boat house and try my hand at fishing. Those poles are insane. I could reel in a whale with fishing line that strong."

Chelsea lay relaxing in a reclining dock chair, working on her suntan. She said, "Go for it. But be quiet. I'm full and I'm going to take a nap."

She saw the girls sitting at the picnic table, playing cards. As usual, they were acting like Mom and Dad didn't exist.

Chelsea watched Jason take a fishing pole from the boat house and bait it with a large plastic minnow. He said, "I keep hearing about giant bass. I'm thinking these local fishermen are doing what fishermen do, exaggerating about the size of their catch. The classic *fishy tale*, as in 'there's something fishy about that story'."

Chelsea stretched leisurely and said, "That's nice, Jason. Very clever. Fishermen often exaggerate. Catch a big one, and you can fry it up for dinner. Please be quiet so I can take a nap."

Just as she was about to doze off, Chelsea heard Jason move to the far end of the dock. She turned to look at him. He cast the lure and began reeling it in slowly.

He yelled, "Chelsea! Wake up! I've got a fish!" Chelsea saw his line go taught. Jason pulled hard. The large pole was bent double. "Chelsea! Girls! I think I've caught a whale, or maybe a monster! Somebody come help me reel this thing in."

Chelsea mumbled, "That's nice Dear." She rolled over on her side to go back to sleep.

Lizzy said to her sisters, "It's just Dad fooling around. Ignore him."

Jason yelled, "Don't everybody come running at once. I'm not letting go. Maybe I caught a Russian spy submarine. It's something very large. Help! I can't hold on much longer."

Chelsea was awake enough to hear the panic in her husband's voice. She sat up and looked in Jason's direction just in time to see him go airborne, hanging on desperately to the fishing pole.

She yelled, "Jason, let go of the pole! We'll buy you another one. You've hooked a boat, jet ski, or something."

Jason responded, "Ahhhh! Help me."

Chelsea watched in horror as Jason did a face plant on the water. He refused to let go of the fishing pole. He was pulled rapidly forward on his stomach, barely skimming the water. It looked to Chelsea like he was trying to water ski on his face, without a boat.

Chelsea said to the girls, "Look at your father. All he has to do is let go of the pole. He's so stubborn I think he'd rather drown."

Lizzy said, "Mom, if he survives, are you going to make him sleep in the car?"

Chelsea looked at Jason again. He did a couple of forward summersaults through the water and then stopped abruptly. He appeared to right himself, tread water to get his bearings, and then he started swimming towards the dock. Chelsea and Lizzy met him at the ladder to the floating dock and help pull him up.

He said, "Did you see that? I was skiing on my face. But there was no boat pulling me. What do you think that was? I thought maybe it was the Lock Ness Monster, trying to drag me back to its lair for lunch. That's why I finally let go of the pole."

Chelsea said, "Yes, Jason. Nessie flew to Virginia, took up residence in Smythe Mountain Lake, and tried to invite you home for a meal. You're delusional as usual. I didn't see anything either, no giant fish. Whatever it was, it pulled a large man around like a rag doll."

Lizzy said, "Well, at least it didn't eat you. So, you're still around to protect me from bears."

***

Chelsea was getting bored without her nursing job. The next steps to getting the PI business up and running were setting up an office and advertising. That's why she was riding around Bedford on a Tuesday afternoon with Carmen the realtor.

Carmen drove while describing the local commercial real estate market, "The economy has boomed at the lake. But things here in Bedford aren't so boomy. The population is shrinking. We should be able to find you a nice office space for a reasonable price."

Chelsea rode shotgun, Jason in back with the girls. Chelsea could tell Jason was depressed. She had decided to take charge of setting up the new private detective agency.

She said, "We're looking for something with an office, waiting room and bathroom. Something I…we…can proudly hang our PI shingle on, *Chelsea Longfellow, PI, and Associate.*"

Chelsea heard Jason groan from the back seat. She turned and saw Lizzy reach up and pat him on the shoulder.

"It's okay, Dad. Mom shoots better than you, detects better than you, wins most of the arguments, is always right, and makes you sleep in the car sometimes, but you're better at...worrying. You worry about us, and that's gotta count for something. You're a great Dad."

Jason said, "Thanks, I think?"

Carmen pulled up in front of a vacant building on Main Street next to a furniture store. Chelsea read the sign in the window, *For Rent. Central Business Location.*

Carmen turned off the SUV and announced, "This is the first property on my list. It used to be a video game arcade, but it's been vacant for quite a while. There's a front room where they sold tokens for the games, men's and a women's bathrooms, and a large room in the back where the games were kept. I already checked the place out, and there's an old Pac-Man, a Mario Brothers, and a Space Invaders game back there that still work."

Lilly spoke up from the back seat. "My friend Samantha's dad has an old Mario Brothers game. She said he still plays it, but she thinks it's b-o-r-i-n-g. It's for old people."

Jason spoke up. "I used to be expert at Pac-Man and Space Invaders. I loved those games. Maybe we could turn the place into an office and keep the games for times when work is slow."

Chelsea wasn't surprised that Lizzy, the teenage expert, had to have her say.

"Oh, Dad. You're so old-school. You should get one of those VR headsets. VR makes those old video games look silly. It's like you're in a whole different world. You can play fun games online, or chat with friends. You can travel all over the world without leaving the house. Mom says you never take her any place. You could go on trips without leaving the couch."

Chelsea wasn't happy. "Can we please look at this place. It doesn't sound very practical as a private detective's office. And your father is NOT going to get away with taking me *traveling* while sitting on the couch. I'm planning to use some of my inheritance to take some actual trips…on an airplane…with live people…to real places. Let's check out this rental space."

Lucy said, "Yeah. Bad Daddy. Mommy wants to go on a trip on an airplane, with people and stuff. Not on the couch. What's Pac-Man?"

Chelsea saw Carmen give her an uncomfortable look. She probably sensed that a family storm was brewing. Carmen hopped out of the SUV and herded everyone into the building.

The realtor said, "It's a little dusty. It's been on the market for almost a year. This is the front room where they sold tokens. This counter could serve as a place to meet new clients. You could put a couch and a couple of chairs over there as a waiting area. The bathrooms are just up that hallway.

The main room is through this archway. Chelsea, you could make this space into a master office suite with window, so you could see the clients as they enter the building."

Chelsea frowned. "It would take a lot of cleaning, remodeling, and furnishing. Although I must admit, it has the right amount of space. I like the idea of a master office suite."

Chelsea and family followed Carmen through the archway into an expansive room. There were electrical outlets placed every few feet, with indentations in the filthy dark blue carpet where the video games had sat. Chelsea was surprised to see that the walls were covered with well-maintained wooden paneling. Several small chandeliers in the ceiling provided adequate lighting. She also saw a tiny manager's office to one side, probably for the guy that maintained the games and collected the coins. Chelsea found the three large video games that Carmen had described sitting side-by-side at the back of the room.

Chelsea saw the expression on Jason's face, like a little boy in a candy store. *He's loving this place. If he had his way, he'd lease it, fix it up into an office and keep the games. Then he'd get so involved in the stupid games I'd end up doing all the investigating. I don't think this is a great idea.* She frowned and stomped her foot in frustration.

Lizzy said, "Mom, are you okay? You look like your head's gonna explode."

Chelsea heard Jason grumble, "Chelsea'll never go for this place. She knows I love old video games. She always has to ruin my fun."

Chelsea walked over to the three video games, and stood in front of Pac-Man. She placed her hand gently on the control lever, smiled a great big smile, threw back her head and yelled, "I can't believe it! It's a sign! We'll take it!"

Jason did a double take. "What the...What did you just say?"

"Jason, it's *Ms. Pac-Man.* I love Ms. Pac-Man. I spent hours playing this game as a kid. I loved the way she chewed up the men, the bad guys. When you think about it, it's kind of symbolic of a female PI. Since this building has been on the market so long, I think we should make the owners an offer to buy. I'll bet we could get a great price. What do you think Carmen?"

Carmen smiled. "I think that's a great idea. It's a small town, I know the owners, and I'm pretty sure they'd be happy to sell. You are in control since there's several other buildings for rent or sale in town and this one's been on the market the longest."

Jason just shook his head and said, "Do I know my wife, or what?"

Lizzy shook her head, and said, "Oh Dad...I'm thinkin' *or what.*"

Chapter 6. Jason Finds a Friend or Two

It surprised Jason how enthusiastic his wife had become about the PI business. He thought the office, remodeled with fresh paint, new carpet, lighting fixtures and furniture, looked modern and professional. A sign above the front door read *Chelsea Longfellow, PI, and Associate.* Jason felt sad about being demoted to *Associate*, but it was Chelsea's inheritance funding the business. His only input had been to count the tiles, make sure the tile guy used an even number. Chelsea let him keep the video games. He decided to take that as a win and move on.

One Monday morning in October, the girls on the bus headed to school, Jason and Chelsea sat in the kitchen of their new home. Jason had made his latest favorite breakfast, burnt pancakes slathered in maple syrup. He hadn't figured out the gas stove yet and was starting to like the charcoal flavored pancakes. He took the last bite, and watched Chelsea sip the black swill she considered coffee. She had made it clear she didn't care for burnt pancakes.

Jason said, chewing as he spoke, "The office renovation in Bedford is nice, but your office is a lot bigger than mine. You've got your *Associate* stuck in a broom closet in the back. That's not fair. The whole PI thing was my idea from the beginning."

"Jason, perhaps you shouldn't have tried to kill me at the shooting range. Besides, it is *Chelsea Longfellow, PI, and Associate.* In what world does *Associate* get the bigger office? I let you keep those video games, back there next to your broom closet…I mean office. Stop feeling sorry for yourself. We need to find some business to pay the bills. Any ideas?"

Jason took a gulp of his now cold decaf coffee and made a face at the foul taste. He knew this discussion was going nowhere, so he relented.

He said, "We could put an advertisement in the local paper and set up a web page. Maybe put a flyer on the bulletin board in the sheriff's office. They must get people coming to them with cases related to divorce, death threats, stalkers, and stuff like that. Lots of cops get killed in domestic violence cases. They might appreciate help with those."

Jason got up, walked over to the kitchen cabinet, and got out a box of glazed donuts. He took two, put them on a plate, and loaded another K-cup into the coffee machine."

"Jason, the police won't like a couple of PIs interfering in their work. The newspaper and website aren't bad ideas. You can take the domestic violence cases. And if you keep eating like that, you're gonna need a bigger office. You won't fit in your broom closet anymore."

Jason carried the coffee and donuts to the table, sat down and took a large bite of donut.

Jason said, "Maybe I should buy a bass boat and join one of the local fishing or boating clubs. I could meet people, advertise our business by word of mouth."

"Jason, if you want to play, you have three video games at the office. And you wouldn't know what to do with a fish if you caught one. You need to focus on the PI business."

"I'd know exactly what to do. I'd bring it home to my loving wife, who I'm sure would be happy to skin it, gut it, filet it and fry it up in a pan. Wasn't there a song like that?"

"You really are an idiot. The only part of that with any possibility of happening would involves the frying pan, and your head. The fishing angle does give me an idea, though. You could ask around about the fishermen disappearing on the lake. Maybe you could get some names, which might lead to a paying client. I realize the concept is foreign to you, but "only paying clients" is the new business model for *Chelsea Longfellow, PI.*"

"And *Associate*... Okay. I'll do it. I'll find some local fishermen to interrogate. If I had a bass boat, it'd be a lot easier though."

Jason flinched when Chelsea gave him her death stare. He kept his eye on her when she got up to make another cup of coffee. She sat down and took a large drink of the steamy hot brew.

No wonder she gets so mean. It must be all that caffeine. How does she not burn her mouth?

"Jason, I need to talk to you about something else."

Jason's stomach tightened. When she started off like that, it never involved good news.

Chelsea said, "Lizzy told me that one of her new friends at school, Kendra, is trying to give away a very pregnant one-year-old cat. Kendra's father wants to put it in a bag and throw it in the lake. I told Lizzy we should rescue it, but I needed to talk to you first. I had a cat when I was little. I loved Priscilla, until Mom ran over her with the car. What do you think?"

Jason said, "My mother had a Pekinese dog. When I was a teenager, I picked it up and blew in its face to tease it. The little monster bit me on the nose. I dropped the dog, and Mom picked it up and hugged it while I sat there bleeding." He pointed to his nose. "I even have a scar."

"Serves you right for torturing a poor animal. And your nose is so crooked nobody notices such a tiny scar. Did your mother take you to the vet to get stitches?"

"Chelsea, my nose isn't all that crooked. I don't want any cats. They shed all over the place. And who's gonna clean the cat box? The girls won't take care of them. More important, how many kittens come in a litter? We could end up with an entire herd of cats."

"Jason, I'm glad you're on board with this. Lizzy promised to take care of Sweety…that's the momma cat's name. This is Sweety's first pregnancy, and a cat only has one or two kittens the first time. I'll enjoy having a kitty in the house."

Jason choked on his donut, took a gulp of hot coffee to clear his throat, and burnt his mouth.

"But Chelsea. I said I didn't think it was a good idea."

"Nonsense. You didn't say no. Besides, you have lots of bad ideas. You'll love having a kitty around. They're so cute. We can take it to the office, put a cat bed in your broom closet. You'll have a friend to share all that space with."

Jason was sad, and his mouth hurt from the hot coffee.

The next Saturday, Jason watched as Chelsea and Lizzy pulled out of the driveway on the way to Kendra's house. They returned with Sweety, a very pregnant long-haired cat, medium-sized, light brown fur with darker patches throughout. Jason had to admit, the cat had a very cute face, but this was just one more time Chelsea got her way.

On Sunday, Jason fled to the office, where he went online to set up a website for their PI firm. His cell phone rang. It was Lizzy.

Lizzy said, "Hello Daddy. Sweety's about to have her kittens. Mom says it's a good thing for us girls to see childbirth in action…teach us about life. Sweety's lying in her new bed raising a fuss. Oh, look! There's a tiny baby kitty. It's so cute. Sweety is licking gooey stuff off it."

Jason said, "Yuck!... I mean, that's nice. So now what? Do we find a new home for Sweety, or the kitten? We can't keep them both."

Lizzy yelled into the phone, "Daddy, here comes another one…and another…and another. There're baby kitties everywhere!"

Jason felt dizzy. "What? Your mother said a cat's first litter only has one or two babies."

Lizzy squealed, "Mom was wrong. Sweety has just delivered one, two, three, four, five, six, seven…seven of the cutest kitties you could ever imagine. Can we keep them, Daddy? Please?"

Jason said, "Lizzy, let me speak to your mother."

He heard Chelsea's voice, "Hello, Jason? We now have seven new kitties. How delightful!"

Jason groaned, "Seven? That's not an even number. We can only keep one…but that's not an even number either. Chelsea, what are we going to do? Maybe we can sell them."

"You're kidding, right? You should come home soon. They are adorable."

Jason disconnected the call, grabbed his laptop, and headed for his jacked up 4 X 4 pickup truck. On the way home, he thought *I'm putting my foot down. We're only keeping one kitten plus Sweety. I'm the husband, the father, and the master of...oh, who the hell am I kidding?*

By the time Jason got home, Sweety had her seven kittens cleaned up. Chelsea had placed them in a large box. The negotiations started immediately; it was four girls to one Jason. He stood his ground, but they were excellent negotiators. They all gave him *the face*. They kept three cats- Sweety, the runt of the litter they named Cupcake, and to Jason's delight, a male orange tabby. Jason named him Herman. Finally, another male in the house.

***

A week after the kitten debacle, *Chelsea Longfellow, PI, and Associate* still didn't have any clients. Jason had put up fliers all over town, advertised in the local paper, and set up a website. The demand for a PI in small town Southern Virginia didn't appear to be all that great. Late on Saturday morning, Jason and Chelsea sat at the kitchen table, Jason working on his second cup of coffee. He watched as the girls went out onto the deck to look at a deer in the backyard.

Jason heard the sliding glass door to the screened porch off the kitchen fly open. Lizzy came running in yelling, "Dad, come quick. Something strange is going on at the neighbor's house."

Jason jumped up, spilled hot coffee on his crotch. He wiped off his pants with a paper towel.

He grouched, "Lizzy, you scared the heck out of me. What's all the commotion?"

Lizzy said, "There's lots of noise coming from the neighbor's house. Can't see anything cause of the trees, but it sounds like someone is being murdered."

Jason threw the paper towel in the trash. "Hey Chelsea, maybe some business. Perhaps a murder? I'll go investigate. There're five houses on this cul-de-sac. Only two of them have year around residents. I've heard some crazy old man lives in one of those. Hope it's not him."

Chelsea laughed, "Change your pants. I'll go with you in case there's trouble."

Jason ran into the bedroom, changed into clean blue jeans, and met Chelsea at the front door.

Jason turned and said, "Lizzy, you stay here with your sisters. Mom and I will check this out. If we're not back in half an hour, call the police. Might be a crime in progress."

Chelsea said, "Jason, don't be so dramatic. The realtor told me there's one old man living in that house, and he has a drinking problem. He probably fell off his deck." To Lizzy, "Keep an eye on your sisters. We're just going next door. I'll yell or call your cell if it's anything serious."

Jason followed Chelsea out the door. He heard Lizzy throw the dead bolt. Chelsea jogged towards the neighbor's gravel driveway with Jason on her heels.

Jason said, "Did you hear that? It sounded like a gunshot, small caliber. I hear a man's voice, lots of cursing. The girls could be in danger. A twenty-two bullet can carry a long way."

Jason took his cell phone out of his pocket and hit Lizzy's number on speed dial.

He said, "Lizzy, keep the girls inside. I heard gunshots. It might not be safe on the deck."

Jason and Chelsea reached the front door of their neighbor's house, a large, open-design log cabin similar to theirs. Chelsea knocked. No one answered, so Jason knocked louder.

A voice from inside said, "Just a damn minute. I'm a comin'. Did someone call the cops on me again? It's those frickin' squirrels. I'm at war with 'em."

The large mahogany door opened. Jason saw an old man standing there holding a twenty-two revolver that looked like something out of the Wild West. The man had unkempt long white hair down to his shoulders, a long white beard and matching bushy moustache, a seriously wrinkled face and one front tooth missing. Medium height, skinny, wiry looking, and barefoot, he wore dingy bib overalls over a ratty T-shirt. Jason could smell the alcohol on the man's breath.

We've moved into the movie Deliverance. I'll bet this guy plays a mean banjo.

Jason saw Chelsea staring at the man's waistline, where the overalls hung loosely over his hips. She whispered, "Jason, he's going commando, he's drunk, and he's armed. Do something."

Jason whispered, "I'd tell him to put on clean underwear, but he has a gun."

The old man said, "Who the hell are you? Whatever you're sellin, I ain't buyin'. Go away."

Jason started to speak, but Chelsea interrupted, "Sorry to bother you, Sir. We're your new neighbors. We heard a loud noise and were concerned there might have been an accident. We came over to make sure no one was hurt. My name's Chelsea Longfellow, and this is my husband Dr. Jason Longfellow." She offered the old man her hand.

Jason was relieved when the man put the gun in his left hand, pointed it towards the floor, and shook Chelsea's hand with his right.

"Howdy Ma'am. The names Horace McDufus. Pleased to make your acquaintance. Sorry 'bout all the ruckus. I got up this mornin', had a little hair of the dog that bit me, if you know what I mean." Jason was amused that the old man winked at her. "Then I see'd a couple'a squirrels down by my boat. I got out my friend, Gertie, to dispatch'em." He pointed at the pistol.

Chelsea said, "Pleased to meet you Mr. McDufus, and your friend Gertie."

Jason said, some concern in his voice, "You were shooting at squirrels? Chelsea, didn't we hear something about killer squirrels from the realtor?"

McDufus said to Chelsea, "This here husband of yers is kind'a a panic puss, ain't he? And he ain't too bright. They's no such thing as a killer squirrel. Y'all must be from the city."

Chelsea said, "Truth be told, we are city folks. I suppose we do have a lot to learn about living in the country. But we both enjoy shooting."

McDufus sounded interested, "Oh yeah? What d'yall shoot?"

Chelsea said, "I have a Desert Eagle in fifty caliber. I think that's right, isn't it Jason?"

Jason was still staring at the pistol in McDufus' hand. "Yes, Dear. You have a hand cannon. And I just bought myself the Judge…fires 410 shotgun shells and Colt 45 rounds. It's bigger than Chelsea's Desert Eagle, I might add."

Jason watched warily as McDufus stepped back, looked at the two of them, and grinned.

"Damn, a fifty cal and the Judge. Great choices if yer gonna live around these parts."

Jason looked surprised. "What do you mean by that? You're holding a twenty-two revolver."

McDufus laughed, "This is my squirrel gun. Them damn squirrels is pests, but you don't need the heavy artillery to dispatch'em. They almost killed me couple of times."

Jason said, "I thought there was no such thing as a killer squirrel."

Chelsea asked, "How does a squirrel try to kill you?"

McDufus said, "Missy, the little bastards'll eat anything. They chewed through my bass boat fuel line and left me stranded in the middle of the lake. Then they ate through the fuel line of my truck, I drove into town, and gas leaked on the hot manifold. If I hadn't smelt the gas it woulda' blowed me up. Couple weeks ago, they ate through my brake line, and I wound up in the ditch. You're gonna need a small caliber handgun and lots of rounds. They multiply faster'n rabbits."

Jason felt anxiety rear its ugly head. "If the squirrels are so dangerous and you take them out with a twenty-two, what do we need a hand cannon or the Judge for?"

Jason kept his eye on the twenty-two as McDufus backed away from the door and gestured for them to enter.

"Come on in and let me enlighten y'all on what you got yerselves into."

Jason placed his hand on Chelsea's back and pushed her through the door. He followed. They entered the kitchen. Jason noticed that the house was similar to theirs, except for the furniture.

Jason saw McDufus point at a rickety metal kitchen table with four vinyl upholstered chairs, the vinyl patched with duct tape in several places. *Great, our neighbor is a crazy old drunk with a house decorated in early hillbilly.*

McDufus said, "Have yerselves a sit down, and I'll fill ya' in on the ways of the woods. Y'all do realize you moved to the country? Right? This here's the real deal."

They all sat at the table. Chelsea said, "So tell us, Mr. McDufus. What have we gotten ourselves into?"

Jason watched with concern as McDufus stood up, went to the kitchen, opened one of the cabinets, and took down a large bottle of whiskey. McDufus took three dirty glasses out of the sink, rinsed them under the tap, and brought them to the table. He poured three fingers into each glass, handed one to Jason, one to Chelsea, and kept the third for himself.

"Y'all might need a little bracer in order to hears what I gots to say. Bottoms up."

McDufus threw back the entire contents of his glass and wiped his mouth with the back of his hand. "Go ahead, drink up, or I'll think you're not being hospitable."

Jason looked at the pistol still in McDufus' left hand, then at Chelsea, and drank down the whiskey in a single gulp. He started choking, and McDufus laughed. Jason finally got his choking spell under control, and watched as Chelsea swallowed the whiskey in a single pull.

McDufus said, "Damn Missy, if y'all ever get tired of old Stretch here, you come on over to my place. I like a woman with some spunk."

Chelsea smiled and said, "I'll keep that in mind, Mr. McDufus. Please continue."

McDufus teetered on his chair. Jason thought the man was going to pass out and hit the floor. But he managed to catch himself, sit up straight, and continue talking.

"Well, let me see. Where to start. This here's a lake in the mountains; yer in real honest to God country, the middle a nowheres. There're the snakes to start, lots of 'em. Theys black snakes; you leave them alone. They're good for keeping the rats and other varmints away. Then there's the copperheads and rattlers. Theys poisonous. They usually hang out in the leaves and bushes, so stay on the path to avoid 'em. Theys also lots of water snakes. No poison ones in this lake. The cotton mouths are further south, in the Carolinas."

Jason did not look happy. "How do you kill snakes? The Judge four-ten shotgun shells?"

"That'd work, but it's kinda overkill. You could get a twenty-two fer the squirrels, and that'll also handle snake shot fer the snakes. Not so much kick with a twenty-two."

Jason said, "Got it, twenty-two for the snakes and squirrels. What else?"

Jason saw the worried look on Chelsea's face. *I'll show her I can protect my family.*

McDufus continued, "There's lots of black bears. You gotta keep yer trash can lid on tight. They can smell garbage a mile away, and they'll come right up to yer house to get to it."

Jason looked shocked. "Bears? What do you use to kill a bear?"

McDufus said, "Best to leave'em alone. They's big. They gonna do whatever they want. If you really need to take one out, yer Judge'd just piss'em off. You need at least a 30-30 rifle."

Jason looked at Chelsea. "Are you getting this? Maybe we should take notes."

McDufus continued, "Then they's the coyotes and mountain lions. The mountain lions are kinda scarce. Lots of coyotes. They specially like to snack on cats, and small chilluns."

Chelsea said, "Oh great. We have both. How do we protect ourselves from coyotes and mountain lions. Perhaps a rocket launcher?"

McDufus laughed. "I like you, Missy. You got a sense a humor. No, save the rocket launcher fer Bigfoot. Your hand cannon'll work fine. Just don't shoot in my direction. I shoot back."

Jason looked at Chelsea. "Did he say Bigfoot? How do we get a hand-held rocket launcher?"

McDufus stopped pouring whiskey in his glass and started drinking from the bottle. Jason thought he was going to topple off the chair. But McDufus took another pull and kept talking.

McDufus said, "Have ya heard 'bout the disappearin' fishermen? In the past month they's been at least three times somebody found a empty fishin' boat with lots a blood. No one has a clue what's goin' on. It ain't Bigfoot, cause he don't like water. My cousin, Bobby, thinks it be aliens takin' 'em, but he drinks like a fish. Ya' can't believe nothin' comes outta his mouth."

Jason saw Chelsea mouth the words silently in his direction, "His cousin drinks like a fish?"

McDufus finished his story, "I'm sorry to say, my other cousin, Earl, was one of the fishermen whose boat was found empty and bloody. Don't git me wrong, Earl and me weren't all that close. He up and stole my wife, Helen, a few years back. She started complainin' bout my drinkin', and next thing I knowed she'd moved in with that rat bastard."

Jason smiled, "Mr. McDufus. I have some good news. I am a PI...that's private investigator...and if you hire me, I could..."

Chelsea interrupted, "What Jason means to say is that I recently opened a new PI agency, *Chelsea Longfellow, PI, and Associate*...that would be

Jason…with an office in Bedford. If you would like, you could hire us to look into the disappearance of your cousin."

McDufus said, "Let me think on that a while. Like I said, me and Earl weren't all that close. I also wouldn't mind a few folks disappearin'. Lake's still a beautiful place, but it's been gettin' crowded lately. They's too many boats in summer, and some make wakes so big they broke my floatin' dock. I'm gonna take out one of them fancy boats one a these days. Some signs of pollution too. A few small algae blooms in shallower coves in peak of summer. It's them leaky septic tanks and fertilizer from them fancy lawns runnin' into the water."

McDufus took a pull on the whiskey bottle, slumped over, and slid to the kitchen floor.

Jason watched as Chelsea got up and walked over to the old, battered couch in the living room. She picked up a ragged blanket and gently placed it over McDufus.

She said, "Poor old man. Reminds me of my mother. She often passed out from drink when I was little, and I always covered her up wherever she landed."

Jason said, consolingly, "Yeah, he reminds me of your mother too. She also drank too much and wanted to shoot me."

Chelsea said, "He did tell us about the dangers of the lake, and what type of firearms to use to protect ourselves. But what is he planning on using to take out a wake board boat?"

Jason said, "He did mention a rocket launcher. But we don't want him to harm himself. He might be our first paying customer."

Chapter 7. Cats, Boats, and Bad Ideas

It was clear to Jason that Smythe Mountain Lake served as a one season resort due to the cold winters. Jason, bored out of his mind, wondered if they'd made the right decision moving to the country. *Chelsea Longfellow, PI, and Associate* only had two cases to date. One involved an old lady from Bedford, a Mrs. Agnes Terwilliger. Someone ran over her cat. The police didn't seem to care, so she hired the PIs. They never caught the cat killer or got paid. But Terwilliger took one of the kittens, which Jason considered a win. The other case included their neighbor McDufus, who hired Chelsea's PI firm to investigate the disappearance of his cousin while fishing last season. They hadn't made any progress on that case either. March was just around the corner, and Jason hoped for new clues to appear with the next fishing season.

End of February, Jason went out of town to attend a two-day PI conference in Richmond. He returned on Sunday evening and found the girls playing with the female cats on the living room floor. Herman lay on the couch at the opposite end from Chelsea. Jason burst into the room, arms open for hugs, and said, "Hello family. Dad's home."

To his dismay, no one jumped up to give him a hug. Lizzy, Lilly, and Lucy looked up and said, in unison, "Hello Daddy." Then they kept on playing with the cats.

Jason was relieved that at least Chelsea got up off the couch and gave him a brief peck on the cheek. "Welcome home, Dear. How was your trip?"

Jason kissed her on the forehead. "It wasn't quite what I expected. I hoped for firearms exhibits, instruction on law enforcement detecting techniques, reports of exciting cases, that sort of thing. It was mostly lectures, the most mundane cases imaginable. Following a cheating husband, getting pictures of him in the act of…you know. One guy, a PI from Virginia Beach, reported on a stolen pet case. A man stole a parrot from an old lady and turned it loose when he couldn't sell it. The bird flew home, told its owner the name of the thief, and the PI made a citizen's arrest. Too bad Mrs. Terwilliger's cat couldn't talk. We might have solved that one."

Chelsea shook her head, "Jason, Fluffy was dead."

"Oh yeah. I forgot. I guess talking wasn't an option."

Jason walked over to the girls. Lizzy was tormenting the cats with a laser pointer. He said, "So, did you girls miss your old Dad?"

To his surprise, none of them responded. He noticed Chelsea was having difficulty looking him in the eye. Then he saw Herman on the end of the couch by himself. Herman looked Jason in the eye. Jason saw what appeared to be deep sadness mixed with anger.

"Chelsea, what did you do? My buddy Herman does not look happy."

Chelsea said, too quickly, "He missed you Dear. He has grown to love and adore you."

Jason said, "That's not a look of love and adoration. He looks like he wants to eat me."

Then it hit Jason like a ton of bricks. Jason had left poor, defenseless Herman at home with his wife and three daughters. And they had done the unthinkable.

"Please tell me you didn't take him to the vet without talking to me first. Poor Herman. I never dreamed you'd do something so cruel."

Jason looked at Herman. Herman, gently licking himself, looked up at Jason and then looked away. Jason felt terrible, and a little dizzy.

"I'm sorry Herman. I never dreamed they'd do such a thing, or I wouldn't have left you alone with them. I would say that I feel your pain…well…I do feel kind of woozy. Please forgive me."

Jason watched sadly as Herman gingerly climbed down from the couch and left the room. Jason realized that his furry friend would not be friendly for a while. *He looks so sad. Leave it to Chelsea. The only other male in the house, I leave him alone with them, and snip, snip.*

Jason said to no one in particular, "How could you? And he's clearly blaming me."

Lizzy finally looked up at Jason, "Mom did it. I told her you wouldn't be happy. And it's obvious that Herman isn't happy. We're sorry Daddy."

Lucy said, "Yeah Daddy. We're sorry. Mommy took Herman to the vet, and he got snipped."

Jason looked at Lucy, "That's not very nice. Don't say that?"

Chelsea said, "Jason, it had to be done. I knew you'd never agree to it. The vet said if we hadn't had him fixed, Herman would have howled, kept us up all night trying to get outside, and ruined the house marking his territory."

"Chelsea, that's terrible. You make poor Herman sound like some kind of animal."

Chelsea mumbled, "Idiot."

Jason went in search of Herman, to pet him and comfort him. But he couldn't find the cat. Apparently, cats were good at hiding. Jason collected everyone in the living room, made a big bowl of popcorn, and they all watched *The Lion King* for the millionth time. After the movie, Chelsea corralled the girls.

Chelsea said, "It's bedtime. Quick take your baths, put on your jammies, and get into bed. Tell Daddy goodnight. I'm sure he wants to get to bed too. He's exhausted after the long drive."

The girls disappeared into their rooms. Jason put the empty popcorn bowl in the sink and walked into the master bedroom. He turned on the light, opened his suitcase on the bed, and began to unpack. Then he glanced at his pillow out of the corner of his eye.

Jason bellowed, "What the hell? Chelsea! What is this?"

He turned and saw Chelsea hurry into the bedroom. She looked at Jason's pillow and said, "Why Jason, you're the expert detective, but I believe that is cat poop."

Jason, still yelling, "I know it's cat poop! How the hell did it get there?"

"Jason, stop swearing. Did you ever find Herman? He appeared to be irritated with you. Perhaps he's sending you a message."

"But why me? You took him to the vet. How'd he know which pillow was mine?"

Chelsea chuckled, "It would seem cats are a lot smarter than we give them credit for. You had better watch your back for the next few days, until your little buddy forgives and forgets. Be sure to wash that pillowcase a couple of times. Actually, just throw it away."

"Chelsea, out here in this godforsaken place there's killer squirrels, snakes, bears, mountain lions, coyotes, giant fish, and an old drunk who runs around on his deck with a gun. But who'd a thought I'd have to deal with cat crap on my pillow? You just can't make this stuff up."

"No Dear, you can't. If I were you, I'd be sure to give your little buddy lots of special treats for the next few weeks."

***

The following week, Jason was hanging out at their PI office building on Tuesday morning, wishing for a client to walk through the door. He always sat at Chelsea's desk when she wasn't there. He replaced her metal nameplate with his and hid hers in the drawer. *Associate* indeed. He heard the bell on the front door jingle, looked through the glass wall of Chelsea's office, and saw a large man enter the building.

Jason met the fellow at the front counter. The man wore blue jeans, a plaid flannel shirt, boots, and a fishing hat adorned with an assortment of lures. Jason offered his hand.

"Hello, I'm Detective Jason Longfellow, at your service. What can I do for you? Is your wife having an affair? Do you want her followed? Should I get juicy pictures? Better yet, was she murdered? What about your mother? Something awful happen to her? Hit by a bus? Or is your brother one of the disappeared fishermen? I hope it's not a lost or stolen pet thing."

The man looked puzzled. He shook Jason's hand.

"Howdy. I'm Oscar Dupris. My wife and mother are fine, thank you for asking. I don't have a brother, or any pets. I work at the boat dealership around the corner and up the block from y'all, and we're havin' a boat sale. I was hoping I could put a flier in your window."

Dupris held out one of the fliers. Jason took it, feeling disappointed.

Jason perked up. "A boat sale, you say. I happen to be in the market for a new bass boat. I'm both an expert fisherman and an awesome PI. I need a new bass boat to compete in local fishing tournaments. I also need access to the local fishing community so I can investigate why fishermen keep disappearing. How about I put your flier in the window. Then I'll close up shop and follow you back to your dealership. Do I get a discount as a local businessman?"

Jason reached behind the front counter for some tape and fastened the flier to the front window. Then he took Dupris by the arm and herded him out the door.

They talked as they walked. Dupris asked, "So, what do you fish for, Detective Longfellow?"

"It's Jason. You can call me Jason. I understand there's some large stripers in the lake. I guess I'll go for a record striper."

Dupris said, "What's your experience on the pro fishing circuit? How often do you fish?"

Jason said, "Well, honestly, I haven't been fishing on the lake yet, or anywhere else to speak of. But I'm sure I'll be a pro. How hard can it be? My wife, Chelsea, refused to let me buy a bass boat. But I'm sure when I tell her about the great deal you're going to give me, she won't be able to say no. She got a large inheritance last year, and she gets all bossy about spending it. By the way, did you or any of your fishermen friends disappear from the lake? It would be great if you disappeared and then came back; you could be very helpful to my investigation."

Jason noticed that Dupris had started walking faster, almost like he was trying to escape.

"Slow down, Mr. Dupris. I'm having trouble keeping up and it makes it hard to talk to you. How much farther is it to your dealership? What type of boats do you sell? How much?"

Jason was relieved when Dupris slowed his pace. "It's just around the corner. My dad started the business twenty years ago, and he recently passed away. I took over last year. We sell Triton, Ranger, and Tracker bass boats, with several difference sized motors. You can spend anywhere from twenty-five thousand for a basic setup to seventy thousand for top of the line. The more expensive ones have up to two-hundred-fifty horsepower outboard motors. If you're serious, I'll give you a good deal. Business has dropped off quite a bit in the last couple of years. It's these darned fishing tournaments. They catch the interest of the large boat dealerships, and most of the fishermen now buy their boats wholesale from somewhere else. It's killing my business."

They turned the corner, and Jason saw a building with a glass front and fenced-in lot. He noticed '*DUPRIS BOATS, for skiing, fishing, cruising, or just taking a nap*' painted on a sign on the roof. There were several boats parked on the lot; the most expensive ones with the larger engines were clearly kept inside. Jason decided he needed one of the more expensive ones. He might end up in a boat chase with the fishermen killer. Besides, it was just Chelsea's money.

Jason followed Dupris into the building. He walked up to a brand new twenty-foot Ranger bass boat with a 250 HP Mercury Outboard, sitting on a shiny trailer. He gave it a thorough examination. The black glossy fiberglass hull sported a white racing stripe with a trace of red and yellow flames near the stern. Two comfortable looking sunken black and white leather seats had been inserted towards the stern, one serving as the helm. This deluxe model included comfortably padded, raised leather fishing seats, also black with white trim, two in the stern and two in the bow. Several storage compartments and a large tank for hauling the day's catch were recessed into the floor in front of the helm. A typical bass boat, the hull only extended a few inches above the floor, creating a large, flat surface from which to fish. A trolling motor on the stern bow rested on the bow floor. This model included a swim platform, ladder, and metal ski rope cleats on the stern, to provide fun for the entire family. The sleek fiberglass hull was clearly designed for speed, with little wind or water resistance when on plane.

Jason placed his hand gently on the gunwale and said, "I'll take this one. How much?"

Dupris gave Jason a quizzical look. "Don't you want to look around? That's a lot of money for your first boat. That one's for pro fishermen."

Jason said, "I like to go fast, that racing stripe is awesome, and my wife has lots of money. Besides, if we don't get some paying clients soon, I'll join the pro fishing circuit to generate some income of my own. Plus, it will give me some cred with the local fishermen. How much?"

Dupris said, "You certainly picked near top of the line. That one's on sale for sixty thousand, with trailer. A great deal at that price. It can take years for a fella to win on the pro fishing circuit. If you want this boat, I'll need a ten percent deposit. How would you like to pay?"

Jason took out his wallet and handed Dupris a credit card. "Put the deposit on this. I'll bring you a certified check later this week." *Once I've convinced Chelsea what a good idea this is.*

Dupris took the card, looked at it, and said, "This is a corporate credit card, with the name *Chelsea Longfellow, PI.*"

Jason took back the card and examined it carefully. He said, "Where's the *Associate*? It's supposed to say…and *Associate.*"

Dupris grinned, "Perhaps there wasn't enough room for the entire name. Since you're not on the card, I need to phone this Chelsea Longfellow to get her permission."

Jason's tone changed from confident to pleading, "There's no need for that. She's my wife and I am a partner is the PI firm. The PI thing was my idea, but her mother left her the money. If you want to make this sale, you'll put the deposit on this credit card and give me time to beg…I mean explain to my wife how important this boat is to our business."

Jason held his breath while Dupris stood there with a thoughtful look on his face. Dupris finally took the credit card back from Jason and ran it for the six-thousand-dollar deposit.

"Detective Longfellow, you've got some stones. I assume you have a good plan for convincing your wife to follow your crazy…I mean excellent plan. I'll have the boat ready for you tomorrow. Hope your wife isn't the violent type. Your deposit is non-refundable."

Jason took the card, "No worries. I can convince her of anything. Besides, once word gets around about my PI skills, we'll be rolling in paying clients. I'll have my own money to spend."

Jason walked over to the bass boat and patted the shiny fiberglass bow. "Don't worry, *Luscious*, I'll be back to get you in a day or two. We're gonna be great friends, catch us some big bass. Might also catch us a killer, with me as the bait."

Dupris shook his head. "I'm not sure you grasp the concept of fishin'. You're s'posed to use bait to catch stripers, not be the bait. Just bring me a check and you can have the boat."

Jason ran back to the office, locked up, and headed for home. Chelsea had taken the day off, and he found it more effective to beg in person. He found her napping on the couch in the living room, and the girls hadn't come home from school yet. He went into the kitchen, took a pan out of the cabinet, and purposefully dropped it on the floor to wake up his wife.

Jason heard Chelsea say loudly, sounding half asleep, "Jason, is that you? What are you doing home so early? I thought you went into the office to drum up some business."

Jason walked into the living room, bent down, and kissed her on the cheek.

He said, "Hi Sweetums, did you get a nice nap? I've got some great news."

He winced when she gave him a suspicious look. She said, "Sweetums? You haven't called me that in…forever. What did you do?"

"I made an excellent investment in our PI business, managed to kill three birds with one stone. Am I brilliant or what?"

"Oh God. Three birds. And how did you do that…dare I ask?"

"I bought us a brand-new fishing boat, a Ranger twenty-footer with 250 HP motor. *Luscious* is a beauty. And the three birds? One, we can paint the name of our PI firm on the side for marketing and deduct the cost from our taxes. Two, I can use *Luscious* to get to know the local fishermen, helping with our investigation of the disappearances. Three, if our PI business fails, I can join the pro bass fishermen's tour and bring in money that way. And four, I can use *Luscious* and me as bait to catch whoever is killing off local fishermen."

"Jason, you said you killed three birds with one stone."

"Yeah, I know. But I just realized three is an odd number, so I had to come up with another one on the fly to make it four, nice and even. What do you think, my little cupcake?"

Chelsea stood up. Jason followed her into the kitchen. She said, "I'm going to get diabetes if you don't stop calling me all those stupid names." Jason watched her warily as she processed his good news. "YOU BOUGHT A WHAT?! We agreed, no boats right now. How much?"

Jason's knees started to feel wobbly. The kitchen contained skillets, knives, and other potentially dangerous things.

"But Chelsea, I just gave you four excellent reasons for buying a bass boat. Plus, we could take the girls for rides on the lake, and tubing, and water skiing and stuff. We're headed into Spring, and boating season's right around the corner." *Damn, that's five reasons. Now I've got to come up with another one to make it even again.*

"How much did you pay for this bass boat? You had better not have written a check from our joint account or the business account."

"No worries, Chelsea. I gave the salesman a deposit with our business credit card. The boat costs sixty-thousand dollars, with all the bells and whistles…depth finder, fish finder, 250 HP Mercury Engine, large fish tank. It's on sale for thirty percent off, and with that large engine I can catch the killers when I chase them down the lake." *That's two more reasons. Now I need another to make it even again. I'm getting a headache.*

Jason followed Chelsea into the kitchen and watched her set up a pot of drip coffee, a French brew he thought was strong enough to choke a horse. Chelsea leaned against the kitchen counter. Jason stood in front of her and gave her his best version of *the face.*

Chelsea said, "Jason, stop with *the face.* You look like you need to go to the bathroom. I did use my inheritance to steal your idea for a PI firm and put my name on it. In fairness, I've solved more of your cases than you have, but I guess it still wasn't very nice. We have plenty of money, and a tax write off is good, if we ever have any income. Go ahead and buy the boat."

"Thank you so much Chelsea. You won't regret it."

"Frankly, Jason, I doubt that. On the other hand, I must confess that I've always wanted a ski boat. But a bass boat with a large engine should suffice for teaching the girls to ski. I'll learn to drive the thing, and maybe I'll even pull you around on water skis. Wouldn't that be fun?"

Jason saw the evil grin and twinkle in his wife's eyes, and suddenly, the bass boat didn't seem like such a good idea. *She's gonna pull me on water skis? Maybe I'll do some night fishing, and I'll disappear myself before she puts me in a tree.*

Chapter 8. GenesRUs

Chelsea paid for the boat. Thursday morning, Dupris delivered it by water. Jason and Chelsea stood on their stationary dock, watching Dupris pull into the boat house. He climbed onto the floating dock, up the three wooden steps onto the stationary dock, and flipped a switch to raise the boat lift out of the water.

Dupris turned from his task and waved to Jason and Chelsea. They stood on the stationary dock behind him. Chelsea saw him point proudly in the direction of the new boat.

Dupris said, "Here she is. You named her *Luscious*. Luscious has found her new home."

Chelsea said, "What kind of name is Luscious? Sounds like a stripper. Jason, why did you name my new bass boat after a stripper?"

"When I saw her, she looked all sleek and alluring. Luscious just popped into my head."

"Idiot."

"Yes Dear."

"We can discuss a more appropriate name for my new bass boat later. It's long, hard, and has plenty of thrust…perhaps Rex, or Rocky."

Jason said, "Wait a minute. What do you mean *your new bass boat?*"

Chelsea noticed Dupris' face had turned red. She said, "This is a discussion for another time, Jason. Let poor Mr. Dupris finish his delivery."

Dupris reached out his hand to Chelsea and said, "Here's the keys. Do you have any questions? One of my salesmen is picking me up. He's probably waiting in your driveway."

Jason answered. "No, We're good. I know how to drive a boat; in fact, I drove one on the Intracoastal Waterway. I even chased a couple of killers."

Chelsea frowned at Jason and shook her head. "Jason, now's not the time to regale Mr. Dupris with tales of your PI misadventures. He needs to meet his ride. We'll give you a call if we have any questions, Mr. Dupris. Thanks again for delivering the boat in person."

"You're quite welcome, Mrs. Longfellow. By the way, my salesman called to confirm that he left your new boat trailer in the communal storage area in your parking spot, number 451."

Chelsea smiled, "Excellent. Let's head up to the house. Jason can take me out on the lake this afternoon and give me a few pointers on how to drive Luscious."

Jason grinned, "I would be delighted to teach you how to captain our new ship."

She started up to the house with Jason and Dupris in tow. Around front Chelsea saw a pickup truck in the driveway with *DUPRIS BOATS* painted on the side.

Dupris shook their hands and said, "Thank you for your business. Enjoy your new boat."

Jason said, "No worries there. We will."

Then Chelsea noticed a distinct change in the tone of Dupris' voice, as he took a step closer to them, leaned in, and said, "By the way, I heard you're lookin' into the disappearance of those fishermen last fall. Do you have any idea what's goin' on? One of the sheriff's deputies came into the store the other day and asked me some questions. Seems one of those abandoned bass boats full of blood came from my dealership. I was wonderin' if you told the police anything that might point them in my direction. I wouldn't be happy about a thing like that. Ya' never know, your Luscious might end up abandoned too. Y'all are new here, and you should mind your own business. We got the police. We don't need no PIs snooping around. Just a word to the wise."

Chelsea took a step back as Dupris got in the truck. He gave them a cheery wave as the driver headed up the driveway. She was struck by the way his demeanor had abruptly shifted to threatening psychopath and then back to friendly boat salesmen again. Jason looked to her like he was oblivious to what just happened.

Jason and Chelsea went into the house. Chelsea said, "I wonder what that was about. I think Mr. Dupris just threatened us. Jason, did you tell the police anything to suggest that Dupris might be a suspect in the case of the disappearing fishermen?"

Jason said, "He did sound kind of grumpy. I was just happy to see someone take my investigating seriously; he thought the police would actually listen to me. I did see Deputy Harbinger in town the other day. I might have mentioned that a local boat dealer could be killing off fishermen that didn't buy their boats locally. But Mr. Dupris just said that one of the boats they found abandoned was from his dealership."

Chelsea said, "That sounds crazy. Killing fishermen because they didn't buy their boat locally? Where'd you get that idea?"

"Dupris told me he'd give me a great price because his business is in trouble. Apparently, because of all the big pro fishing tournaments most of the fishermen around here are buying their boats wholesale from larger dealerships. A small local dealership can't compete."

Chelsea said, "I guess it's also possible Dupris could have murdered one fisherman who bought one of his boats to deflect suspicion from himself. The real question is, why would he threaten us unless he is doing something illegal?"

Jason said, "Deputy Harbinger seemed interested in my theory. I never dreamed he'd follow through. If he took me seriously, maybe there is something to it. I knew I was a great detective."

Chelsea said, "You better keep your yap shut, great detective, or you're going to get us killed. Also, we have a boat now, but I don't think it's a good idea to use you as bait to catch the killer. How about a peanut butter and jelly sandwich for lunch, and then a boat lesson."

Jason said, "Are you kidding? You with your hand cannon and me with Blaster? Use me for bait. Those thugs won't know what hit 'em."

Chelsea didn't feel like arguing. She'd deal with his stupid plan and stupid name for her new boat later. She slapped together a couple of peanut butter and jelly sandwiches and told Jason to pour two glasses of milk. They took their lunch out onto the table in the screened porch.

Chelsea took a bite of her sandwich and looked up at Jason. His PB&J and milk were gone.

She said, "Did you inhale that?"

"Come on, woman. I'm in a hurry to run Luscious through her paces. Mr. Dupris said she'll do sixty on the water, and these fishing boats are so sleek they barely touch the surface."

Chelsea took another small bite and followed it up with a sip of milk.

"Jason, it's not an offshore racing boat. Maybe you should have named the thing *Zippy*."

"Chelsea, are you jealous of my new girlfriend, Luscious? I promise not to run off with her."

Chelsea grinned, *If only…*

They finished lunch, and Chelsea followed Jason down the path to the dock. He walked onto the stationary dock, went to the boat lift, and hit the switch. Chelsea stood behind him.

"Jason, shouldn't we check for life jackets, a fire extinguisher. And where's the boat key?"

"Chelsea, you worry too much. Mr. Dupris took care of all that stuff, and the key's in the ignition. Although probably not a good idea to store the boat that way. I'd hate to watch a thief drive off with my new sixty-thousand-dollar boat."

"Don't remind me. I must be crazy for agreeing to this."

Chelsea watched as Jason ran the boat lift, the electric motor humming smoothly. He stopped it when Luscious was floating free. Chelsea watched him climb down to the floating dock.

"Come on Chelsea. You have to come down here to get in."

Chelsea climbed down the three wooden steps. Jason had boarded Luscious and sat in the captain's chair. Chelsea stepped into the boat just as a ski boat pulling a tube full of children passed within twenty feet of the dock. The huge wake hit Luscious, and Chelsea almost went over the side. Jason grabbed her arm and pulled her into his lap.

Chelsea said, "Oh Captain, my Captain. Are you trying to kill me? Get us out of here. These steel pylons are going to turn my brand-new boat into shredded fiberglass on the first day."

Jason said, "Sorry. I didn't see that boat. It's nice having you sit on the captain's lap."

She whacked Jason on the back of the head, got up, and moved to the seat next to him.

"Ouch! Now I know why it was considered bad luck to have a woman on board a ship in the old days. They're really grouchy."

"Jason, get us out of here before that boat comes back and turns Luscious into the Titanic."

"Chelsea, the Titanic was an ocean going…"

Chelsea tried to whack him again, but Jason ducked. He started the big Mercury outboard, placed the throttle in reverse, and managed to hit each pilon twice as he backed out.

Chelsea said, "We need rubber bumpers for the floater and pilons. Our captain in a klutz."

Chelsea watched as Jason turned Luscious towards the *big water*, the main part of the lake. She saw that look in his eyes that appeared when

Little Jason took over. She grabbed the seat frame for dear life as he shoved the throttle all the way forward. The boat leapt clear out of the water and shot forward like a rocket.

Chelsea felt woozy as the houses, trees, and mountain flew by as a colorful blur.

"Jason, are you crazy?! You're supposed to teach me how to drive the boat, not kill me. Let me take over the helm and show me how to drive like a normal human being." *Who am I kidding? There's nothing normal about my husband. I married a wackadoodle.*

They reached a broad expanse of the lake next to the mountains, and Jason slowed Luscious to a stop. Chelsea looked around, the dizziness subsided, and she noticed how beautiful it was.

"Jason, remind me to smack you one later. But right now, look at that view. The blue sky and the gorgeous expanse of sparkling water, with that spectacular mountain as a backdrop. I hate to admit it, but this boat was an excellent idea. We'd never get to see views like this without it."

Jason said, "You're welcome."

Chelsea enjoyed the view some more. Then said, "Okay Captain. How do I drive this beast?"

She watched as Jason placed his hand on the throttle to demonstrate.

"The center position is neutral, the engine idling and not engaged. If you want to go forward, you squeeze the handle to engage the clutch and gently but firmly push the throttle forward. The further forward, the faster the boat will go. Once you reach the desired speed, you adjust the trim with this button to push the boat up onto plane. Same for reverse; you squeeze the handle and pull the throttle firmly backwards. Going in reverse is the same as with the car; if you want the rear to go left, you turn the wheel to the left, and vice-versa."

Chelsea listened intently, then said, "Okay, how do you stop? Where are the brakes?"

"There aren't any brakes. You put the throttle in neutral and let the water slow the boat to a stop. You need to give yourself plenty of room. If you're going slow and you get into trouble, you can put the boat in reverse and the propeller will pull in the opposite direction, stopping you. But you can't do that when you're flying down the lake, or bad things will happen. If you want to go really slow, like when parking at a dock, you can put it in forward for a couple of seconds and then slip it back into neutral. The boat will continue to float forward slowly. I'll show you all this when we get back to the dock. I'm an…"

"I know. You're an expert boatsman. Is that even a word? Okay, let me give it a whirl."

Chelsea sat down in the captain's chair and took over the helm. Jason kneeled behind her. She squeezed the clutch and gently pushed the throttle forward. The boat began to move.

Jason said, "Okay, good. Now give her more gas, and when I tell you push the trim button."

She shoved the throttle forward, the boat lurched, and Jason fell over the side. Chelsea was so exhilarated by the speed that she didn't notice at first.

She turned around and said, "Jason, how am I doing? When do I push on this trim thingy? Jason? Where did you go? Leave it to you to abandon ship when I need you."

Chelsea pulled the throttle back to neutral. She stood up and looked around the lake.

She yelled, "Jason Bartholomew Longfellow! Where are you? Get back into this boat right now! How dare you abandon me like that!"

Chelsea saw a tiny person in the water off in the distance, frantically waving his arms. She pushed the throttle forward, turned the boat around, and headed in that direction. When she reached Jason, she aimed the boat directly for him, planning to pick him up.

She saw Jason waving and choking. He yelled, "Help! Help!" Then, "Stop! Stop!"

Chelsea saw Jason dive for deep water as the boat ran over top of him.

She yelled, "Jason, what was that about stopping? I still don't understand the brakes."

After she went over him, she saw Jason come back up to the surface. She slowly turned the boat around and put it in neutral.

Jason yelled, "Chelsea, for the love of God, stay there! Please! I'll come to you."

He swam to Luscious, grabbed the side of the bass boat, and pulled himself onto the deck.

"You almost killed me! I showed you how to stop. Why'd you try to run me over?"

"It's not my fault. You buy a boat with no brakes. Then abandon me when you're supposed to be teaching me to drive. Sixty-thousand-dollars? How much were the boats *with* brakes."

Jason shook his head, and said, "There's no such thing as a boat with…Oh, never mind. Let me take over, and we'll go back to the dock. That's enough excitement for one day."

Chelsea felt angry, both at herself and at Jason. He could have explained things better. And who buys a vehicle that goes this fast without brakes? She sat down, grabbed onto the seat, and hung on tight. Jason was like a child. He only had one speed, go fast. He shoved the throttle forward and they flew towards their dock. Then Jason unexpectedly pulled back on the throttle and stopped in the middle of the lake near the dam.

"Jason, why are you stopping? I thought we were going home."

"I thought this electronic thingy on the dashboard was a depth finder, and the digital readout does show the lake is two hundred feet deep right here. But I just noticed this button on it that says *fish*. This must also be one of those fish finders. I thought I'd stop and turn it on; try it out."

"You mean you were flying down the lake at sixty miles an hour, and you were looking at this thingamajig instead of watching where you were going?"

Chelsea watched as Jason pushed the button marked *fish*. A computer screen came to life with avatars of fish of all sizes.

Jason said, "Chelsea, look. There's a school of fish below us. If we had our fishing poles, we could stop and reel 'em in. This fishing thing's gonna be a piece of cake. I could win lots of money on the pro fishing tour with a gadget like this."

Chelsea became impatient as Jason moved Luscious forward slowly so he could look for fish. As he entered their cove, she saw another bass boat headed in their direction.

She said, "Jason, you need to look out for that boat. He's going to cross in front of you on the way to our dock, and we're going to crash if someone doesn't change course."

She looked at Jason. His eyes glued to the fish finder, he pointed at the device.

"Chelsea, look! There's a whale underneath us! That fish is almost as big as Luscious."

Chelsea looked at the digital screen, and she saw an avatar of a gigantic fish.

"Jason, there are no whales in this lake. I don't know what that is, but it can't be a fish."

Jason said, "Maybe it's a submarine. The Russians are invading the lake! Or maybe it's a freshwater shark."

Chelsea heard the roar of an engine and looked up. She saw Jason do the same. The other boat had moved between them and their boat house. The driver sped up to avoid a collision.

Chelsea pointed and yelled, "Jason, we're gonna crash!"

Jason swerved hard, producing a large wake. The other bass boat slowed, bouncing around violently. Jason headed to their dock. Chelsea saw the other boat driver pull up to their floater.

Chelsea said, "What's he doing? He looks mad. Maybe we should come back later."

Jason said, "This is my dock, and he went too close. I read in the online boating course you're supposed to stay fifty feet from docks. He also cut me off. I've got this."

Chelsea couldn't resist, "Perhaps you should have taken the boating course where you actually drive a boat…oh, never mind."

Jason aimed Luscious between the two front pilons, moving very slowly. This was the first time he had put the boat on the lift. Chelsea heard him counting under his breath, a sign that he was stressed and upset about the near crash. The man in the other boat sat watching.

Chelsea put her hand on Jason's shoulder and squeezed gently. "Jason, you can do this. It's just like parking a car, only not."

Chelsea watched with dread as Jason crashed into the right pilon. He backed the boat up and started forward again, just as a strong cross wind blew by. Jason put the throttle into neutral to coast slowly, and the wind blew him into the left pilon. On the third try he had the boat centered perfectly. Instead of coasting, he shoved the throttle forward, forcing the boat between the pilons. Chelsea was impressed, until the boat crashed into the dock at the end of the boat house.

"Nice job, Captain. I hope we have insurance to repair the crack in the fiberglass hull."

Chelsea saw the sad look on Jason's face. He stepped onto the floating dock and gave her his hand to help her out of the boat. He climbed onto the stationary dock, hit the switch on the lift, and stopped it when the boat was out of the water. He walked back down to the floating dock to where the other boat was parked. Chelsea followed.

Chelsea guessed that the man sitting in the captain's seat was in his fifties, a crown of gray hair encircling his sunburnt bald head. He wore a green bathing suit, no shirt. He stood, stepped onto the floating dock, and walked towards Jason. Around five-foot-nine and shaped like someone who had difficulty pushing himself away from the table, his gut hung over the front of his suit and bounced in synchrony with each step. When he turned his head, Chelsea saw a large wart on the left side of his nose. To make matters worse, the wart had sprouted its own bush of gray hair. Chelsea couldn't help but stare at the thing. The man offered his hand to Jason.

He said, "Hi there. The names Dr. Gene Sorgensenovitch. My father's ancestors were Swedish and Polish, so now I can't spell my own last name. I wanted to apologize for cutting you off. I didn't know anyone lived here. I'll give your dock a wide berth from now on."

Chelsea felt relief as Jason shook the man's hand. "Nice to meet you, Dr. Slogwartovitch."

Chelsea cringed.

Jason continued, "No worries. I'm an expert boatsman and was able to avoid a crash. This is my wife, Chelsea. Do you live around here?"

Chelsea stepped back as the man stumbled towards her due to a wake from a passing boat. She feared his gut might knock her off the floating dock. He offered his hand, and she shook it.

He said, "Pleased to meet you, Ma'am." To Jason, "I live right over there, in the house next to yours. Are you here full time? Most homeowners are only here in the spring and summer."

Chelsea had to fight the urge to stare at that hairy wart. She answered his question.

"Yes, we live here year-round. Our three daughters are in school, and the school bus will be here soon. I should go on up to the house to meet them. Nice to meet you, Dr…Gene. Hopefully we'll get to know each other better, since we're neighbors. Are you married?"

"Yes. My wife works in Bedford, and I'm vice president of a local company. Mary is at work today. I took the day off to do a little boating. I'm sure Mary would love to meet you. Would be nice for her to have a friend nearby."

Chelsea said, "I look forward to meeting her."

Chelsea climbed up to the stationary dock and started to walk up to the house. She stopped and turned when she heard Jason speak.

Jason said, "I'm a private eye. We opened an office in Bedford last year."

Gene said, "So you're the PI guy that looked into who ran over Mrs. Terwilliger's cat. Mary knows Mrs. Terwilliger, and she told my wife that your solution was to try to sell her one of your cats. Hopefully you've found more interesting work since then."

Chelsea decided to keep quiet. Jason wanted to be the lead PI, so she let him continue this particular conversation on his own. She'd step up later when they had a case worth discussing.

Jason countered, "It's true the case of the cat murderer went unsolved. But we are heavily involved in investigating the disappearance of several fishermen from the lake. We have a client who hired us to find his cousin, one of the aforementioned fishermen. I bought this boat so I could use myself as bait to draw out the fishermen murderer. Tell him, Chelsea."

Chelsea felt her face turn red. She wished she'd walked up the hill faster.

She said, "It's true we have a client who hired us to investigate the disappearing fishermen. But the idea of Jason acting as bait is still up for debate."

Gene chuckled. "Sounds like an interesting plan. I look forward to hearing how it works out."

Jason said, "You said you are the VP of a local company. What company is that? Is it in Bedford? Is your wife having an affair? Has anyone robbed your business? Someone embezzling funds from you? Any lost or stolen pets, especially parrots?"

Gene said, "You certainly are direct. I don't have the need for a PI right now. If the need arises, I'll be sure to give you a call. I'm the VP of Manufacturing for GenesRUs, a local medical biotech company. Our facilities are located on fifty acres just outside of Bedford on Route 29."

Jason perked up. "A biotech company? I used to work for the FDA, and we regulated biotech products. I'm a Doctor of Pharmacology…and a PI. What types of products do you make?"

Chelsea noticed that Gene looked wary. "You worked for the FDA? And now you're a PI? That's kind of an unusual transition, isn't it?"

Chelsea said, "When you get to know him better, you'll see that unusual isn't the half of it. But yes, Jason used to work for the FDA. He went insane and started doing PI work on the side. I'm a nurse, worked in hospital administration. Northern Virginia got too crowded, so we moved here. I apparently lost my mind too and we opened a PI firm. We haven't had time to get established. If you know of anyone who might require our services, we'd appreciate a referral."

Jason jumped in. "We both have our PI licenses from the internet, and a great office in Bedford. It's got three old video games that I can play when times are slow, like since we opened several months ago. That's another reason I bought a boat. I'm bored."

Gene said, "Sorry to hear that. I'm sure things will pick up now that spring is almost here."

Jason repeated his question, "What kinds of products does GenesRUs manufacture?"

Gene said, "We have a couple of monoclonal antibodies for eczema and MS and one gene therapy for Parkinson's disease. Our latest thing is recombinant human growth hormone. Since you don't work for the FDA anymore, I guess I can tell you. We submitted an Orphan Drug Application for idiopathic growth hormone deficiency in children and Turner's syndrome in young girls. I'm sure you remember what an Orphan Drug is."

Jason said, "Yes, a drug developed to treat a rare disease with a small patient population. The drug company gets certain regulatory and financial dispensations for developing these types of drugs. With so few patients such a drug would not otherwise be economically feasible."

Chelsea watched from the stationary dock as a new flurry of wakes rocked the floating dock. Jason grabbed a steel pilon to support himself, and Gene's gut bounced along with the waves.

"Yes. I'm very proud of the work we've done, and it looks like the FDA will approve our Orphan Drug Application. It's quite exciting, being able to help these children."

Chelsea watched in terror as a large wakeboard boat zoomed by, only thirty feet away. The massive wake caused the floating dock to bounce violently. Jason and Gene grabbed the side of the stationary dock. To Chelsea's surprise, even the stationary dock, with steel pilons driven into bedrock, shook with this gigantic wake. She stumbled and had nothing to grab onto.

Chelsea righted herself and said, "I didn't realize these boats made such a large wake. I'm surprise our floating dock is still attached. Is it always like this?"

Gene, hanging onto a dock pilon, said, "It can get crazy. There're these damn wakeboard boats. Then there's that crazy old man that lives on the other side of you. I've heard gunfire and seen him running around on his deck in his underwear shooting at squirrels. But the freakin' fishermen are the worst. They think they own the lake. Pull right up next to your dock, cast their lures underneath it where stripers like to hang out, and usually hook your boat or jet ski cover. I replace one or two a year because of them. They also have no problem tossing their empty beer cans in the water next to your dock or shoreline. If I could, I'd make them all disappear. But this is a beautiful place to be. Welcome to Smythe Mountain Lake, the middle of nowhere."

Jason said, "Do you know Mr. McDufus very well? We met him the other day, and he seems kind of unstable. Drinking, shooting a handgun in a development…not good."

Chelsea looked down from the stationary dock as Gene smiled and said, "Unstable sounds about right. First time I met him, I asked him how long he'd lived here. He started ranting about how he was one of the first people to move to the lake, it got discovered, and now it's being ruined. He also hates squirrels. Your place provides Mary and I cover from his stray bullets."

Chelsea said, "In spite of his odd ways, he seemed like a harmless old man. I'm sure he's just lonely and has the crotchety old man syndrome. He does seem to drink a lot."

Chelsea gave a sigh of relief when the water smoothed out. Gene untied his bass boat and climbed in. He started the engine and waved at Jason and Chelsea.

"It was nice to meet you. My wife will be thrilled to hear we have new neighbors. Stay safe and watch out for stray bullets."

Chelsea watched as he backed away from the floating dock, turned his bass boat towards the big water, and shoved the throttle forward. The bass boat took off like a rocket. Jason climbed the three wooden steps up to the stationary dock and stood there with Chelsea.

Jason pointed and said, "See Chelsea. That's the way you're supposed to drive a bass boat. They're called *go-like-helly-boats*. Apparently, you need to get to the fish as fast as possible."

Chelsea shook her head, "I don't think the boat is the problem. It's the male child in adult's clothing driving it. I'm beginning to wonder if those fishermen were murdered, or they just fell overboard driving around the lake like maniacs in the middle of the night."

Jason said, "I sure hope they were murdered. No one's gonna pay us to find out they accidentally suicided themselves."

Chapter 9. The Longfellows Go Fishing

April rolled around, and the Longfellow family were finishing up dinner. Jason helped Chelsea clear the dishes, and then he sat at the table drinking coffee while she loaded the dishwasher. Chelsea never let him do the dishes because he did it wrong. Striving for symmetry, he always placed the breakable glasses too close to the rinsing arm and the pots and pans in the four corners where they never got clean.

Jason said, "Chelsea, fishing tournaments are in full swing. According to McDufus they're reeling in some really big stripers this year. It's time to take the family fishing. It's Wednesday night, and I propose that we take the entire family out tomorrow after school to buy fishing gear. Only you, I and Lizzy need licenses. The other girls aren't sixteen yet. What d'ya think?"

Chelsea loaded the last cup, added a detergent pod, and started the machine. She sat down at the table, took a gulp of her now cold coffee, and made a face.

She said, "Yuck. I need to nuke this. A family fishing trip sounds good. Let's make it a competition. Whoever catches the biggest fish gets to pick the type of pizza we have for dinner. No pepperoni. I'm tired of that."

Jason started to speak, "Chelsea, if you'd learn to cook..."

"I cook just fine. Besides, you get upset when I prepare a meal. It also seems like a waste of time with all the restaurants out there. Better to help them stay in business."

Chelsea got up, walked over to the microwave above the stove, and heated her coffee.

"Chelsea, your home cooked meals often include bad news. So, pepperoni pizza it is."

"Jason, you never pay any attention to me. I just told you, I'm tired of pepperoni pizza."

"Yes, Dear. About the fishing thing. What do you think? Should we take everyone out for fishing licenses and all the trimmings?"

"I already said it would be okay."

Jason said, "Great. Tomorrow evening we'll go to the local sporting goods store to buy fishing stuff. I think it's called *The FishingAndShooting House.* This is truly the country. You can buy a gun anywhere."

Thursday afternoon Jason and Chelsea were waiting at home when the girls got off the bus. Chelsea watched and laughed when Jason struggled to herd everyone into her SUV. The girls were all wound up from school. Jason drove, and Chelsea sat in the passenger's seat.

Lizzy spoke up, "Why couldn't we do this on the weekend. I've got homework tonight, and I'm supposed to video chat with my friend Charlene at nine."

Lilly said, "I'm hungry. What are we going to have for dinner?"

Lucy added her two cents worth, "Pizza, I want pepperoni pizza!"

Chelsea sighed and gave Jason an annoyed look.

Jason said, "What? I'm trying to be a good father. I'm buying fishing licenses and equipment so we can all go fishing together."

Lizzy, ever the teenager, "Yeah. You're buying us all this stuff, with Mom's money."

Jason said, "It's not Mom's money. It's *our* money. I earned some money last Fall. Mr. McDufus gave me a fifty-dollar retainer to look for his cousin."

Chelsea said, "Lizzy, be nice. Daddy earned plenty working for the federal government. He retired and moved down here because I wanted us to get out of Northern Virginia. It's not his fault that Chelsea Longfellow, PI, and Associate hasn't taken off yet. We need to be patient. And Jason, that fifty-dollar retainer check was made out to Chelsea Longfellow, PI."

Jason frowned, "McDufus said there wasn't enough room on the check to add the *and Associate* part. I don't think he likes me."

Jason pulled into the sporting goods store parking lot. They entered the store and Chelsea herded them towards the fishing and camping section. They were greeted at the sales counter by an old man. By his frail appearance, complete lack of hair, skin mottled by age spots, and shaky voice, Chelsea guessed him to be in his early eighties.

The man said, "Howdy folks. The name's Howard. What can I do ya' for?"

The girls started to wander off. Chelsea herded them back just as Jason spoke to Howard.

"I'm Dr. Jason Longfellow, PI. I'm here to equip my family for striper fishing. I'm a professional fisherman, so I need your best equipment. We also need three fishing licenses."

Howard came out from behind the counter. He was so skinny, his legs so spindly, Chelsea worried his pants would fall down. They followed him to the fishing pole aisle. He turned and pointed to an entire wall filled with fishing rods of all sizes, complete with reels and fishing line.

"So, Dr. Longfellow, PI. You're gonna want these larger rods and reels for striper fishin'. I recommend at minimum a thirty-pound test line. They've been pulling some doozies out of the lake this year. You'll want a couple of different sized bucktail lures and some hinged minnows. Pick out your equipment and bring it to the counter. I'll get the forms for your fishing licenses. You'll need ID and lots of cash."

Chelsea watched as Howard left Jason standing there, looking confused. Finally, he grabbed four of the largest poles and one smaller one. He handed them to Chelsea.

Chelsea said, "If one of the girls hooks into something large enough for these poles, it's going to pull them into the water. Maybe we should fish for something smaller."

"Don't be daft. Our daughters are Longfellows. They're tough. Those stripers are in trouble."

Lizzy caught Chelsea's eye, and said, "Oh Dad. What are we going to do with you?"

Chelsea heard a scream and turned around. She saw Lucy standing in the aisle with a large fishing net over her head. Lilly stood next to her, an evil grin on her face.

Lucy cried, "Mommy, Lilly caught me in a net. I'm not a fish. Make her stop."

Chelsea scolded Lilly and sent her to get a cart. Lilly returned, and Chelsea dumped poles, lures, and assorted fishing gear in the cart. She found Jason in a nearby aisle looking at filleting knives. She walked up and whacked him on the back of the head.

"We've got enough gear for an entire deep-sea fishing trip. Let's check out. It's dinner time."

Lucy stood next to Chelsea, looking bored. She perked up when she heard her mother.

"Pizza! I want pepperoni pizza."

Chelsea groaned. "You already said that. Jason, there's a Pizza Hut just around the corner. Load up the SUV, and let's head over there. I'm hungry enough to eat an entire pizza myself."

Jason said, "I think I'll have anchovies on mine. I've got fish on the brain."

Idiot.

At the counter, Chelsea watched Howard ring up their fishing gear. He said, "If'n you're plannin' on fishin' on the lake, you might want to buy a gun." He pointed to a nearby display case that contained several handguns. "I've sold a bunch since them fishermen started disappearin'. I've got a nice three-fifty-seven magnum on sale."

Chelsea said, "That's just great. Our neighbor shoots squirrels off his deck, and all the fishermen on the lake are armed, and scared. So much for moving here for peace and quiet."

Jason said, "Howard, we're good to go. Chelsea has a fifty-cal and I've got the Judge."

Howard said, "What about the kids? My daddy gave me a twenty-two rifle when I wuz seven. Maybe you oughtta arm them too. There's safety in numbers."

Lizzy said, "Yea Mom. You should buy me one of those three-fifty-seven magnet things."

Chelsea said, "It's magnum...and we're not arming our children. I'm not even sure it's safe to arm Jason."

Jason said, "You're being mean. I'll be fine with Blaster. Just stay out of the blast area."

Chelsea said, "That's what I'm afraid of. We're gonna be in a boat, so there's not much room for us to get out of the way."

Howard said, "I just hope y'all don't show up in the newspaper as the next victims of the fishermen killer. Keep your eyes open while you're out there."

Chelsea watched the tally as Howard rang up their purchases. The total came to six-hundred-twenty-five dollars and change. Chelsea handed him a credit card.

Chelsea said, "Jason, do you know how much fish I could buy at the grocery store for six-hundred-dollars? This is another one of your hair-brained ideas."

"But Chelsea. Think of all the fun we'll have catching those big stripers. And think of all the fun you'll have gutting, cleaning, filleting, and cooking them."

Chelsea scowled at Jason. She saw Howard wince.

"Howard, I'll need a fillet knife, a big one, for a six-foot-seven, two-legged, hair-brained fish. I'm gonna gut him, clean him, fillet him, stuff him, bread him and fry him up real nice."

Lizzy said, "Dad, are you sure you want anchovies on your pizza?"

Jason gulped. "No, how about we let your mother choose."

***

Friday night after dinner Chelsea sat in the living room drinking white wine. She watched as Jason rounded up the girls for bed. He told them they had to get up at three AM to go fishing. Apparently, stripers were allergic to sun and sleep. Chelsea was not happy, but she needed to keep Jason busy until they got some work. He was unbearable when he was bored.

Saturday morning Chelsea heard the alarm at two-thirty. She saw Jason get up, and she dragged herself out of bed. She made two cups of coffee, three glasses of milk, and placed a box of Krispy Kreme Donuts on the table. Everyone appeared to eat breakfast in their sleep. After breakfast, Chelsea led them down to the dock. She was glad to see Jason had already loaded everything into the boat. With everyone on board, he headed for deep water. He stopped near the shoreline at the base of one of the mountains.

Chelsea said, "Jason, are you sure this is a good idea? The girls are all huddled in the bow, asleep. I'm drifting off myself. It is only three in the morning. Are you sure the fish are awake?"

Jason smiled, "I talked to McDufus, and this is the best time to fish for stripers. We stop the boat near the shoreline, listen for shad...small fish that travel in schools near the surface. When we find shad, stripers are not far behind. We'll hear tail slaps as they come to the surface to feed. Then we start casting with our bucktails, and whammo! We've got us a fifty pounder!"

"Captain. Set up the trolling motor. I'll wake the girls. I'd rather be in bed asleep. But with all the disappearing fishermen, I'd probably have nightmares. Are you sure we're safe out here?"

"Chelsea, hush, you'll scare the girls. You're scaring me. It's really dark. Did you bring your hand cannon?"

"No, and it's probably a good thing. Right now, I'd like to shoot the captain."

Chelsea woke the girls, sent Lilly and Lucy to the stern seats behind Jason. Lizzy sat in a bow seat. Chelsea gave them each a pole and told them to listen for the shad. She watched Jason's silhouette as he set up the trolling motor and moved them closer to the shore.

Jason pointed and whispered, "Look. See the shiny fish in the moonlight, and hear the gurgling sound? Those are the shad. I'll move us over there, and everyone cast your lures and begin reeling them in. We'll have a boat full of stripers in no time."

Lizzy grouched, "This is stupid." Chelsea saw her cast her bucktail. It landed near the shad.

Chelsea said, "Good job, Lizzy. Now reel it in slowly."

Chelsea heard Lilly groan and saw that her daughter had gotten her lure hooked onto her blouse. She was struggling to get it loose. Chelsea was afraid Lilly would fall overboard as she danced around, tugging on the lure, the boat rocking with her gyrations.

Chelsea whispered, "Lilly, stop hopping around. I'll come help you get unhooked. Your idiot father bought poles that are way too big for us. We're not fishing for whales."

Chelsea heard Lucy crying. She turned and saw that the child was all wound up in excess fishing line that had been released when she tried to cast. Chelsea was relieved the lure was still attached to one of the rungs on the pole. At least she wasn't getting stabbed by the hooks.

Chelsea turned to Jason, standing at the bow. "Jason, quit fooling around with the motor and help your children. These poles way too big for us. Lilly's hooked, Lucy's all tied up, and…"

Lizzy yelped, "Dad, I've got something."

Chelsea shined a flashlight on Jason and saw him stop the trolling motor. She watched him run to Lizzy; fishing pole bent double as she struggled with something large.

Chelsea whispered loudly, "Jason, help Lizzy. She's got a whale by the tail."

Chelsea turned back to Lucy and continued to untangle her from the fishing line. She glanced back at Jason; she could see his silhouette in the moonlight reaching for Lizzy's pole.

He said, "Here Lizzy. Let me help you. Looks like you hooked a monster."

Chelsea saw Lizzy push Jason away and keep reeling.

Lizzy said, "Dad. Get off. This is my fish. Go catch your own fish."

Chelsea gasped as she saw the line pull tight and Lizzy almost go overboard.

Lizzy screamed, "Dad, help! Are you just gonna let me fall in the water?"

Chelsea finished unwrapping Lucy. She moved to Lilly, where she started working the lure loose from the child's blouse. She saw Jason take Lizzy's pole and finish reeling a very large fish up to the side of the boat. Lizzy shined a flashlight on the monster.

Jason held onto the pole for dear life. "Lizzy, get the net. Help get this thing into the boat."

Chelsea worried that Jason was going overboard as he held the pole with one hand while trying to help Lizzy net the fish with the other.

Jason said, "Lizzy, we're almost there. Take the pole, so I can get the net around this monster and pull it into the boat. It looks like a forty pounder. Congratulations, Daughter."

Chelsea finished unhooking Lilly. She took out the hand-held scale. She helped Jason haul the fish onto the boat, remove it from the net, and attach it to the scale. When Jason raised it up, he shined the flashlight on the dial.

"Wow Lizzy. Forty-three pounds. McDufus wasn't kidding when he said there were some large stripers in this lake."

Chelsea rubbed her hands on Jason's blue jeans and said, "You were right. Fish are slimy and stinky. You'll need to wash your pants tonight. You smell like fish."

Jason said, "Thanks. I can see that. Help me get this thing in the tank and let's catch more."

They wrestled the giant striper into the storage tank, and then Chelsea excitedly casted her bucktail into the water near the school of shad. She immediately felt a strong tug.

"Jason, I've got one. What do I do?"

"Reel him in. Keep the tip of your pole up to set the hook in his mouth, and reel, reel, reel."

"I can barely hold on. My pole is bent double. I think it's going to break. Help!"

She felt Jason beside her, as he reached out and took the pole. She watched as he fought with the fish, alternately pulling, and reeling.

"Don't lose him, Jason. I think this is Moby Fish. We should form another company, Chelsea and Lizzy Longfellow, PF, *professional fisherwomen*. And we won't be needing an associate."

Lizzy said, "Yeah. No associate. Just an assistant reeler-inner."

Chelsea and the girls watched as Jason fought the fish for several minutes before pulling it up next to the boat. Lizzy held the flashlight while Chelsea netted the huge fish. Then Chelsea and Jason worked together to haul it into the boat and mount it on the hand-held scale.

Chelsea said, "Fifty-five pounds! This really is Moby Fish."

Jason said, "Shhhh. You'll scare away the rest of the fish before I catch mine."

Lizzy laughed, "Dad, these things are monsters. I doubt if they scare easily."

Chelsea said, "Where's your Moby Fish, Jason? You're the professional fisherman."

She watched as Jason turned and moved to the trolling motor in the bow.

"I'll show you. I'll move closer to the shad and catch one bigger than either of yours."

Just then Chelsea felt the boat bump against something large. and lurch sideways. She saw Jason fall overboard and disappear into the deep, dark water. She ran to the bow, leaned over the side, and looked for her husband.

"Jason Longfellow, you come back here right now! Just because Lizzy and I caught fish and you didn't, that's no excuse to run away."

Lizzy said, "Mom, I don't think he did that on purpose. I think he fell. He's kind of a klutz."

Chelsea said, "I guess you're right, but he should be coming up soon. Your father can swim, but he still needs to breathe."

Chelsea felt another hard knock on the bottom of the boat, causing it to rock violently.

Lizzy grabbed onto her mother and said, "What was that? Mom, I'm scared. Those are really big fish. One of them could swallow Lucy in one gulp."

Chelsea heard Lucy scream, "Mommy, am I gonna get eated? I don't wanna be fish food. Where's Daddy? He should be here to protect me."

Chelsea heard rapid footsteps and felt Lucy grab her by the leg.

"I don't know where your father is. But I agree, he should be here to protect us. Pretty rude of him to leave us alone in the dark. Remind me to whack him one when he gets back."

Lizzy said, "Mom, I don't think he left on purpose. I hope one of those fish didn't eat him."

Chelsea said, "Don't be silly. Your father's too big for a fish to swallow. Besides, it'd spit him out. I doubt he'd taste very good. He's just lost out there in the dark. He'll be back soon."

Chelsea, with Lucy permanently attached to her leg, took a flashlight, shined it out over the water and began to call for her husband.

"Jason Longfellow, you come back here right now. Your daughters are afraid, and you need to be here to comfort and protect them."

Chelsea heard and felt another thud as something large bumped hard against the bottom of the boat. The boat lurched and Chelsea almost went overboard.

Lizzy grabbed her mother's arm to keep her from falling.

"Mom, something big keeps crashing into us. It's trying to knock us in the water, like that scary movie *Jaws*. There's no sharks in a lake. Right?"

Lucy, still hanging onto her mother's leg, said, "Yeah Mommy. No sharks, right?"

Chelsea heard Lilly's voice from the stern of the boat, "Maybe if there's a shark, it ate Daddy and it's full. It won't be hungry anymore."

Lucy said, "Poor Daddy. Do you really think a shark ate him?"

Chelsea started to answer when she felt the boat tilt sharply to one side. She heard coughing and choking. She shined the flashlight in the direction of the noise. There was a soggy Jason, hanging onto the boat, trying to pull himself over the side.

"Jason! Where did you go? We've been scared to death. Something keeps banging into the boat, trying to capsize us. And Lucy thought you got eaten by a big fish, maybe even a shark."

She heard Jason trying to speak while water spewed out of his nose and mouth.

He gasped, "No sharks in lake. Sharks only in ocean. Boat hit log. Fell overboard. Why no one help me?"

Chelsea said, "We thought you abandoned us. You were gone a long time. And that monster kept crashing into the bottom of the boat, trying to knock us overboard so it could eat us."

Chelsea watched Jason drag himself onto the boat. He continued to cough and choke.

"I'm the monster. It's pitch black down there. I got stuck under the boat. Kept hitting my head trying to swim to the surface. Why didn't you move the boat so I could come up?"

Chelsea shook her head, "It was you trying to knock us out of the boat? You nearly scared us to death. You've traumatized your family. It'll take years of counseling for the girls to recover."

"But, I was stuck under the boat. I almost drowned. Strangely enough, I did sense something big down there. I thought I was a goner, either drown or get eaten. Whatever it was just checked me out and then left. I wonder if it does have anything to do with those missing fishermen."

Chelsea shined the flashlight out over the water. "Probably just your imagination. Or were you trying to scare us, banging your head on the bottom of the boat like that? Sounds like something you'd do. Would serve you right if something had nibbled on you a little. Let's go home. I've had enough fishing for one night. I can't wait to take you water skiing though. After tonight, I'll be driving the boat, and you'll be a'skiin'…in the trees.

Chapter 10. A New Client

It was early June; the first Monday after the school year ended. Jason convinced Chelsea they should go into the office and leave the girls with Lizzy. Now sixteen, he felt his oldest daughter was trustworthy enough to watch her sisters. Lizzy had agreed to do it, for a small fee. He had stopped off at the local donut shop, three chocolate covered cake donuts for him and a plain one for Chelsea. They sat in Chelsea's front office drinking coffee and munching donuts. She sat in her cushy office chair behind her fancy wooden desk with the spectacular teak top. Jason sat at one of the small, low slung guest chairs across from her.

Jason said, "We need better client chairs. I can barely see over the desk, and I'm six-seven."

Chelsea wiped donuts crumbs off her blouse, took a sip of coffee, and looked down at him.

"These chairs are fine. You wouldn't understand because you're tall. People sitting in those chairs are forced to look up at me, here in the power seat. I'll get more respect."

Jason bit off half of a donut, chewed a couple of times, swallowed, and washed it down with a gulp of decaf coffee. Then he laughed.

"You'll get plenty of respect if you leave that hand cannon on your desk next to you. Might scare the clients away though. I hope it's not loaded."

"We don't have any clients. And I want anyone who comes into this office to know I mean business. Who wouldn't respect a woman that can handle that thing? And no, it's not loaded. With your shenanigans, I'm afraid the temptation to shoot you might overwhelm me."

"Good thing I have my own office in the back, with a wall between us."

Chelsea smiled, "No worries. My firearms instructor assured me that a fifty-caliber bullet will easily penetrate wooden walls. Besides, if you don't bring in some business soon, I'm going to need to remove the *Associate* from my PI firm's name and you won't need an office."

Jason said uneasily, "I'd prefer to be fired, not fired at, thank you very much."

"Jason don't be silly. You're the father of my children. I would never intentionally shoot you, although I do plan on cleaning my gun at my desk. I understand that accidental discharges are not uncommon when cleaning a weapon, especially when that person's husband has been acting badly. Did I mention that I also increased your life insurance policy?"

Jason decided to change the subject. "I haven't learned anything more about those disappearing fishermen. Although I do wonder about that giant thing I saw in the water when you tried to run over me with our boat."

"Which time, Dear?"

"The other night when we were fishing at three in the morning. Remember? I fell out of the boat and you had me trapped underneath it for about an hour. I still don't understand why you didn't just move the boat so I could come up."

Jason wiped chocolate frosting off his mouth and took another sip of lukewarm decaf coffee.

"Jason Longfellow. You were only under there for a couple of minutes. And you scared the heck out of me and the girls. We thought you were some kind of monster fish, trying to knock us out of the boat and eat us. It's a good thing I didn't have my hand cannon with me, or there'd have been another missing fisherman."

"But Chelsea…"

Jason heard the door chime ring. He turned to look through the window in Chelsea's office to see who had entered the building. An alluringly beautiful brunette walked through the door, dressed in a black tube top struggling to contain its abundant contents. Her top and expensive looking black denim jeans matched her dark eyes and long, wavy black hair. She had completed the outfit with spiked high heels that pushed up her perfect buttocks, which Jason couldn't help but notice when she turned around to close the door. She looked to be in her early thirties.

Jason stood up. Jaw hanging down, eyes wide open, he pointed through Chelsea's window.

"Chelsea, client."

Chelsea walked around her desk and whacked him on the back of the head.

"Yes Jason, client. All of a sudden, you're Tarzan the Ape man? Use your words."

Jason turned to rush through the door of Chelsea's office to meet their potential new client and fell over one of the client chairs. He crashed headfirst into the wall and slid slowly to the floor. He saw a blurry Chelsea step over him and walk through to door. Shaking his head to clear the cobwebs, he pushed himself onto his feet and cautiously stumbled towards the front of the office. He imagined himself to be one of those hardboiled detectives from an old noir murder mystery...Philip Marlowe, Sam Spade, Inspector Clouseau. The gorgeous babe comes into the office, him propped on the corner of his desk smoking a cigarette, looking calm, cool, and confident. Except for the fact that he had walked into a wall, his wife met the gorgeous babe first, and he didn't smoke. At least he was still conscious.

Jason staggered up just as Chelsea took the young woman's hand and introduced herself.

"Hello. I'm Chelsea Longfellow, PI. Pleased to meet you. What can I do for you?" Jason nudged his wife. Chelsea said, "Oh yes, and this is *Associate*, as it says on the sign."

Jason forced a smile and shook the young woman's hand. He smelled l'air du lilacs.

"I'm Dr. Jason Longfellow, PI. I'm the associate because this woman put up the money to start the business. But the whole thing was my idea. I'm the real detective."

He winced as Chelsea stared daggers through him. "*This woman* is his wife, and if he doesn't let go of your hand, I'm going to have to remove his for him. I'm a retired surgical nurse, my instrument bag is in the back, and I'm experienced at amputations."

Jason saw the dark-haired beauty take a step back, a startled and confused look on her face. She said, "My name is Veronica Fairchild. My husband is Harold Fairchild, President and CEO of GenesRUs, a local medical biotech company."

Jason stepped forward, moving in front of Chelsea. "What can we do for you, Mrs. Fairchild? I'll bet your husband is a lot older than you. If he were your age, he'd be very young for a CEO. Is he having an affair? Do you want me to follow him, catch him in the act, get some juicy photos? Maybe you're having the affair, and you want me to follow you."

Jason felt a sharp pain in his ribs as Chelsea elbowed her way between her husband and the young beauty.

"Forgive my husband, Mrs. Fairchild. He just fell and hit his head, and he's even more confused than usual. What can I do for you? You've obviously come to a PI for some reason."

"No worries. And you can call me Veronica. Your husband is right about one thing. Harold is quite a bit older than me…in his early sixties. I'm worried about him. He went out fishing last night with one of his buddies. He didn't come home this morning, and he didn't call me. With the rumors about fishermen disappearing, I called the police. They told me he'd have to be gone at least twenty-four hours before they could do anything. Some rude deputy suggested Harold had gone to an all-night bar, gotten drunk, and found a lady friend. I know my husband better than that. He takes two naps a day, and he always calls when he's going to be late. I even checked with his younger brother, Lucas, who lives here in Bedford. But he hasn't seen Harold for days. I'm afraid something has happened to him. Since the police were no help, I thought I'd pay you a visit. Can you please help me? Money is no object."

Jason stepped between Chelsea and Veronica. He said, "Money no object? We'd be happy to help. We have a contact in the sheriff's office we can call to find out if anything untoward has been reported. We're already on the case of the missing fishermen, so we'll hear if anyone finds your husband's half eaten body on the lake…if they find a body at all. No worries. I've got this."

Jason felt a pain in his gut as Chelsea elbowed him out of the way again. She turned toward him, moved in close, and he heard her whisper in his ear.

"Jason, it's a bad idea to take Mrs. Fairchild as a client. If I catch you staring at her backside again, I might be compelled to Velcro you to the wall and use you for target practice. We should only take clients with behinds larger than mine. That's a new rule."

Jason whispered back, "Chelsea, Honey, your derriere is perfection. I wasn't staring at her behind…I didn't even notice it for that tube top…I mean…I was just impressed with the lady's fashion sense. We need a paying client. Come on. I promise to close my eyes when Mrs. Fairchild's rear end is around."

He saw Chelsea give him the death stare, shake her head in the affirmative, and make the *I'm keeping an eye on you* signal. Then Chelsea turned back towards Mrs. Fairchild.

"Pay no attention to my drama queen of a husband. I'm sure your Harold is fine. Perhaps he and his fishing buddy caught a record striper and wandered into an all-night bar to celebrate. Or maybe they're stubborn, like my husband, and refused to quit fishing until they caught a big one. If you leave us a retainer, we'll do what we can to find your Harold. How does that sound?"

Jason watched unhappily as Chelsea placed her hand on Veronica's shoulder and led her into her office, leaving him alone out front. Through the window Jason saw the dark-haired beauty sit down, reach into her purse, pull out a checkbook, write out a check, and hand it across the desk to Chelsea. A few minutes later they came out of Chelsea's office and Veronica waved and walked out the front door. Jason's eyes seemed to have a mind of their own as they tracked those tight jeans walking away. Then, he caught Chelsea's eyes watching him. He didn't duck in time and felt another blow to the back of his head.

"Chelsea, would you please stop it. The ocular center is located in the back of the head, and I see stars when you do that. Besides, I don't understand how you do it. I'm so tall."

"Jason, better you see stars than stare at that woman's behind. You're such a sexist."

"You're just jealous. I used to stare at your…"

Chelsea turned on him, fire in her eyes. "What do you mean, used to?"

Jason panicked, turned, and ran out the front door, yelling behind him as he went.

"I'll be back in a while. I'm going to pay Deputy Harbinger a visit. Ask if he's had anymore reports of missing fishermen. And you have the derriere of a twenty-year-old! See you later."

***

Jason walked around downtown Bedford, waiting for Chelsea to cool off. He knew Deputy Jim Harbinger ate lunch at a diner called *Jake's House of Burgers*. Their patty melts and milkshakes were excellent. Jason entered Jake's at eleven thirty, smelled his favorite aromas, fried beef and french fry oil. He saw the deputy sitting at the counter. The deputy looked official; clean shaven, a crisply pressed uniform, hat on the counter next to him, eating a cheeseburger and fries. Jason took the stool next to the deputy, said hello, and picked up a menu. Barb, the short, middle-aged waitress that clearly enjoyed her fair share of Jake's burgers and shakes, took Jason's order, a patty melt, fries, and a chocolate milkshake.

Jason struck up a conversation, "Hey there, Deputy Harbinger. I'm PI Longfellow. Nice to see you. Remember when you came to our place to investigate the abandoned fishing boat? All that blood and guts. I think the mess included part of a colon, spleen, liver, and kidneys. Have you made any progress on the case? You said you'd keep Chelsea and I informed, but we haven't heard anything back from you."

Jason had seen the deputy take a large bite of his cheeseburger, dripping with catsup and special sauce. He waited while the deputy gagged on his sandwich.

Jason said, "Are you okay? Burger go down the wrong pipe? I had a friend once choked on a piece of bacon. I gave him the Heimlich maneuver. Nod once if you need the Heimlich."

Jason watched with concern as the deputy choked and finally washed the bite of sandwich down with a full glass of water.

Harbinger held up his hand and said, "I'm fine. I don't remember any body parts, just a lotta blood. No, we haven't made any progress on that case. That was last fall, and fishin' was light over the winter. I haven't forgot my promise. If we find out anythin', you'll be the first I call."

Barb came by and sat a plate with a patty melt and fries in front of Jason. She said, "Your shake'll be here in a minute. I gotta get some more ice cream from the freezer in the back."

Jason thanked her and turned back to the deputy. "I was just asking, because a very pretty young woman came into our office this morning. Her husband, one Harold Fairchild, went fishing with a friend last night and hasn't come home. She's worried he might have disappeared like the others. She reported it to your office, but you guys told her that twenty-four-hour thing."

Harbinger said, "I wasn't in the office this morning. I'm sorry I missed her. I've heard she's quite a looker. If he doesn't turn up in the next twenty-four-hours, we'll file a missing person's report. Nothin' ever comes of those, but we gotta do 'em. Says so right in the manual."

Jason wouldn't let it go. "Deputy, do you know anything about the Fairchilds? For example, she said her husband is much older than her…in his early sixties. Perhaps there's a young gentleman in town with an interest in the fair Mrs. Fairchild? Wouldn't be the first time a young wife and her lover knocked off her rich old man. Know what I mean?"

Jason took a bite of his patty melt. The burger was cooked to perfection, the fries hot and crispy. Barb returned with his chocolate milkshake, so thick he took the first taste with a spoon. He was enjoying the food immensely until he remembered that Chelsea was mad at him. *Why did I have to look at that woman's rear end? More important, why did I let Chelsea catch me?*

The deputy said, "Yeah, I get it. I watch TV. But rumor has it lots of young fellas have tried to hit on the Fairchild woman, and nobody's gotten anywhere. She's faithful to her old man. Strange, ain't it?"

Jason said, "Good one. Her *old man*. A double entendre. Clever."

The deputy said, "I don't know anything about that, but I did hear somethin' about the old man. I shouldn't be tellin' you this, but you are kind of a bastard kin of law enforcement, bein' a PI. And, that PI wife of yours, she's something special, especially going away, if you know what I mean." He laughed and elbowed Jason, just two good old boys joking around.

He's talking about Chelsea's derriere. Why, I outta…Wait a minute. Maybe I can keep him talking and he'll tell me what he knows about Harold Fairchild. "Yes, my wife has a spectacular behind. How nice of you to notice. Now, what's this about Harold Fairchild?"

The deputy continued, "Well, this Fairchild guy owns a company just outside of town. It's a drug or biotech company…somethin' like that. I think it's called GenesRUs, whatever-the-fuck that means. Anyhow, one of my poker buddies told me the other day he was fishing out by the dam. He swears he saw one of their trucks on the old fireman's trail road down by the water. He said he saw a guy throwin' a couple of boxes in the lake. It was almost dark, so he didn't get a good look. But he was sure the logo on the side of the truck said *GenesRUs*. Anyhow, that's all I know. How's about that Fairchild woman? How'd she look walkin' away?"

Jason ignored the question. He said, "What do you think? Is it possible the young wife might have knocked Fairchild off for his money? She might have a lover. She did mention that Fairchild had a younger brother who lives in town. Or maybe his disappearance is related to his company dumping stuff in the lake. Maybe Fairchild found out about that, it was something illegal like toxic waste, and someone in his company killed him to keep him quiet. Or maybe old man Fairchild was having an affair with his administrative assistant, and his young wife offed him for that. Then there's the giant stripers people have been pulling out of the lake. Would a striped bass eat a fella? Have you learned anything to point in any of these directions?"

Jason saw the amused look on the deputy's face as he chewed his last french fry. The deputy swallowed, and said, "Or maybe aliens came over the mountain and carried him off. Where'd you learn investigating? One of them online courses? You're just makin' shit up. You gotta have some kinda evidence of somethin' afore accusin' someone of somethin'. Now, what about the Fairchild woman? A good looker? What did I miss?"

Jason grinned. *Wow! There's the perfect motto for our PI firm. "You gotta have some kinda evidence of somethin' afore accusin' someone of somethin, and we'll get you that evidence, or die tryin". I can't wait to tell Chelsea and have a sign painted up.*

Jason took another drink of his milkshake. As the rich chocolate syrup tickled his tastebuds, he conjured up a picture of Veronica Fairchild's derriere. Then he pictured Chelsea's derriere. Then he pictured Chelsea, face filled with rage. He felt a whack on the back of the head and saw stars. *How'd she do that? She's not even here. And she has that hand cannon.*

Jason said, "Have I mentioned that my wife, PI Chelsea Longfellow, has a fifty-caliber hand cannon, and she's a crack shot with it? Perhaps we shouldn't discuss women's posterior anatomy anymore. If it gets back to Chelsea, I fear I might become the next disappeared fisherman. If anyone files a missing person's report on me, you might consider investigating my wife first."

"We always do, Jason. We always do. It's usually the wife. And they don't always stick to poison. That's just an old wives' tale."

Jason said, "Thanks for the information on Mr. Fairchild's company. Don't worry. I won't tell anybody where I got it. Unless Chelsea gets out her hand cannon. Then all bets are off."

Chapter 11. Jet Ski of Death

That same Monday afternoon, Chelsea was waiting for Jason in her office. She heard someone walk through the front door. Sitting at her desk, she saw him through her office window as he walked in her direction and cautiously stuck his head in through her doorway.

Jason said, "Hello Sweetums. How ya' doin'? And where's Bertha? Have I told you today how young and beautiful you look? You look mighty fine. And you have the behind of a…"

Chelsea grinned an evil grin, "Enough about my rear end. Apparently, my husband isn't interested in looking at it anymore. I locked Bertha in the gun safe. I'm concerned I might be overcome with the urge to shoot the father of my children. Come in and have a seat."

Jason entered Chelsea's office cautiously and sat in one of the low-slung client chairs.

He said, "Why would you do that? I hear he's a really nice guy, and a helluva PI. I had lunch with Deputy Harbinger. Remember him? Came to our dock to investigate the bloody bass boat?"

Chelsea's anger hadn't completely subsided from the Veronica Fairchild incident, and she felt it start to rise again.

"You had lunch without me? I've been waiting for you to come back so we could go to lunch together. I'm starving." She looked at the gun safe.

Jason said, "Let me finish before you do something I'll regret. I took a walk to give the mother of my children time to calm down, and I wandered into Jake's House of Burgers for a cup of coffee. I ran into Deputy

Harbinger, and great PI that I am, I joined him for lunch. By the way, I had a patty melt, french fries, and a chocolate shake, and it was delish. I took the opportunity to interrogate the heck out of him."

Chelsea rubbed her stomach, "Jason, really? I told you I'm starving."

"Sorry. I asked the deputy a lot of questions. He knows nothing about the disappearing fishermen. He did say that Mrs. Fairchild reported her husband missing. He told her he couldn't do anything for twenty-four hours. He agreed that the burgers and shakes were outstanding."

"Jason, I hear Bertha calling. You best shut up about the food."

"Yes, Dear."

Chelsea sat there, her stomach grumbling, while Jason reported his conversation with Deputy Harbinger. This included Fairchild's biotech company, the dumping of boxes in the lake, Fairchild's younger brother, and Mrs. Fairchild's reported devotion to her much older husband. Jason also ran through a list of possible reasons for Harold Fairchild's disappearance, including everything from the young wife killing him for his money to the Lock Ness Monster, or SML Monster in this case. Chelsea's hunger finally overwhelmed her, and she interrupted him.

"Jason, you have a lot of speculation, no evidence, and I'm starving. Take me to lunch, now."

Jason said, "Okay. We probably shouldn't go to Jake's though. Someone might have heard the deputy and me comparing your derriere to that of Mrs. Fairchild. Might be embarrassing."

Chelsea growled, leapt up, and went for the gun safe. By the time she got it opened, Jason was out the front door and long gone.

***

Chelsea hadn't gotten the gun safe open in time to shoot her husband. Frustrated and hungry, she drove her SUV to Dairy Queen. After a burger and a strawberry milkshake, she calmed down and drove around town looking for Jason. She found him walking on the sidewalk near the boat dealership, hands in his pockets, shoulders slumped forward. He turned, saw her, and kept walking when she pulled the SUV up next to him.

"Hey there, tall, lean, and crazy. Need a ride?"

Jason stopped and said, "Well, it's the mother of my children, the one who wants to make herself a widow. Just so you know, it's illegal to run over your husband on the sidewalk."

"Jason, just get in. I'm not going to shoot you or run over you, at least not today. Although I better never hear of you discussing my derriere with anyone in public again. You seem to have more of a death wish than usual. What's going on?"

Jason walked over to the truck, opened the passenger door, and climbed in. "I guess I'm just bored. When we opened the PI office, I thought it'd be all fun and excitement. Instead, all we've got is this one client, albeit with a really good looking…"

"Jason…"

"Yes Dear. Anyhow, we've got no solid leads. Deputy Harbinger provided some information, but I'm not sure how to proceed from here." He paused, then Chelsea saw him smile and perk up. "I know. I should follow Mrs. Fairchild around. I'll bet that'd get me…"

"Killed, Jason. That'd get you killed. I have a much safer idea for you. Why don't you spend tomorrow morning down at the docks in Bridgewater…you know…the place where most of the fishermen hang out, put their boats in the water. You need to chat up some of those guys, ask questions about the fishermen that have disappeared. Also ask around about Harold Fairchild and his young wife, see what you can find out. Meanwhile, I'll follow and question Mrs. Fairchild. That way I might not be forced to make myself a widow and single mom."

Chelsea pulled away from the curb and headed towards home. She looked at Jason. He had one of those *I've got a really bad idea* looks on his face.

Jason said, "I like your suggestion. But how about we work in the morning and play in the afternoon. We could take the boat out, do some water skiing with the girls."

Chelsea thought maybe it would help with his boredom and depression if they had some fun. She reached the main highway where the speed limit increased to sixty-five, and she punched it. Jason's desire to go fast was rubbing off on her. That was something to be concerned about.

Chelsea said, "Okay. Let's do it. We can work in the morning. We'll take the boat out around one and have the entire afternoon to play. I'll tell the girls."

Next morning after a quick cup of coffee and a couple of donuts, Jason and Chelsea headed off to work. She watched Jason pull out of the driveway in his jacked-up pickup truck, headed for the marina in Bridgewater to question the local fishermen. Chelsea took the SUV into

Bedford to stake out Veronica Fairchild's house, to watch for any young men who might pay her a visit. It didn't seem quite right that this woman was their client, and also a suspect.

Chelsea got back to the house at eleven-thirty. She saw Jason pull into the driveway fifteen minutes later. When he came in the front door, she told him to meet her in the living room. They needed to talk about their morning. She'd bring coffee and bologna sandwiches for them and take sandwiches on the boat to feed the girls later. She brought three sandwiches on a tray and went back to the kitchen for the coffee. When she returned, two of the sandwiches were gone.

She said, "Hungry, were you? Inhaling bologna is probably not good for the lungs."

"Thanks for the sandwiches. I worked up an appetite interrogating all those fishermen. How'd it go with the stakeout of our client?"

"You're welcome. I saw something interesting, although I'm not sure what it means. I parked up the street from the Fairchild house at eight-thirty. Around nine a BMW sports car pulled into the driveway. A man got out and knocked on the front door. Mrs. Fairchild answered the door, appeared to recognize the man, and let him in."

Jason took another sip of coffee. "Very interesting. Did he grab her and lay a big kiss on her with lots of tongue? Was she dressed in a skimpy nightie?"

"Jason, I was at a stakeout, not a porno movie. No, they didn't appear to show each other any signs of affection at all. She opened the door, nodded at him, and he walked past her into the house. She appeared to be fully clothed. I found a photo of Harold Fairchild's younger brother, Lucas, online, and I'm almost positive it was him. That's the interesting part."

"So, maybe the porno part started after he entered the house. Did you peek in the window?"

Chelsea finished the last bite of her sandwich, took a sip of coffee, and gave Jason one of her disapproving looks.

"Jason Longfellow, I hope you don't run around peeking in windows. That's not a PI, that's a PT, peeping Tom. You can get arrested for that. Truth is, all we know is that Harold's younger brother visited Veronica this morning. Perhaps he was there to discuss the fact that Harold is missing and console her. She might have told him that she came to us for help. It wouldn't have gone over well if they'd caught me peeping in the window when she just hired us to find her husband. How did you do at the docks? Any luck with the fishermen?"

"I talked to five different fishermen, and they all said the same thing. There are fewer and fewer professional fishermen showing up for the tournaments, and everyone's on edge. No one goes fishing overnight without being armed. These guys are carrying everything from thirty-eight specials to one guy who had a thirty-ought-six rifle, big enough to kill a grizzly bear. I wouldn't be surprised if there's somebody out there with a hand-held rocket launcher."

Chelsea shook her head, "So much for the firearms lesson. Did you hear anything useful that might help us figure out where Harold Fairchild went, or why these fishermen are disappearing?"

Jason finished his coffee and laughed. "All five guys had a different take on what's happening to the fishermen. One guy thinks it's the giant stripers. According to him they are a hybrid fish that somebody caught in the ocean and released in the lake, and they're meat eaters. Another said he'd seen a monster in the lake, and it looked like a dinosaur. I smelled whiskey on his breath. The third guy also smelled of alcohol. He assured me there are aliens abducting the fishermen and probing them. He was disappointed they hadn't taken him for a good probing yet. The other two fishermen mentioned how cutthroat professional fishing has become. They think someone on the pro bass tour is eliminating the competition. I don't know any more than I did last night, except these guys drink way too much to be flying around on the lake in bass boats."

Chelsea said, "So all we really know is that Harold Fairchild's younger brother visited Mrs. Fairchild this morning, the striped bass in the lake are larger this year than ever before, and fishermen drink way too much. Not exactly riveting progress. Let's go water skiing so this day's not a complete loss."

Chelsea told the girls to get their bathing suits on. She packed some sandwiches and sodas in a cooler. Chelsea herded everyone down to the dock and watched as Jason loaded the skis, rope, and life jackets into the boat. He lowered the boat, everyone climbed on board, and he pulled out of the boathouse, headed for the big water.

When they reached the middle of the lake Chelsea said, "Okay Jason, I'll take over the helm. Put on your life jacket and get your skis. You've never water skied, have you? I watched a YouTube video. You sit in the water, knees bent, skis forward, tips up and hang on tight to the rope. I'll take off really fast to pull you up on your skis. Then I'll tow you around the lake for a while. Sound good?"

Jason said, "I've got this. No problemo. Let's do it."

Chelsea turned off the outboard motor. She watched Jason attach the ski rope to the chrome fasteners on the boat. He tossed the rope in the water, threw the skis in after it, and jumped in. She laughed as he rolled around in the water trying to get the skis on. He finally managed the seated position, ski tips up, hanging onto the rope. He gave her the thumbs up.

Chelsea started the boat motor and yelled, "Ready? Here goes."

Lizzy said, "Don't look, girls. Daddy's gonna die."

Lucy said, "Oh no! Poor Daddy."

Jason yelled, "Let'er rip!"

Chelsea rarely agreed with Jason, but perhaps he was right about going fast. It was fun. She looked at the girls, Lucy and Lilly in the stern seats and Lizzy in the bow, and yelled, "Hang on!"

She shoved the throttle all the way forward and the large outboard roared to life. She saw the girls hanging on for dear life, eyes the size of silver dollars.

All three girls yelled, "Aaaah!"

Chelsea watched as Jason flew violently forward, his skis launching themselves in opposite directions. He went airborne headfirst, let go of the rope, and did a spectacular face and body plant on the water. Chelsea turned around and gunned the engine again to get to him before he drowned. Forgetting about the no brakes thing, she swerved just in time to miss him. She did another turnaround and approached him more slowly.

"Jason Longfellow, you're supposed to be water skiing, not flying. What's wrong with you?"

Jason floated on his back, coughing, choking up lake water, trying to catch his breath. Then he swam around retrieving his skis.

"Honey Bun, maybe you could start out at something less than warp speed. I thought I was going into orbit. Worse, you almost tossed our daughters over the side. Good thing they're wearing life jackets. I'll swim to the rope, and let's try again, perhaps half throttle. Please, do not kill me in front of our children."

"Jason, stop it. It wasn't my fault, and you're scaring our children. I'll try half throttle as you wish, but you need to hang on, stand up, and keep your skis on this time. No more flying."

Chelsea brought the boat around slowly and stopped. Jason took hold of the rope and assumed the position. Chelsea noticed the boat was aimed at the shore. She felt she had plenty of distance for Jason to get up on his skis before hitting land. Jason gave her the thumbs up.

He yelled, "Let'er rip!"

Chelsea gave the boat half throttle, the engine roared, and the boat surged forward. She turned and looked at Jason, and to her surprise he was up and skiing. He looked a little wobbly, squatted down to keep his center of gravity low, his butt almost touching the water.

The girls yelled in unison, "Look at Daddy! He's skiing! Go Daddy!"

Chelsea turned to look ahead. The shore, lined with thick fir trees, was coming up fast.

Chelsea heard Jason yell, "Yahoo! Look at me! I'm an expert water skier!"

Chelsea panicked and made a hard left turn to avoid crashing. She turned and looked at Jason, racing towards shoreline faster and faster due to the slingshot effect.

The girls yelled in unison, "Daddy's gonna die! Mommy, don't kill Daddy!"

Chelsea heard Jason yell, "Aaaahhh! Help me!"

Chelsea watched in horror as her husband's water skis hit the muddy shoreline. They stayed stuck in the mud as he flew forward, crashing headlong into a fir tree. His upper half disappeared into the greenery. His bright blue bathing suit and sunburnt legs hung from a low branch. She aimed the boat at the spot where her husband's rear end stuck out from the thick, green forest.

Chelsea yelled, "Jason, if you're alive, say something, or move something!"

Lizzy said, "You killed Dad. Why did you toss him into a tree? I don't think that's how you're supposed to water ski."

Chelsea heard a loud moan as she watched Jason dislodge himself from the thick vegetation and fall a couple of feet to the ground. She pulled the boat up next to the shoreline. Jason lay nearby, his face and chest red with multiple scrapes, his hair filled with pine needles.

"What the hell, wife? It's called *water* skiing, not tree skiing. Which YouTube video did you watch, the one about how to murder your husband and make it look like an accident?"

Chelsea said, "Jason, if you really knew how to ski, you would have turned and missed the shoreline. I managed to miss it with the boat. It's not my fault you decided to ski into a tree."

Lucy said, "Yeah, Daddy. Why'd you try to ski into a tree? Hey, that rhymes. Cool."

Chelsea watched as Jason stood up slowly and brushed the pine needles out of his hair. He limped to his skis, pulled them out of the mud. Then he limped to the boat and climbed aboard.

Lizzy said, "Dad, you don't look so good. Maybe we should take you to the ER."

Jason said, "Thank you for your concern, Daughter. It's nice to know that one of the women in this family is worried about me. I'm okay, just a few scratches and bruises. I'm done with water skiing though. Next time I ask your mother to do something outdoorsy, I'm gonna pick the YouTube video. I find it hard to believe there's one about water skiing in the woods."

Chelsea said, "Jason, take the helm. You've hurt my feelings. You obviously don't think I can drive this boat, or you'd stop whining. I toss you into one little tree and you get all upset."

"No worries, Chelsea. I'm not upset. I'm clearly too tall to water ski anyhow; my center of gravity is too high. So, I'm gonna rent a jet ski instead."

Lizzy said, "Oh boy. Dad's going to die, again."

***

Chelsea sat sullenly as Jason drove to the dock, unloaded their gear, and put the boat up on the lift. Chelsea and the girls followed him as he limped up to the house. He told Chelsea he was going to take a long, hot shower. Then they were going to Bridgewater to rent a jet ski.

At two o'clock in the afternoon Chelsea sat on the couch in the living room finishing off a cup of her favorite dark roast coffee. The girls were sprawled out on the floor playing a board game. They had their bathing suits on, waiting for Jason. He finally came hobbling out of the bedroom in his bathing suit. He looked raring to go, despite all the cuts and scrapes.

Jason said, "Let's go girls. It's jet ski time. Your mother might have put me in a tree, but nothing's gonna stop me from having fun. What d'ya think, Lucy? Want to ride on a jet ski?"

Chelsea didn't like the expression on her husband's face, the stubborn look of a three-year-old determined to ride his tricycle down a set of stairs, again. Chelsea realized that Jason had been humiliated in front of his family, and he wasn't going to be happy until he redeemed himself. Apparently, that meant demonstrating his prowess on a jet ski.

Chelsea said, "Jason, two things. First, you've never driven a jet ski. I'm not so sure it's a good idea to include one of our children in your first attempt. And second, where'd you get that bathing suit? That's the brightest red I've ever seen. And I've never seen one with a draw string that long. Dangling there, it looks like a great big worm."

Chelsea recognized Jason's indignant look. "Chelsea, you worry too much. A jet ski is just like a motorcycle, but in the water, that goes really fast, and jumps wakes, with no brakes. Where's the danger in that? And I happen to think this bathing suit is very stylish. Besides, I'll wear it if you ever take me water skiing again. The bright red color will hide the blood stains."

Chelsea helped Jason herd the girls into their SUV. Jason backed out of the garage and headed for Bridgewater. Chelsea noticed that the girls were unusually quiet. She couldn't decide whether they were worn out from boating or terrified at the idea of jet skiing with Dad.

Chelsea's nerves were frayed as Jason crossed the bridge into the town of Bridgewater. He drove into the jet ski rental parking lot, parked, and turned to the girls in the backseat.

"Come on girls. You're coming with us. I don't want to leave you in the car in summer. It can get up to two hundred degrees, hot enough to cook you."

Lilly said, "Mommy, I don't wanna be cooked.

Chelsea said, "Jason, you're scaring the children again. Stop it."

Jason said, "But, I said they were coming with us. We'll all go inside and rent a couple of jet skis. You want to give it a try too, right Chelsea? I looked online, and they have two- and three-seaters. I'll get a two-seater for me and Lucy, and a three-seater for you, Lizzy, and Lilly."

Chelsea didn't want to drive a jet ski, but she was afraid to turn Jason loose on the lake alone with poor Lucy. She knew he loved his children and would never intentionally harm them. But he often got carried away with new things. Who was she kidding? He always got carried away.

"Yes, Dear. I'd love to try a jet ski. Wouldn't you rather take Lizzy with you, though? I could take our youngest with me."

Lizzy spoke up, "Oh no you don't Mom. I've seen Dad drive the boat, and he only has one speed…zoom. I'm going with you. I'm young, and I've got my whole life ahead of me."

Jason said, "But Mom put me in a tree."

Lizzy countered, "Yeah, she put *you* in a tree. We were all safe in the boat."

Lucy said, "I'm the youngerest, and I don't wanna die."

Jason said, "No worries, Lucy. I'll take it easy. I promise."

Jason led everyone into the store and approached a woman standing behind a glass counter full of fishing gear. The woman looked to Chelsea like she was in her late forties or early fifties. Chelsea's height, she wore a yellow one-piece bathing suit with a pair of blue jean shorts. Her graying hair was tied in a short ponytail, and her round face and exposed skin looked dry and wrinkly, tanned to a dark brown. She gave them a big smile.

She said, "Howdy, folks. The name's Dee. What can I do for you? Beautiful afternoon for a boat ride. Or maybe a jet ski is more to your liking."

Jason walked up to the counter and said, "We'd like to rent a couple of jet skis, a two-seater, and a three-seater."

Dee said, "I've got just the thing for you, a couple of Sea-Doos. Plenty of power, very reliable, and great mileage. Have either of you ever driven a jet ski? Are you Virginia residents? If so, have you taken the state boating safety course online?"

Chelsea stepped up to the counter beside Jason just as he said, "I'm Dr. Longfellow, PI…you can call me Jason. This is my wife, Chelsea. We've both driven our new bass boat, and Chelsea took me water skiing. She put me in a tree on the second try."

Chelsea saw Dee wince as she examined Jason more closely. "That would explain all the scrapes and bruises, and the limp, but it don't answer my questions."

Chelsea said, "Never mind my husband. He's always complaining about something. To answer your questions, neither one of us have driven a jet ski, and we are Virginia residents. I don't know anything about an online boating safety course."

Jason said, "We've watched a video on YouTube. It looks easy. You can go really fast."

Chelsea was amused by the look that Dee gave Jason. She knew how the woman felt. Dee turned around, bent over, and took a handful of forms out of a cabinet. She placed them on the counter and handed a pen to Jason and one to Chelsea.

Dee said, "You'll both need to sign these forms. I shouldn't rent you jet skis until you've taken the state boating safety course. But things have been a might slow, what with all the missing fishermen. So, I'm gonna make an exception. You look like a reasonably sane couple...well, you anyhow Ma'am...and I assume you'll be careful since you're taking your children. The husband and I wish all the fishermen would disappear. They're bad for business. They're always complaining about jet skis buzzin' by them and scarin' the fish. The local fishin' association tried to get jet skis banned from the lake. My husband, Joe, hates fishermen."

Chelsea began reading the forms. She looked over at Jason. He had already signed all the forms in front of him and was waiting for her.

"Jason, these forms absolve the rental agency of all responsibility for bodily harm to you, me, and our children, including death, dismemberment, and damage due to fire and explosion. Are you sure about this? Are these things likely to explode? Sounds like a floating bomb."

Jason said, "Come on Chelsea. Sign the forms and let's get out on the water. Jet skis are perfectly safe. If anything, they're more like *flying* bombs. Did I mention that they go really fast, jump wakes, and then there's the no brakes thing. I might have read online that occasionally a small fuel leak can occur from all the bouncing and wake jumping. If that happens, one might catch fire or explode. But all you have to do is lift the seat and take a sniff, make sure you don't smell gas before you start it up. And there's a fire extinguisher. So, no worries. Now let's go!"

Chelsea went into mild shock. Her mind couldn't process what she heard fast enough to put her foot down. A flying bomb? She also felt bad about skiing Jason into a tree. So, she signed the forms. On the dock, Dee pointed to two jet skis, explained how to start, and make them go.

After the demonstration, Dee left them with the two jet skis, the keys, and five life jackets. Chelsea watched the woman as she walked back into the store, shaking her head and mumbling to herself. Chelsea looked at Jason. She became overwhelmed by a feeling of doom.

"Jason, I'm not sure we should take the girls out on these things. Why don't you go, and we'll stay here on the dock and watch you explode. It'll be kind of like the Fourth of July."

Jason said, "Chelsea, don't be silly. We'll have loads of fun."

Chelsea saw the look of excitement on Lizzy's and Lilly's faces. Lucy looked terrified.

Lizzy said, "Wow, cool! These things look like a blast."

Chelsea saw two jet skis zoom by the dock out in the main channel. They were driven by kids not much older than Lizzy, and they were swerving, bouncing, and squealing with joy.

Jason said, "Look at that. Those kids are having a great time. Won't this be fun?"

Chelsea smiled. *Yeah, and neither one of them have exploded. Yay!*

Chelsea said, "Okay everyone, put on your life jackets. Safety is important."

Chelsea watched everyone put on their life jacket. She heard Lucy whimper.

Chelsea untied the three-seater jet ski, climbed on, and grabbed hold of the dock to steady the machine. Lizzy and Lilly got on behind her. Chelsea watched as Jason untied the two-seater, stepped over the jet ski, planted his foot on the opposite side, flipped it and fell in the water. Chelsea felt bad at the sight of poor Lucy, standing there looking like she was about to cry.

Lucy said, "Mommy, can I ride with you?"

Chelsea saw Jason's head pop up. He swam to the ladder, climbed onto the dock, and stood scratching his head and staring at the jet ski. It had righted itself and still floated next to the dock.

Chelsea said, "Jason, perhaps you should approach the thing more cautiously, try to balance yourself side to side. You're going to break your neck. Oh God, Lucy, I'm so sorry."

Jason said, "Chelsea, you're scaring our child. I've got this. I'll mount this thing like Roy Rodgers mounted his horse Trigger."

Chelsea watched in horror as Jason took a couple of steps back, ran forward, threw his right leg over the seat, and leapt onto the machine. The jet ski was no Trigger; it flipped again, tossing Jason into the water. Chelsea saw his head pop up, and once again he swam to the ladder and climbed onto the dock. Chelsea heard footsteps, turned, and saw Dee walking towards them. Dee went to the jet ski, bent over, and took hold of the handlebar.

Dee said, "Sir, I was watching through the window, and you look liked you could use some help. Climb on while I hold the thing steady. Are you sure you want to take your youngest daughter with you? Your wife has a three-seater, but the child is small. Perhaps it would be safer to squeeze her in behind her sisters. I promise not to tell anyone."

Chelsea felt relief when Jason managed to mount the stabilized jet ski. He said indignantly, "Dee, I would've gotten it eventually. You clearly gave me a defective machine. Come on Lucy, climb aboard and let's get going."

Chelsea shook her head as she watched Lucy climb on behind Jason. She put her little arms around him, squeezed him tight as she could, and closed her eyes.

Chelsea said, "Jason, follow me. We're going to take it easy."

She started the jet ski, pushed off the dock, and squeezed the throttle gently. She heard a roar as Jason flew by, his jet ski bouncing violently and Lucy holding on to her father for dear life.

Idiot. I'm going to kill him.

Chelsea sped up, trying to catch Jason. She looked on in horror as she realized what her husband had in mind. A cabin cruiser motored up the main channel, and Jason aimed his jet ski for the large wake behind the boat. His first time on a jet ski, and he was clearly planning to jump the wake. And with poor Lucy on board. Chelsea was definitely going to kill him.

Chelsea yelled, "Hang on Lucy. Your father is a lunatic. I'm so sorry! I love you!"

Chelsea could barely hear Lizzy as she said to Lilly, "Poor Lucy. Dad's gonna kill them both. At least Mom won't have to investigate this disaster. We're all witnesses."

Chelsea watched in terror as Jason hit the large wake. The front end of the jet ski pointed skyward, and it flew straight up in the air. When it reached the apex, Jason flew off in one direction and Lucy in another. The machine did a perfect nosedive, completely submerging in the lake. Chelsea saw the jet ski pop up, right itself, and go into circle mode as it was designed to do when the idiot pilot fell off. Overwhelmed with rage, Chelsea scanned the water for Lucy.

Chelsea turned to Lizzy and Lilly, "Do you see Lucy anywhere? I pray her life vest works."

Chelsea saw Lizzy point at the middle of the channel. "Look Mom. There's Dad, swimming towards something. I think it's Lucy."

Chelsea looked on, fearing the worst, as Jason frantically swam towards Lucy. Chelsea gently engaged the throttle and aimed her jet ski towards Jason, considering whether to run him over or not. She pulled up alongside Lucy just as Jason got there. She was surprised to see Lucy bobbing up and down in her life jacket, laughing hysterically.

Jason said, panic in his voice, "Lucy, are you okay. I'm so sorry. I didn't mean to do that! I mean, I did, but I had no idea we'd both go flying. Please tell me you're okay."

Lucy, still giggling and laughing, "Let's do it again, Daddy! That was fun!"

Chelsea, obviously not sharing in Lucy's enthusiasm, said, "Jason, lift our daughter and put her on my jet ski behind Lilly. We're going back to the dock, where there are no crazy people." She pointed in the direction of Jason's jet ski. "Your jet ski is running around in circles. Good luck with that. You better swim fast. I still haven't decided whether or not to run you over."

Chelsea hit the throttle and headed for the rental place. She pulled up to the dock, dismounted, and held the handlebar to stabilize the machine while her daughters climbed off. They all looked out into the channel where Jason was trying to catch his jet ski.

Chelsea said, "Girls, your father loves you. But sometimes his childish side takes over. Seems to be a man thing. I'm sorry. I should never have agreed to any of this." She looked out at the water. "What is he doing?"

Chelsea watched as Jason finally caught up with his jet ski. He reached up, grabbed hold of the seat, and tried to climb on board. Suddenly, it looked like something pulled him underwater.

Chelsea said, "What's he doing? Why can't he just get on the thing and return to the dock?"

Lizzy pointed and said, "Mom, I saw something really big in the water next to him."

Chelsea watched as Jason popped up, grabbed onto the jet ski seat, and tried to pull himself on board. He had barely made any progress when his body jerked backwards, turned around, and began to skim over the water facing forward. From a distance, it looked like he was water skiing on his butt, away from the jet ski. Chelsea heard him yell, gasping and choking.

"Chelsea, help me! Something's got hold of my drawstring. I wanna go home!"

Chelsea said, "Lizzy, did you hear that? Something about his bathing suit?"

Lizzy said, "I think he said something has hold of his drawstring. Mom, you told him not to wear that stupid bathing suit."

Lilly said, "Wow! How's he doing that? It's like magic."

Lucy said, "I hope that Lock Nestle Monster hasn't got him. It might eat him."

Lizzy said, "Loch Ness Monster. Nestle is a type of chocolate."

Chelsea pointed and said, "Wow. Look at him go. I'd be impressed, except I'm afraid Lucy's right. Something big has got hold of him and is dragging him away."

Chelsea saw Jason slow abruptly. Whatever had hold of him let go, and his forward momentum caused him to do a summersault in the water. Jason's head popped up again, he looked around, and started swimming frantically back to the jet ski. He reached it, approached it from the back and quickly climbed onboard.

Lizzy pointed at Jason and said, "Mom, I think Dad's mooning us."

Chelsea watched as Jason stood up on the jet ski and adjusted his bathing suit. Then he sat back down and aimed the jet ski towards the dock. He arrived a couple of minutes later. When he dismounted, Chelsea noticed that his drawstring was untied, dangling down, and shredded.

"Jason, how were you moving through the water so fast? Lucy thought the Loch Ness Monster was taking you home to meet the family."

Chelsea saw Jason stare down at his bathing suit. He took the dangling string, ran his hand along it.

He said, "What's happening? I finally caught the damn jet ski, tried to climb on, and next thing I know I'm being pulled along at warp speed. There was something large in the water, like what I saw when you tried to drown me under the boat the other day. I think it liked my bright red bathing suit. It was pulling me along by the drawstring."

Lizzy said, "Dad, aren't worms used for bait? Maybe it was a big fish, it saw your drawstring, thought it was a worm, and it was trying to take it away from you."

Chelsea said, "Yes, let's go with that. A big fish and a worm. Much better than the Loch Ness Monster. And it makes sense, because when the fish got a good look at you, Jason, it let go of the worm. No sensible fish would drag a crazy man home to its family. Which makes me wonder if I'm the one should have my head examined."

Lizzy had the last word, "Speaking of head examining, now you're going to have to pay for a shrink to treat us girls for jet ski PTSD. I'm never going near one of those things again."

Chapter 12. Expired

The Longfellow's neighbor, Horace McDufus, invited Jason to go fishing with him on Saturday night. McDufus professed to know the best spots for catching stripers. Chelsea had objected, telling Jason she thought the man might be crazy. Jason was aware that McDufus had a proclivity for getting drunk and shooting at squirrels from his deck. Chelsea had told Jason that if the fishermen killer didn't murder him, McDufus probably would. Jason ignored her concerns.

According to McDufus, the best time to catch stripers occurred between midnight and sunrise. Jason headed for McDufus' dock at midnight, fishing pole and tackle box in hand. Jason could see where he was going without a flashlight since it was a clear night with a half-moon and a sky full of stars. He walked carefully, concerned about stepping on a copperhead. He saw McDufus' silhouette in the moonlight, standing on his dock loading fishing gear into his boat.

Jason yelled, "Hey Mr. McDufus! PI Longfellow here, reporting for duty!"

To Jason's surprise, McDufus twisted around, pistol in hand, and fired off a round in his direction. Fortunately, the shot missed Jason by several feet. Jason dove behind a tree.

"Hey! It's me, Jason Longfellow! Why are you shooting at me? You invited me here!"

Jason heard McDufus say, "Sorry there PI Longfeller. You startled me. You need to be more careful sneakin' up on a fella like that. Everyone's nerves are edgy, what with all the disappearin' fishermen. It's just Gertie, my little ol' twenty-two. Wouldn't a done much more than wing ya' a little bit, lessen' you were a squirrel. Are ya' ready to catch some big'uns?"

Jason cautiously stepped out from behind the tree and walked the rest of the way to McDufus' dock. He climbed onto the dock, found McDufus standing in his bass boat, and handed him his fishing pole and tackle box. McDufus took them, sat them down, shook hands with Jason with his right hand and handed him a cold can of beer with his left.

McDufus said, "Climb aboard, Neighbor. She's a beautiful night fer striper fishin'."

Jason stepped into the boat and said, "Mr. McDufus, are you sure we should be drinking alcohol and driving a boat. Won't the police frown on that?"

McDufus scoffed at him, "Come on young feller. What's yer problem? Nuthin' wrong with a beer or six while fishin'. Besides, them police ain't gonna ever catch me and Nellie 'less we want to be caught." He pointed to the outboard motor. "Old Nellie here's sportin' three-hundred horses of pure power. Once we get movin', her hull never touches the water."

Jason took a pull on the cold beer. "That's a lot of power. But I'm not sure it's safe to levitate over the water in the dark."

"Won't matter anyway's. I'll be three sheets to the wind by the time we get outta the cove. I got me four more six packs in the cooler. Did you bring some sorta' protection? Gertie here's great fer squirrels, but she ain't much fer bears, or people. I was hopin' you had somethin' bigger in case we run into them dudes whats disappearing fishermen. Happens mostly at night, and as you can probly tell bein' a fancy detective and all, it's night."

Jason smiled. *I hate to admit this, but maybe I should listen to Chelsea once in a while.* He said, "I'm proud to say I came prepared." Jason reached under his jacket and pulled *the Judge* out of a large hip holster. "I brought Blaster. He's loaded with five four-ten shotgun shells."

Jason saw a worried look on McDufus's face. McDufus said, "That oughtta do it. D'ya know how to handle that thing? It's kinda big, and I wouldn't want to come home dead."

Jason said, "I can handle Blaster. I hope we run into this fishermen killer. You're not our only client. A Mrs. Fairchild hired us to find her husband, who also recently disappeared."

McDufus took his seat at the helm. "Are you talkin' about Veronica Fairchild? That's one fine lookin' woman. Did you get a look at that rear end...?"

"Mr. McDufus, my wife Chelsea has informed me that I'm not allowed to discuss women's posterior parts. Apparently, they take offense at that."

McDufus said, "Jason...can I call you Jason...Jason, grow a pair. You can't let yer wife tell ya' what ta do. It just ain't natural. Yer the man. Yer s'posed to tell her what's what."

"But my wife is a nurse. She knows how to inflict pain. She also packs a Desert Eagle in fifty-caliber. And she just joined the Bedford women's shooting team as their best shooter."

McDufus said, "Damn Man. What did'ya do to yerself, marryin' a woman like that. Maybe it's better you don't grow a pair. She'd prolly just shoot'em off. Well, let's get ta fishin'. Sit yerself down, have another beer or three, and hang on tight ta' somethin'."

Jason watched as McDufus untied the boat, handed him another beer, and pointed the boat towards the big water. He punched the throttle just as Jason took a drink, and beer poured all over Jason's face and jacket. *Great. Now I'll go home smelling like beer. Chelsea'll be pissed. I better catch a fish, rub fish smell all over myself. Maybe that'll help.*

Everything appeared as a blur as the three-hundred horsepower outboard pushed the boat along at warp speed. Jason apparently wasn't the only one with a need for speed. Then, McDufus pulled the throttle into neutral and stopped near the shore next to the mountains. Jason's dizziness cleared, he released his iron grip on the seat frame and looked around. He had to admit the moon and stars made for a spectacular sight, and the peace and quiet calmed his nerves. He could see why fishermen might enjoy this.

McDufus whispered, "Okay Jason. We'll give'er a try here first. I've caught some beauties in this spot. Keep yer eye out fer a school of shad; they'll look all shiny in the moonlight. Then listen fer the tail slaps, and there's yer stripers. That's when ya' start castin' yer bucktail lure. Let's catch us a record; I'm lookin' fer a seventy pounder."

Jason watched McDufus lower the trolling motor. They sat there quietly for half an hour.

McDufus whispered, "Hear that sound? That's shad bubbling up on the surface. Them stripers should be along shortly."

Jason listened. He heard a whap sound. "Is that what you were talking about, Mr. McDufus?"

"That's it. See them shiny things by the shore? Them's the shad. The stripers'll be in there. Cast yer bucktail over there and reel'er in slow. We'll be haulin' 'em in afore ya' know it."

Jason picked up his fishing pole, turned on a flashlight, and fastened a bucktail to the clip at the end of his line. He released the line from the reel, cast the bucktail towards the shore, and hooked a tree branch. He spent the next five minutes tugging at his line, trying to dislodge the lure. Meanwhile, he saw McDufus haul in two stripers in the ten-to-twenty-pound range.

Jason continued to tug and jerk his line. "Damn pole. Damn lure. Damn tree. Damn fishing."

Jason watched McDufus catch his third striper, take it off the hook, and place it in the storage tank. McDufus rested his pole on the side of the boat and shined his flashlight in Jason's eyes.

"I see you caught yerself a tree branch. I thought you'd been fishin' before. I'll move us over ta' the shore, and ya' can fetch yer bucktail. Them lures ain't cheap. No sense loosin' it."

Jason watched McDufus' silhouette as he guided the boat up next to the shore with the trolling motor. Jason stepped off the boat, followed his fishing line, and retrieved his lure from a low-hanging branch. He boarded the boat, and McDufus returned them to their fishing spot.

Jason saw McDufus retrieve his pole and cast into the school of shad. McDufus whispered, "PI Longfeller, get to it. Them stripers'll eat their fill and move on."

Jason sent his bucktail flying towards the shad, and into another tree. Jason heard McDufus whisper, "Ya' gotta be kiddin'. Ya' do know the fish are in the lake and not in them trees, right?"

Jason said, "It's not my fault. The action's too light on this reel, and the lure really flies." Jason tugged on the line. "I'm stuck again. Stupid rod, stupid lure, stupid trees, stupid fishing."

McDufus said, "Yer forgettin' ta mention the most stupid thing. I think I unnerstand why yer wife bought that fifty-cal."

Jason flew into a tantrum, yanking and pulling on his line, stomping his feet, and cursing.

McDufus said, "Give it a rest there, PI Longfeller. Yer gonna capsize the boat, and yer scarin' hell outta the fish. Hold still, and I'll take us ta shore, again."

Jason felt frustrated, angry, and embarrassed as McDufus once again moved the boat up next to the shore. As Jason stepped out, pole in hand, he turned his head towards a noise in the woods.

Jason said, fear in his voice, "McDufus, did you just growl at me? There's no reason to growl. I promise not to catch any more trees."

Jason saw McDufus point towards the shoreline, just behind where he was standing. McDufus whispered, "I didn't growl at you. It must have been that there bear."

Jason turned and looked behind him. A large black bear was visible in the moonlight. It appeared to be drinking from the lake. Jason looked at the bear. The bear stood up on its hind legs and looked at Jason. The bear sniffed the air.

McDufus said, "Jason, I think he smells our…I mean my…fish. Bears likes 'em some fish. Maybe you should hop on back into the boat, and we oughtta skedaddle. Hungry bears have been known to also likes 'em some human, and I don't wanna find out if this one's hungry or not."

Jason said, "How about pee? Do they like the smell of human pee? I just peed myself."

McDufus said, "Then you ain't gettin' in my boat."

Jason tossed his fishing pole into the boat, reached under his coat, and pulled out Blaster. He aimed the large revolver in the direction of the bear, his hand shaking violently. He tried to steady the gun with both hands. *Damn fishing. Damn lure. Damn bear. Damn shaky hands.*

McDufus said, "You got that loaded with four-ten shotgun shells? That'll just piss him off."

Jason turned around to answer McDufus, and as he did so the gun swung around and pointed at the old man. Jason said, "You mean shotgun shells won't stop a bear?"

Jason saw McDufus' silhouette hit the deck, trying to get out of the line of fire. Jason turned back around. His hands were shaking so violently he dropped the cocked gun. It hit a rock and went off. Jason heard the clanking of buckshot bouncing off the aluminum hull of McDufus' boat. Then he heard a growl, and watched as the bear went down on all fours and fled.

McDufus said, "You shot my boat! Why'd you shoot my boat! What'd it ever do ta you?"

Jason bent down to pick up Blaster. He heard footsteps as McDufus joined him on the shore. McDufus shined a flashlight on the side of his bass boat.

"Look at all them dents. You shot Nellie. Yer wife is right, you're a crazy person. At least none of the buckshot went clean through, and that bear hightailed it outta here. But you could'a shot me. I need another six pack or six to calm my nerves. I've always been partial to drink, but I'm gonna have to drink lots more if'n I'm gonna live next to the likes of you. Get in the boat, and we'll try trollin' in the middle of the lake. They ain't no trees or bears there. Holster that hand cannon. Are you sure them other fishermen didn't disappear cause they took you fishin'?"

Jason felt sure he wasn't the reason for all the disappearing fishermen. But after catching two trees and the bear debacle, he could understand how McDufus might think so. And he had shot Nellie. He took a knife out of his tackle box, cut the bucktail lure off his fishing line, collected his rod and reel, and sat down. McDufus pulled in the trolling motor, fired up the engine and moved them to a spot several yards from a small island in the middle of the lake.

Jason watched McDufus set up the trolling motor. McDufus said, "Add a lead sinker about a foot above yer bucktail, so's it'll stay on the bottom. We're gonna troll over the deep hole just off this little island. Drop yer lure over the side and let out a bunch of line. My fish finder is showin' a school of big fish below us. We'll get you a striper, if'n you don't kill us first."

Jason did as he was told, and McDufus started moving the boat back and forth over the deep hole. Jason felt disappointed when they made several passes with no fish. Then there was a large tug on his line; his pole bending dramatically as it was almost pulled out of his hands.

Jason whispered loudly, "McDufus, I've got something. It feels like a whale."

McDufus said, "Pull and reel, keep yer tip up so ya don't lose it. Looks like you got a doozy. Keep reelin', and I'll get the net. I'll snag the thing when you get it up next to the boat."

Jason pulled and reeled for half an hour before something broke the surface of the water, a dark form in the moonlight. McDufus shined a flashlight on the giant fish.

McDufus said, "Pull it over here next to the boat. You must'a wore it out, cause it don't seem to be fightin' much."

As he pulled the fish closer to the boat, Jason said, "Are there any fish that are square in shape?"

Jason saw McDufus reach towards the fish with a long-handled net and pull it closer to the boat. "No, there ain't no square fish. So far, you've caught two trees, and now you snagged yourself a soggy old cardboard box. I'm not sure you unnerstand the concept of fishin'."

Jason helped McDufus lift the box into the boat. Jason carefully removed the soggy cardboard box from the net and examined it with his flashlight.

Jason said, "The top is sealed with duct tape. Chelsea swears by this stuff. She got mad at me once and tried to duct tape me to the wall. I ran away. Anyhow, I'll cut it open with my knife."

McDufus said, "That wife of yers is kinda scary. You could always blast it open with that hand cannon of yers." Jason reached for Blaster.

"Just kiddin'. Use the knife, please."

Jason took a pocketknife from his tackle box, opened the box, and shined a flashlight inside.

"It's a box full of small vials, filled with some kind of liquid. The vials are all labeled."

Jason reached in, pulled out one of the vials, and shined the light on it.

"The print is blurred from being wet, but I can still make it out. It says *Recombinant Human Growth Hormone.* And there's a logo with the name *GenesRUs* printed under it. Harold Fairchild, the man whose wife hired us to find him, is the CEO of that company. And, come to think of it, our other neighbor is a scientist and VP there. I shouldn't have told you about our other client, confidentiality, and all, but we're looking for your cousin too, so I guess it's okay."

McDufus said, "What's a recom…whatever…human growth hormone thingy? And what the hell's it doin' in my lake?"

"I worked for the FDA, which is the doctor part of my name. I worked some with medical biotechnology products, a type of medicine. You can extract human growth hormone from the human body and use it to treat diseases. Scientists can also synthesize some of these substances in a lab rather than taking them from a human being. Those are called recombinant hormones."

McDufus said, "Synthesize? Ya' mean like cookin' meth in the bathtub?"

"Not exactly. More like mixing chemicals in a laboratory to make medicine to treat diseases, not explode your heart and rot your teeth. Human growth hormone is used to treat things like growth hormone deficiency in children, causing children of short stature. It's also used for Turner syndrome and wasting syndrome with AIDs. If I remember correctly, it's been approved by the FDA under the Orphan Drug Act. That's where companies get special perks for developing drugs to treat diseases with so few patients that it would not otherwise be profitable."

McDufus said, "What's this Turner Syndrome thing?"

Jason said, "That's a disease where a female is missing part or all of the *X* sex chromosome, resulting in short stature, failure of the ovaries to function, and heart problems."

"Jason, stop speakin' all sciency. I think what yer sayin' is this medicine thing can make short people taller?"

Jason gave up. "Yes, that's about the size of it. It can make short people taller, sometimes."

McDufus shined his flashlight into the box. "Well, can this human growth hormone thingy also make fish taller? It looks like some of these here vials are leakin'. Could that maybe explain them really big stripers that started showin' up this past year?"

Jason was impressed that after drinking almost two six-packs of beer, McDufus could connect the dots and come up with this theory. Or remain conscious for that matter.

"McDufus, I see where you're coming from. This is *human* growth hormone, and it shouldn't work on fish. But it's recombinant and was made in the lab instead of extracted from people. If GenesRUs made mistakes when they synthesized the stuff, who knows what they actually came up with. Their quality control guys should have tested it to make sure that it was *human* growth hormone, and not fish growth hormone. But I've seen some strange things since I started working as a PI. I once investigated a murder case with a drug that had a side effect involving some very odd hallucinations. But that's for another book...time. Anyhow, human growth hormone should not affect fish. But if it did that could explain all the very large stripers."

McDufus said, "Could the stuff also turn normal fish into meat-eaters? That might explain all the disappearin' fishermen. Wouldn't that be somethin'? Them damned boats knockin' down a fella's dock, all them old septic tanks leakin' and messin' up the water. They's even a guy on our cove what feeds the geese; there's goose crap everywhere. Now they's some nut case dumping stuff in the lake making giant, man-eatin' stripers. I'm gonna need more beer."

Jason watched as McDufus reeled in his line, sat his pole down, raised the trolling motor, and started the big outboard. It was clear McDufus had enough fishing for one night. Next thing Jason knew, they were skimming along the surface of the lake at warp speed, in the dark. Jason held on for dear life. *Well, this was fun. I hear you can fish with dynamite. Maybe I'll try that next time. Probably safer than fishing with McDufus.*

McDufus pulled up to his floating dock and unloaded the remaining six-packs of beer along with his fishing gear. Jason took his pole, tackle box, and the soggy cardboard box, climbed out of the boat, and thanked McDufus for the fishing trip. Then he headed home.

When Jason got home, he left his fishing gear and the cardboard box in the garage and entered the house. It was three o'clock in the morning. He went into the bedroom and tapped a sleeping Chelsea on the shoulder.

"Chelsea, Chelsea. Wake up. I had an interesting fishing trip."

Chelsea grumbled at him and placed her pillow over top of her head. Jason kept tapping her on the shoulder. Finally, she removed the pillow and said, "What! What time is it?"

Jason said, "I think I solved the case, with some help from our neighbor McDufus."

Chelsea said, groggily, "What are you babbling about?" She looked at the clock on her nightstand. "Jason, it's three AM. Can't this wait until morning?"

Jason sat on the bed next to her. He bounced up and down to make sure she was awake.

"It is morning. I had a great fishing trip. I caught two trees and a soggy cardboard box."

Chelsea said, "That's nice. Don't get into this bed until you take a shower. You smell like swamp and fish. What's this about trees and cardboard boxes? Didn't you go fishing for fish?"

"Oh yes. I forgot. I also shot Nellie with Blaster."

Chelsea, now wide wake, sat up and put her pillow behind her back.

"Oh God! You killed somebody. Who's Nellie? It isn't McDufus' wife I hope."

"What are you, asleep or something? Wake up and listen to the words coming out of my mouth. Nellie is McDufus' boat. I got attacked by a bear. I shot McDufus' boat to scare it off."

Chelsea took the pillow from Jason's side of the bed and hit him with it. He put up his arms to protect himself.

"Jason, stop it. I'm getting a headache, in the middle of the night. Forget the bear. You look like you've still got all your parts. What's this about solving the case?"

"Yes! We went trolling for stripers in the deep water, and I caught a soggy cardboard box. When I looked inside, it contained vials of recombinant human growth hormone. The label said the drug was made at GenesRUs. The company where Harold Fairchild is CEO. The guy we've been hired to look for. Anyhow, McDufus suggested that the human growth hormone might be leaking into the lake, causing the stripers to grow into giants. I told him I didn't think human growth hormone would affect fish, but I'm not so sure. The company could have screwed up the synthesis, and who knows what they actually made. Maybe that's why they threw it in the lake."

Chelsea took the other pillow and placed it behind her head to get more comfortable.

Chelsea said, "Why would a drug company toss boxes full of drugs in the lake? Isn't that stuff expensive to produce?"

Jason said, "I found the expiration date on a couple of vials. The product expired six months ago. Maybe they had to dispose of it, and it's cheaper to toss it in the lake than to pay a disposal company to get rid of it properly."

Chelsea, now interested, said, "That would make sense. But, even if this growth hormone is responsible for the giant stripers, aren't they just lake bass? They don't eat meat, at least not human meat, do they? So, how would that explain the disappearing fishermen?"

Jason said, "McDufus suggested the growth hormone might have changed the stripers in other ways too, like giving them a taste for other types of food, such as people. Or perhaps the fish are growing so fast they need a larger food source, like humans. I'm not sure he's right, but it's something to think about. I was surprised that he came up with such creative ideas."

Just then, Jason and Chelsea heard several gunshots and a lot of cursing coming from next door. Jason heard McDufus yell, "Damn squirrels! I'll kill everyone a'yus! Eat lead!"

Chelsea said, "You mean that McDufus, our *creative* neighbor? I think you better phone the police, before he shoots himself, or one of us."

Jason said, "He did drink a six-pack of beer or three. Perhaps it wasn't so much that he came up with creative ideas; more like alcohol-induced hallucinations. I'll phone the police, Dear."

Chapter 13. Jason Catches a Big One

Chelsea did not want to report the box of recombinant human growth hormone to the authorities until they figured out what, if anything, it had to do with the disappearing fishermen. Tuesday morning the private detectives sat at the kitchen table finishing their Eggo waffles and coffee. The girls were still in bed. Chelsea had burnt Jason's waffles, so he slathered them with butter and syrup and placed a scoop of vanilla ice cream on top to improve the taste. She watched in amazement as he took his final bite and washed it down with decaf coffee.

Chelsea took a bite of her perfectly toasted waffle, sipped her coffee, swallowed, and said, "We're not getting anywhere. I suggest we dial it up a notch and you go fishing tomorrow night. We can use you as bait for the fishermen killer. I'll rent a second boat and hide nearby with my fifty-cal and a flashlight, ready to jump into the fray when they show up. The girls will be fine. We won't leave until they're all asleep, and Lizzy will be here with them."

Jason said, "Are you sure you want to use me as bait? I'm not thrilled about being bait. Especially since we don't know what we're fishing for, fish, human, or something else. Did I mention the bear? Why can't you be bait too?"

"Jason, you're such a baby. If you insist, I'll go along fishing with you and act as bait too. I just thought it might be better if one of us survived to raise our children. But if you want to be selfish... I'll take Bertha, and you can carry Blaster, as long as you promise not to shoot me, or the boat. And we can avoid the bears by staying away from the shoreline."

Jason said, "That sounds good. Two guns are better than one. And how do I know you wouldn't just fall asleep lying in wait in the dark? Better we're on the same boat. That way you'll stay awake, and I'll know who to shoot at."

Chelsea said, "That's reassuring."

Chelsea told the girls their plan to go fishing, and Lizzy agreed to take care of her sisters. Wednesday night just before midnight, the girls in bed asleep, Jason and Chelsea headed for the boat. Chelsea stood on the dock and watched while Jason loaded the boat with fishing gear and a cooler full of sodas. She took out Bertha and made sure she was loaded.

Jason said, "You could help me load the boat. Please be careful with that hand cannon. Remember, I'm the father of your children. You want to shoot kidnappers, killers, and bears."

Chelsea said, "No worries, just don't start talking about other women's behinds, or comparing them to mine, and you should be fine."

"Yes Dear."

Chelsea boarded Luscious and sat down next to the helm. She watched as Jason untied the boat, climbed in, and started the engine. He pushed off the floating dock, pointed Luscious towards the big water, and shoved the throttle all the way forward. They blasted off.

Chelsea grabbed the seat frame and held on for dear life. "Jason, take it easy. It's pitch dark out. The clouds are covering up the moon and I can't see a thing."

Jason said, "No worries, Darlin'. I've got the running light on, so nobody's going to run into us. And I know this part of the lake like the back of my head...I mean...hand."

Chelsea squealed as Jason swerved violently to the right, just in time to miss the shoreline. She almost fell out of the boat despite hanging on tight with both hands.

"Jason, slow down. Or when I can finally let go of this seat frame, I'm going to wing you with Bertha. Maybe if I shoot you in the leg, it'll slow you down."

"If you shoot me in the leg with Bertha, I'll need another leg. Remember that father of your children thing?"

"I have my own PI firm, my inheritance, and you've already fathered my children. You might just be expendable at this point, especially if you don't stop being so irritating."

Chelsea was relieved to see Jason slow the boat to three-quarter throttle. He stopped in the middle of the lake, several yards off a small island barely visible in the nighttime light.

Chelsea heard Jason say, "Okay, we're here. This is where McDufus caught a couple of stripers, and I caught the cardboard box. We can either look for schools of shad over next to that island or troll the bottom out here. What do you think?"

Chelsea scanned the area. "It looks scary. It's dark, and there's nobody else around. Are you sure it's a good idea for us to be out here? I'm thinking this was a bad idea."

"Chelsea, it was your idea. You said we weren't getting anywhere with the case, so we needed to come out here fishing and use ourselves as bait."

"Yeah, but now that we're out here I'm thinking this was really your idea. You're the one with all the hairbrained ideas. Come to think of it, my original idea was to use you as bait."

Jason said, "This idea was yours. Besides, we have Blaster and Bertha if any killers show up. Meanwhile, what will it be? Bottom fishing or a school of shad?"

Chelsea looked around some more, still not convinced they should be using themselves as bait. "What does that fish-finder thingy say? Are there any big fish under us?"

Jason said, "I forgot about the fish finder. I'll just flip this switch and we'll see what's what." He reached down and turned on the fish finder screen. "Wow, there's a school of big fish down there. Let's do some bottom fishing. Put a large sinker on your line to keep your lure on the bottom. We'll have a boat full of stripers in no time."

Chelsea turned on a flashlight, opened the tackle box, and tied a large sinker to her line. Then she held the flashlight for Jason as he did the same. Chelsea followed Jason towards the bow of the boat. She sat in the portside seat, Jason on the starboard side near the trolling motor.

Jason said, "I'll release a bunch of line here on the starboard side. You watch me and then release a similar amount on the port side. Then we lock our reels and I move us back and forth with the trolling motor. You'll be scaling, gutting, cleaning, and fileting fish for dinner in no time. McDufus says these things taste great when breaded and fried up in a pan."

Chelsea looked at Jason as she released fishing line, letting her lure sink to the bottom. "That sounds awful. No way I'm cleaning all the fish. Yours are your problem. I've heard that it takes forever to get that fishy smell off your hands." *Translated, I catch the smelly things and you clean them. And I've never fried anything in my life.*

They were half-way through their second pass when Chelsea's pole jerked. She yanked to set the hook like Jason had told her to do.

"Jason, I've got one! It feels like a monster."

Jason said, "Pull and reel. Keep your tip up. Let me know if you need any help."

"The only help I need is for you to get the net to haul this monster into the boat."

Chelsea saw the beam as Jason shined a flashlight onto the water. Something broke the surface several yards off to the side of the boat.

"Jason, get the net ready. I don't want to lose this fish after all this work."

Chelsea watched the water as she reeled the fish in next to the boat. Jason scooped the fish up in the net, and she put down her pole to help him haul the large striper into the boat. She felt proud as Jason untangled the large fish from the net and used needle-nosed pliers to remove the lure. He attached the fish to a hand-held scale and struggled to lift it high enough to weigh it.

Jason said, "Jeez, Chelsea. This thing weighs forty-three pounds. I've never caught a fish this big in my life."

Chelsea, doing a victory dance, said, "You still haven't. That's Chelsea one, Jason zero."

She worried that the fish might escape as Jason placed it in the storage tank. She worried more that he might accidentally let it go on purpose. He could be overly competitive at times.

Jason said, "Don't be such a showoff. Stop dancing, or you'll swamp the boat. Besides, we've just gotten started. And the good news, no one has killed us yet."

Chelsea stopped dancing and released her bucktail into the water. Jason started the boat moving with the trolling motor again. Chelsea fell in love with fishing as this same scenario repeated itself two more times in the next half hour. Each time she reeled in a large striper and watched as Jason netted it, hauled it into the boat, weighed it, and placed it in the storage tank.

After her third fish, Chelsea sat, resting with her bucktail beside her in the boat.

She bragged, "Wow, I'm all worn out from pulling and reeling. My bucktail even needs a rest. That's Chelsea three, Jason zero. And that last one is over fifty pounds. What's wrong, Mr. Professional Fisherman? These stripers don't seem to be at all interested in your lure."

Jason said, "I don't know. Maybe you have the lucky bucktail, and mine's jinxed."

Chelsea smirked, "That's the silliest thing you've ever said, which is hard to believe. Would you like to trade lures, just to test your theory?"

Jason said, "No thanks. I'll catch something eventually. You're all tired out from reeling, so perhaps you could give your lucky bucktail a rest for a couple of passes. Maybe that would give the stripers a chance to find mine."

Chelsea smiled, "Okay, you've got it. Me and my bucktail will rest and give you a chance to catch something."

She saw the determined look on Jason's face as he drove the trolling motor while hanging onto his fishing pole. On Jason's second solo pass, Chelsea saw his pole jerk and bend. She watched Jason jump up and start reeling frantically, almost falling overboard in the process.

"Chelsea, I've finally got one! It's a doozy. It's a lot bigger than the ones you caught. Look, my pole is bending double."

Chelsea turned on her flashlight and aimed the beam out over the water. She watched Jason's silhouette in the sparsely moonlit night as he struggled, pulling, and reeling with all his might. She felt some disappointment. Perhaps he had caught the biggest striper of the night after all. She dutifully picked up the net and continued to scan the water for signs of the giant fish.

"Jason. There it is. It's big alright. But it doesn't appear to be putting up much of a fight."

Jason said, "What do you mean? It's taking all my strength to reel the thing in."

Chelsea kept watching the water as Jason pulled and reeled. She saw something large moving slowly in their direction. When the fish got close enough for Chelsea to see it more clearly, it took her brain a few moments to process what floated up next to the boat.

"Jason, I can see your striper. There's something very wrong here. Have you ever heard of a fish wearing a suit? I'd run away, but my legs won't work, and I can't walk on water."

Jason held tight to his fishing pole, keeping the tip up. "Chelsea, what are you talking about? You're making stuff up because you're jealous I caught something bigger than you did."

Chelsea said, "That may be true. It's also true that yours is much better dressed. And I don't think we'll be cleaning and eating it unless you're into cannibalism. You're not into cannibalism, are you Jason?"

"Chelsea, stop joking around, get the net, and help me haul this monster into the boat. I'll bet it's at least sixty pounds; bigger than any of yours. Take that! Chelsea three, Jason the biggest."

She just sat there staring at the thing. She saw Jason put down his pole, grab the net, and hurry towards what he obviously believed to be the winning fish.

"Chelsea, I'm going to be mad if this thing gets away. What's the matter with you?"

When Jason arrived at her side, she pointed into the water. "Jason, that's no fish. And it's not going anywhere. You've caught a dead person; looks to be an older man dressed in a business suit. I don't know if you snagged him off the bottom or he was just floating by. But you win. I'm guessing he weighs more than fifty pounds. I'm really scared. Can we go home now?"

Jason said, "What are you scared of? We're both armed. And this guy's obviously dead."

Chelsea said, "Well, for one thing it's the middle of the night, we're in the middle of nowhere, and you managed to haul in a dead body. Then there's the issue of who, or what, made him dead, and whether or not it's still around."

Jason said, "That's a lot more than one thing. You're scaring me. Should I pull Blaster out of his holster?"

"Jason, shooting the boat isn't going to scare this guy away like it did the bear. He's not going anywhere. I've got a cell signal, and I'm going to call the police. They have a police boat that patrols the lake. We can't really haul this fellow back to our dock. Our fishing licenses don't include dead bodies. Also, we'd destroy the crime scene, such as it is."

Jason said, "Don't call it a crime scene. We're the only ones here besides the dead guy. The police will think we killed him."

Chelsea said, "Good point. We'll tell the police we stayed here with the body so they could see where *you* found it. It was you who reeled him in. I caught three giant stripers. Only you caught a dead human. You seem to be some kind of crime magnet. My associate, Dr. Jason Longfellow, PI, CM…private eye, crime magnet. That's just great."

"What's wrong with being a crime magnet? A good skill for a PI. Bring in lots of business."

"Or land us in jail."

Jason said, "Well, there's that."

Chelsea phoned the police and gave them her position on the water. They told her they'd send their boat out right away.

Chelsea pointed her flashlight at the body. "Jason, you have a knack for finding dead bodies. If I'd known that twenty years ago, I probably would have said no to your marriage proposal. While we're waiting for the police, we should examine the body. Look for a cause of death. Could you please turn him over so we can see his face."

Jason said, "I'm not touching that soggy old dead body. Who knows where it's been."

"It's been in the lake, and it should be very clean. Stop being a big baby and turn him over so we can see his face. We might recognize him."

Jason said, "In a horror movie he wouldn't have a face. The fish, or a monster, would have eaten it. I don't wanna touch him."

Chelsea said, "Jason, do I have to get Bertha?"

Chelsea winced as Jason bent down, reached into the water, and turned the floating body over. She shined the flashlight on the man's face, hoping Jason was wrong.

Jason wiped his hands on his pants and said, "At least he has a face. I don't see any giant bites or teeth marks, do you?"

Chelsea bent down to get a closer look. "No, I don't see any teeth marks. So much for the giant man-eating fish theory. He's all bloated, and his skin is discolored from being in the water for a while. There's not a lot of decomposition, although the water has been cool, which can slow decomposition down. He probably hasn't been dead very long, a matter of days."

Jason said, "His face looks kind of familiar, although it's hard to say in the dark with him all bloated up like that. Does he look familiar to you?"

Chelsea said, "He does look familiar. Oh my God. I think that's Harold Fairchild."

Jason said, "Chelsea, you're right. This guy looks like that photo of Mr. Fairchild his wife gave us if he had been submerged in a bathtub for a couple of weeks. Maybe that's how he died. Someone drowned him in the bathtub and tossed his body in the lake to make it look like an accidental drowning. I saw that in an episode of Columbo once."

"Jason, this man is dressed in a business suit and tie. I doubt he drowned in the bathtub."

"Come on, Chelsea. I'll bet his sweet young wife is having an affair with his younger brother. She drowned Harold in the bathtub, dressed him in one of his business suits, hauled his body out here to the lake, and tossed him in. Made it look like he accidentally fell in and drowned. She probably thought it would be the perfect crime. But the autopsy will reveal he has soapy bathtub water in his lungs. That'll be the key."

"Jason, you're delusional. Why would he be at the lake in his business suit? Wouldn't she have dressed him in his bathing suit?" She shined her flashlight on a spot on the side of the man's head. "This dent in his skull looks like blunt force trauma. Someone whacked him on the head with a hard object and cracked his skull like a melon. Probably no water in his lungs at all since he didn't drown."

While they waited for the police boat to arrive, Chelsea and Jason continued to investigate. She told Jason to search for a wallet. Jason found it in the breast pocket of his suit jacket.

Chelsea held the flashlight while Jason went through the wallet's soggy contents. "The driver's license confirms that this is Harold Fairchild. He has several credit cards, and a fishing license. You don't suppose he was out here fishing, and the fishermen killer got him, do you? That would be great. It would mean his sweet young wife is innocent. No woman with a rear…"

"Jason Bartholomew Longfellow, DO NOT say it, or the police will need two body bags."

"Yes Dear."

Chelsea felt her anger subside a little, "I seriously doubt that Mr. Fairchild went fishing in his business suit. I think that we can rule out the fishermen killer. Looks like the *sweet young wife* may be on the hook for this murder."

Chelsea heard a boat off in the distance and saw running lights headed their way. "The police boat is almost here. So, let's get our story straight."

Jason said, "Okay, so I caught three very large stripers, and you reeled in Mr. Fairchild. Don't worry, I'll be sure to tell them you didn't kill him."

Chelsea reached for Bertha, in a hip holster under her jacket. "Jason, I'm warning you."

Jason said hurriedly, "Chelsea, don't pull that thing out right now. We need to keep Blaster and Bertha under wraps. The police might not like the idea of our being out here armed to the teeth. They will for sure think we killed Mr. Fairchild."

"Jason, he doesn't have any gigantic holes in him. Someone whacked him on the head, much like I'd like to do to you right now. Tell the police the truth, or you will regret it."

The police boat pulled up next to Luscious. Chelsea heard a male voice yell, "Ahoy! We're from the Bedford Sheriff's Office. Are you the lady who called about a body, a floater?"

Chelsea yelled back, "Yes Sir. I'm Chelsea Longfellow. I called it in. The body is floating here next to our bass boat. My husband caught a giant striper that turned out to be a Mr. Harold Fairchild, according to his driver's license."

A tall man in a deputy's uniform tied a line to the bass boat. He leapt down from the deck onto Luscious. The moon had come out from behind the clouds, and Chelsea could see a handsome man with dark brown hair, sculpted features, broad shoulders, and a thin waist. She thought he looked more lumberjack than policeman. He gave her a big, friendly smile, his teeth so white they glowed in the dark. He took Chelsea's hand and gave it a very friendly shake.

"Hello, Ma'am. I'm Deputy Andrew Hawkins, Bedford Police. Pleased to make your acquaintance. What is such a beautiful woman doing out on the lake in the middle of the night?"

Chelsea saw Jason tap the man on the shoulder. The deputy turned and looked surprised when he saw Jason.

Jason said, "Excuse me Deputy Hawkins. I'm Dr. Jason Longfellow, PI, and that's my wife's hand that you are fondling. I'm the one who found the body. I brought Chelsea out here to teach her how to fish for stripers, and I reeled in Mr. Fairchild by mistake. He has some nerve floating around in the lake at night like that. He gave us quite a scare."

Chelsea couldn't help but notice that the deputy continued to hang onto her hand while speaking to Jason. It felt strong and warm.

The deputy said, "So, you're the one that found the body. That makes you the prime suspect. Perhaps you'd like to come downtown, and I'll put you in an interrogation room."

Chelsea noticed Jason's voice begin to sound a little shaky. Jason said, "I'm the victim here. I thought I'd caught a giant striper, and all I got was this old dead body. Chelsea, tell the deputy I didn't kill anyone. You were in the boat with me the entire time."

Chelsea smiled at Deputy Hawkins, "I can't actually account for the whereabouts of my husband for the entire time. I was occupied for quite a while reeling in the three very large fish that are in our storage tank. I guess Jason could have stepped out during that time, and I might not have noticed. Isn't that right, Jason?"

"But Chelsea, we're on a boat. Where could I have gone? Chelsea? Earth calling Chelsea."

Chelsea was busy staring up at the deputy's handsome face. She came back to earth when she felt Jason step up, take hold of her hand, and remove it from Deputy Hawkins' grasp.

Jason said, "Mine. The woman attached to it is mine too. About the dead body over there."

Chelsea saw the deputy take a step back. He put his hand on his sidearm and said, "Don't get aggressive with me Sir. You're the prime suspect in a murder. In fact, we've had several fishermen disappear from this lake under suspicious circumstances. I can't help but wonder if you might have something to do with that too."

Jason said, "I'm a licensed private eye. And this Harold Fairchild, the aforementioned dead body, happens to be wearing a business suit. I'd hardly call him a fisherman."

Chelsea said, "But Jason, you just called him a fisherman a few minutes ago."

Jason said, "Wife, whose side are you on? Besides Officer, it's my wife's private eye business. I'm just the *Associate*. So, if anyone should be the prime suspect here, it's her."

Chelsea said, "So now it's *my* PI firm. That doesn't make any sense. Besides Jason, you were right here hauling the giant stripers that I caught into the boat, so you know I didn't go anywhere. Therefore, I have an ironclad alibi. Don't you agree?"

She smiled when she saw the confused look on Jason's face. She knew the way his brain worked, or didn't work. He had what she called a *box brain*. He could only focus on one thing at a time, which is why she was always three steps ahead of him. She didn't really plan on letting him remain the prime suspect…or did she?

Jason said, "Wait a minute. How's come you can't give me an alibi, but I just gave you an ironclad one? That can't be right."

Deputy Hawkins started to laugh, "What is this, your Abbott and Costello act? Who's on first? I get it. You came out here fishing. Mrs. Longfellow, PI caught all the fish, and Dr. Longfellow, PI caught a dead body. And it's embarrassing, amusing, and terrifying all at the same time. So, tell me, do you two PIs have any thoughts as to how this Mr. Fairchild managed to find himself dead, in a business suit, floating in the lake?"

Chelsea said, "I'm Chelsea Longfellow, PI. He's my husband, *Associate*."

Jason said, "Chelsea, stop being mean. You know the PI thing was my idea."

Deputy Hawkins said, "You two sound a lot like a married couple. Please focus. Any ideas about how this guy got out here?"

Chelsea didn't want to mention that Harold Fairchild's wife was their client yet. There was the matter of client confidentiality. She also wanted to figure out if the wife had anything to do with this first.

Jason said, "Well, Deputy Hawkins. Having had my online PI license for a year longer than my wife, perhaps I should speak first. According to the wallet I found in the dead man's pocket, his name is Harold Fairchild. About a week ago, his w....ouch!"

Chelsea had kicked Jason in the shin, hard. Deputy Hawkins obviously hadn't seen her do so in the dark. He looked confused.

The deputy said, "His w...? What is his w...? Please continue."

Chelsea had given Jason one of her most threatening looks. She saw Jason reach down, rub his shin, and take a step back.

Chelsea said, "What my husband...*Associate*...means to say is that we have no idea who Harold Fairchild is, how he got out here in the lake, or why he is wearing a business suit. I can say with some confidence that he was killed by blunt force trauma. I used my flashlight to examine the body and part of his skull is clearly fractured."

The deputy said, "I'll mention that to the coroner. Did you find any bite marks on the body? Some of the crazier folks around here think the large striped bass that started showing up in the lake recently have something to do with the disappearing fishermen. I can't imagine that's the case, but people are scared."

Chelsea said, "No, there were no bite marks."

Jason blurted out, "Being the more experienced PI, I have several theories about what happened to Mr. Fairchild. For one thing, this Harold Fairchild has a sweet young wife..."

Chelsea shot him another threatening look, but to her surprise he continued.

"One of my theories involves Mr. Harold Fairchild's younger brother, who we know visited the young Mrs. Fairchild after Harold disappeared. Perhaps the younger brother was having an affair with her, and the two of them made Mr. Fairchild the elder disappear into the lake. My second theory is there's a rumor that Mrs. Fairchild was having an affair with the young realtor that sold her the house. Perhaps she got together with him and knocked off her husband to clear the path for young love. My third theory is that perhaps the serial killer of fishermen has changed his modus operandi, and instead of leaving behind body parts he is now whacking them on the head. And finally, the most interesting. I don't believe these giant stripers are killing and eating the fishermen. Based on Mr. Fairchild's injury, perhaps these giant bass have developed an unusual defense mechanism. When threatened, they swim up to a person, or a boat, and head butt it as a form of self-protection. That might explain Mr. Fairchild's skull fracture, and the fact that something kept crashing into our boat the last time we went fishing."

Chelsea shook her head in amazement and gave her husband the look of the damned.

"Jason, have you entirely lost your mind? Bass that head bump fishermen, and their boats, in self-defense? Mr. Fairchild is wearing a business suit, so clearly not a fisherman. And a serial killer that whacks fishermen on the head while they are fishing in the middle of the night? How would this serial killer get into the boat without the fishermen noticing him?" *At least the idiot didn't tell them that young Mrs. Fairchild is our client. That would be a real problem based on the clear conflict of interest.*

Jason said, "By the way, the sweet young Mrs. Fairchild happens to be one of our clients."

Chapter 14. Notification or Interrogation

Jason answered the office phone, and it was Mrs. Fairchild. She told him the police had notified her that her husband's body had been found. She sounded inconsolable, crying uncontrollably. After he got off the phone, he told Chelsea. She suggested they meet with their client as soon as possible. Friday morning, Jason, Chelsea, and Veronica Fairchild sat in Chelsea's office drinking coffee. Jason and Veronica sat in the low-slung clients' chairs in front of the gigantic wooden desk, looking up at the owner of Chelsea Longfellow, PI, and Associate.

Jason said, "Well, this is nice. The *Associate* gets to sit in the kiddie's section. How's the weather up there, Chelsea?"

Chelsea took a sip of hot coffee, "Jason, stop whining. Now you know how I feel when we're standing up."

Jason looked at Veronica, who didn't appear as distraught as she had sounded on the phone.

Jason said, "So Mrs. Fairchild…"

Veronica reached over, put her hand on Jason's knee. She winked at him, and said flirtatiously, "No need to be so formal, Dr. Longfellow. You can call me Veronica."

Jason smiled, turned red behind the ears, and said, "I'd like that. And you can call me…uh… Jason. My name is Jason."

Chelsea interrupted, "Actually, you can call him Associate, or PI Associate, or PI My Husband Associate. And if you don't get your hand off his knee, you can call him my late husband. Now let's get on with it."

Jason liked the attention and was sad when the young woman removed her hand.

Jason said, "Anyhow…Mrs. Veronica, the police told you that your husband's body has been found. Did they mention who found the body, or how your husband might have died?"

Jason saw Veronica's flirtatious face turn serious. "Jason, the deputy told me that you and Mrs. PI Longfellow found my husband's body while you were out fishing. They didn't tell me how he died, but they said you are a suspect in his death? The police want to talk to you because I am your client, I hired you to find Harold because your online photo is so handsome, Harold is now dead, and you found the body. Did you kill Harold, Jason? Why would you do that?"

Jason panicked, "Chelsea, help! I'm supposed to be asking the questions here." He turned to Veronica, "Did you say handsome?"

Chelsea stood. Jason almost flipped his short-legged chair over backwards looking up at her.

She said, "Jason, I told you not to tell the police that Mrs. Fairchild was our client. Veronica, it's true we did find your husband's body. We went out fishing the other night, with the intent of catching the fishermen killer. I caught three record stripers, and Jason managed to reel in your husband. When the police got there, Jason provided me with the perfect alibi, because he spent all his time netting and putting my fish in the storage tank. I couldn't provide him with an ironclad alibi, because he could have gone anywhere while I was distracted reeling in those big fish, and I never would have noticed."

Jason said, "Chelsea, that's…"

"Jason, let me finish. I just wanted to say I don't think Jason killed your husband, even though I can't give him an ironclad alibi. And I don't think he's the fishermen killer, either. He's been with me way too much since we moved here from Northern Virginia. I wish he'd get a hobby, so I could have some time to myself."

Jason said, "If I were gonna get a hobby, it'd be something manly like riding a Harley, or off-roading in my truck. It wouldn't be riding around the lake at night knocking fishermen in the head. Which brings us to how your husband died, Mrs. Veronica. Someone, or something, whacked him on the head with a blunt object and cracked his skull."

Veronica stood up, pointed down at Jason, and gasped, "How do you know that? What did you hit him with? The police are right. You killed him."

Jason was concerned about his neck. He now sat there looking up at both women. He said, "Chelsea, she's asking the questions again, and I'm getting a sprained neck."

Chelsea said, "Jason, if you want a promotion, stand up, take control of the interrogation."

Veronica said, "Wait a minute. You're interrogating me? I'm paying you to find my husband, and now I'm a suspect. Are you trying to deflect suspicion away from your husband?"

Jason tried to get up out of the low-slung chair but couldn't manage it. It was too low, and his butt was stuck in the small chair. He gave up the struggle, continued sitting there looking up.

He said, "Let's get back to me being the suspect, okay? I didn't hit Harold with anything. When we found his dead, discolored, bloated body, Chelsea discovered that your husband's skull was fractured. I have a couple of theories on that."

Chelsea said, "Oh please God, no."

Jason struggled to get up again, to no avail. He spilled the last of his coffee on the carpet.

He said, still looking up at Veronica, "We went fishing a week ago, and something kept bumping into Luscious. There were several very large striped bass in the area, and it's my theory that they kept banging into Luscious with their heads, trying to chase us away."

Jason's neck was starting to cramp as he continued looking up. He saw Veronica turn to Chelsea, and say, "Who's this Luscious, and why were fish head-butting him, or her?"

Chelsea said, "Jason named his bass boat Luscious. Don't ask. Also, I've heard his theory, and it's nuts."

Jason pointed up at Veronica and said, "Yes, Luscious is my sweet, sweet bass boat. And my theory makes perfect sense. It's a science thing. These striped bass are an anomaly. They've grown very large for some reason. Whatever caused them to grow so large could have also made them more aggressive, thus the head-butting. It's my theory that those same fish found your husband swimming in the lake and attacked him by head-butting him, fracturing his skull."

Veronica looked down at Jason, shook her head. "You're trying to tell me that you didn't kill my husband. He was head-butted to death by some freakishly large fish. I think you must have hit your head. Or perhaps your mother dropped you on your head, several times."

Chelsea finished off her coffee, sat her cup down, and said, "Jason, you do remember that Mr. Fairchild was wearing a business suit when you reeled him in. I don't think it's likely that he went swimming in his business suit. So, your head-butting fish theory is a non-starter. Mrs. Fairchild, you seem quite perceptive. Perhaps I should fire my current Associate and hire you."

Jason said, "Chelsea, you can't hire her. She's a suspect in her husband's murder. And Mrs. Veronica, did your husband ever go swimming in his business suit? Perhaps he stopped by the lake to take a cool dip after work, forgot his bathing suit, went swimming in his suit, and the bass were offended by his being overdressed. Maybe that's why they attacked him."

Chelsea said, "A woman who murdered her husband? That's a concept I could get behind. Which is it, Jason? Is the killer Veronica the wife, or these imaginary head-butting bass?"

Jason began to feel extremely vulnerable sitting down there at floor level with both his irritated wife and a female murder suspect standing over him, and his neck really hurt.

"Ladies, could one of you please give me a hand getting out of this chair. My rear end seems to be stuck, and gravity is not my friend."

Veronica reached down, offered Jason her hand, and helped pull him to a standing position.

Jason looked down at Veronica and his wife. "Thank you. That's much better. I have more questions."

Jason felt Veronica place her hand on his shoulder in a friendly gesture. He heard Chelsea growl and saw her look at her gun safe. He stepped back out of Veronica's reach.

Veronica said, "You're welcome, Mr. Associate. To answer your question, no my husband never went swimming in his business suit. Also, my husband's younger brother, Lucas, has disappeared. Do you know anything about that? You didn't knock him in the head too, did you?"

Jason shook his head, took another step backwards, and almost fell over a low-slung chair.

He said, "I didn't knock anyone in the head. I'm working for you, trying to find out who killed your husband. Now you seem to be more concerned about his brother." He looked at his wife, "Chelsea, help. Work with me here."

Chelsea placed her hands on her desk, leaned forward, and said, "Jason, you're on your own. I can't provide you with an alibi for her husband's murder, or for his brother's disappearance."

Jason placed his hands on his head, feeling dizzy. *Why do women always gang up on me? It's like when my daughters always side with Chelsea.*

He said, "Mrs. Veronica, it's my turn to ask the questions. I am the PI…Associate."

Veronica looked up at him and said, "Don't forget, I hired you."

Jason stepped forward towards Veronica, carefully navigating around the chair. He thrust his hands into the air to emphasize the seriousness of what he was about to say.

He said, "Yes, I work for you. It's also my job to find your husband's killer. Please, let me continue. I have a couple of theories as to what may have happened to Harold. Is it possible that you and Harold's younger brother are more than friends, perhaps lovers, a little hanky panky? Perhaps you and Lucas got together, bashed Harold's brains out, and tossed his body in the lake. We also found several boxes of expired human growth hormone from your husband's company that had been thrown in the lake near where we found Harold's body. They had the GenesRUs logo printed on them." He pointed at Veronica for emphasis. "A coincidence? I think not. With your husband gone, you could take over the company, marry Lucas, and live happily ever after. Illegally destroying expired drugs was just icing on the cake. Dump the drugs and the body at the same time, killing two birds with one stone."

Jason had worked himself into a frenzy, waving his arms around, pointing, gesturing. This interrogation thing felt righteous. He was onto the truth.

Chelsea, still leaning on her desk, said, "Jason, calm down before you hurt yourself. And what's this *we* stuff? Need I remind you that it was you who reeled in the body? I was an innocent bystander. More importantly, how could Mrs. Fairchild take over the company? Wouldn't she need a medical, science, or business degree to run a biotech company?"

Veronica, switching into flirtatious mode again, winked at Jason, and said, "Actually, I am Dr. Veronica Fairchild. I have an MD degree from Harvard. I met Harold while working on one of the GenesRUs clinical trials. He was sexy, kind of like you. We hit it off and married. With Harold's millions I didn't need to work, so I quit, stayed home, and enjoyed the good life."

Jason said, "Aha! So, you do have the credentials to take over the company. Did you and the younger brother knock off your husband? More importantly, how sexy am I?"

Chelsea stood up straight, waved her hand in Veronica's direction, and said, "Sexy like Harold. He was in his sixties. Jason, you suck at interrogation. She's manipulating you. If you wink back at her, I'm coming over this desk."

Veronica shook her head, gave Jason a hurt look and said, "No, Lucas and I did not harm my husband. We are just friends. He came over to console me after Harold disappeared. That's all. And on a scale of one to ten, you're about an eight."

Jason said, "What about your realtor? The deputy mentioned you might have had an affair with the realtor that sold you your house. Apparently, that realtor is also a younger man. Did you get together with your realtor and knock your husband in the head? Again, you would get the company, and a younger man to meet your...needs. Did you hear that, Chelsea? I'm an eight."

Chelsea shook her head. "Yes, an eight in the elderly category." *Idiot.*

Veronica said, "No, Mr. Associate PI, I am not having an affair with my realtor. Don't be ridiculous. He's married and has five children. What would I do with five children?"

Jason said to Chelsea, "That's a fair point. I have no idea what to do with three." He turned to Veronica, put his hand on her shoulder, and said, "Well, are you planning on having an affair with anyone else? The deputy suggested that you have a lot of needs. Am I really an eight?"

Chelsea walked around her desk and whacked Jason in the back of the head. She said, "I apologize for my Associate PI. He gets carried away sometimes. And if he doesn't stop it, he's gonna get carried away in a box."

Jason removed his hand from Veronica's shoulder to rub his head.

Veronica said, "How often do you smack him on the head like that? I'm not surprised he seems so confused. Explains a lot."

Jason saw the angry look on Chelsea's face and retreated to a spot behind her desk. Chelsea said, "Jason, you're getting nowhere, and if you put your hands on her again, you're in danger of losing an arm. I need to create a position lower than Associate to demote you too. Meanwhile, I'm taking over this interrogation."

Jason, safe on the other side of the desk, got distracted by Chelsea's desk chair, large, heavily padded, lush leather. He sat in the chair, started rolling around and spinning in circles.

Chelsea looked at him and said in disgust, "Dear God, I'm raising four children, and this one's hopeless." Then she said, in a much louder voice, "Earth calling Junior Associate, I'm taking over this interrogation. That doesn't mean you can just go away. Perhaps you'd like to take notes or record the rest of this conversation on your cell phone. Do something!"

Jason stopped the chair, stood up, and faced the two women from across the desk. "Sorry Mrs. PI Longfellow. Can I have a chair like yours? It's very nice. Wait, what? Junior Associate?"

Jason saw the concerned look on Veronica's face and realized he might be in danger again. Veronica said, "I get it now. I'd like to whack him one myself, and I'm not married to him."

Chelsea glared at Jason, "Please make yourself useful and take notes on the rest of this interrogation." She looked at Veronica and said, "Now let's get to it. Your husband is dead, he's a millionaire, and he owns a biotech company called GenesRUs. Who stands to gain from Harold's death? Do you inherit everything, including his millions and the company?"

Jason spoke up, "Yeah, do you inherit it all? That's called motive."

Jason cringed as Chelsea pointed at him and said, "More writing, less chatter, Junior Associate. And Junior Associates definitely *do not* get a new chair."

Jason frowned, took a pen and notepad from Chelsea's desk, and wrote something down.

Jason saw Veronica's face change again, this time a puppy face, the picture of innocence.

She said, "Well, full disclosure, according to Harold's will I do inherit everything. That includes his bank accounts, stock portfolio, the house, our summer home in the Virgin Islands."

Chelsea said, "What about the company?"

Jason said, "Wow! How much is all that worth?"

Veronica continued, "I'm not sure of the actual value of the bank accounts, stock portfolio, and houses, but it's in the millions. Harold was about to take GenesRUs public, in which case the value of the company would have skyrocketed even more. Lucas wanted to keep it in the family rather than go public and have to deal with a board of directors, public stocks, and all that mess. I agreed with Lucas. If the company stays private, I become the President and CEO. And since I am inheriting, that decision is mine. So, you have to help me. All that money, and the company, are pretty good motives. Things don't look so good for me as far as the police are concerned. With Lucas disappearing, it looks even worse, like maybe we conspired to get rid of Harold."

Chelsea said, "So you do understand how bad this looks for you."

Jason said, "Yeah, and you're our client. If you killed your husband, we won't get paid."

Veronica continued, "But I didn't have anything to do with my husband's death. I loved the man, despite his age. He was good to me, and a great lover; he definitely took care of my needs."

Jason looked at Chelsea and said, "Chelsea, look at her. She looks so sad. Like a lost puppy. She has lots of needs, and Harold was a great lover. I think she's innocent."

Chelsea said, "Jason, a jury would convict her based on what she just told us, even though it's all circumstantial. She's our client, and she looks guilty as sin. I'm not sure how to proceed."

Jason tried to put on his own puppy face, and said, "But Chelsea, if she were guilty of murdering her husband wouldn't she have disappeared along with Lucas? I think the fact she's here talking to us proves her innocence."

Chelsea said, "First of all, stop the puppy face. She can get away with it, but you just look demented. As to Veronica not running away, perhaps that's because she gains a lot more by staying put and taking over the company. Maybe she knocked off both Harold and Lucas; more money for her. And a woman can always find another man who's a great lover, especially if she's wealthy. What do you have to say to that, Veronica?"

Jason said, "Yeah, what d'ya have to say to that?" Then to Chelsea, "Wait a minute. You just inherited a bunch of money from your mother, so you're wealthy, too."

Jason did not like the whimsical expression that appeared on Chelsea's face.

Veronica said, "Guys, I really need your help, and I am innocent. I didn't kill my husband, and I have no idea where Lucas has disappeared to. I wasn't having an affair with him. I swear. I'll pay you double your regular fee to help me prove my innocence."

Jason looked at Chelsea, and they said in unison, "That sounds like a plan."

Chelsea said, "For once we agree on something."

Jason said, "Can I have a new office chair now?"

Chelsea shook her head and said, "Idiot." Then she looked at Veronica and said, "Okay, we're going to assume you're innocent for now. We still need to address a couple of things. If you didn't kill your husband, then

Lucas is the logical suspect. Do you have any reason to believe he murdered Harold, other than that he wanted to keep the company in the family?"

Jason watched as Veronica stood there, obviously deep in thought. Finally, she said, "No, I honestly do not think that Lucas killed Harold. He loved his older brother. And Lucas stood to gain a lot even if Harold did take the company public. Lucas was slated to join the Board of Directors and receive a lot of stock options. I wish I knew where Lucas is. I'm worried that someone has killed him too."

Chelsea said, "We'll leave it at that for now. There's also the issue of the expired human growth hormone that we found dumped in the lake. Do you know anything about that?"

Veronica said, "I have no idea what that's about. Harold rarely discussed company business with me. It'd be easier for me to take over the company if he had. I do know there are government regulations requiring proper disposal of expired drugs. There are also companies that charge a lot to dispose of such things properly. It would be cheaper to sneak out to the lake and dump them under the cover of darkness. So, saving money is a possibility."

Chelsea said, "I wonder if that had anything to do with Harold's murder? Perhaps he found out about it, and someone killed him to keep him quiet and stay out of prison."

Veronica said, "That doesn't make sense. Harold was the current CEO, and he would have been held ultimately responsible. He would have been the one to be fined or go to jail."

Jason chimed in, "That's true. Remember Chelsea, I used to work for the FDA, and what she's saying is correct. So that probably has nothing to do with his murder."

Chelsea said, "Jason, less talk, more notetaking."

"Yes Dear. Is that what Junior Associates do, take notes?"

Chelsea said, "Okay, we're not sure why the company dumped the expired human growth hormone in the lake, although saving money sounds plausible. Jason and I noticed that a couple of the vials were leaking. Veronica, do you know if this recombinant human growth hormone could also affect fish? It seems that the striped bass in the lake have grown exponentially over the past couple of years. There are even those who think it's the huge bass that are responsible for the disappearing fishermen. I personally think that's nonsense, but how about it?"

Jason was impressed with the way Chelsea had abruptly changed the line of questioning to keep Veronica off balance. He chimed in, "Yeah, giant head-butting stripers. I still think that's a possible explanation for all the murders and disappearances. What say you, Doctor Veronica?"

Jason saw that Veronica looked confused. She said, "Again, Harold seldom discussed the business with me. I have no idea if this human growth hormone would have any effect on fish. However, it is called *human* growth hormone. It's not called *fish* growth hormone. As a doctor, I'm not sure how *fish* growth hormone would be of much use in medicine."

Jason said, "I do know one thing…"

Chelsea interrupted, "Only one thing? Now that's plausible."

Jason continued, "Chelsea, stop being so mean. I remember from the FDA that these recombinant protein products are made in the lab using genetic engineering. It is possible to make mistakes when building the messenger RNA that codes for the final proteins. If this happened, you could get a recombinant human growth hormone that acts differently from the original human growth hormone. Perhaps affect other species, like fish for example? How about that Dr. Veronica? Isn't that possible?"

Veronica looked even more confused. "I'm a medical doctor, not a molecular biologist, geneticist, or ichthyologist. I guess what you're saying sounds possible."

Jason said, "Did you hear that, Chelsea? What I said sounds possible. How about that? And an ichthyologist? That's a fun word. Say it. Ich-thy-ol-o-gist. Say it, Chelsea. It's fun."

Chelsea shook her head. "Idiot. Even if this growth hormone is somehow affecting fish, making them grow larger, that doesn't mean the fish are responsible for anyone's death. Especially Harold, who was found in his business suit."

Jason argued, "What about my head-butting fish theory? We already saw some head-butting fish. They kept bumping into our boat. This could provide an explanation for at least some of the murders. We need to ask one of those ichthyologists. Are there any of those around here?"

Jason saw Chelsea shake her head in dismay. "Veronica, you may be right. I probably shouldn't whack him on the head anymore."

Veronica smiled sadly. "You got that right."

Chelsea said, "I think the best explanation for Harold's murder is that he found out someone was dumping expired drugs into the lake. That person killed him to keep him quiet, or to keep from being fired. Maybe they didn't know the President and CEO would be held responsible. Corporations are sometimes known to pull stunts like that to save money. Veronica, was Harold an honest man? Would he have allowed his company to do something like dump the drugs?"

Veronica said, "My Harold was as honest as the day is long. And did I mention he was great in bed? He would have never stood for anyone in the company polluting the lake to save money. If he'd found out, he would have fired them on the spot."

Chelsea said, "This could also explain the disappearing fishermen. If someone from GenesRUs killed Harold to keep him from reporting the dumping of expired drugs in the lake, that person might also kill off any fishermen that stumbled onto the discarded drugs. Jason, do we know where the fishermen disappeared? Was it near where you found the discarded drugs?"

Jason said, "I do not know. That's something we need to investigate. Let me write that down on our to do list." He put pen to paper and scribbled something. "I would also like to point out that any respectable fisherman who found out about the growth hormone would most likely keep his or her mouth shut. Why would a fisherman report something that created record-sized bass?"

Chelsea said, "Veronica, what do you think? Would a company employee kill fishermen to keep the secret that he was dumping expired drugs into the lake? It scares me, but Jason might have a point. Why would a fisherman report the growth hormone if he thought it was creating giant stripers? Jason, keep it up and I might promote you back to Associate…but no new chair."

Veronica threw up her hands. "I have no idea about any of this. I know nothing about fishermen, where they fish, or why they are disappearing. And large head-butting bass sounds insane. Until Harold disappeared, I was an attractive young woman, with a wealthy husband and no responsibilities. All I know is my husband is dead, his brother disappeared, and I'm the prime suspect. Can you help me, or not?"

Jason said whimsically, "And don't forget, you said the sex was great. Poor Harold."

Jason failed to duck when Chelsea walked around her desk and whacked him on the head.

"Ouch, that hurt. You've got to stop doing that."

Jason saw Chelsea reach for his notepad. He tried to keep it away from her, but she managed to wrestle it from his hands.

She looked at the pad and said, "Jason, where are all your notes? You've written *'My wife is mean'* over and over. What is wrong with you?"

She whacked him on the back of the head again. Jason said, "Chelsea, you need to stop doing that, or unlike Harold, I'm not going to be able to provide you with great sex anymore."

"No worries, Junior Associate. As you pointed out, I'm a wealthy woman now."

Chapter 15: The Brother Returns

The next morning at ten o'clock Chelsea sat at her office desk drinking coffee and thinking about the case, when Veronica Fairchild phoned. She reported that her brother-in-law, Lucas, had shown up at her house the night before. He had apparently been wandering around lost for a couple of days with a serious head wound. He couldn't remember where he had been or how he'd gotten injured. Chelsea found Jason in the back room trying to beat her Ms. Pac-Man score. She drove them to Veronica's house to interrogate Lucas Fairchild.

Chelsea turned the SUV onto a long, narrow paved driveway lined with neatly trimmed six-foot shrubs. At the end of the lane, they pulled up beside a spectacular lake-front home.

Jason pointed and said, "Chelsea, look at that. It's humongous. Must be at least twenty or thirty thousand square feet, all brick, and stone. Look at the size of that deck with a huge hot tub. The view, the wide water, and the mountains. This Harold Fairchild must have been loaded."

Chelsea climbed out of the SUV and joined Jason at the paved walkway to the front door.

"Focus, Jason. Yes, it's an impressive house, but we're here to interrogate Lucas Fairchild. Find out where he's been. If he knows anything about his brother's death."

Jason said, "You grill him, and I'll go out on the deck and check out the view. Might be a clue out there."

Chelsea led the way to the large solid mahogany front doors and knocked. She looked at Jason and said, "What's lower than Junior Associate?"

Veronica opened the door. It surprised Chelsea to see her wearing pink silk pajamas at mid-morning, the top buttoned partway down and the bottoms very short. Seemed like a provocative thing to wear to receive guests. Chelsea noticed that Jason didn't seem to be offended.

Veronica said, "Come in PI Longfellow and Associate, or Junior Associate?"

Chelsea smiled. "I'm looking for something lower than Junior Associate. Got any ideas?"

Veronica laughed. "I slept in this morning. I'm still on my first cup of coffee. Give me a little while and I'll think of something. Come on in. Lucas is in the living room having his morning coffee and icing the knot on his head."

Chelsea looked around as Veronica led them through a massive foyer. The foyer included a large circular staircase. They walked past the staircase, past a huge dining room on the right, what appeared to be a large guest bedroom on the left, and towards a sunken living room straight ahead. Chelsea looked through the open bedroom doors and saw an unmade king size bed, with a sheer black lace nightgown on the floor nearby. Chelsea's perception of Veronica and brother-in-law Lucas changed when Veronica hurriedly closed the doors on their way by. They continued to follow Veronica into the sunken living room full of expensive looking leather furniture. Then Chelsea noticed Jason. He appeared to be detecting the rear end under the short silk pajama bottoms as Veronica walked ahead of them. Chelsea raised her hand to whack him on the head. But they arrived in the living room and Veronica turned to speak. Chelsea lowered her hand and thought better of it. Her arm was getting sore from whacking him.

Chelsea saw a man approximately the same age as Veronica lounging on a comfortable looking black leather couch built into the perimeter of the sunken living room. Veronica waved her hand in the man's direction and said, "This is my brother-in-law, Lucas Fairchild. Lucas, I'd like you to meet PI Chelsea Longfellow and her husband and Junior Associate, Dr. Jason Longfellow. I hired them to look for Harold. They have some questions for you."

Chelsea noticed the man's sandy brown hair, deep blue eyes, handsome and youthful face, and charming smile. The smile appeared incongruous with the ice pack that he held on the side of his head, partially covering a substantial wound. Lucas stood and extended his right hand to Chelsea while continuing to hold the ice pack with his left. She couldn't help but notice that the man was slender and muscular. He stood almost as tall as Jason. She preferred tall men.

Lucas said, "Pleased to meet such a beautiful private eye. I usually think of private detectives as grisly old men, ex-cops, or ex-military adrenaline junkies. This is quite a nice surprise."

Chelsea blushed and continued to let him hold her hand well after the handshake had ended. She saw Jason step forward and extend his hand to Lucas.

"I'm the original PI Longfellow, but you can call me Dr. Longfellow, or Jason will do. I'm not an old ex-cop. Actually, I'm a doctor. But this whole PI thing was my idea. I got my PI license online first, and then Chelsea inherited a bunch of money and took over. She used to be a nurse. She looks sweet, but don't turn your back on her. It's not safe. You think you've got a head wound? She's a head-wounding machine." He rubbed the back of his head.

Chelsea got an amused look on her face as Lucas released her hand and shook hands with Jason. Lucas said, "Pleased to meet you…Jason."

Chelsea said, "Don't mind my Junior Associate, and husband. He's having an identity crisis. He recently retired from the FDA, where he was an actual doctor. Now he works for me as a PI, and I can't decide what title to give him. He started as Associate PI, then I demoted him to Junior Associate. His last evaluation wasn't very good. I'm thinking perhaps a demotion to PI-in-training, or PI Intern. He does play a mean game of Ms. Pac-Man though."

Chelsea was surprised when Jason said, "Chelsea, I'm a great detective. I'm the one who reeled in Harold Fairchild's disgusting, bloated, discolored corpse. The man was fish food."

Chelsea saw Jason's face turn red as he clearly realized what he'd said. "Lucas, Mr. Fairchild, I'm sorry. I forgot Harold is…was your brother. He didn't look that bad. He *was* dressed in a business suit. There wasn't a lot of bloating, mostly teeth marks where things had been gnawing on him. He looked like a floating zombie, having been in the water and all."

Then Chelsea saw Jason pause in thought for a moment. She cringed as his voice changed from apologetic to aggressive, and he pointed at Lucas.

"Wait a minute. We're here to interrogate you. To find out who knocked Harold in the head. Lucas, did you hit your brother on the head with a blunt object, crack his skull? You were on the boat with him that night, probably the last one to see him alive. Why did you kill him? Are you having an affair with his sexy young wife Veronica?"

Chelsea watched as Jason pointed his finger at Veronica for emphasis, and his expression changed again, this time from accusation to apparent lust. His emotions were all over the place.

Jason continued, "After seeing her in these skimpy pajamas, I can see why you might do that. Why is she wearing slinky silk pajamas this late in the morning? What were the two of you doing before we got here? Was it fun? Feel free to include details. Chelsea and I have three kids, and we don't get a chance to…"

Chelsea whacked him on the back of the head. "What kind of interrogation is that? You're supposed to gently sneak up on him, not mount a vicious attack against a man who just lost his brother. And stop staring at her. Now you've done it. *PI Intern* it is. Interns don't get their own office. I could use another file room. We'll set up a folding card table out in the hallway for your office, until you convince me to hire you as a full-time employee."

Chelsea saw Lucas smile at her, and she couldn't help but smile back. He appeared surprisingly calm as he sat down, leaned back, and drank the last of his coffee.

Lucas looked up at Jason and said, "Jason, you seem to be setting all kinds of records for demotion. Perhaps you should consider not working for your wife. Seems like a bad plan. I do understand your questions though. You show up here this morning, and Veronica is still in her pajamas. I can assure you there is nothing going on between us. I came here last night because of my head injury and confusion. I didn't know where else to go, and she is family. She was kind enough to take me in and treat my head wound. She's still in her PJs because we were up late last night talking and slept in. I slept here on the couch."

Chelsea thought she should take over the interrogation before Jason ran off the rails again. She said to Lucas, "Speaking of your head wound, where have you been for the past two days? How did you get that head wound? Veronica was afraid you'd been killed too."

Lucas removed the ice from his head and said, "I'm still dizzy and have a terrible headache. Why don't you all sit on the sofa, so I don't have to look up. I'll do my best to answer your questions. I know Veronica hired you to search for Harold, and then to help clear her as a suspect in his murder. Perhaps after you hear what I have to say you will work for me as well."

Everyone sat down, Chelsea and Jason on Lucas' left and Veronica on his right. Chelsea was not happy when Jason bounced his butt up and down on the padded sofa and said, "Wow! This thing is comfy. Chelsea, we should get one of these now that you're rich."

Chelsea shook her head at Jason, turned to Lucas, and said, "Please continue. You were about to tell us where you've been for the past couple of days."

Chelsea watched attentively as Lucas placed the ice pack on the bump on his head again and said, "I remember the first evening, and then it gets kind of fuzzy from there. Harold had asked me to go fishing. That surprised me since he didn't fish. He had a bass boat, but I don't remember him ever using it for fishing, just for cruising around the lake. He liked it because it went so fast. I met him at his house, and we launched his boat from the dock at eight-thirty."

Jason leaned forward and asked, "Was he wearing a business suit when you left the dock? Why would he do that? It seems a little odd."

Chelsea elbowed Jason in the ribs and said, "Jason, don't interrupt. That's something an intern would do. Let the man finish answering my questions."

Jason said, "Chelsea, stop demoting me. I'm going to sue you for unfair business practices."

Chelsea said, "I don't pay you enough to hire a lawyer. Be quiet and let Lucas continue."

Jason argued, sounding like a defiant teenager, "You said the inheritance was our money."

Chelsea said, "That was before you were demoted to PI intern. Interns don't get any benefits. Now hush!"

Lucas said, "Hello, I thought you were here to interrogate me. The way you two squabble, perhaps you should forget this case and speak to a divorce lawyer."

Chelsea said, "Don't be silly. I could never divorce Jason. He's the father of our three beautiful daughters. If you think I'm going to raise them by myself, you're nuts. Now shut up, mind your own business, and continue with your story."

Chelsea realized she'd lost it. She sounded like Jason there for a moment. She saw Lucas look at Jason with an expression of pity.

Lucas said, "I'm beginning to understand your problem, PI Intern Longfellow. Your wife is great looking and comes off as a sweetheart at first. But there's some nasty in there. Veronica tells me she whacks you on the head a lot. Would you like Veronica to get you some ice too?"

Jason said, "No thanks, but thank you for understanding. Please do go on and answer Chelsea's questions, before I get anymore demotions."

Lucas laughed. "As you wish. Like I was saying, Harold and I headed out in his bass boat around eight-thirty night before last. It had just started getting dark, and he had turned on the running lights. It took us about twenty minutes to get to the fishing spot he'd chosen, near the shore at the base of the mountain."

Chelsea interrupted, "You said Harold never fished. How did he pick a fishing spot that night?"

Lucas said, "I never asked. I guess someone from work must have told him about it. Anyhow, Harold turned off the engine, set up the trolling motor, and we sat there waiting for a school of shad to show up. Nothing happened for at least half-an-hour, and then suddenly something banged against the bottom of the boat."

Chelsea saw Jason thrust his fist into the air. "Aha! The head-butting stripers. I knew it."

Lucas said, "What? I've never heard of a head-butting striper. Is that a new species of fish? People are always trying to introduce invasive species into the lake. Damned idiots. One time some kid released a baby crocodile into the lake. It was a salt-water croc and didn't make it."

Chelsea shook her head in frustration. "Just ignore Jason. A head-butting striper is not a species of fish. It's only in the mind of a delirious private investigator, or rather PI intern."

Veronica said, "In your husband's defense, you do whack him on the head a lot."

Chelsea was losing her patience with this interrogation. "Jason, would you please be quiet. The only thing lower than PI intern is unemployed PI, and you're getting there."

Chelsea watched as Lucas held the ice bag out towards Jason, mockingly offering it to him.

Lucas said, "Ouch. Being fired by your wife. Now that hurts. Allow me to continue. Something, I don't know what, banged on the bottom of Harold's bass boat several times. One of the blows was so hard it made the entire boat lurch. Harold lost his footing and fell overboard. We were close to the shore. When he never came back up to the surface, I was concerned he had hit his head on a rock or something. I used a flashlight and the trolling motor to search the water all up and down that shoreline, but I never found him. I was terrified he had drowned, or something had dragged him off and killed him. There're all kinds of things out there in the woods. If he reached the shore, a mountain lion, bear, or rattlesnake could have gotten him."

Jason said, "So what did you do? Did you dive into the water and look for your brother?"

Lucas said, "It was too dark to find him in the water. Since we were close to shore, I hoped Harold had managed to find his way onto the bank. I pulled the boat up next to the shore, took my flashlight, and searched the area on foot. I stumbled around in the weeds, stumps, roots, and mud for over an hour without any sign of Harold. I had just gone back to the boat to call the Bedford Sheriff's office when something hard hit me up the side of the head. I blacked out. I don't know how long I lay there. When I came to, it was morning."

Chelsea asked, "Why didn't you call for help at that point?"

Lucas said, "I tried to stand up, but I was dizzy. My head hurt, and I couldn't think straight. I looked for my cell phone. It was gone along with my wallet and keys. After laying there a while longer, I managed to get to my feet. I stumbled back to where the boat had been, but it was gone. No boat, no cell phone, and stuck out there at the foot of the mountain in the middle of nowhere. I waited by the shoreline a long time, but I never saw anyone. So, I started walking. I spent two days and nights wandering around in the woods. Yesterday morning I climbed up high enough to find a road that goes around the mountain towards North Carolina. I flagged down a passing car, a local man my family has known for years. He was kind enough to bring me to Veronica's place. I have no idea what happened to Harold or his boat. I also don't know why he was wearing a business suit when you found his body. He had on blue jeans, a long-sleeved flannel shirt, and tennis shoes when we left his dock."

Jason said, "Your story checks out in one way. I spoke with the police, and the autopsy showed that the blow to your brother's head is what killed him. That would be consistent with hitting his head on a rock when he fell overboard."

Chelsea shifted in her seat, looked around at the magnificent house, and said, "The police are going to want to speak to you, Lucas. Do you plan on calling them today? There are a couple of things they are going to want cleared up. First, who hit you on the head, and did they leave you for dead? Second, why was your brother dressed in his business suit when Jason found him? And third, two days is a long time to wander around lost in the woods. Are you sure that's where you were the entire time?"

Chelsea saw a wicked smile on Jason's face. He said, "Chelsea, you didn't happen to be out there that night? You like to whack people on the head."

Chelsea looked daggers through her husband. "Jason, I'm sure there's nothing lower on the corporate totem pole than fired PI...except maybe deceased PI? Stop talking."

Out of the corner of her eye, Chelsea saw Lucas place his free hand on Veronica's bare knee and begin to rub gently. It looked more sensual than consoling. Chelsea gently elbowed Jason in the ribs to get his attention and whispered in his ear.

"Jason, did you see that? I'm not buying this guy's story. Wandering around lost in the woods for two days? Now he's fondling his sexy sister-in-law's knee. And I still can't understand how Harold ended up in a business suit if he died while fishing with his brother."

Jason whispered back, "Maybe the blow to Lucas' head has confused him, and his brother went straight to the dock from work, still wearing his business suit. I agree that two days is a long time to wander around lost in the woods, but fondling her knee? Speaking as a guy, well, it's a very nice knee."

Chelsea whacked him on the back of the head again. She didn't have to reach very high to do it since they were both sitting down. Chelsea saw Veronica and Lucas look at her when they heard the thud of her hand on Jason's head. She felt embarrassed.

"Sorry. My hand slipped. I can't seem to help myself."

Jason said, "Ouch. You need help, Wife. Maybe you should seek out a self-help group. Is there such a thing as Head-Whacker's Anonymous?"

Chelsea said, "Yeah. I'll take you to the meetings with me. Once they get to know you, they'll all understand my affliction. You've heard of Whack-a-mole? How about Whack-a-fired-PI, feel better, and win a prize. Could turn out to be a great new therapy."

Lucas said to Veronica. "I'm going to end up a person of interest in my brother's murder. You hired these two to find Harold, and then to prove you had nothing to do with his murder. We're actually thinking about hiring them to clear my name too? It's more likely Mrs. PI is going to end up in jail for murdering her husband. Come to think of it, didn't you tell me

Mr. Junior PI here is a person of interest in Harold's murder? Maybe we need a Plan B."

Chelsea tried not to take offense at this. Veronica came to her defense, "No worries, Lucas. Chelsea is a great detective. I've known them a little longer than you, and she has every reason to whack Jason on the head. He can be very irritating. He did find Harold's body, and he also discovered a box of discarded expired drug from GenesRUs in the lake. They're familiar with the case. If we hired anyone else, they'd have to start over."

Chelsea jumped in again, trying to save actual paying clients. "Yes Lucas, we're familiar with the case. I promise to try to stop whacking Jason on the head if it really bothers you. Do you know anything about expired recombinant human growth hormone from your brother's company? Somebody threw some leaky vials of the stuff in the lake. I believe it's a clue to what's going on, either with your brother's death, or the missing fishermen, or both."

Chelsea saw Lucas move his hand from Veronica's bare knee to her shoulder and start rubbing gently again. The way he was touching his sister-in-law, Chelsea felt sure that it was more of a sexual nature.

Lucas said, "I honestly have no idea what you're talking about. It was like pulling teeth getting information about the company out of my brother. He treated his company like a top-secret government agency, always concerned there were spies trying to steal information about GenesRUs drug development. He didn't trust anyone, including me. I don't know anything about any expired drugs. I do know that Harold would have never done anything to purposefully pollute the lake. He was a staunch conservationist."

Jason said, "Do you know if human recombinant growth hormone would affect fish?"

Chelsea saw the look Lucas gave Jason. She had just convinced Lucas to hire them, and she feared Jason was about to blow it.

Lucas said, "Mrs. PI Longfellow. I just said I didn't know anything about Harold's company. I'm beginning to understand this head-whacking thing."

Chelsea realized they'd better get out of there before they lost their only paying clients.

"Jason, I think we have enough information, and we've bothered these two long enough. We should leave, and we can circle back again after the police have had some time with Lucas. By then we'll know if they consider him a person of interest in Harold's murder."

Chelsea stood, grabbed Jason's hand, pulled him to his feet, and dragged him to the door. She saw Veronica stand and follow them. Veronica opened the door and let them pass.

Veronica said, "Don't worry. I'll set Lucas straight. He's still a little woozy from the head wound. I'm sure he'll want to hire you as well. I'll talk to you later."

Chelsea held tight to Jason's hand, hauling him out the door and towards their SUV. When they got into the vehicle, she was tempted to whack him again. But she thought better of it. Perhaps she was causing some permanent brain damage.

"Jason, did you see the way Lucas rubbed Veronica's leg and shoulder? That wasn't a consoling type of rubbing. That was more of a *let's get it on* massage."

"Chelsea, I love it when you talk dirty. But if you don't stop hitting me on the head, you might break something. Then I won't be able to *get it on* anymore."

"I'm sorry. I'll try to not whack you so often. You're just really annoying. Do you buy Lucas' story about the fishing trip with Harold? Someone hit him on the head, and he wandered around in the woods for over two days? Then we find him at Veronica's mansion, and her in those sexy silk pajamas mid-morning. I also saw a lacy black negligee on the floor in that guest bedroom before she closed the doors. Lucas didn't explain how Harold ended up in the lake in his business suit. There're too many inconsistencies with his story."

Jason said, "I agree. And he never said anything about my theory of the head-butting fish. That's pretty suspicious."

Chelsea's hand started to raise up on its own, and she had to argue with it to make it stop.

"Jason, don't you think it's more likely that Veronica and her husband's younger brother conspired to kill Harold and steal his company? They have the most to gain. That's where the investigation takes us if we follow the money."

Chelsea saw Jason's eyes light up. He said, "Not only that, but what if they were the ones responsible for tossing the expired drugs in the lake? Just because they told us they know nothing about Harold's company, doesn't mean it's true. Poor Harold turned out to be fish food, and he's not going to tell. If Harold found out about it, knocking him off would have solved that problem for them too. Even better, what if Veronica and Lucas are also the ones killing the fishermen? They could be murdering fishermen as a cover for Harold's murder, to make it look like Harold was just another victim of this fishermen killer. Or maybe they're also killing fishermen that fish near where they disposed of the drugs, to prevent them from running across cases of the expired drugs like we did. We have plenty to investigate."

Chelsea reached out, whacked him on the back of the head, and drove off towards home.

"Jason, you come up with a couple of decent theories that could solve the case, and they all lead to the clients who just hired us. We're not going to get paid again."

Jason rubbed the back of his head and said, "Good thing you're still rich. And since you agree I solved the case, can I have a new office chair like yours?"

Chapter 16. That Crazy Cat

Herman and Jason had become best friends. This surprised Jason after he had abandoned the poor cat with Chelsea, resulting in that life-altering visit to the vet. Jason had another male, well…almost male…to bond with in an otherwise female household. Whenever Chelsea started to fight with one of their daughters, Jason and Herman would hide in the basement. Jason was like Dr. Dolittle; he could carry on a conversation with his orange tabby buddy. Jason enjoyed having someone sane to talk to until the storm blew over.

The Saturday after the interview with Lucas Fairchild, Chelsea and Lizzy started arguing. On house cleaning day, Chelsea wanted Lizzy to do more than hide her dirty clothes under the bed. Jason sat in the living room drinking coffee and eating a chocolate donut when the yelling began.

He heard Lizzy bellow, "Why do I have to do everything? What about Lilly and Lucy? You're the mother. Housework is your job! I'm just a kid!"

Jason recognized Chelsea's frustrated scream, "Lizzy, you're the oldest! You need to set an example for your sisters! And I have a job as a PI! Get off your butt, dust, and vacuum!"

Jason hated it when Chelsea fought with the girls. His first inclination as a man was to fix things. He got up, walked into the kitchen, and went into peacemaker mode. Chelsea had Lizzy backed into a corner of the kitchen, pointing, and shaking her finger at her. Lizzy leaned forward as if to launch herself at her mother.

Jason said, quite reasonably, "Ladies, what's this about? Calm down. Lizzy, you need to help your mother with the chores. And Chelsea, there's no need to scream. The neighbors will think somebody's being killed. Take a breath, give each other a hug, and talk it out. See how easy this is to resolve. My work here is done."

Jason immediately sensed his mistake. It was as if his wife and his daughter had been pointing shotguns at each other, and suddenly they turned both barrels on him.

Lizzy said, "Daddy, why do you always take her side? It's not fair. I'm just a kid. I should be having fun, not doing Mom's work for her."

Fear grasped Jason. Chelsea looked as though she were about to explode, eyes bugged out, face bright red. He cringed as she started walking towards him, arms waving randomly in the air.

Chelsea screamed, "Mom's work?! Why is everything Mom's work?! There are four other people in this house. Jason, you need to make your daughters do their chores. I have my own PI firm, and I'm trying to solve this crazy case. I can't do that, keep the house clean, buy the groceries, cook! I'm tired all the time! Jason, what's wrong with you?"

She approached Jason, reached up, and whacked him on the back of the head. He tried to duck out of the way, but she was too fast.

Jason said, "Ouch! Why'd you do that? You're fighting with Lizzy. Whack her one."

Chelsea shook her head sadly. "How could you even suggest such a thing? I would never hit our darling daughter. That would be child abuse. Shame on you."

Jason rubbed his head. He watched Lizzy walk up to her mother and give her a hug.

"Thanks Mom. Dad's really mean, telling you to hit me. That's just wrong. I love you. Why don't you hire someone to clean the house? You can afford it. You have that inheritance. Or maybe you could order your Junior Associate to do it. He doesn't do much besides play those stupid old video games at your office."

Chelsea hugged Lizzy back and said, "Excellent idea. Jason, why couldn't you come up with something constructive like that? I'll make a few calls and see if I can find someone to clean the place. Maybe I should make house cleaning part of the job description for my Junior Associate."

Jason looked confused. He picked up Herman and ran for the basement.

Carrying the cat down the stairs, he said to Herman, "What just happened? I made a perfectly good suggestion that they calm down and talk it out. They both turned on me. Now they're best buddies, I'm a nervous wreck, and my head hurts. I need a nice soak in a hot tub."

Herman looked Jason in the eyes, shook his furry head, and said, "Meow."

Jason said, "You're right. Women are a kinda crazy. And yes, you can sit on the side of the tub and keep me company."

Jason walked into the large downstairs bathroom. It had an extra-long soaking tub with circulating jets, and a separate shower. He often read or napped in the tub, while the hot water relaxed his muscles and steamed his troubles away. Jason turned on the water and adjusted it to steamy hot. He undressed, climbed in, and got comfortable. Herman jumped up onto the side of the tub and lay down. When the tub was full to the overflow drain, Jason turned off the water.

Herman lay with his head resting on his paws. He looked at Jason. "Meow."

Jason smiled and said, "I agree, it's so peaceful, my favorite place. I'm glad you like it too."

Herman stood, bent down, dipped a front paw in the water, and licked it. "Meow."

Jason smiled. "That's fine. If your thirsty you may drink all the water you want."

Jason lay back, resting his head on the tub. He closed his eyes and was almost asleep when he heard a splash. He opened his eyes and saw Herman standing in the water near his feet.

Jason was surprised. He said, "Herman, old buddy, I thought cats hated water. You seem to like it."

Herman took another drink of bath water. "Meow, meow."

Jason said, "Yes, I see you like the water. Just don't drink it after I use the soap. Since you like water, I'll take you fishing. You can protect me from the giant head-butting stripers."

Herman looked at Jason, shook his head in the affirmative. "Me-ow!"

Jason said, "Great. I'll take you next time instead of Chelsea. I won't have to worry about getting whacked on the head by those crazy fish, or Chelsea."

Jason watched as Herman walked around in the water. Then the cat jumped back onto the side of the tub, laid down, and began licking his paws and purring.

Jason washed, exited the tub, and dried himself, and Herman. He got dressed and Herman followed him to the bottom of the stairs. Jason stopped and listened for signs of arguing.

He said, "Herman, it sounds like all's quiet. Think it's safe to go back upstairs?"

"Meow."

Jason said, "I agree. We'll sneak up the stairs. Keep a low profile until we're sure it's safe."

Jason quietly ascended the stairs with Herman following close behind. He found Chelsea in the kitchen, preparing dinner. Jason walked into the kitchen, smiled, and gently touched her shoulder, prepared to duck. He saw Herman jump up on the kitchen counter.

He said, "Is everything okay? Herman and I retreated to the basement and took a bath."

Chelsea said, "Yes, things are fine, no thanks to you. I made a few calls and found a woman who cleans houses. She comes highly recommended, but it's going to cost a pretty penny."

Jason said, "That's okay. You're rich." He reached over and petted the cat on the head. "Guess what? My good buddy Herman likes water. He joined me in the bathtub. I'm taking him fishing next time I go. He agreed to protect me from those giant head-butting bass."

Jason watched as Chelsea took milk and butter out of the refrigerator, sat them down on the counter, and pointed at him. He took a step back.

"Let me get this straight. Now you can talk to our cat? And he agreed to protect you from giant head-butting bass that only exist in your head? That's nice. Will he protect me too?"

Jason watched Herman jump down from the counter and hide behind his legs.

Jason said, sadly, "Not after what you did to him."

"You men are all alike. A little snip-snip, and you freak out. It had to be done. He'd have marked his territory all over the house. Good thing you don't do that. I am a nurse."

Jason felt a wave of nausea pass through him. He said, "Hey, tomorrow's Sunday. The weather's supposed to be nice. How about we take the family fishing? Striper fishing's better late at night, but we could still go during the day. Get everyone out on the water, and we can fish for smallmouth bass, perch, catfish. We could make this Herman's maiden voyage."

Herman said, "Meow."

Jason said, "Herman says it's a great idea, Chelsea. What do you think?"

Chelsea laughed. "I'm thinking it's dinner time, and you don't speak cat as well as you think. He's asking for food."

***

Sunday morning, Jason got up early. He made a pot of coffee and took an assortment of Pop-Tarts out of the pantry for a quick family breakfast.

Herman joined him in the kitchen. He gave the cat a small bowl of milk. Then he woke Chelsea and the girls. A few minutes later Chelsea joined him in the kitchen in her ratty old cotton bathrobe.

She said, "What the hell, Jason? It's seven o'clock in the morning. You said we were going to go fishing during the day. It's not day yet."

Jason, pouring himself a cup of coffee, said, "Good morning, Darlin'. You look ravishing. I made us a nutritious breakfast. Eat up and let's hit the water. Herman's anxious to get started."

Chelsea poured herself a cup of coffee and placed a cherry Pop-Tart in the toaster. Then she put the toasted pastry on a plate and settled down at the kitchen table.

Jason watched as Lizzy, Lilly, and Lucy stumbled into the kitchen, still in their pajamas. He was surprised to see Lizzy pour three glasses of milk for herself and her sisters. They toasted their own Pop-Tarts. Jason ate his last chocolate donut.

Lizzy said, "Dad, we're taking Herman on the boat? Don't cats hate the water?"

Chelsea said, "Your father has become a cat-whisperer. He says Herman told him that he likes the water, wants to go fishing with us, and will protect us from the killer bass."

Lucy perked up. "Killer bass? Are we gonna die?"

Herman said, "Meow."

Jason said, "Herman says he will protect us. I'll bring along Blaster too."

Chelsea said, "Herman, he's going to bring his hand cannon. Would you like to change your mind about going fishing? We'd all be a lot safer if we went back to bed."

Herman looked at Chelsea. "Meow."

Jason took the last bite of his donut, followed by a large gulp of his second cup of hot coffee to wash it down. He burned his mouth.

"Ouch, damn coffee. Herman's glad I'm bringing Blaster. He thinks we'll be a good team."

Chelsea said, "Now I'm really confused. I don't know if I need a shrink for my husband who talks to cats, or a shrink for a cat who thinks it's safe in a boat with my armed husband."

Lizzy said, "Sounds like a little of both. Can we please go back to bed?"

Jason raised a fuss until the women got dressed. Then he herded them down to the dock. He lowered Luscious into the water and loaded his family and their fishing gear onboard. Jason had carried Herman down to the dock to make sure he didn't run off to chase a squirrel or chipmunk. He sat the cat down on the captain's seat next to him, started the motor, and they were off. Jason was pleased to see that Herman sat quietly, like he was meant to be there.

Jason looked around at his crew. Lucy and Lilly sat in the fishermen's seats in the bow, Lizzy in a seat in the stern, and Chelsea sat next to Jason, at the helm. Herman was perched between Jason and Chelsea, his fur blowing in the wind.

Chelsea yelled, trying to talk over the roar of the wind as they flew up the lake, "Jason, you were right. This crazy cat appears to be just fine on the boat. Don't you find that a little strange?"

Herman said, "Meow."

Jason said, "I know, Herman. Women just don't get it. We're manly men, and cats. Well, you not so much thanks to Chelsea…sorry about that. Anyhow, we're here to protect them. It's our job. Between your teeth and claws and my Blaster, we've got this. Bring on those killer fish."

Jason saw Chelsea shake her head, give him a look of concern.

Herman shook his head, his voice low and uncertain. "Meow?"

Jason stopped Luscious in deep water, near the shore at the base of the mountain. He chose a different spot from where they had found Harold's body or the discarded drugs. He wanted the family to have fun, not become the latest victims of the fishermen killer. They should be safe in the daylight. Plus, he had Blaster and Herman, to fight off both man and head-butting fish.

Jason turned off the engine, moved to the bow, and lowered the trolling motor.

"Okay girls. I've given each of you a fishing rod with a bucktail or minnow lure. Cast your line in the direction of the shore, wait a couple of seconds to give the lure time to sink, and then slowly reel it in. The best time to catch stripers is at night, but we can still try. If they don't bite, we'll switch bait and go for other fish. More important, it should be a lot safer during the day."

Jason watched as the girls tried to cast their lures. Within minutes, each of them had a hopelessly twisted mass of fishing line. Jason watched Herman, standing on the bow of the boat, reach down, dip his paw into the water, and lick it. Then Jason heard Chelsea yell.

"Jason, I've got one! It's a big one."

Jason rushed to her side, "Keep your tip up. Pull, reel, pull, reel. I'll get the net."

Jason saw Herman walk over next to Chelsea. The cat began to rub against her leg, walking around her in circles.

Chelsea said, "Jason, get your furry friend away from me. I think he wants my fish. He's going to trip me, and if I fall in the water, I'm going to kill you."

Jason used his foot to nudge Herman away from Chelsea's leg. Chelsea managed to reel the fish, a smallmouth bass, up next to the boat. Jason netted the fish, pulled it into the boat, and bent down to remove the hook from its mouth. The fish slipped out of Jason's hands. To Jason's surprise, Herman pounced on the flopping bass, biting, and clawing furiously.

Chelsea said, "Jason, your furry friend is ruining my fish. I think he's trying to eat it."

Herman yelled, "Reowwww!"

Jason said, "Herman's not trying to eat your fish. He's protecting us from it."

Jason saw that Lizzy and her sisters had already given up on fishing. They stood watching with fascination as Herman wrestled with the fish."

Lizzy said, "Dad, I think Herman's pulling your leg. That fish isn't very big, and it's not doing any head-butting. Looks to me like it's Herman's lunch."

Jason wrestled the smallmouth bass away from the cat and placed it in the storage tank.

Chelsea said, "My poor fish. Thanks to your crazy cat it looks like it's been through a woodchipper."

Herman looked up at Chelsea. "Meow."

Jason said, "Herman says he was just trying to help. I've got to pee. I'm going to pull up next to the shore and go behind a tree. You guys stay in the boat. I won't be gone long."

Jason parked the boat next to the bank. He reached into his tackle box, got Blaster out of its holster, and handed it to Chelsea. "Here, feel free to shoot anything that looks unfriendly."

Chelsea said, "Then you better be smiling when you get back."

Jason tied the boat to a small tree, stepped onto the shore, and started walking into the thick woods. He heard leaves rustling, turned around, and saw Herman following him.

Jason said, "Well, Herman. I guess you need to pee too. We should hurry. Don't want to leave the girls alone for very long."

Jason walked between two tall bushes and behind a tree. He did his business, and then turned to look for the cat. He saw Herman run off into the woods in pursuit of a squirrel.

He yelled, "Herman, let's get back. We're supposed to be protecting Chelsea and the girls."

It was clear to Jason that Herman preferred to chase the squirrel. Jason walked back to the boat. As he stepped out of the woods, he saw Chelsea raise Blaster and point it in his direction. She appeared to be on edge.

"Chelsea, don't shoot! It's your loving husband and Junior Associate. See, I'm smiling."

He relaxed when she lowered the gun and said, "That didn't take long. Where's Herman?"

Jason took Blaster from her, placed it back in its holster. He said, "Herman ran off after a squirrel. I told him not to, but you know cats."

Chelsea looked him in the eyes and said, "Yeah. They're just like husbands. They won't do what they're told. Not even after the old snip-snip. I thought sure that would help."

Jason said, "Chelsea, I don't think they do that to male cats to make them obedient."

Jason didn't like the look on Chelsea's face as she said, "Too bad. I'm a nurse, and we sleep in the same bed. If Herman had become more obedient, well...I might have had thoughts."

Jason cringed. "Really bad thoughts. I'm sleepin' with one eye open from now on."

Chelsea said, "No need. It obviously didn't work on the cat. How about you go find your buddy so we can get back to fishing. The girls are getting bored, and that never ends well."

Jason stood up, formed a megaphone with his hands, yelled, "Herman, come back! We're goin' fishing. I don't want to leave you here by yourself. There're lions, and tigers, and bears."

Lizzy said, "Oh Dad. Don't worry. There're just coyotes, mountain lions, bears, and snakes. No tigers. Herman's fine. He'll get tired of chasing squirrels and come back. Also, we have his fish in the storage tank."

Jason heard Chelsea start to argue, but she obviously thought better of it. He was glad. He had no basement here to retreat to, and no cat to take with him.

Jason said, "I'll pull the boat along the shoreline by hand using these protruding tree roots. Everyone shout out Herman's name, and maybe he'll come back."

Jason sat on the bow of the boat. He grabbed one of tree roots sticking out of the shoreline and pulled Luscious along. He did this repeatedly, until one of the roots slithered through his hands and into the boat. Jason yanked his hand away from a large water snake.

Chelsea screamed, "Snake! There's a snake in the boat! Jason, what did you do now?"

Jason watched the large water snake coil up, ready to strike. It had him trapped in the bow. Chelsea and the girls fled to the stern and huddled together on the floor.

Jason sat as far up on the bow as he could without falling out of the boat. The snake was obviously agitated. Jason whispered in Chelsea's direction.

"Chelsea, Blaster is in the holster in my tackle box. Could you please take it out and carefully hand it to me. I'll use it to dispatch this snake before it bites someone, like me for instance."

Chelsea sat with her arms around the girls, comforting them. She said, "Bad plan. The tackle box is too close to your scary friend. I'm not getting bitten. That thing might be venomous. Also, I really don't want you shooting holes in your stupid boat. We kind of need it to get home. Can't you just grab the snake by the head and toss it in the water like they do on TV?"

Jason pulled his legs up under him to get as far away from the snake as possible.

"Chelsea, can you tell if the snake's head is round or triangular? If its round, it's just a water snake. But if it has a triangular head, it could be a poisonous copperhead. What do you think?"

"Jason, I can't tell from here. If I were to guess, I'd say it has a round, fat head, like someone else I know. So, it's probably safe for you to grab it and toss it off the boat. If it turns out to be triangular, don't let it bite you. If it bites you, maybe you could jump in the water while it's still attached and take it with you. I like that plan better than you shooting holes in the boat."

Jason said, "Wife, your concern for my safety is underwhelming. I told you I'd keep you safe. I'll grab it behind the head like they do in that swamp show. How hard can it be?"

As Jason was about to grab for the snake's head, he heard Lizzy say, "Look. Here comes Herman. He's got something in his mouth. I hope it's not a poor chipmunk."

Jason turned and saw Herman jump into the boat near the girls. When the cat saw the snake, he dropped the thing in his mouth.

Chelsea screamed, "Ahhhh! Finger! It's a human finger!"

Herman moved towards the bow, went into pounce mode, and hissed at the coiled serpent.

The snake appeared startled by all the commotion. Jason watched it uncoil, slither over the gunwale and into the water.

Jason saw Herman walk back to the stern, sit down, lick his paws, and pick up his prize again. He carried the finger to the bow and proudly dropped it on the floor in front of Jason.

Herman looked up at Jason. "Meow."

Chelsea said, "Jason, your furry friend caught something during the hunt. He's presenting it to you. It looks like a man's ring finger, with a gold ring on it."

Jason said, "Chelsea, I can see it's a finger. Herman chased that snake away and saved my life. I could've been bitten. Thank you, Herman. You are a true friend."

"Yes Jason. He saved you. Then he gave you the finger. You're a detective. Don't you want to know where the rest of the person is? Ask Herman to show you. It might provide us with a clue to our case. We could use a clue."

Jason said, "But what about the snake? If there's one snake, he's probably got brothers and sisters out there. Suddenly, I'm not all that anxious to go stomping around in the woods."

Chelsea said, "Jason, stop it. You and your cat are scaring the children with your snake and severed finger. Girls, I'll get Blaster and keep you safe. I promise not to shoot any holes in the boat. Your father won't be so lucky if he doesn't find the body that goes with that finger."

Lizzy said, "Mom, don't shoot poor Dad. He's got enough problems."

Jason sat in the bow of the boat staring at the finger laying at his feet. Herman had become bored of the whole thing and sat washing himself.

Jason said, "Chelsea, please don't shoot me. I've got a better idea. Since I'm only a Junior Associate, I'm not qualified to go hunting in the snake-infested woods for a dead body. I suggest that we take the finger, and your impressive fish, back to our dock and call the police. We can describe this place to them, and they can bring a search team out here to dance among the snakes. If they find a body, they'll tell us, and we'll still have a clue."

Chelsea said, "Jason, I'm finding it harder and harder to believe you've ever had a clue. I'll leave it to you to handle the evidence…the finger. Here's an empty paper bag that held the new lures. Put it in there and let's head for home. I've had enough excitement for one day."

Jason took the small paper bag, picked up the finger, and gingerly placed it inside. He put the bag in his tackle box. Then he looked around and saw the girls still huddled together in the stern of the boat.

Chelsea said, "It's okay girls. We're heading for home. We had an exciting day, with the snake and Herman giving your father the finger. It hasn't been all bad. I did catch the only fish."

Jason said, "Yeah, and the fishermen killer didn't murder us, so there's that."

Chelsea said, "Idiot."

Jason drove the boat back to the dock. He got everyone unloaded and safely up to the house. Then he phoned the police and told them about the family fishing adventure. An hour later a couple of deputies pulled into the Longfellow's driveway. Jason and Chelsea met them on the front stoop. Jason saw the lead deputy was Tim Harbinger, the Bedford police officer the Longfellows had been dealing with since the start of their investigation.

Jason shook the deputy's hand. Then Chelsea handed Jason the paper bag.

"Here Jason. Give Deputy Harbinger the finger."

The deputy looked confused. He said, "Excuse me, Mrs. Longfellow?"

The two PIs told Deputy Harbinger what had happened on their fishing trip. Jason described their location when Herman had found the mysterious body part. Jason followed as Deputy Harbinger went to his car. The deputy called it in, initiating a search of the area for the body.

Deputy Harbinger and Jason walked back to where Chelsea stood on the front stoop. The deputy said, "Dr. and Mrs. PI Longfellow, you'll be glad to hear that, for now, neither of you are persons of interest in this…whatever it is. Presumably there's a body out there somewhere. But you were obviously on a fishing trip with your daughters. There's no reason to suspect you of anything. You do have an uncanny way of turning up at the wrong place at the wrong time."

The deputy took the finger. He told Jason he'd look for a fingerprint match in all the law enforcement databases the Sheriff's Office had access to. He promised he'd let them know if he got an ID from the print.

After the deputy left, Jason and Chelsea told the girls they could watch TV. The two PIs went into the kitchen, brewed a pot of coffee, and spent the next two hours discussing the case while sitting at the table sipping the hot brew and munching on the remaining Pop-Tarts.

Jason said, "It's nice to know that if I ever plan a serious crime, all I need to do is take the children with me. I won't even be considered a person of interest."

Chelsea sipped her hot coffee, took a bite of a cherry Pop-Tart, and said, "Idiot. Don't even kid about such a thing. You scared our poor children half to death today, what with the snake, the cat finding that finger, and you running off and leaving us on the boat alone. Our daughters are going to need a lot of therapy. So, no more stupid jokes."

Just as they were finishing up their second pot of coffee, Jason's cell phone rang. He put it on speaker phone so Chelsea could hear. Jason heard Deputy Harbinger's voice.

"The search is over already. Our search team found two bodies, or at least parts of two bodies. Both men, dressed like fishermen. The heads and hands were missing. Someone didn't want the bodies identified. But we got a hit off the finger that your cat found. It belongs to one of the fishermen that disappeared about a month ago. The guy worked for the County Government, so his prints were on file. He was fishing with his brother-in-law, and the killer must have murdered them and dumped their bodies out there in the wilderness."

Jason said, "Was there any evidence of a blow to the head? One of my theories for the fishermen killings involves giant stripers that butt heads with the victims, either killing them outright with blunt force trauma or knocking them out and drowning them."

Chelsea said, "Are we on the same call? Deputy Harbinger just told us that the bodies were missing their heads."

Jason said, excited, "Of course. The killers took the hands so no one could identify the bodies by fingerprints. They took the heads so the police couldn't determine cause of death as blunt force trauma to the head. These guys, or fish, are ingenious."

Jason heard silence from the other end of the phone. He thought perhaps the deputy was left speechless because of his clever deductions.

Chelsea said, "Jason, you can't have it both ways. How does a fish kill a person by knocking them out of their boat, head-butting them to death in the water, then taking them on shore and cutting them into pieces to keep them from being identified. Oh God. You're dragging me into insanity with you."

Jason said, "Thank you?"

Chelsea continued, "It sounds to me like there's two different things going on here. There appear to be very large striped bass growing in the lake. That may, or may not, be due to the GenesRUs human growth hormone. It's highly unlikely that these large bass are killing anyone. Now we have two bodies found on land that were chopped up to prevent identification. I repeat, that's not a thing that a fish is likely to do. These fishermen murders are clearly being done by a human or humans unknown. As to motive, I have no idea whether the discarded growth hormone or

GenesRUs have anything to do with this mess. We don't seem to be much farther along than we were before. What do you think Deputy Harbinger?"

The deputy said, "I agree. There seems to be more than one thing going on."

Jason said, "I still think the most important clues are the giant head-butting fish and the recombinant human growth hormone. I get that the giant fish probably aren't cutting up the bodies and dumping them."

Chelsea said, "Probably…?"

Jason continued, "Maybe the fish are killing people, and someone from GenesRUs is trying to cover it up by mutilating and dumping the bodies to avoid identification. Chelsea, I think I did good today. I saved our family from that deadly snake and found a finger, an invaluable clue. I think I should be promoted back to Associate."

Chelsea said, "If I remember correctly, it was Herman that chased the snake away. Herman also gave you the finger. I'm liking that cat more and more. I'm thinking I should promote Herman to Associate PI, and you can be his PI Intern."

Chapter 17. Nature Fights Back

The following Saturday morning, Jason sat on the lower level of their lake house, staring out the picture window. Chelsea had taken the girls to the grocery store with her, and he was enjoying the peace and quiet. The beginning of a warm, sunny, spring day, the cloudless sky appeared a bright luminescent blue that reflected in the calm, clear mountain lake. Tired of the swill Chelsea called coffee, he had made a cup of tea, four teaspoons of sugar. He sipped it while munching on a chocolate covered cake donut. His mind ran over the facts of the case repeatedly, and he kept coming to the same conclusion. He had no idea what was going on. He began to regret leaving the FDA. He had provided medical risk assessments for new drugs submitted to the Agency for licensing, and he was good at it. He had been promoted several times. As a PI, he was clueless. Even worse, his wife was his boss, and she kept demoting him.

Herman sat on Jason's lap. Jason rubbed the cat's ears and said, "Herman, old buddy, maybe I should look at this case like a risk assessment. If I don't catch this killer, the *risk* is that he will keep killing…or *they* if it's those giant head-butting fish. Just last week, my *reward* was that I almost got bitten by a snake, and I got demoted, again. This really sucks."

Herman smiled. "Meow."

Jason said, "You're right. I need to keep it positive. I didn't get bitten, and Chelsea didn't fire me, or shoot me." He paused and thought for a moment. "Nope, I'm still sad."

Jason saw movement out of the corner of his eye. He bent forward to see out the picture window more clearly. A squirrel had run across the paved walkway just outside the window. It now sat on the other side of the sliding glass door to Jason's left, staring in at him.

Jason said, "Herman, I feel strange, like I'm the caged animal in the zoo and that little guy is looking in at me. I wonder what he wants."

Herman said, "Meow."

Jason said, "I see it's a squirrel. Normally you would want to chase him down and eat him. Why aren't you more excited?"

Herman started cleaning himself, licking his paws and rubbing his face.

Jason said, "You might not be curious. But I've got to find out what this little guy is up to. He's just sitting there staring in at me. It's kinda spooky."

Jason sat Herman on the floor, got up, and walked to the sliding glass door. Jason looked down at the squirrel. The squirrel looked up at Jason.

Jason said, "Herman, this little guy doesn't appear to be afraid of me. I could squash him with my number twelve shoe. I'm going out there to chase him away. He must be up to no good."

Herman sat down, shook his head. "Meow."

Jason said, "Why don't you think it's a good idea? It's just one little squirrel. I'm going to chase him away before he chews another hole in my garden hose."

Jason unlocked the sliding glass door. He opened it just enough so he could squeeze through without the squirrel running into the house. He shut the door behind him and stood there, foot to face with the squirrel. The squirrel didn't move. Jason felt strangely uncomfortable.

Jason kicked at the squirrel. "Shoo. Go away you pest."

The squirrel back up a little but held its ground.

Jason saw Herman saunter up to the inside of the sliding glass door, a bored look on his furry face. Jason kicked at the squirrel again.

"Shoo, you little varmint, before I squash you like a bug.

Jason became more concerned the longer the squirrel refused to leave. His concern increased exponentially as two more squirrels came hopping along the paved walkway, one from the front of the house and the other up the path from the dock. They sat on either side of the original.

Jason still felt he had the upper hand. He was a giant compared to these furry creatures. To his surprise, multitudes of squirrels came running from the front of the house and up from the dock. Jason's OCD kicked in; he found himself staring down at over one hundred squirrels. The lead squirrel began to walk slowly towards Jason's pant leg. Jason turned and looked at Herman, sitting complacently on the other side of the closed sliding glass door.

"Herman, what the hell? It's squirrel-mageddon. Help me! They're gonna eat me!"

Jason turned and slowly reached for the handle to the sliding glass door. When he got hold of the handle, he yanked the door open, thrust his body inside the house, and slammed it closed behind him. He turned to look, and the squirrels were still there, staring up at him. They appeared to be waiting, perhaps for the right time to attack? Jason's imagination conjured up visions of squirrels piling on top of him, chomping away with their pointy teeth. Then, just as suddenly as they had appeared, the squirrels turned tail and went away.

Jason looked down at Herman, who sat, calmly cleaning himself. "Meow."

Jason, fear in his voice, said, "What do you mean you told me so? I didn't know there were that many squirrels in the world. Why didn't you do anything?"

"Meow. Meow. Meow."

Jason said, "You don't have to get snippy. I realize there were a lot of them, but you're a cat. You're supposed to be a hunter and a killer. Just because Chelsea promoted you to Junior Associate, doesn't mean you're my boss."

Jason heard the front door open upstairs, followed by the yelling of squabbling sisters.

He said to Herman, "Sounds like Lizzy and Lilly are going at it. Normally I'd just stay down here. But I've got to tell Chelsea what happened. Let's go greet the noisy side of the family."

Jason walked through the door to the stairwell and ascended the stairs, Herman on his heels. Jason entered the kitchen where Chelsea was unpacking the groceries, placing loaves of bread in the pantry. He smelled the unmistakable aroma of coffee and donuts. The girls had fled to their rooms, no doubt to avoid helping.

He said, "Hello, Dear. How'd it go? Did you find everything you wanted at the store?"

"Jason, I don't think you've ever had the pleasure of grocery shopping with our little darlings. You need to give it a try sometime. I found everything on my list. I somehow managed to come home with a few extras…a bag of Snickers bars, two bags of Twizzlers, and a half gallon of chocolate milk. There are three of them and only one of me. I never had a chance."

Jason said, "Sorry to hear they misbehaved. Thanks for getting the groceries. And speaking of being outnumbered, I had a strange experience this morning."

Jason walked into the kitchen, took some cans out of a bag, and started to put them away.

Chelsea walked over and took the cans, bean and bacon and chicken noodle soup, from him.

"Jason, please don't help. Last time you put the groceries away I couldn't find anything. You put everything up on the high shelves where I can't reach. Stand over there and tell me about your morning, when you weren't chasing children around the grocery store."

Jason told her about his bizarre encounter with the squirrel army, and how Herman had refused to help. Chelsea put away groceries, and Herman searched for escaped food to attack.

After Jason had finished his story, Chelsea said, "First, your two-sided conversations with our cat are becoming disturbing. You realize Herman doesn't really talk, right? Having said that, your story is unusual. I know you're OCD, so I don't doubt there were over a hundred squirrels. I don't understand where they all came from, or what they wanted. I do have a suggestion. Our neighbor, Horace McDufus, has apparently lived here forever. If anyone should be able to explain this odd squirrel behavior, it's him. I saw his car in the driveway. Why don't we pay him a visit after I finish here, and we can ask him."

Jason leaned against the kitchen counter, tore open the bag of snickers. He ripped the wrapper off one and tossed the bite-sized candy bar into his mouth. He started to speak and choked on a partially chewed peanut. Chelsea filled a glass with tap water and handed it to him.

Chelsea said, "Here, drink this before you choke to death. I've told you over and over, don't talk with food in your mouth. Now what were you trying to say?"

Jason took a drink, cleared his throat, and said, "Are you sure you want to visit McDufus? Last time we saw the man, he had a snoot full and was running around with a twenty-two-revolver threatening the squirrels. Hey, maybe that's what this was about."

Chelsea said, "Let me guess. The squirrels mistook you for a sixty-year-old drunk and were planning on exacting their revenge. Were any of the squirrels armed? Jason, do you ever think before you speak? The filter between your mouth and your brain is more like a sieve if there's one at all. I'll tell the girls we're going next door. Maybe we can talk to McDufus and solve at least one mystery. At this point I'd be happy to solve anything."

When Chelsea came down the hallway from the girls' bedrooms, the PIs headed for their next-door neighbor's house. Jason followed his wife around the heavily wooded cul-de-sac. He was amazed at how far out in the middle of nowhere they lived. They climbed the steps onto McDufus' porch and approached the front door. Chelsea knocked. Jason heard footsteps, and Horace McDufus opened the door. McDufus wore his usual uniform, a dirty white T-shirt, and coveralls. Jason noticed the hand grips of a twenty-two revolver sticking out of his pants pocket.

McDufus said, "Well if it ain't my new neighbors, the private eyes. Come on in and take a load off. What can I do ya' for?"

Jason smelled alcohol on the man's breath. Then there was the body odor mixed with alcohol; he appeared to be sweating the stuff.

Chelsea said, "We have a question for you, if you wouldn't mind."

McDufus waved them into the living room. He walked over to a ratty old couch, picked up an armful of dirty clothes, and tossed them on the floor.

"Make yerselves comforble. I'll get us a drink, and then y'all can tell me what it's about."

Jason and Chelsea took a seat. Jason watched as the man walked out of the room, presumably headed for the kitchen. Jason looked around, uncomfortable with all the chaos. A couple of minutes later McDufus returned with three Mason jars half-full of clear liquid. He sat one down on the floor next to a chair and handed the other two jars to the visiting PIs.

"I got me a cousin lives way back up in the mountains, makes some of the best shine in these here parts. This is from his latest batch; a mighty fine brew aged a full twenty-four hours. Drink up and tell me what's goin' on. Y'all haven't found my cousin have ya'? That'd be just great."

Jason watched Chelsea place the Mason jar against her lips and pretend to take a drink. Intent on showing his wife who wore the pants in the family, he took a large gulp of the home-made rocket fuel. Suddenly his mouth, nose, throat, and eyes were on fire. He choked violently. Chelsea started to slap him on the back. He ducked, thinking she was aiming for his head.

Jason finally stopped choking, looked at McDufus, and said, "Wow, that's smooth. And aged a full twenty-four hours? The stuff you age for a week must be really awesome."

It annoyed Jason when Chelsea gave him that pitiful look. She said, "Horace, last time we talked, you told us you've lived here a long time. Jason had a strange experience this morning, and we thought you might be able to explain it to us. Jason, tell Mr. McDufus what happened."

Jason told McDufus his squirrel story. He finished with, "I swear, I thought they were going to eat me. Have you ever had an experience like that? Is that why you shoot them?"

McDufus laughed. "Well, Mr. PI, yer partly right about the eatin' thing. Some other dumbass moved here recently, lives on the next street over. I hear tell he started feedin' the animals, puts out food fer the deer, geese, birds, and squirrels. Ain't nothin' worse than a city slicker movin' to the country and thinkin' he knows what he's a doin'. If'n ya' feed the wild animals, they get used to it, and it causes all manner of problems. Them squirrels weren't there to eat you. One of 'em just saw ya' through the winder, thought you was a gonna feed him, and rang the dinner bell fer his friends and family. They was waitin' to be fed."

Chelsea said, "That's all it was? Somebody has trained the squirrels to believe that people will feed them, so when they see a person, they come running. That's why Herman didn't come to your rescue, Jason. You weren't in any danger."

McDufus drank down his entire Mason jar full of moonshine in one pull and wiped his mouth with the back of his hand.

He said, "Ahhh. You're right there, Mr. PI. That's some smooth stuff. You weren't in any danger with them squirrels this morning. But this dumbass feedin' the wild animals is causin' all kinds of problems. Brings loads of the pests to our area of the lake. Squirrels don't eat people, but they like to chew on things, like gas lines, brake lines, plastic lawn chairs. One of the little bastards chewed through the gas line of my outboard motor, and I got stranded on the lake t'other day. I coulda' been blowed up."

Jason said, "I see your point. Wouldn't be good if a squirrel chewed through our SUV gas line or brake line. Chelsea, I need to get a twenty-two revolver for shooting squirrels."

McDufus pulled his twenty-two out of his pocket and began waving it around. "I'm not sure ya' want ta' do that. The bullets travel a long ways. It's dangerous to shoot one of these things where there's people around, unless ya' really know what yer' doin'."

Chelsea said, "That would not be Jason."

McDufus said, "I figured as much. Ya' need to get yerself a pellet gun. It'll take out a squirrel, and the heavy brush and weeds'll stop a pellet. That way ya' don't accidentally shoot one of yer neighbors, like me fer instance."

Jason said, "A pellet gun. I'll look into it. What about the geese and deer? You said feeding them is also dangerous."

McDufus said, "Hang on just a minute."

Jason watched as the man got up, walked towards the kitchen, and came back with two more Mason jars full of liquid. He handed one to Jason and sat back down. Then he threw the entire jar of rocket fuel down his throat in one gulp, wiped his mouth, and continued.

"Drink up, Mr. PI, and I'll tell ya' the problem. When Mr. Dumbass feeds the deer, them animals tell their friends, and pretty soon we're overrun by 'em. They eat everythin', yer' garden, flowers, grass, anythin' that's a plant. With herds of 'em, it ain't safe to drive on the road. It got so bad the county government let bow hunters hunt a couple days a week in some of the neighborhoods to thin out the deer population. Ifn' you take yer girls fer a walk, be prepared to dodge arrows. Them guys ain't to bright. Some of 'em can't tell a deer from a person."

Jason saw Chelsea pretend to take a sip of moonshine. She said, "That's terrible. I thought we'd be safe out here in the middle of nowhere. There were no random flying arrows up north."

Jason said, "What about the geese? How's feeding them a problem?"

McDufus snorted, "Let's just say be careful when ya' walk on yer dock, or swim in the lake. When that dumbass feeds the geese, they come from miles around, and crap all over everythin'. There're docks in some places covered in goose poop. I've seen neighbors out shovelin' piles of goose poop into the water. It just ain't sanitary."

Jason looked around McDufus' house. *If this guy thinks it's not sanitary, it must be bad.*

Chelsea sat her Mason jar down on the floor next to her feet. She said, "That's disgusting. Can't anyone make this guy stop feeding the animals?"

McDufus said, "It's more'n just disgustin'. The county government, another bunch of dumbasses, decided to let hunters with shotguns hunt the geese from their boats, somethin' that used to be illegal. Now it ain't unusual ta' go out on the lake and see a guy in a bass boat takin' pot shots at geese. T'other day one of my bar buddies told me some crazy hunter shot up his dock trying to bag hisself a couple of geese. It's nuts."

Jason watched with concern as McDufus made a third trip to the kitchen, returned with another Mason jar full of the clear liquid, and drained it in one gulp. The man was clearly drunk and getting agitated telling his stories. He started waving his twenty-two revolver around.

Suddenly McDufus growled, "Damn squirrels. Damn dumbasses."

Jason watched in horror as McDufus stood up, staggered to the sliding glass door, out onto the deck, and started shooting at squirrels.

Jason stood up, grabbed Chelsea by the arm, and said, "Time to go."

Jason was glad that Chelsea did not argue. In fact, she beat him to the door and was halfway home before he got off McDufus' porch. Lizzy met them at the front door.

Lizzy said, "Mr. McDufus going to war with the squirrels again? I put Lilly and Lucy in the bathroom just in case a stray bullet heads our way. Can't you do anything about that crazy man?"

Jason said, "I don't think we have to worry about McDufus. He only shoots at the squirrels on the lakeside of his house, the part of his lot that's cleared. It's the only place he can see the squirrels. He's not shooting in our direction. He's only dangerous to people on the water."

Chelsea said, "I think Lizzy's right. McDufus is a drunk. He shouldn't be allowed to have a gun. Let alone blasting away at squirrels in a populated neighborhood, especially since we are part of that population. And the whole purpose of living on a lake is to go out on the water."

Jason said, "I just thought of something. I have another theory as to what's happening in our case of the missing fishermen. Nature has been here a lot longer than we have. What if McDufus was wrong, and those squirrels really were planning to eat me. Maybe nature is fighting back against the invading humans, killing us off. Maybe the squirrels are only part of the problem."

Chelsea shook her head, "Let me guess. You think someone's been feeding the bass, and they've turned into head-butting monsters. They're killing fishermen as a way of fighting back against the humans who have invaded their territory. They're taking back the lake. Jason, you're like a dog with a bone…a really dumb dog. Once you get an idea in your head, you couldn't knock it out with a brick."

Lizzy said, "So is that why you're always whacking him?"

Jason was sad, again.

Chapter 18. Jason, The Bait

The following Monday and Tuesday, Jason and Chelsea had gone into the office in the morning. They left at noon on Tuesday because nothing was happening with the case. No new bodies or information had turned up. On their way home, Jason discussed the case with Chelsea while at the wheel of his jacked-up pickup truck.

"Chelsea, I'm confused. I can't figure out if these killings involve someone murdering fishermen, or if it's really a case of nature fighting back against humans. It could be someone from GenesRUs trying to cover up the illegal dumping of that drug by killing all the fishermen who fish that part of the lake. Although that feels kind of extreme. At worst the company would have to pay a fine, hardly worth murder. Also, Harold Fairchild's murder doesn't fit that theory. He was wearing his business suit when I reeled him in. That killing feels different somehow."

Jason drove around a hairpin turn, and a large deer appeared, crossing the road at a leisurely pace. Chelsea screamed, "Jason, look out! Deer!"

Jason yanked the steering wheel to the right. The truck's front wheels dove into the ditch and stopped abruptly, throwing both PIs against their seat belts. Jason watched the deer run off into the thick woods. He got out of the truck, walked around it, and re-entered the driver's seat.

Jason said, "Wow! Good thing this truck's jacked up so high. Doesn't look like it's damaged at all, although my neck hurts. How about you, Chelsea? Are you okay?"

Chelsea said, "I'm fine. Get us out of this ditch and watch where you're going. I'm not sure if it's the deer or you that's trying to kill us. On the subject of the murders, for once I agree with you. There must be something else going on. How could a killer expect to murder every fisherman that fishes the area where the drugs were dumped? It's usually pitch dark at night, it's a big lake, and they're bound to miss someone. If that's the motive, it's not a practical plan. More like something my husband might do."

"Be nice Chelsea. I would never dump drugs into the lake. It's awful to pollute such a beautiful place. On the other hand, those stripers we caught were huge. If the human growth hormone caused that, maybe this particular pollutant isn't so bad. I'm guessing most fishermen would be happy about something that creates gigantic stripers. So why kill them?"

Jason shifted into reverse, pulled the front wheels out of the ditch, and headed for home.

"Jason, you mean the huge stripers that *I* caught. You caught a dead man in a business suit."

Jason ignored the gibe. "I can't think of a motive for a person to kill all those fishermen that makes any sense. Which is why I believe this really is a case of nature fighting back. Think about it. McDufus keeps shooting the squirrels, so they started fighting back by eating car and boat gas lines. Then they escalate to killing and eating humans; those squirrels really were gonna eat me. Man is the stripers' enemy. Fishermen catch them, kill them, and eat them. Then, the growth hormone makes them huge. They start fighting back by head-butting bass boats, head-butting the fishermen, killing them, and chewing on them. And that deer that put us in the ditch tried to kill us too. I'm sure this is a case of nature declaring war on humans. It just makes sense."

Chelsea shook her head. "Jason, you've watched too many science fiction movies. I agree the squirrel thing was a little unsettling. You almost hitting that deer scared the crap out of me. But the idea of giant head-butting stripers? You're out of your tiny mind. How is Deputy Harbinger going to solve that crime? Arrest a fish?"

Jason looked serious. "I guess he'd have to call in the game warden, although I don't know how you handcuff a bass."

Chelsea shook her head. She said, "Don't be ridiculous. Stop with the killer bass and get serious for a minute. We need to come up with a motive for someone, as in a human, wanting to kill all those fishermen, and Harold Fairchild. It's possible that they are two different crimes. Another possibility is that someone killed all the fishermen to mask Harold's murder and make it look like there's a serial killer on the loose."

Jason saw Chelsea shake her head in frustration, and they said in unison, "But, Harold was wearing a business suit when he was killed. He wasn't fishing."

Jason reached their driveway, pulled in, and parked the truck in front of the house. He looked at Chelsea, a determined expression on his face.

He said, "It's only one o'clock. I'm going fishing tonight by myself. I'll load up Luscious with some snacks and sodas and pull an all-nighter on the water. With any luck, I'll catch a couple of those humongous stripers, which you can clean and cook for supper. And hopefully the fishermen killer will come after me. I'll be waiting with Blaster."

Jason climbed down from the cab of his truck and walked around to help Chelsea down.

She said, "Jason, I'm not comfortable with your plan. I don't want anything bad to happen to you. You're the father of my children, I love you, and I'm not raising the little darlings by myself. Please don't do this."

Jason led the way to the front door, unlocked it, and opened it for Chelsea.

"Chelsea, I'm your Junior Associate…"

"PI in training."

"Okay, PI in training. I need a promotion, and the only way for me to get it is to catch this killer and solve the case. So tonight, I'm the bait. I'm going to take a nap. After dinner I'll pack a cooler and some snacks and get ready to head out. Why don't you check on the children."

At eleven o'clock, Jason kissed Chelsea and the girls goodbye and hauled a cooler and snacks down to the dock. He turned on the dock lights, lowered Luscious into the water, loaded her up with his gear, and pointed her towards the big water. The sky included a heavy cloud cover. Jason needed the large spotlight to find his chosen fishing spot, a deep hole near the shoreline in an area where other fishermen had disappeared. He stopped Luscious, killed the outboard, set up the trolling motor, and maneuvered the boat into position to fish the deep hole.

Jason looked through the darkness that surrounded him. The extreme quiet was deafening. He mumbled to himself, "It's kinda scary out here all alone. I'll set Blaster down here next to me on the seat in case I need to get to him in a hurry."

Jason removed the gigantic revolver, loaded with five 410 shotgun shells, from its holster and placed it on the seat beside him. Then he took a fishing pole and made his first cast towards the shore, giving the bucktail a few seconds to sink before slowly reeling it in.

Maybe this wasn't such a good idea. It's very isolated out here, and there's no one to help if I get into trouble. I'm thinkin' I should just head for home and forget the whole thing. I'll bet Chelsea and the girls miss me.

Jason heard the burbling sounds of a school of shad moving into the area between him and the shoreline. Then came the tell-tale tail slaps as stripers began to feed.

Jason perked up at the thought of catching a record sized bass. He would enjoy taking home a fish larger than the ones Chelsea hauled in on their last outing. Jason stood in the bow near the trolling motor, casting and reeling in his lure. Something crashed hard into Luscious' bow, causing Jason to stumble. Irritated, he dropped his fishing pole and picked up the spotlight in his left hand and Blaster in his right. He shined the light into the water and saw something large swim out from under the boat. He pointed Blaster and emptied all five chambers into the water.

He said, "Take that, you murdering fish. You might have been here first, but I'm here to stay. Besides, I need to solve this case so I can get promoted back to Associate PI."

The spotlight revealed a large fish floating to the surface. Based on all the holes and the fact that part of the head was missing, Jason's fear subsided.

Yep, it's nature declaring war on us humans for invading their space out here in the wilderness. That'll show 'em. Now I can get on with the real business at hand, catching a fish bigger than the ones Chelsea caught. I'd take that one, but it's full of bullet holes. Chelsea'd say I cheated. Oh well, I like a challenge! At war with nature. Catch a big fish, before it catches me.

Jason decided that to catch a striper larger than Chelsea's, he needed to use bigger bait. He sat down, took a knife and large artificial minnow out of his tackle box, and got to work. Just as he started to cut the line to remove old lure, something large bumped the boat and caused it to rock. The knife slipped and he sliced his hand. He grabbed the first aid kit. Blood collected on the seat and floor before he got the cut bandaged. He felt a little woozy, fought through it, put away the first aid kit, and finished attaching the large lure to his line. He returned to the bow, used the trolling motor to maneuver into position, cast his new lure, and began reeling it in.

He mumbled, "Damn dark night. Damn fishing lure. Damn knife. Damn nature. I'm gonna catch a striper bigger than Chelsea's if it kills me."

Something very large bumped into the bow of the boat. Jason still felt woozy, the boat floor shifted under his feet, and he fell overboard. As something pulled him down into the deep cool water, his last thought was, *Well, this sucks. I was just kidding, but I guess Chelsea wins.*

Chapter 19. PI Chelsea Longfellow, Widow

Next morning, Chelsea woke at seven-thirty, turned over, and no Jason. Not quite awake, she said in a loud voice, "Jason, are you in the bathroom?"

She heard no response. More awake, she sat up and looked around. Jason's side of the bed had not been slept in. Concerned, she got out of bed and walked into the kitchen, expecting to see Jason sitting at the table drinking coffee. No Jason. With a heightened sense of anxiety, she walked through the house checking on the girls. She found them all asleep in their beds.

Chelsea brushed her teeth, went back to the kitchen, and brewed a pot of her high-octane coffee. She poured a cup, made a piece of buttered toast with raspberry jelly, and sat down at the table to eat and think.

I knew it was not a good idea for Jason to go fishing alone. I should have stopped him, whacked him one on the head. I need to stop doing that, or I'm going to cause brain damage. Oh, who am I kidding? His brain is already damaged. That's why I keep needing to whack him. It's a vicious cycle. Jason, where are you? I told you; I'm not raising our three little angels alone. What to do? I should try calling his cell, although reception is spotty on the lake. If he doesn't answer, I can phone the police just in case they've heard anything. Knowing Jason, he probably fell asleep and is snoring away on the lake somewhere.

Chelsea sipped hot coffee and nibbled on her jelly toast. After finishing breakfast, she poured another cup of coffee. Then she went into the living room to keep from waking the girls and hit Jason's number on her cell's speed dial. No answer, and it went to voice mail. She tried again and got his voice mail.

She said, "Jason Bartholomew Longfellow, what have you done now? You're not home yet, and I'm worried. I do love you, in spite of how irritating you can be. Call me back, now!"

She disconnected and dialed the police.

Chelsea heard, "Hello, Deputy Harbinger, Bedford County Sheriff's Office."

She said, "Hello Deputy Harbinger, it's Chelsea Longfellow."

"Well, hello, Mrs. PI Longfellow. What can I do for you? We still don't have any new leads in the case of the missing fishermen. Hopefully you have something to report."

Chelsea said, "Jason went fishing last night, with the idea of catching the fishermen killer. I'm worried. He's not home yet, and he was supposed to be home long before now."

Deputy Harbinger said, "Do you have any reason to believe something bad has happened? Did you try to call him on his cell?"

Chelsea felt a surge of panic. "Nothing concrete, just a bad feeling. I tried to call him. He doesn't answer, but cell service on the lake is spotty. For all I know, he could have fallen asleep and is floating around in his stupid boat somewhere. Have you heard anything in the Sheriff's office? You know, like my husband's empty bass boat turning up with blood or body parts in it?"

Deputy Harbinger said, "No, we haven't heard anything. I'm sure you're right, though. Dr. Longfellow probably fell asleep and is floating around the lake. I can't file an official missing person's report until he's been gone for twenty-four hours. Since I've worked with you and your husband before, I'll unofficially check it out, just in case he did trip over a clue."

Chelsea said, "Thank you Deputy Harbinger. I really appreciate it. Please call me at this number if you find out anything. It's my cell."

Deputy Harbinger said, "No problem. Talk to you soon."

Chelsea disconnected the call. She heard someone moving around. Lizzy, rubbing her eyes, came walking from the direction of her bedroom.

"What's going on, Mom? What time is it? What did Dad do now? Is he okay? Isn't he back from his fishing trip?"

Chelsea said, "No, he's not back yet. I just spoke with Detective Harbinger at the Bedford County Sheriff's Office, and they haven't heard anything. I'm sure your father's fine. He probably fell asleep and is floating around aimlessly on the lake. Hopefully someone will find him, wake him up, and he'll come home soon."

Lizzy, awake now, said, "Poor Dad. Why did you let him go out there alone? He's always hurting himself. If he's got that hand cannon thing, he probably shot a hole in the boat and sank. Then there's this person that's killing fishermen? Oh well, at least now he won't have to suffer the embarrassment of being demoted to PI in training."

Chelsea felt bad. "Lizzy, what a terrible thing to say. First, there's no reason to think there's anything wrong. He's just a little late. Second..."

"Mom, face it. You sent Dad out on the lake in the middle of the night, armed with something called Blaster. This man who fancies himself a private detective believes that there are giant head-butting fish out there that will try to murder him. What could possibly go wrong?"

Apparently, Lizzy paid more attention to current events than Chelsea realized. This was difficult to believe considering the amount of time the teenager spent plugged into her music, phone, social media, and binge-watching TV.

Chelsea relented. "Honey, you're right. I should have tried to stop him. Daddy's a good guy, but he's not great at the PI thing, or the being armed thing, or the staying alive thing. The police are going to call me back if they hear anything. Hopefully he's fine, and just fell asleep, or caught lots of fish...maybe is still catching fish...hopefully not killer fish. Oh God!"

Lizzy said, "Mom, you need to whack yourself on the head. You're delusional. This is Dad, the original PI Longfellow, you're talking about. We should rent a boat and go out looking for him ourselves. God only knows what kind of mess he's gotten himself into."

Chelsea sent Lizzy to wake her sisters. She prepared a healthy breakfast, cereal with chocolate puffs and marshmallows and a glass of orange juice. Chelsea had hated the fact that her mother, the controlling alcoholic, had insisted on a traditional breakfast, the same bacon, eggs sunny-side-up, and buttered toast. She had decided to re-live her childhood vicariously through her daughters by providing fun breakfasts. A breakfast smelling of chocolate, sugar, and diabetes went against everything she'd learned in nutrition class, but it was fun. The girls showed up in their pajamas and dug into their tasty breakfast. Chelsea poured herself a third cup of coffee. Her cell phone rang. She glanced at the caller ID.

Chelsea answered the phone, "Hello, Deputy Harbinger? Is there any news? Is Jason okay?"

Chelsea didn't like the fact that the deputy paused for a long time before speaking.

"Mrs. PI Longfellow? This is Deputy Harbinger. There's no easy way to say this, so I'm just going to spit it out…well…your husband…Jason…boat…blood…gone."

Chelsea wanted to reach through the phone and whack the man on the head. "Deputy Harbinger, speak up. You're not making any sense."

The deputy said, "Sorry Mrs…PI Longfellow. I'm not good at family notifications. I should be doing this in person. But I hate being there when people get all sad and weepy. It's depressing. We got a report that an abandoned bass boat has been found floating in deep water off the shoreline in the vicinity of the dam. An early morning water skier apparently found it."

Chelsea's anxiety dialed up several notches. "What do you mean, *abandoned*? Does that mean it was empty? Was it Jason's boat? What about blood, bodies?"

The deputy said, "Our police boat is on the way, but hasn't reached the crime scene yet. According to the skier, there was blood in the bow of the boat and on the seat. We'll know more when the crime scene investigator gets there. He'll go over the boat with a fine-tooth comb."

Chelsea said, her voice getting more high-pitched, "Crime scene? Blood on the bow? How much blood? Do we know whose boat it is? It might not even be Jason's."

Lizzy placed her hand on her mother's arm for comfort. "Calm down, Mom. It probably isn't even Dad's boat. Ask the deputy if there are any bullet holes in the bottom."

Chelsea said into the phone, "Jason named his boat *Luscious*. The name is painted on both sides of the bow in bright blue paint. Did the water skier mention anything like that?"

Chelsea heard Deputy Harbinger speaking to someone in the background. Then she heard him say, "I'm so sorry, Mrs. PI Longfellow. It would appear that the skier did mention something painted on the bow. We have him on the landline, and he says he thinks that was the name. The good news, the skier said that the pool of blood was fairly small. So, if your husband was in the boat, he could still be alive…unless he finished bleeding out after he fell in the water, or the killer finished him off somewhere else, or a bear got him."

Chelsea grimaced. "Deputy, you really are not very good at this. You remind me of Jason. So, it is Jason's bass boat. And we think there's a pool of blood on the floor and seat, and no Jason. This sounds like the crime scenes of the other missing fishermen. Were there any cracks in the hull? Any scratches or other evidence that something had crashed into it?"

The deputy said, "No, the skier didn't say anything about scratches or cracks in the hull. We'll know more once our crime scene investigator gets there."

Chelsea couldn't help but think about Jason's crazy theory of giant head-butting striped bass, but she thought it wise not to mention this to the deputy. He might rightly conclude that Jason was crazy, and it would be better if they didn't find him. The deputy didn't have any additional information, so Chelsea thanked him and disconnected the call. She turned to Lizzy.

"Lizzy, tell your sisters to brush their teeth and get dressed. I want everyone in the SUV in fifteen minutes. We're going into Bedford to talk to the deputy in person. Hopefully they'll have more information by the time we get there. I know the blood doesn't sound good, but it's likely fish blood. He probably caught a large bass and cleaned it in the boat."

Lizzy said, "Mom, whack yourself again. Dad would never clean a fish. He'd give it to you to clean. Dad's always hurting himself. Maybe he cut himself and bled in the boat before the giant head-butting bass knocked him overboard and ate him."

Lucy looked up from a spoonful of chocolate cereal, her eyes really big.

"Don't say that. Daddy didn't get eaten by any fish. Didn't he have that big gun of his? Maybe he shot himself in the foot, and that's why there's blood. He's probably at the doctor."

Chelsea said, "Lucy, you'll make a great PI. You're right. The most likely explanation is that Daddy hurt himself. We'll examine Luscious when the deputy gets her hauled into the dock."

By the time Chelsea finally got her daughters loaded into the SUV, it was early afternoon. They really were like herding cats. Chelsea used hands-free Bluetooth to call Deputy Harbinger to let him know they were coming. The deputy told Chelsea they would put Luscious on a boat trailer and haul her to the Sheriff's impound area near the main office in Bedford.

Deputy Harbinger met Chelsea and the girls at the front desk of the Sheriff's office. He suggested they leave the girls in the office with a female deputy. Chelsea agreed it would be better if they did not see the bass boat. The deputy led Chelsea to the impound out behind the office, where they found Luscious sitting on a boat trailer. Chelsea was glad to see that the pool of blood was not huge. Someone might survive that much blood loss.

Deputy Harbinger said, "Well, Mrs. PI Longfellow, here's your husband's boat. You can see the amount of blood on the bow floor and seat. I don't have to tell you this doesn't look good. As you said on the phone, the crime scene resembles that of the other fishermen who disappeared. Didn't you say your husband was armed? He might still turn up if he got off a shot or two."

Chelsea looked at Luscious and said, "Something big must have banged into the boat to cause such large scratches and cracks in the hull. Is it possible that my demented husband could be right? Could there be giant head-butting bass in the lake, and they knocked him overboard and ate him? I feel really bad that I demoted him to PI in training. Jason, I'm so sorry. Please come home, and I'll make you Associate PI again."

Deputy Harbinger said, "Don't give up yet. We're going to continue searching. We've got some volunteers from town to help. We'll find him, hopefully still alive and with all his parts."

Chelsea looked sad. She said, "Thank you, Deputy Harbinger, for your kind words. I tried to tell him not to go out there by himself, but Jason never listens to me. None of the other missing fishermen have been found. It's going to be hard on the girls if Jason really is gone. But it'll be harder on me. I loved him. Also, all the time I've spent training that man, and now I'll have to start over. As I told him repeatedly, I'm not raising those three angels all by myself."

Chapter 20. PI Chelsea Longfellow, Bait

While she realized it was likely that Jason had become the latest victim of the fishermen killer, she decided to take an optimistic approach with the girls. After arriving home from the Sheriff's office, she sat them down in the living room. They were obviously tired and upset. Lilly sat on the sofa, and Lucy plopped down next to her.

Lilly turned and shoved Lucy off the couch. Lucy lay on the floor screaming hysterically.

Lilly said, "Mom, get her off me. I need some space. She's breathing my air."

Lizzy sat in an adjacent armchair, out of reach of her sisters. She said, "Stop it. Dad's in trouble, and the police think he's…you know…dead. We know better. We all know Dad, and he probably shot himself in the foot and is wandering around lost in the woods. Or he fell out of the boat, hit his head, crawled onto the shore somewhere, and is taking a nap. I'm sure he'll turn up later today, bragging about the giant fish that got away. I'm sure it'll be bigger than Mom's."

Chelsea sighed. She was impressed with Lizzy's optimism. Lizzy also knew her father well.

Lucy climbed back onto the couch, just out of Lilly's reach, taunting her older sister. "I can sit here if I want. Dad would let me."

Lilly said, "Yeah, but he's not here. According to the deputy, Daddy's probably fish bait. I don't think he's taking a nap in the woods. I heard the deputy say there was blood in the boat, lots of blood. I'm afraid Daddy's not coming home."

Lucy said, "Don't say that! He is too coming home. He just got lost. Mom, you know Daddy. He could get lost in our driveway. Why don't you go out and look for him. He needs you."

Lucy started crying. Lilly joined in. Tears formed in Chelsea's eyes, as grief swept over her.

Lizzy said, "What's wrong with you guys? You're acting like Dad's dead. No way. He's survived a hurricane, crashed his truck, ran over an alligator with a motorcycle, got rescued by the Coast Guard in the middle of the ocean, got shot at, and some lady tried to beat him to death with a rubber…well…you remember Mom."

Lucy chimed in. "It was a rubber tenacle."

Lizzy continued, "He even got lost in a nuclear missile base, and he turned up there, eventually. This is Dad we're talking about. He's PI Longfellow, the original. Mom, Lucy's right. You need to get a boat and go looking for him. I can stay here with my sisters."

Lilly and Lucy both looked at Chelsea and said, in unison, "Yeah Mom. Go find Daddy. He's lost, and he needs your help."

Chelsea believed that Jason was gone, but she wanted to give her girls hope.

She said, "Lizzy, thank you for that speech. I needed to hear it, all but the tenacle thing. You're right, Jason needs me. But I have a better plan. Instead of wandering all over this large lake, I'll go fishing by myself tomorrow night. This time I'll be the bait, and maybe the killer will come after me. I'll take Bertha, my trusty Desert Eagle. That'll even the odds when this fishermen killer shows up. I can catch the killer and bring Dad home. Kill two birds with one stone, or fifty-caliber bullet in this case."

Lizzy said, "Sounds like a great plan, Mom, but poor choice of words. Just make sure Dad isn't one of those birds. Hey, why don't you take Herman with you. Dad took him out in the boat before. Herman and Dad are best buddies, and he might be able to use his sniffer to find him."

Chelsea said, "Great idea. I'll rent a boat first thing in the morning. Tomorrow night I'll bring your father home, one way or the other."

Lizzy said, "Alive and in one piece would be good."

***

The next morning, Lizzy stayed with her sisters while Chelsea went to a local marina and rented a bass boat. Chelsea left her SUV in the marina parking lot and drove the boat home to their dock. She saw no sign of Jason's body floating in the lake on her way home.

As Chelsea drove the boat down the lake her anger grew, and she drove faster and faster. *How could he abandon me to raise our three little angels alone? I told him not to go out fishing overnight. But he had to play hero. Now I have to solve Jason's murder, in addition to catching the fishermen killer. Did the fishermen killer also murder Jason? Is it possible that Veronica and her husband's younger brother thought we were on to something, like dumping the expired drugs, and they found Jason on the lake and killed him? I can't remember if we mentioned anything about his planned fishing trip to them or not. Jason's kind of a klutz. It's more likely that he just fell out of the boat and drowned, although that doesn't explain*

the blood. I'm going to find out what happened to him. And if he's still
alive, I'm going to kill him.

Chelsea parked the boat rental at their dock and went up to the house to fix lunch. She served the girls banana splits and chocolate milkshakes to try to cheer them up. At least lunch included a banana, which was more fruit than they usually got. Chelsea sat at the table eating with her daughters and laying out her plans for the night. She noticed that their father's disappearance, and possibly the massive sugar rush, had made the girls jumpy.

"Girls, tonight I'm going to pretend to go fishing. I'm really going hunting for your father and the fishermen killer. I'll take Bertha with me. As per Lizzy's advice I'll also bring Herman along. He's your father's best friend, and maybe he'll be able to sniff Jason out."

Lizzy said, "Mom, I think you're confusing Herman with a bloodhound."

"Don't get smart with me, Young Lady. If you haven't noticed, things are tense at the moment. It was your idea for me to take the cat in the first place. So, if you don't have anything constructive to say, just hush."

Lilly said, "Mom, you are planning on coming back. Right?"

"Yes, Dear. I'll be back first thing in the morning. I'm going to take the boat out around eleven tonight, and hope to be back home, with your father in tow, by five or six in the morning. In the meantime, you, and Lucy mind Lizzy. She's going to be in charge. I'll call her on my cell phone to check on you or if anything happens."

That night at eleven Chelsea set out in the rental boat for the same
fishing spot where the water skier had reported finding the empty and
bloody Luscious. She had loaded fishing equipment, a cooler with soft
drinks and snacks, Bertha, and one orange tabby cat. She wasn't entirely
sure why she had brought Herman. Lizzy had suggested it and it just felt
right."

As Chelsea flew up the lake, she began to understand Jason's obsession
with speed. It felt good to move so fast, the wind blowing through her hair,
the warm late spring air so soothing on her face. As she looked around, she
realized how little she could see, even with a cloudless night, half moon,
and a sky full of stars. She slowed the boat.

Chelsea looked at Herman, sitting in the bow, face to the wind. She
said, "Herman, I'm starting to think and act like Jason. That's not good.
This family needs one sane parent."

Herman said, "Meow." It sounded to Chelsea like he agreed.

"I'm also talking to a cat. This is getting serious."

"Meow." Chelsea, just beginning to learn to speak cat, didn't
understand.

Chelsea stopped the boat at the spot near the shoreline where Jason's
boat had been found. She turned off the motor, walked to the bow, and set
up the trolling motor like Jason had taught her. Herman hopped up onto the
fishing seat next to her and rubbed his face against her hand. She took the
hint, petted him, and rubbed his ears.

"What about it, Herman? Do you sense Jason nearby? Would be nice if
we could find him and take him home alive. We're really going to miss

him; despite all the ways he screws up. He always does his best, and it's actually quite endearing the way he makes us laugh."

Chelsea intended to look like a fisherman, trying to draw out the killer. She baited one of her fishing poles with a large bucktail. Then she stood in the bow and used the trolling motor to position the boat. She began casting the lure towards the shore and slowly reeling it in. Herman sat next to her, inspecting the lure each time it returned to the boat.

After a half-hour of casting and reeling, something large bumped against the side of the boat at the bow near where Chelsea stood. Herman froze into pounce position. Chelsea stumbled but managed to keep her footing. A second hard bump, Chelsea found herself next to the gunwale on the starboard bow, and a hand reached up and grabbed her ankle.

Chelsea screamed, "Ahhh! What the hell?! Herman, something's got me by the ankle."

Herman sprang into action. Claws bared, he swiped at the hand, inflicting long, deep scratches. The hand held on tight in spite of the damage. Struggling to stay in the boat, Chelsea pulled a fully charged taser out of her tackle box. She turned it on and slammed it against the wrist attached to the hand. The hand went limp, and she bent down and grabbed hold of it.

Chelsea said, "Herman, I think we've just caught ourselves the fishermen killer, and it's not a fish. Last I checked, fish don't have hands. What do you think?"

"Meow." Herman took a bite out of the hand. Chelsea pulled with all her strength, intent on pulling whatever was attached to the hand into the boat.

Chelsea said, "Down Herman. I'm going to haul this thing in. You should probably go to the stern just in case I need Bertha to put a couple of holes in our catch."

Herman fled to the stern and sat watching Chelsea. Chelsea kept pulling until she had a full arm, then a shoulder, and finally an unconscious head attached to said shoulder.

She said, "Herman. You're not going to believe this. It appears our neighbor Horace McDufus is the fishermen killer. I didn't see that coming. Why on God's earth would McDufus want to kill fishermen?"

"Meow, meow."

Chelsea said, "I think I'm starting to understand you. I agree. I would have thought McDufus would have shot the fishermen. He's in love with that twenty-two he carries around. Looks like he's got a couple of tools attached to his belt, a crowbar, and a hammer. This could explain the banging on the boats, and the blood. Jason was wrong with his head-butting bass theory. It was a hammer-banging McDufus."

Chelsea kept tugging, and she finally pulled McDufus' barely conscious body into the boat. She pulled his legs over the side, and his body collapsed onto the floor of the bow. He lay on his back, dressed in a wetsuit. He moved his hand slightly. Chelsea fired up the taser and hit McDufus again. Then she took out Bertha, aimed it at McDufus' head, and slapped him to wake him up. McDufus regained consciousness and took in a large gulp of air.

Chelsea said, "Horace McDufus. What are you doing swimming around in the middle of the night imitating a fish? I'm guessing you're the fishermen killer. But why? And more important, have you seen Jason? He disappeared last night, and his bass boat turned up empty this morning. You better not have hurt him. Bertha here has a hair trigger, and I'm not a happy woman."

Chelsea watched his face as he realized he was staring down the barrel of a fifty-caliber pistol. She saw him glance down at his crotch.

"Horace, did you just wet yourself? No worries. No one will notice since I just pulled you out of the lake."

A groggy McDufus said, "Chelsea? My neighbor PI Chelsea Longfellow? What the hell'er ya' doin' out here in 'ta middle the night? I mighta kilt ya. Please point yer very large gun somewheres else, if ya wouldn't mind. I kinda like my head where it is, on my shoulders."

Chelsea said, "I repeat, have you seen Jason? Did you kill him? His empty bass boat showed up with blood on the seat and floor. And why on earth are you killing fishermen? What did they ever do to you? Does it have anything to do with dumping expired drugs into the lake?"

Herman said, "Meow" and swatted McDufus on the left cheek, claws out.

McDufus squawked, "Lady, call off that crazy cat! What in hell's goin'on?"

Chelsea said, "I just told you. Jason is missing, and you appear to be the fishermen killer. I want to know if you killed Jason and why you are killing fishermen? And I want to know now! By the way, this is Jason's cat and best friend, Herman. And this is my best friend, Bertha."

McDufus, now coherent, said, "Damn, woman. I can't believe you catched me. I been doin' great 'til now. I been killin' fishermen ta' scare off as many damned fools from the lake as possible. I've lived here fer a long time, and at first the water were so clean I could see the bottom twenty feet down. Now it's full of algae…damn leaky septic tanks, boat exhaust, oil, crap folks throw in the lake. Then they's those infernal jet skis; the buzzin' noise drives me crazy. Them new wakeboard boats keep knockin' down my dock. Cost me thousands to repair. With all the boat traffic, ya' can't go out on the water without bouncin' around so much it jars my false teeth. I figured if'n I killed off a few fishermen, folks would get scared and stay away."

Chelsea felt the anger welling up inside. This crazy old man killed her husband, and for what? To scare people away because the lake was too crowded for his liking. She shoved Bertha's barrel up against McDufus' temple and cocked the hammer.

"You're crazy. I'll admit, you do have people scared. But why did you have to kill Jason? Now what am I going to do? He was kind of irritating, but the girls and I loved him. And you just tried to murder me. I should blow your stinking head off right now."

McDufus said, "Hold on there, Missy. PI Longfellow is fine. I didn't kill him. I pulled him outta his boat, dragged him to shore, and whacked him on the head with my crowbar. That boy's got one hard head. Didn't even knock him out. Just made him kinda woozy."

Chelsea whimpered, "Jason isn't dead?"

"No Ma'am. After his head cleared, we got ta talkin', and I realized I didn't wanna kill him. He's my only friend. You prolly don't know this, but some days when you weren't around, I'd sneak into your PI office and your husband and me would play them video games fer hours. Ain't ya ever noticed the initials HM has the high score on that there Ms. Pac Man? And HM is second on Space Invaders. HM, that's me, Horace McDufus. Also, yer husband and me both hate them danged squirrels. We's at war with them furry buggers. If'n I killed him, I wouldn't have nobody to fight them squirrels with. We're kinda kindred spirits."

"So, Jason's alive? Where is he?"

McDufus continued, "I tied him up while he was still woozy, put him in my boat and took him to my place. I couldn't turn him loose right away since he knowed I was the one killin' the fishermen. He's tied up and gagged in my basement. Don't worry, I been feedin' him. He's fine. I planned on letting him go once he agreed ta' not tell anyone what I been up to. Now the both of yuz know. I don't wanna kill you either. You all got a nice family and make fer good neighbors. I guess I'm screwed. You might as well just blow my head off."

Chelsea used her left hand to untie one of the lines from the side of the boat. She told McDufus to place his hands behind him, and then she tied his wrists tightly together.

"Okay, let's go get Jason. Just a couple more questions. You admit you have been murdering fishermen. Are you sure it doesn't have anything to do with drugs being dumped into the lake? And did you kill Harold Fairchild, the CEO of GenesRUS? He was the body in the business suit that Jason reeled in the other night."

McDufus sounded sincere, "I don't know nothin' 'bout no drugs bein' dumped into the lake. If'n I'd have known about it and who was doin' it I woulda' killed them too. I also never killed nobody wearin' a suit. Why would any damn fool in his right mind wear a suit to go fishin'?

Chelsea aimed the boat towards McDufus' dock. She said to Herman, "McDufus sounds like he's telling the truth. If he didn't kill Harold Fairchild, who did?"

Herman said, "Meow."

McDufus said, "This here lady talks to cats. And she says I'm the crazy one."

Herman walked over and bit him on the hand, again.

Chapter 21. Who Really Dunnit?

Chelsea pulled the rental boat up to McDufus' dock. Bertha in hand, Chelsea walked McDufus up the path to his house. Herman followed along behind them.

McDufus said, "You can untie my hands. I'm not gonna run off. You got me dead to rights."

Pressing Bertha's barrel into his back, Chelsea talked as they walked up the path. "McDufus, keep quiet. Take me to Jason. Then we'll figure out what to do with you."

McDufus kept walking and said, "We need ta go in through the back door on the lake side. I keep a key under a rock back there. Once we get inside, yer husband's in the room on the left. He's gagged and tied to a chair. I offered ta leave off the gag, but he wouldn't shut up. That man can sure talk when he's scared."

Chelsea knew this was true; when Jason was nervous, he couldn't stop talking. She felt a wave of relief flow through her, as her mind fully processed that Jason was alive.

Chelsea retrieved the key. She forced McDufus through the door first, then followed him into the dark basement. When they got inside, she cautiously looked for Jason.

She called out, "Jason, are you in here? Make some noise for me to follow."

Chelsea heard a loud thud. Bertha still in her hand, she followed the sound, forcing McDufus to walk ahead of her. They entered another room, and McDufus said, "There's a light switch on the wall over there. Turn it on and we should see your husband."

Chelsea reached out and flipped the wall switch. The dark, dank basement room filled with blinding light. She saw Jason, laying on his side on the floor, gagged, hands tied behind him. He had rocked his chair over sideways to make noise.

Chelsea pointed Bertha at McDufus and said, "Sit in that chair and scoot up close to the table, so you can't jump up and run away. I'll untie Jason. I'm on the Bedford County women's shooting team. If you run, I'll ventilate you with fifty-caliber rounds, which will hurt, a lot."

She watched as McDufus did as he was told. Then she rushed to Jason, removed the gag, and untied his hands. He looked unconscious, probably from bouncing his head off the wooden floor.

Chelsea placed her hand gently on Jason's face, kissed his forehead, and said, "Jason, are you okay? I thought you'd been murdered by the fishermen killer. Thank God you're alive."

Jason didn't move. He was still out. Chelsea felt something furry rub against her leg. Herman had followed her into the house. She watched as he walked up to Jason and licked his face.

Jason moaned and opened his eyes. Chelsea took his arm and tried to help him stand up. He said, "Chelsea, is that you? How'd you find me?"

Chelsea held onto his arm to provide support. She said gently, "We thought you were dead. I'm very relieved to find you alive." The expression on her face changed abruptly. Her arm came up and she whacked him one on the back of the head. "I told you not to go fishing alone. What's wrong with you! I thought you'd abandoned me to raise our three daughters by myself!"

She watched as Jason rubbed his head in two different places, and then shook it, apparently trying to clear out the cobwebs.

Jason said, "Jeez Chelsea, you've got a funny way of showing you're glad to see me. I didn't abandon you." Jason saw McDufus sitting in the chair, hands tied behind him. "McDufus is the fishermen killer, and he almost took me out. We bonded over Ms. Pac Man, and he couldn't bring himself to kill me. It's a guy thing. You wouldn't understand."

Chelsea walked over to McDufus and put her hand on his shoulder. She said, "You're right, I don't understand why he didn't beat your brains out like he did all those other fishermen. It's got something to do with machismo and Ms. Pac Man. I won't even pretend that I get it. What I really don't understand is that McDufus admits he's the fishermen killer. But he claims he didn't kill Harold Fairchild. You know, the guy whose killer we were hired to find. We're not going to get paid if we don't get some answers."

Chelsea noticed that Jason looked thoughtful, or perhaps his eyes were just crossed from being hit on the head so often.

Jason said, "I've been thinking about that ever since Horace knocked me out, tied me up, and left me in his basement. That's not a very nice way to treat your gamer friend by the way. I'm not going to let you win at Ms. Pac Man anymore. You're goin' down."

It took all of Chelsea's resolve to keep from whacking her husband yet again. "Jason, focus! What were you thinking? Did you figure out who killed Harold Fairchild?"

Jason looked a little woozy to Chelsea, and she rushed to him and caught him as he started to collapse. She helped him sit down in one of the chairs next to the table.

Jason shook his head again. "Give me a minute. I hear church bells ringing in my head. As soon as they stop, I'll tell you what I know." He paused for a couple of minutes, and then continued, "That's better. The bells stopped. Church must be over. Anyhow, after my friend McDufus here tied me up and gagged me, he admitted he was the fishermen killer. I was relieved when he said I was his only friend, and he wasn't going to kill me. But Horace, old buddy, we're gonna have to turn you over to the police. I'll miss having a video game buddy, but you can't go around killing half the town and get away with it. It just wouldn't be right."

Chelsea saw McDufus nod in agreement. "I wuz just tryin' ta' save the lake, like one of them environmental folks. But I unnerstand. You're a big PI here in town, and ya gotta do what ya gotta do. I warn ya though, I hears they got them video games up at the state penitentiary, and I'm gonna practice up so when I get out, I'll kick yer ass."

Chelsea shook her head. "Jason, get on with it. What did you figure out?"

Jason said, "Oh yeah. I figure that Horace here killed the fishermen. But Harold Fairchild was wearing..."

Chelsea said, "...a business suit. Yes. We already discussed that."

Jason continued, "So I figure there must be two different killers. Horace took out a lot of fishermen. But someone else killed Harold Fairchild."

Chelsea said, "I'm with you so far. But who? And what's the motive?"

Jason said, "It must have something to do with the drugs that were dumped into the lake. It was no coincidence that I reeled in Harold's body in the same area of the lake where we found the drugs. And in the movies, it's always the spouse, in this case the wife."

Chelsea said, "You mean our employer, the one who hired us to find her husband, and his killer. We won't get paid if she's the killer. Come up with a different theory. Do better."

Jason said, "No, I definitely think she has something to do with it. Harold was a lot older than her, and we know she's acquainted with his younger brother, Lucas. Maybe Mrs. Fairchild decided she wanted the younger brother. So, the two of them got rid of the old guy. And boddabing, boddaboom, she gets GenesRUs, Harold's millions, the younger brother, and a lot more activity in the bedroom. What better time to kill Harold and throw him in the lake? Just another poor fisherman killed by the notorious fishermen killer. They screwed up by leaving him in a business suit. But that's how murderer's get caught, by makin' dumb mistakes."

Chelsea said, "I have to admit, that sounds surprisingly reasonable. But we don't have any proof. No evidence that Lucas and Veronica were having an affair, and no proof that either the wife or the brother killed Harold. We also know nothing about who dumped the drugs or why.

We've got lots of work to do, just to prove that *our client* murdered her husband. Why did I have to follow you into this PI thing? I was better off as a stressed-out ICU nurse, or in hospital administration. At least I actually got paid for my efforts."

Jason said, "What are you complaining about? You weren't demoted from head PI all the way down to PI in training. Maybe Veronica and Lucas didn't kill her husband. There's still the human growth hormone and the giant bass. Harold did have a head wound. We could go back to the giant head-butting bass theory for Harold's murder."

Chelsea shook her head. "Jason, you're out of your mind." She looked at McDufus.

McDufus smiled, "I ain't sayin' nuthin'. I don't wanna get whacked on the head."

Jason said, "I feel you. I love Chelsea, but sometimes she's mean. Horace, while you were running around on the lake killing people, did you see anyone dump drugs into the water? I can't shake the idea that the box of drugs has something to do with Harold Fairchild's murder."

McDufus said, "Well, now that ya' mention it, one night last fall I did see a feller throwing somethin' in the lake off the shoreline out near the dam. It wuz dark, but there were a full moon, so I could see some. I can't say for sure it wuz boxes, but it wuz somethin' big. I wuz also busy lookin' for fishermen ta' kill, so I didn't pay much attention."

Chelsea walked over to McDufus and whacked him on the back of the head. "I asked you that when we were on the boat. You told me you never saw anyone dumping boxes in the lake. What's that about?"

McDufus said, "Ouch. Jason, make her stop. I was all upset about you catchin' and hog-tying me when you asked me the first time. You ruined my plans and I saw myself headed for prison. Plus, I'm an old man. 'Scuse me all ta hell if my memory don't work so good no more."

Jason said, "Chelsea, could you please stop playing whack-a-mole with Horace's head so maybe he can provide us with a clue. Horace, did you get a good look at this person? Only one person? Was it a man or a woman? Can you describe them?"

McDufus said, "The moon wuz out, but it were dark. I'm pretty sure it were a man. Medium height, not a bean pole like Jason. Medium weight, short hair, a might on the pudgy side."

Jason said, "That could describe Harold Fairchild. But why would he be dumping expired drugs in the lake? He's the CEO. Wouldn't he order one of his employees to do it?"

Chelsea said, "Jason, that could describe most of the men in Bedford County. Mr. McDufus, did you happen to notice if the man was wearing a business suit?"

McDufus said, "You already asked me that."

Chelsea said, "That was on the boat when you said you had never seen anyone dumping boxes in the lake."

Jason said, "Chelsea, what kind of interrogation is that? If he didn't see anyone, how could that person be wearing a suit? And I'm the PI in training?"

McDufus said, "Duck man. She's gonna whack you again."

324 John J Jessop

Jason stood up and ran around to the other side of the table from Chelsea. Chelsea ignored him and said, "Again, Horace, was this man wearing a business suit?"

McDufus said, "Hard to say. It were too dark. Coulda' been I guess."

Chelsea said, "Come to think of it, why didn't you kill him? That's what you were doing out there."

McDufus said, "I were out there to kill fishermen. This feller weren't fishin'."

Jason, still on the opposite side of the table from Chelsea, said, "So, we now know that a man was seen dumping something, possibly expired human growth hormone, into the lake. But we don't know who it was."

Chelsea added, "And we don't know if it has anything to do with Harold Fairchild's murder. We're going around in circles."

Jason said, "We need to interrogate Veronica and Lucas Fairchild again, separately. We need answers. We'll get them to come into the office, and I'll grill'em with my relentless interrogation techniques. I'll get them to talk."

Chelsea said, "Yeah, you're crazy enough to play good cop and bad cop at the same time, PI in training Longfellow."

McDufus said, "I got a suggestion. Lock 'em in a room with your Misses here, and she can whack'em on the head 'til they talk. You'll get yer answers in a heartbeat."

Chelsea went upstairs, took a sheet off one of the beds, and tore off a strip of cloth. She took it downstairs and used it to gag McDufus.

Chelsea said, "Horace, we're going to leave you tied up here through tomorrow. That should give us enough time to interrogate Veronica and Lucas Fairchild. I don't want to turn you over to the police until we've had a chance to catch Harold Fairchild's killer. If the killer finds out you've been caught, he might make a run for it. He'll realize he won't be able to claim the fishermen killer did it if you deny it. I don't feel too bad, since you left poor Jason tied up the same way. I'll send him back to feed you and let you go to the bathroom."

Jason said, "It wasn't all that bad. I spent the time counting the pine boards on the wall and the floorboards. There are two hundred and twelve floorboards and four hundred and thirty-seven separate wallboards. Feel free to check my math, Horace."

Chelsea took pleasure when she saw the dazed and confused look on McDufus' face as they walked out the door. She felt even better when she saw Herman jump up on the table, bite McDufus on the nose, and then jump down and follow them out the door.

Chapter 22. All in the Family

Jason and Chelsea walked home from McDufus' house. They quietly entered through the front door, trying not to wake the children. When they stepped into the living room, a light came on. Jason saw the girls sitting on the couch, clearly waiting for Chelsea to return with their father in tow. He felt the love when all three of them ran towards him, until they grabbed hold of Chelsea and smothered her with hugs and kisses.

Chelsea said, "I told you I'd bring him home. Give Dad a hug too. He got knocked on the head and has been tied up in a basement for the past two days."

Lizzy stepped back and looked Jason over. "I told you he was too tough to kill. That looks like a pretty good bump on your head there Dad. Don't you need to go to the emergency room and have that looked at? You take us to the ER for X-rays when we get hurt."

Jason said, "Actually your mother gave me this particular bump. I'll be fine. I've got a hard head. Mostly I'm hungry. How about we have some popcorn and watch a movie."

Lizzy said, "Can we Mom? Please, oh please!"

Chelsea looked at Jason. "Are you daft? It's three o'clock in the morning."

Jason said, "I know. But I've been locked in McDufus' basement for two days. The only thing I've had to eat was moonshine and toast. I'm hungry, and a little drunk. I was also bored, so I want to watch a movie. How about *The Lion King*. Everybody likes that one."

Jason smiled when Chelsea gave up and got up to go to the kitchen. He heard the sound of popcorn popping. When Chelsea returned to the living room, Jason saw her carrying two large bowls of popcorn and several sodas on a large tray. Jason and the girls were already snuggled up on the couch watching *The Lion King*. Jason thanked Chelsea for the snacks.

Lizzy took hers and said, "Thanks Mom. You're the greatest. You rescued Dad and we're having a party in the middle of the night. Only thing, he kinda smells bad. You said he was locked in a basement for two days. Why was he locked in Mr. McDufus' basement?"

Jason overheard Lizzy's question. He looked around, and the other two girls were busy munching and watching the movie.

Jason whispered to his eldest daughter, "Lizzy, you can't tell anybody about me being locked in McDufus' basement. I mean it. Mom and I will explain later. For now, just enjoy the party."

After the movie, the girls gave Jason a hug and headed off to bed. He knew they wouldn't get up before noon. Jason heard Chelsea tell Lizzy that they would be gone by the time the girls got up. They had to go into the office in the morning, in just a couple of hours. Chelsea told Lizzy to feed her sisters and watch them until she and Jason got home. Jason chuckled when Lizzy grunted and headed for her room, already half asleep.

Chelsea said, "I'm going to tuck the other two in and let them know Lizzy will be watching them tomorrow. Meet you in the bedroom."

Jason was almost asleep when Chelsea entered the room. He heard sniffing sounds, and then he felt a tap on the shoulder.

She said, "Jason, wake up. You smell like damp basement and body odor. I can't sleep next to you until you shower." She poked him again.

Jason groaned, "Chelsea, you woke me up. I was dreaming I caught the fishermen killer, he got away, and you were whacking me on the head."

"If you don't get up and take a shower, part of that dream's going to come true."

Jason said, "Yes, Dear."

Jason took a shower, and a few minutes later he returned to bed smelling like Jason, which was to say *Ivory* soap. He got into bed and set the alarm for eight AM, only two hours away, and drifted off to sleep. Last thing he heard was Chelsea snoring softly.

It seemed like two minutes later when Jason heard the alarm. He hit the off button, rolled over and shook Chelsea awake.

"Wakey wakey PI Longfellow. Time to get up, consume mass quantities of coffee, and pay a visit to GenesRUs. I'm going to use my infamous relentless interrogation technique to force them into confessing. Or maybe I will play good cop-bad cop by myself. I'm that good."

Chelsea rolled over, still half asleep. She said, "Don't you mean bad cop-idiot cop? You babble, confuse and irritate the suspects mercilessly until they confess to shut you up. That's not in any PI manual. More like part of the Geneva Convention, under inhumane treatment."

Jason said, "Don't knock it if it works. But what if the lovely Veronica and her brother-in-law Lucas are innocent? What if the killer really is a giant head-butting bass?"

Chelsea chuckled, "Then you're going to have to learn to speak fish to do your interrogation. Enough with your stupid theories. While it's true there are some large bass in the lake this year, including the record-breaking ones I caught, no one in their right mind thinks those fish are killing anyone. Get your butt out of bed and let's get moving."

"We'll see, Wife. I promise you if Veronica or Lucas Fairchild know anything, I'll get it out of them. I'm one determined PI."

"PI in training…"

"Stop it."

Jason heard Chelsea get up, brush her teeth, and get dressed. Then he heard the coffee pot gurgling in the kitchen and smelled coffee and burnt toast. When Jason walked into the kitchen, Chelsea was seated at the table. He saw burnt toast, butter, and jelly, along with a cup of coffee for him. He sat down in front of his coffee.

Chelsea said, "Help yourself to breakfast. Hurry up. I want to get to GenesRUs by ten. Hopefully we can catch their new CEO, Veronica Fairchild, off guard and get some answers."

Jason scraped the black off his toast, slathered it with butter and jelly. They ate and drank two pots of coffee. Jason felt Chelsea's impatience as he recycled his coffee before heading out.

Chelsea said, "I don't know why you bother to drink coffee. You pee it out faster than you put it in. Let's go."

Jason followed Chelsea into the garage. Chelsea told him she'd drive because he didn't look awake yet, and she didn't want to end up in the ditch. They both climbed into the SUV.

Jason said, "Sure you don't want me to drive? I love these curvy roads. GenesRUs is forty-five minutes from here, just outside the Bedford city limits. I could get us there in half that time."

Chelsea said, "No thanks. I'll drive. I prefer to get there alive. I'm not up for one of your dodge-the-deer games. You know, where you go around curves at seventy-five-miles-per-hour with your eyes closed. You really are a crazy person. You know that. Right?"

Jason gave her shoulder a friendly shove. "Maybe. But you love me anyway. Right?"

Chelsea said, "Yes, you know I love you. Although for the life of me I can't figure out why."

Forty-five minutes later Chelsea pulled into the GenesRUs parking lot. She and Jason climbed out of the SUV and entered the building through the front door. They found a male receptionist at the front desk. Jason was impressed by this clean-cut young man, wearing a button down light blue shirt and dress pants, and sporting a short, stylish haircut. But when the man turned towards them, the large nose ring looked a little out of place. A large black man in a uniform and hat with the word SECURITY sewn on it stood at the end of the front counter. The man wore a military sidearm in a hip holster. He looked like he just came off the battlefield.

Chelsea and Jason walked up to the front desk, and the young man approached. He said from across the counter, "Hello. Welcome to GenesRUs. What can I do for you?"

Jason decided to take the lead. *PI in training indeed. I'll show her.* He took his laminated PI license out of his wallet and flashed it at the young man.

Jason said, "I'm Dr. Jason Longfellow, PI, and this is my wife and colleague, Chelsea. Your CEO, Veronica Fairchild, hired us to carry out an investigation for her. We have some new information, and it's urgent that we see her immediately."

The young man said, "Yes, Dr. Fairchild informed me that I should send you up to her office when you arrived. But she said PI Longfellow was a woman."

Chelsea stepped forward, elbowed Jason out of the way, and said, "That would be me, PI Chelsea Longfellow. I'm the owner of our PI firm. This is my husband. He's irritated that I recently demoted him. But we do have new information and need to see Veronica immediately."

Jason's face turned red when the young man smirked at him and said, "I'll call to tell her you're on your way up. And ouch! Working for the wife. That must hurt."

Jason growled.

Jason felt better when the young man took a step back and said to Chelsea, "Did he just growl at me?" The man pointed across the hall. "Take that elevator to the top floor, executive suite. You can go on up. Maybe you should muzzle your husband, put him on a leash."

Jason turned, charged towards the elevator, and pushed the call button. He tried to ignore Chelsea as they stood waiting for the elevator.

Chelsea said, "Jason, you've got to get over this. I can't help it you weren't making any money as a PI. You should be grateful I took part of my inheritance and started my own PI firm. I probably shouldn't have demoted you, but you can be so irritating."

Jason repeatedly pushed the call button. The elevator arrived. They entered and Jason pushed the button for the top floor. When it arrived at their destination the doors opened, and Jason charged out first. He saw a beautiful cherry desk sitting beside an expensive looking set of double oak doors with a gold-plated sign that read *Dr. Veronica Fairchild, CEO, GenesRUs.*

Jason felt Chelsea walk up behind him. She said, "We suspected with Harold's death the fair Veronica would take over the company. She said she wasn't interested, but this suggests otherwise. Her name's already on the door."

Jason was further frustrated because there was no one at the desk to announce their presence. Anger pushed him into action, and he knocked loudly on the door.

He said, "Hello, the PI Longfellows are here. Can we come in?"

Jason heard a flurry of activity and loud whispering on the other side of the oak doors. Veronica Fairchild's voice sang out, "Just a minute. I'm on the phone. I'll be right with you."

Jason heard more noise. He imagined giant squirrels scurrying around the room. He tensed up, remembering his previous encounter with squirrels.

Then he heard, "Okay, come on in."

Jason opened the door and walked in, followed closely by Chelsea. He found Veronica Fairchild sitting behind a very large teak desk that probably cost more than Jason's truck. The desktop contained a phone and the usual office supplies, tape dispenser, stapler, laptop, cup full of pens, container of paper clips, along with several small piles of file folders full of papers. Jason thought it odd that everything had been pushed to the far end of the desk.

As Jason and Chelsea approached the desk, Jason whispered to his wife, "She's not very neat. Way too much chaos, lopsided, everything stored at one end of the desk. Who does that?"

Chelsea whispered back, "Jason, I'm thinking that desk has seen a lot more chaos very recently than you might imagine."

Jason didn't understand, but that wasn't all that unusual, so he let it pass. He looked at Veronica, sitting in her plush padded leather office chair. She wore a white button-down blouse and a short red skirt. Her chair was pushed back from the desk, her legs crossed, revealing attractive long legs and more thigh than one might expect for a proper CEO. Upon closer investigation, he noticed that the top button of her blouse had been placed in the second hole, and things were askew all the way down the front. Her cheeks were unusually red, and she was breathing like a long-distance runner who'd just completed a marathon.

Chelsea spoke up. "Hello Veronica. We didn't mean to interrupt anything. We thought we should bring you up to date on your case."

Veronica waved her hand, said, "No worries. You're not interrupting anything. I got the call that you were here, and the elevator just brought you up faster than I expected. So, what's up?"

Jason looked at Chelsea and saw that twinkle in her eyes that said things were getting interesting. He just didn't know what things.

Jason watched as Chelsea stood over the desk, looking down at Veronica. Chelsea said, "Jason, don't you see it? The smeared lipstick, blouse buttoned wrong, the crooked skirt. Then there's the desk with everything shoved to one end to make room for...well...you know."

Jason felt confused. "I know what? What do I know? So, the desk is a mess, and she did a lousy job putting on her makeup and getting dressed this morning. I forgot to wear underwear one day last week. It happens."

Jason saw Chelsea shake her head. She gave him that *what's wrong with you* look. "Jason, read the room. Don't you feel the sexual tension? And yuck. We went out together somewhere and you didn't have on any underwear? Please tell me that doesn't happen often."

"No Dear. Just the once." He turned and looked at Veronica again. "Now that you mention it, her blouse is buttoned up wrong...all asymmetrical. Here Veronica, let me fix it for you."

Jason started to step around the desk, hands in front of him, intent on setting the chaos right by rebuttoning Veronica's blouse. Chelsea stepped up behind him and whacked him on the head.

Jason said, "Ouch! Now what did I do? I was just going to help her re-arrange her blouse so it's symmetrical. Symmetrical is obviously better."

Chelsea said, "Jason, I know you're OCD, but sometimes I have to wonder. Undressing this young woman in front of your wife isn't going to bring order to your universe. It will get you killed. Besides, there's already been enough fooling around in here recently."

Jason looked confused again. "What is it you think has been happening?"

Chelsea said, "Jason, let's put it this way. I don't think that Veronica is alone. You should look around, open doors, see if you can find someone else...not wearing any underwear."

The light finally went on in Jason's head. "Ahhh. You think Veronica here has been doing the happy dance with someone, and on this beautiful teak desk." Jason looked from Veronica to the empty desktop and back again. "I see what you mean, Mrs. PI Longfellow. Clever deduction, although that desktop looks uncomfortable. I'll look around, see if I can find her dance partner."

Jason started searching the large office. He looked in the executive bathroom, several file drawers, a couple of desk drawers, and finally moved towards the door to a supply closet.

Chelsea said, "Jason, I doubt you're going to find her lover in a filing cabinet or drawer, unless he's a munchkin. But you're getting warmer with that closet door. Veronica flinched when you started moving in that direction."

Veronica said, "I don't know what you're going on about. You've got no right coming in here, searching my office, and accusing me of doing inappropriate things at my own company. I hired you to find my husband, Harold, and who killed him. What's the matter with you?"

Chelsea turned and pointed towards the closet door. "Jason, please look in that closet. I'm pretty sure there's more in there than a broom, a mop, and some office supplies. If this woman hasn't had sex, apparently really good sex, very recently, I'll be surprised. The way she's glowing, I'm anxious to find out who the man is."

Jason said, "I hope it's not her husband Harold. I know he's dead because I reeled him in the other night. I hate zombies."

Chelsea said, "Jason, at the risk of stating the obvious, you need help. First head-butting killer bass, and now zombies. Just open the freakin' closet door."

Jason walked the rest of the way to the closet, turned the doorknob, and threw it open. There stood a fully naked Lucas Fairchild, holding his clothes in one hand. He held a file folder in the other hand, trying to cover a large bulging object extending surprisingly far out into the room.

Chapter 23. Whodunnit Some More

When Jason opened the closet door, he heard Chelsea gasp. She said, "No wonder the fair Veronica is still smiling and panting like she just finished a hundred-yard dash. That thing would put a smile on any girl's face. How in the world did he close the door?"

Jason pointed and said indignantly, "Mr. Lucas Fairchild. Come out of that closet, put your pants on. And put that away. My poor wife doesn't need to see a thing like that. It's frankly embarrassing, a little scary, and it makes some of us look bad…I mean…Chelsea, close your eyes. And what's that file folder about?"

Lucas bent down, placed the file folder on the floor, and quickly put on his boxers and pants. Jason noticed that Chelsea had not, in fact, closed her eyes.

"That's it, Chelsea. Keep a close eye on him so he doesn't get away."

Chelsea said, "No worries. I've got both eyes on him. If he tries to escape, I'll jump him."

Jason said, "I was thinking more along the lines of shooting him, but okay."

Chelsea took Bertha out of her purse. She said, "Lucas, when you get your parts rearranged…and take your time…looks like it could take a while. When things are rearranged, take a seat next to Veronica. You know, the sister-in-law with which you have a platonic relationship. Platonic must mean something very different here than where I come from."

Jason said, "Chelsea, focus. The man has his pants and shirt on now, stuff no longer in the upright position. We need to interrogate these two." To Lucas, "Bring that file folder with you."

Jason watched carefully as Lucas picked up the file folder, walked over to the desk, moved one of the guest chairs next to Veronica, and sat down.

Chelsea said, "Sorry Jason. You're right. Veronica, you've been lying to us from the beginning. How long have you and Lucas been having an affair? You realize this gives you both a strong motive for killing your husband."

Jason watched as Veronica reached out, took Lucas' hand.

Veronica said, "At first, Lucas and I were just friends. Harold was all about the business. He was never around. When we did spend time together, he drank too much and either fell asleep, complained about work, or became physically abusive. I turned to Lucas for comfort."

Lucas said, "My brother had a mean streak. He was a bully; used to beat the crap out of me when we were kids. That was long before he took to drinking heavily. I've always been attracted to Veronica, but she was married to Harold. I knew he treated her badly, but I only recently learned it had advanced to physical abuse. When she came to me and told me he was beating her, I couldn't help myself. I revealed my true feelings. We became more than just friends."

Chelsea said, "An excellent motive for murdering your brother."

Lucas continued, "You've got no proof that I did anything to Harold. He was found in the lake. In fact, PI Longfellow here reeled him in like a bloody bass. It's my understanding that he is a person-of-interest in

Harold's murder. I was surprised when Veronica hired the two of you to find his killer. Seemed like a conflict of interest, the suspected killer investigating himself."

Jason looked at Veronica and said, "I'm sorry to hear your husband was abusing you. I can see why you might turn to another man for comfort. I am great at comforting and consoling women. Just ask Chelsea."

Chelsea walked up to Jason and whacked him on the back of the head. "You're gonna need more than comforting if you don't stick to the subject of the murderer."

Jason decided to switch subjects. He looked at Veronica and turned aggressive again.

"Enough of this lovey-dovey stuff. Let's get to the point. Mrs. Fairchild...Veronica...what about the human growth hormone? You're the CEO of GenesRUs. Do you know who tossed those expired batches in the lake? More importantly, does this human growth hormone also work on fish? Did someone in your company dump the drug in the lake to create these head-butting monster fish, perhaps for the purpose of killing off fishermen?"

Veronica said, "Do you hear yourself? You sound insane. It's no wonder your wife demoted you. I don't know anything about human growth hormone or dumping drugs into the lake. I wouldn't do that. It would be bad for the environment and my company would have to pay major fines if we got caught. And head-butting monster fish?"

Chelsea spoke up. "Jason, McDufus already confessed to killing the fishermen. Remember? Enough with the head-butting fish. She's right.

You sound like a crazy person. Harold Fairchild's murder has to be about something else, a different killer than McDufus, and definitely NOT a fish. I guess I do need to stop whacking you on the head so often."

Jason saw Chelsea point at the file in Lucas' hand.

Chelsea continued, "It's my guess that Lucas showed up here today looking for something. Veronica invited him into her office, their passion overwhelmed them, and that's how the desk got trashed. We showed up at an inopportune time. Does that sound about right folks?"

Jason realized he needed to let go of the head-butting fish theory. Chelsea was right. McDufus had confessed to killing the fishermen and denied killing Harold Fairchild. Jason really liked that fish theory though. That fishy tale was a lot more interesting than some old geezer trying to chase people away from the lake. That story along with a couple of photos of Jason with giant striped bass would have gone viral. He could have become a social media influencer. That would have shown Chelsea, and maybe got him promoted back to Associate PI.

Jason stepped towards Lucas and Veronica, a serious look on his face.

Thinking through his next steps, he mumbled, "Chelsea's right. We already caught the fishermen killer, and he swore he didn't kill anyone in a business suit. Someone else must have murdered Harold Fairchild. Now for some serious interrogation. I'm guessing Veronica is the weak link, so I'll start with her." He looked around. "Wait...did I just say that out loud?"

Chelsea said, "Idiot. About time you caught up."

Jason pointed at Veronica and spoke aggressively, shaking his finger for emphasis. "It's obvious from the closet that Lucas is fond of you. And it's not good for my marriage for Chelsea to see things like that. Tell your lover to keep his pants on...anyhow...how long have you been having an affair? And shame on you. Your husband's younger brother. Come on. How long? Spill it. How long? This clearly wasn't the first time. Tell me now. Okay, now. How about now?" Jason waited a minute. "How about now? Come on. I need to know. Tell me now."

Veronica said, "PI Longfellow, is your husband okay? He seems to be having a seizure."

Chelsea said, "No worries. This is his version of a serious interrogation. I've seen him throw himself down and bang his head on the floor until he gets answers. It's surprisingly effective. If he were interrogating me, I'd just sit quietly and let him knock himself silly. But I've been married to him for twenty years. Most folks are more compassionate."

Veronica said, "Calm down, Dr. Longfellow...PI in training. I'll answer your questions. Please don't bang your head on the floor, or my desk. I don't want blood stains in my office."

Jason said, "Wise choice. Now spill it, or I'll bleed on your stuff. How long have you and Lucas been having an affair, knocking boots together, doing the happy dance, riding..."

Chelsea said, "Jason, I think she gets it."

Veronica said, "It's been a little over a year. A year-and-a-half ago Harold told me he had been diagnosed with advanced cancer. With treatment he might last a year. That's when his drinking got worse, and he started the physical abuse. He was very angry. I was distraught, and I turned to Lucas for comfort. At first, he just listened, and tried to offer advice."

Jason interrupted, "But eventually he offered more than just comfort and advice."

Chelsea said, "From what I saw in that closet, that would be *a lot more*."

Jason said, "Chelsea, stop it. I'm on a roll." He turned back to Veronica. "You found out your husband was dying, he got physically abusive, and you turned to the Lucas for comfort. That doesn't explain how your name ended up on the CEO's door so soon after Hubby's death."

Veronica looked at Lucas, then back at Jason. "When Harold found out he wasn't going to live much longer, his drinking increased, and that's when the abuse started. I considered leaving him. But when he was sober, he would struggle with guilt for the way he treated me. In an attempt to make up for it he began grooming me to become CEO. He started teaching me the ropes, giving me more responsibility. At first, I wasn't interested. I still had to put up with a lot from him when he was drunk. But when I found out how much money was involved, the profit potential of the company, I decided to go along."

Chelsea said, "So you lied to us. You did know something about running the company. And I'll bet that didn't sit well with little brother. I'm guessing he wanted a piece of the company too. Harold wouldn't have been so anxious to turn the reigns over to you if he knew you were banging his little brother."

Veronica said, "So I lied about that. The truth made me look guilty. And I certainly couldn't tell Harold about Lucas. He was already beating on me. He might have killed me. He certainly would have divorced me, and with my pre-nup I wouldn't have gotten anything."

Chelsea said, "Lying seems to come naturally to you. And this way you get Lucas, his impressive doorstop, and the company."

Jason said, "Chelsea, stop it. I told you to close your eyes. And stop interrupting. I've got her on the ropes." To Veronica, "After you and Lucas started with the sex, he must have found out about Harold's plan to turn the company over to you. How did Lucas react to that information?"

Jason saw Veronica look at Lucas again. "You're right. I had no choice but to tell Lucas what was happening. I didn't want to lose him, so I decided to share the wealth. As Harold's disease progressed, he came to the office less frequently. Eventually he stopped coming at all. That's when I had my name put on the door. Without telling Harold, I invited Lucas to help me run the business. He was already somewhat familiar with the company, and he took to the task well, in fact, a little too well. It was his idea to save thousands of dollars by tossing expired drugs into the lake instead of paying to have them disposed of properly."

Jason looked at Lucas, whose face had turned red. Lucas said, "That's not true. We were having an affair, and she did agree to share management of the company with me. In fact, she actually asked for my help. But, the dumping of the drugs was her idea, not mine."

Jason winced when Veronica let go of Lucas' hand, turned and whacked Lucas on the head.

Jason said, "You must be related to Chelsea. Perhaps a long-lost cousin?"

Veronica said, "He's lying. I assigned him the task of hiring a certified company to legally dispose of all the expired drugs in the warehouse. He decided to dump them in the lake and pocket the money instead. Take a look at that file folder he's trying to hide behind his leg. It contains records of the batches of expired drug that ended up in the lake, copies of forged bills from a fake drug disposal company that he submitted to the GenesRUs accounting department, and the fake amounts charged for each disposal. Lucas managed to direct the GenesRUs payments into his own personal account."

Jason walked over to Lucas and took the file folder. He scanned through its contents.

Jason said, "She's right. These are disposal records for several batches of expired growth hormone. It should be easy to find out if this disposal company exists, and if they disposed of these drugs. This doesn't look good for you, Lucas. What do you have to say for yourself?"

Lucas said, "She's lying. These are the original records for batches of expired drug that I disposed of properly. My signature is on the forms. I came to her office to find this file, as proof that I didn't do anything wrong. Talk to the disposal company. She replaced this original file with a set of forged records, including batches she dumped in the lake. She stole this file to cover her tracks. She dumped the drugs, pocketed the money, and killed Harold to keep him quiet."

Jason watched as Veronica jumped out of her chair, leaped at Lucas, and began strangling him. She had her hands around his neck, shoving his body hard enough to bend him over the back of his chair. Jason realized she had the leverage she needed to strangle the man she just had sex with. Jason stood there watching, amazed at this turn of events.

Chelsea yelled, "Jason, stop her. She's killing him!"

Jason was dumfounded when Chelsea picked up a laptop from the desk and whacked Veronica on the head. Veronica collapsed to the floor, releasing her grip on Lucas' throat.

Jason felt bad for Lucas, who was rubbing his throat, choking, and gasping for breath.

Lucas managed to speak, "Did you see that? She tried to kill me. I thought she loved me, but I'm having second thoughts."

Jason reached over and patted Lucas on the shoulder. "No worries. Chelsea is always whacking me on the head and threatening to kill me in my sleep, and we love each other." Jason looked concerned when he glanced at his wife, still holding the laptop. "Isn't that right Chelsea?"

He saw her put the laptop down. She smiled. "Yes, Jason, we still love each other. It's just that you're so irritating sometimes. Can we get on with interrogating these two before Mrs. Fairchild goes all psycho again?"

It appeared to Jason that Veronica, having moved from the floor to a chair, had pulled herself together. Chelsea pointed at her and said, "Now for the million-dollar question, the one you hired us to find out. Who killed your husband? Come on Veronica. Spill it!"

Jason watched as Veronica's face turned red. She said, "I don't have any proof, but I think it was Lucas. After I decided to share the CEO responsibilities with him, he became more aggressive. He wanted to be involved in every aspect of the company, every decision. He wanted me to take him to the Board of Director's meetings and introduce him as my partner. I told him that would be a bad idea, at least until after Harold died. But he kept pushing. I'm beginning to doubt that he loved me at all. He said he didn't care about his brother's company, but he was actually using me to take over the company. And it was Lucas who dumped the drugs in the lake. I had nothing to do with that."

Jason thought Lucas looked genuinely surprised. Lucas said, "That's nonsense. I never cared about the company. Dad liked Harold better, and it was obvious that he would inherit. I've always had to fend for myself, except for that measly ten-million-dollar trust fund set up for me when Mom died. And I only get half-a-million a year from that. This was about you, Veronica. I loved you, and I thought you cared for me too. It's you who wanted the company. In fact, I think that's the reason you married my brother. You're nothing but a gold digger. You also claimed you weren't interested in the company, but now your name is on the CEO's door. You are the one with the motive for killing him. The sooner he was gone, the sooner you'd have full control."

Veronica said, "I'm not falling for that line about you loving me anymore. And what a load of crap. Why would I kill Harold? My poor husband was going to die soon anyway. And like you said, my name's already on the CEO's office door. So, what's my motive?"

Jason had lost control of his interrogation. He said, "I still think Harold's murder is all about the drugs that were dumped in the lake. Which one of you was really involved in that scam?"

Lucas spoke up first. "Think about it. It had to be Veronica. She's now the CEO, and the CEO knows everything that goes on in the company. Harold must have found out that she had been dumping the expired drugs and keeping the money for herself. He probably confronted her, and she had someone kill him for it. Or maybe she killed him herself. Didn't matter that he was dying. She had to get rid of him before he told anyone about the drugs."

Jason said, "Chelsea, she did just try to strangle Lucas. She also whacked him on the head a couple of minutes ago, kinda like someone else I know. Maybe she lured Harold down to the lake and hit him on the head with a blunt object, a stick or rock. In my experience, women seem to like whacking men on the head. The things us poor guys have to put up with."

Jason looked at Veronica, then at Chelsea. His knees felt weak when he saw the angry looks from both of them. He didn't know which way to run. He moved in the direction of Veronica, who stood up, raised her hand, and whacked him hard on the back of the head.

Jason yelled, "Ouch! What the hell! Crazy women everywhere."

Much to Jason's surprise, Chelsea reached over to the desk, picked up the laptop, and handed it to Veronica. Jason stood there terrified, rubbing the back of his head, and watching as chaos overtook the room. Veronica turned, smacked Lucas upside of the head with the closed laptop and pulled it back in preparation for more of the same.

Jason stepped back, pointed at Chelsea, and said, "Are you crazy? Why would you give that insane woman a weapon? If she beats him to death, you'll be an accessory to murder. And what about me?"

Chelsea gave Jason a *just trust me* look, and said, "Wait for it."

Lucas held up both hands to ward off the incoming blow, clearly fearing the insane look on Veronica's face.

"Somebody stop her! She's going to kill me."

Chelsea pointed at him and said, "The only thing that will save you is the truth. Tell us what really happened, and we'll make her stop."

Jason said, "Clever wife. Confession by crazy lady."

Lucas sat there, hands up in defense, a terrified look on his face. "Okay, I'll tell you. Just take that damn laptop away from her. She's out of her mind."

Veronica, voice choked with emotion, "Lucas, I didn't kill my husband. It must have been you. Why did you kill him? Your plan to get control of the company through me was working. I suspected what you were up to, but I didn't care. I just wanted you to love me. You could have had the company, and me, after he died from cancer."

Jason watched as Veronica drew the laptop back further, fury in her eyes, on the brink of delivering a fatal blow. Jason looked at Chelsea, expecting her to spring into action to stop Veronica. But Chelsea stood there, relaxed, hands on her hips, waiting.

Lucas spoke up in a quiet, shaky voice, "Okay. Just don't kill me. I don't want to be beaten to death with a laptop. I killed Harold. I admit it."

Jason saw Chelsea do a fist pump, heard her say under her breath, "I knew it was him. I knew he would talk. A scorned crazy woman trumps a crooked, lying con man every time." The hair raised up on the back of Jason's neck. He tried to focus on what Lucas was saying.

Lucas continued, "Harold found out about the drugs, and he began to suspect me. He approached me in the parking garage a couple of weeks ago and asked me about it. I was surprised, since he wasn't supposed to know I was involved with Veronica or the company business. But he must have figured it out. I guess a husband just knows. I had Veronica wrapped around my little finger. My brother was much older than her, he was never one for affection, and physical abuse opened the door for me. Veronica came to me, starved for affection, and just plain old human physical contact. The rest was easy. But I knew if he found out I was dumping the drugs, or having an affair with his wife, my plan for taking over his company was finished."

Jason said, "Physical contact is good. Feel free to share details."

Chelsea turned to him, "Jason, shut up."

"Yes dear."

Lucas said, "I had to do something. I denied having an affair with Veronica, or anything to do with company business. I told Harold she had talked to me about his drinking, and that was the extent of it. I also told him that Veronica had come up with the plan to dump the drugs. I said she had told me about the scheme, and she was pocketing the money. He was furious. He was such an honest businessman, it was disgusting. He was determined to find out when she planned to dump the next load of drugs and catch her in the act."

Jason said, "This is getting good. Like one of those murder mysteries on TV."

Chelsea said, "Jason, shut it."

Jason said, "Yes Dear."

Lucas continued, "I suggested that a dock worker was helping her dump the drugs, and I could try to find out a date, time, and location from him. I made it late at night in the middle of the lake near a small island where I had been disposing of the drugs. I had been dumping them in several different places, sometimes from the shoreline and a couple of times from my own boat out in the deep water. I took him there late at night in my own twenty-two-foot wakeboard boat. When we got to the spot, I pretended to wait a while for them to show up. He turned his back on me, and I hit him in the head with a ball peen hammer from my garage, several times to make sure he was gone. I pushed his body into the lake, tossed the hammer into two-hundred-feet of water, and headed home. I was actually doing Veronica a favor, getting rid of him for her. She'd have a lock on the company, along with me of course. I could give her all the things he couldn't, great sex, affection, companionship...great sex."

Chelsea said, "That sounds about right, except for one thing. Truth is if Harold had found out about your drug dumping scheme and that you and Veronica were having an affair, he would have divorced her and made sure neither of you ever went near his company. By killing him, you got the company, his wife, and still got to pocket the money from dumping the drugs. You didn't do any of this for Veronica. This was all about you. And don't get me started on men and sex. A man would cut off his leg if he thought it would get a woman into bed with him."

Jason had trouble keeping up, what with his box brain that could only focus on one thing at a time. He finally said, "I would never cut off my leg. Maybe a finger or a little toe."

He flinched when he saw Chelsea raise her hand. When he was sure she wasn't going to whack him one, he continued, this time to Lucas.

Jason said, "You were clever trying to blame the murder on the fishermen killer. That was a stroke of genius. By the way, I'm still upset that when I reeled in Harold's body, I thought I'd caught a striper bigger than Chelsea's. That sucked."

Veronica added, "I'm glad this is over, and I didn't marry you, Lucas. You're such a pathetic loser. If you were going to blame the fishermen killer for Harold's murder, why on God's earth didn't you talk him into dressing in something besides a business suit to go out there into the middle of nowhere in your boat? None of the other dead bodies were found wearing business suits. They were fishermen. You really screwed the pooch there."

Lucas said, "You were married to Harold. He was a hard-headed old man. He would never go anywhere without wearing a suit. He was my brother, and it would have been cruel to try to talk him into wearing anything else."

Chelsea said, "Yes, the business suit is what got us...and by us, I mean me...to thinking that Harold was killed by someone other than the fishermen killer. You screwed up there. Men seem to screw up a lot. And cruel to talk him into wearing something besides a suit? You do realize that you murdered him." She looked at Jason.

Jason said, "But Chelsea, men don't always screw up. I got a confession out of Lucas. My interrogation techniques are awesome."

Chelsea reached out and took the laptop from Veronica. "Jason, you live in a dream world. This was clearly a confession-by-laptop, and two determined women pulled it off."

Jason looked sad. "I still think my interrogation techniques helped. At least I didn't try to stop you or Veronica from killing him. I'm not that stupid. I'm a survivor. I get my promotion back to senior PI, right?"

Chelsea shook her head and said, "We're talking Junior PI at best."

Chapter 24. A Fishy Tale

Still in Veronica Fairchild's office, Chelsea felt elated that her PI firm had solved the case, actually two cases. She walked over to Jason and raised her hand for a high five. She felt bad when he misunderstood her intentions and ducked.

She said, "Jason, I'm trying for a high five to celebrate. PI Chelsea Longfellow's company solved two separate murder cases, the fishermen killer, and the murder of Harold Fairchild. I'll call the sheriff's office and have them send someone to arrest Lucas. I'm not sure our client's hands are completely clean here, but Lucas did all the confessing. Veronica denied any involvement in the murder, which I believe. I'm not so sure about the drug dumping, although Lucas did tell us he disposed of the drugs in several different places in the lake. We'll leave that to the police to sort out. Hopefully she's clean of that too. I'd like to get paid. After the police take Lucas away, we need to go to McDufus' house and call the sheriff again. Our fishermen killer is handcuffed and locked in his own basement. I want to present these cases to the police separately to avoid any confusion."

Jason said, "I had no doubt we'd solve the case of the fishermen killer, and this other thing is a bonus. Two separate cases with different killers. Wow! I'm good. We're gonna be famous!"

As Chelsea took her cell phone out of her pocket to dial the police, she said, "Jason, need I remind you that your main suspect was a bunch of *'giant head-butting fish'*?"

Chelsea and Jason sat in Veronica's office keeping an eye on the couple until the police arrived. When Deputy Harbinger got there, Chelsea stood to greet him. She was surprised that Jason hung back, probably still sulking about his demotion. She shook hands with the deputy.

"Hello Deputy Harbinger. Nice to see you again."

Chelsea waited impatiently as Jason took a couple of steps forward and nodded at the deputy. He made no effort to shake hands. The deputy nodded back.

Chelsea said, "Jason and I have solved Harold Fairchild's murder. Harold's younger brother, Lucas, confessed to us an hour ago. Harold's wife, Veronica, has agreed to testify to witnessing his confession. There's also another crime of an environmental nature. Lucas confessed to dumping expired human growth hormone in the lake to save money on proper disposal. It's not clear if Mrs. Fairchild knew anything about this crime. I'll leave that for you to sort out."

Chelsea smiled proudly as Deputy Harbinger walked over to Lucas and Veronica, seated next to each other. The deputy said, "Mrs. Fairchild, is it true that you heard Lucas confess to murdering his brother, and your husband? Are you willing to testify to this in court?"

Chelsea felt relief when Veronica stood up, faced the deputy, and said, "Hello, Deputy Harbinger. Yes, I heard Lucas confess to Harold's murder. And yes, I am willing to testify in court. I loved Harold. It's true he was dying, but he could have had a year or more of life left. He didn't deserve to die like that, knocked in the head by his greedy brother."

Deputy Harbinger turned to Lucas and said, "Please stand up, Mr. Fairchild, and put your hands behind your back." The deputy handcuffed Lucas' hands and then said to Veronica, "Mrs. Fairchild, I'd like for you to ride downtown with me and provide us with a statement regarding the crime. I'll have someone drive you home when you're finished."

Chelsea, a big smile on her face, said, "By the way, Deputy Harbinger, we have another surprise for you. I was going to wait until you had a chance to book Lucas to avoid confusion. But I'm too excited. We also solved the case of the fishermen killer. At first, we thought Harold was murdered by the fishermen killer, but as it turns out they are two separate cases with different killers. Lucas murdered his brother Harold out of greed. But our next-door neighbor, Horace McDufus, killed all those poor fishermen. He's lived on the lake for a long time, and it seems he's angry that it has become so crowded. His plan was to kill several fishermen for the purpose of scaring off as many people as possible. McDufus also confessed to us. We have him handcuffed and locked in his own basement. You can collect him at your leisure."

Chelsea was surprised when Jason finally stepped forward and said quietly, "McDufus is not really such a bad fellow, except for the killing thing. Now I'll have to find somebody else to play video games with. You need to know that Chelsea figured it all out. I thought the fishermen killer was a bunch of giant head-butting striped bass, and that those same bass had murdered Harold Fairchild. Then when Chelsea pointed out it must be two separate cases and murderers, I thought sure Mrs. Fairchild had killed her husband. I only figured out the McDufus thing when he knocked me on the head, locked me in his basement, and confessed. Chelsea had to rescue me. I guess that's why it's Chelsea's PI agency. She's good at figuring stuff out. Me, I take the more direct approach, solving the case by getting knocked on the head and taken prisoner."

Chelsea watched as Deputy Harbinger took Lucas by the arm, herded him towards the door. The deputy turned and said, "Dr. Longfellow, it's clear that you and your wife have different approaches to crime solving. I can see why she's the senior PI. As a fellow investigator, I'd recommend you find a safer way to catch a killer than letting him hit you on the head and lock you in his basement. Sounds painful, and a little sad. Then to be rescued by your wife?"

Chelsea felt bad for Jason. Still, she thought, *That's the problem, the killer hit Jason on the head? What about Jason's insane theory that the killer was a bunch of giant head-butting fish?*

She said, "Jason's not such a bad PI. He did learn that McDufus was the fishermen killer. And he survived being knocked out, handcuffed, and locked in a basement for two days. He clearly has a hard head. So, there's that."

Chelsea felt a little better when Jason appeared to perk up. But this was short-lived when he said, "I did discover Harold Fairchild's body. I reeled him in the night Chelsea and I went fishing, hoping to lure out the fishermen killer. I'm still a little disappointed though, cause at first, I thought I'd caught a bigger fish than Chelsea."

Chelsea and Jason followed Deputy Harbinger as he led Lucas Fairchild towards the building exit, with Veronica in tow as well. The

Deputy said back over his shoulder, "Of course you did. Your wife figures things out, but you're a man of accident…I mean action."

Outside, Chelsea and Jason followed the deputy to his car, prisoner in hand. Chelsea said, "Jason and I will head home. When can we expect you at McDufus' house to arrest him?"

Deputy Harbinger put Lucas in the back seat and directed Veronica to the front passenger's side. Then he said, "It'll be a couple of hours by the time I get Lucas down to the jail, process him, book him, put him behind bars, and talk with Mrs. Fairchild. It's an hour drive to your place. I'd say late afternoon. Please check on McDufus when you get home to make sure he's still locked in the basement. I should cite you for failing to call us when you first caught him. But you did solve two murder cases, so I'm willing to let that go, unless he's escaped."

Chelsea said, "No problem. We'll head home right now and make sure he's still there. If there's any problem I'll call you immediately, although we had him locked up pretty tight. Otherwise, we'll see you in a few hours."

Chelsea agreed that Jason should drive home. She felt exhausted, and they still had to turn McDufus over to Deputy Harbinger. She felt confident that McDufus was still locked safely away in his basement, but she started to get a little worried. Had she let Jason handcuff the man? Had she checked to make sure he was secure?

They arrived home an hour later, went inside their house. Chelsea checked on the girls while Jason went to the bathroom. She found them in the basement watching *The Little Mermaid*.

Chelsea walked over to Lizzy and tapped her on the shoulder. She wanted to speak with her without the other two hearing. She whispered, "Are you guys okay? Have you eaten today?"

Lizzy said, "Hey Mom. Yes, I fed the monsters. Yes, we're fine. Is Dad still alive? Have you solved the case, caught the killer? You didn't kill Dad, did you? You gotta stop whacking him on the head. I'm afraid he's gonna get brain damage. It's a good thing he doesn't have that job working as a scientist for the FDA anymore. He needed his brain for that. I'm not so sure with this PI thing. Seems like you do most of the thinking. He just stumbles around all confused, and usually ends up getting hurt."

Chelsea said, "Lizzy, be nice. Your father is a fine PI. It's like I've told you before. Men have this thing called a box brain, where they can only think of one thing at a time. Sometimes solving a crime requires that you think about more than one thing at once. Women are much better at multi-tasking, so that's probably why I'm better at this than Dad. Also, now that you're older I can tell you this. The one thing that men think about the most is…"

Lizzy smiled, "Yeah, I know Mom. I'm sixteen, and you've already given me the talk."

"Yes, Dear. I know. And, just so you know, when men are thinking about that one thing you have the advantage. They can't think about anything else. Which makes it even more difficult for your father to do the multi-tasking required to solve a case."

Lizzy said, "Mom, you're a smart cookie. And ick. No daughter wants to think of their parents that way."

Chelsea said, "Never tell your father about my theory. And how do you think you got here? A clue, there's no such thing as the stork."

Lizzy laughed. "Don't worry. I won't say anything. It would only confuse him anyhow."

Chelsea said. "Go on and finish your movie. Your father and I are going to meet a deputy over at McDufus' house, to turn him over to the police. I'll be back in time to make dinner. Keep an eye on Lilly and Lucy."

Lizzy waved, "Go on. No worries. These two love this movie. You couldn't pry them off the couch until it's over."

Chelsea went back upstairs and made a pot of coffee. She and Jason sat down at the kitchen table, and each had a cup. She served Jason her strong brew, refusing to make him a separate pot of his decaffeinated swill. They sat sipping and talking.

Chelsea said, "The kids are fine. They're watching *The Little Mermaid*. Lizzy said she fed them lunch. I told her we had to meet the deputy over at McDufus's place in a little while, but I'd be home in time to make dinner. This has been quite a day."

Jason appeared to her to be sulking. He said, "Yeah, it was okay. We did solve two separate murder cases. I'm sure once the word gets around, we'll be swimming in new clients. I just wish I could have done more. And I don't know what I was thinking. Giant head-butting fish? I guess I always try to make things too sciencey. Makes more sense that McDufus and Lucas Fairchild were the killers. I'll try to think more rationally in the future, more like a senior PI."

Chelsea felt bad. She tried to comfort him. "Yeah, you kind of suck at this PI thing. Maybe you have too much education and you overthink things. You also seem to wander off into the Twilight Zone a lot. Just try to remember one simple rule: if a murderer plans to kill someone in advance, that murderer is most likely human. Can you remember that?"

Chelsea chuckled as Jason took a drink of the strong coffee and choked. Jason said, "God Woman, this coffee is like drinking battery acid. I don't know how you do it. And yes, I will try to remember that in a premeditated murder case, the killer is often human. Although it could be a pet lion, or a trained killer pit bull…"

Chelsea said, "Jason, stop it and drink your delicious coffee. You're overthinking things again. There probably aren't a lot of pet lions here on the lake."

A few minutes later Chelsea heard a knock at the door. She said, "Jason, would you please get that. Deputy Harbinger must be early."

She heard Jason open the front door and greet the deputy. She took the last drink of her coffee and joined the men at the front door.

She said, "Hello, Deputy Harbinger. You're early."

The deputy said, "Yes, I decided to assign someone else to process and book Mr. Fairchild. I wanted to bring in the fishermen killer as soon as possible. Shall we go collect Mr. McDufus?"

Chelsea led the way around the cul-de-sac to McDufus' house. She used his key to enter the front door, and they went down to the basement. McDufus was still handcuffed and tied to the chair. His head had flopped back, and he was snoring, sound asleep.

Jason said, "I hope he's okay. Looks like he's breaking his neck. I'm gonna miss Horace when you haul him off to jail. I will have to find someone else to play video games with. He's a good friend, and a real pro at Ms. Pac Man."

Chelsea saw the deputy give Jason a strange look. She said, "No worries, Deputy. It's all innocent. Jason had nothing to do with the murders."

Deputy Harbinger shook McDufus by the shoulder to wake him. When he didn't wake up immediately, Chelsea thought perhaps they shouldn't have left him tied up like this. Then she saw McDufus' head spring into the upright position. He blinked his eyes several times, clearly trying to get his bearing. Chelsea took the gag out of his mouth.

Deputy Harbinger stood in front of McDufus and said, "Horace McDufus, I hereby arrest you for the numerous fishermen murders." Then he read him his Miranda rights.

McDufus said, "I unnerstan'. Please take these here cuffs off. My hands and arms are numb."

Deputy Harbinger said, "In a moment. First, PI Longfellow tells me that you knocked him in the head and kept him hostage down here for a couple of days. During that time, you confessed to murdering all those fishermen; that you are the fishermen killer. Is that true?"

McDufus said, "Yep. I give up. Like I tol' Jason, I been here fer a long time, and more folks just keep a comin' and comin'. They ruined the water, keep knockin' over my dock with their devil boats, make it so crowded it ain't possible to fish or boat no more. I just wanted to scare as many of'em away as possible. I guess I got a little carried away. I think maybe I been puttin' down a little more of that moonshine than a feller outta. Must've done somethin' to my brain. That's it. It be the shine. Maybe I'll claim…what's it called…insanity…alkyholism."

Chelsea and Jason followed as the deputy untied McDufus from the chair and led him upstairs to the squad car. She felt a little sorry for the man. He wasn't all that bad, if you ignored the drinking, shooting a pistol in the neighborhood, and all the murders of course. *Oh God. I am starting to think like Jason.*

They reached Deputy Harbinger's car, and Chelsea watched the deputy put McDufus in the back seat. The deputy approached Chelsea and Jason, standing nearby.

Deputy Harbinger said, "The two of you should be proud. You solved two cases, the fishermen killer, and the murder of Harold Fairchild. You delivered the guilty parties in both cases, complete with confessions. I can't pay you anything for catching the fishermen killer. I hope your client pays you for finding Mr. Fairchild's killer. We can use a couple of good PIs around here. We have a small police force and not a lot of resources. Your help is appreciated."

Chelsea felt flattered when the deputy gave her a big, flirtatious smile.

She felt even more flattered when Jason stepped between them, shook the deputy's hand, and said, "We're glad to be of service. And I might only be the PI in Training, but Chelsea's my woman. So, turn that smile down a notch or two."

Chelsea smiled. *He might have some problems doing the PI thing, but he's always protective of me. That's not such a bad thing.*

The deputy stepped back and said, "Message received. Attractive but unavailable."

Just then, the deputy's phone rang. He answered. Chelsea couldn't help but hear his side of the conversation. Her face turned red, and she began to feel first confused, and then a little woozy. The deputy disconnected the call and turned back to Jason and Chelsea.

Deputy Harbinger said, "That was the sheriff on the phone. Someone just reported finding a bass boat with blood in it, all banged up on the bottom and the sides. It was floating next to the shoreline near the dam. There were two dead bodies lying half out of the water nearby, two fishermen. They've only been dead a few hours, and McDufus could not have killed them since you had him locked in his basement. Both bodies had fractured skulls and were covered with bite marks; they appeared to have been bitten repeatedly. The sheriff said there are places on the bodies where large chunks of flesh had been removed. It doesn't sound good."

Chelsea looked at Jason, and his face lit up. He interrupted Deputy Harbinger, "Well, I guess we have the answer as to whether human growth hormone has an effect on fish. That would be *three* sets of murderers, *three* separate cases. The third clearly involves giant head-butting bass."

Chelsea looked from Jason to the deputy, reached up, and whacked herself on the head.

ACKNOWLEDGEMENTS

I would like to thank my loving wife for helping me with numerous edits and proof-reads of *A Fishy Tale* and for her support as I continue to write and publish. I would also like to thank my youngest daughter for teaching me about editing, formatting book text and cover for self-publishing, and instruction in various Adobe software that allowed me to design my own book cover for *A Fishy Tale*.